COLDFALL WOOD

COLDFALL WOOD

STEVEN SAVILE

St. Martin's Press
New York

COLDFALL WOOD. Copyright © 2018 by Steven Savile. All rights reserved. Printed in the United States of America. For information, address St. Martin's Press, 175 Fifth Avenue, New York, N.Y. 10010.

www.stmartins.com

Designed by Devan Norman

Library of Congress Cataloging-in-Publication Data

Names: Savile, Steve, author.
Title: Coldfall wood / Steven Savile.
Description: First edition. | New York : St. Martin's Press, 2018.
Identifiers: LCCN 2018010651 | ISBN 9781250077875 (hardcover) |
    ISBN 9781466890206 (ebook)
Subjects: | GSAFD: Fantasy fiction.
Classification: LCC PR6119.A95 C65 2018 | DDC 823/.92—dc23
LC record available at https://lccn.loc.gov/2018010651

Our books may be purchased in bulk for promotional, educational, or business use. Please contact your local bookseller or the Macmillan Corporate and Premium Sales Department at 1-800-221-7945, extension 5442, or by email at MacmillanSpecialMarkets@macmillan.com.

First Edition: August 2018

10 9 8 7 6 5 4 3 2 1

For two men who changed my life without ever realizing it:

Alan Garner for writing Elidor, *my favorite book of all time.*

And Al Mendes for reading it to us in class all those years ago.
Coldfall Wood *would not exist without you.*

In the deepest part of the ancient woods
He stirred, crying out against the land's pain.

Hwaet! Áríseaþ!
Hark! Rise up!

PART 1

Albion is sick! said every Valley, every mournful Hill
And every River: our brother Albion is sick to death. . . .

Arise! awake O Friends of the Giant Albion

—WILLIAM BLAKE, *JERUSALEM*

1

They found what remained of Huw Carter's body six months later.

It wasn't much: part of a jawbone, a fragment of skull, and a few teeth. The coffin was so much larger than it needed to be, the Union Jack draped across the lid.

There was a narrative being woven around Taff's death, the hopeless bravery of the Welshman standing up—tragically—to one of the oldest crime families in the city. It was a big fat steaming pile of bullshit, of course, but the truth didn't help anyone.

There were no pretty words or fond remembrances. No one stood up to give the eulogy. Things were kept simple. A few lines from the priest who could have been talking about anyone, so bland were his platitudes. Julie kept his head down, mumbled a few prayers and shuffled out of the church to watch them put what little remained of his old partner in the ground while history was rewritten to give Taff a kinder end.

Julie stuffed his hands into his pockets.

It really should have been raining, he thought. Rain was the right kind of weather for this.

The priest led them to the graveside and waited while the pallbearers folded the flag and lowered the coffin into the ground.

There were a few nods exchanged by the mourners. Everyone knew each other, which wasn't particularly surprising given there were only half a dozen people there. It was hardly the mark of a life lived well. Julie knew all of them: Ellie Taylor, his new partner; Melissa Banks and Sara Sykes and their solemn-faced gaffer, George Tenaka, representing the station; and Alex Raines, who held onto Julie's hand when it finally came out of his pocket. She was the only good thing to come out of the last few months. He looked at her and tried to smile as the priest offered his well-rehearsed last farewell to the flesh, of ashes and dust.

Beyond her, across the tops of the headstones, he saw the ancient forest that bordered the cemetery.

Coldfall Wood.

Once upon a time the trees had stretched for miles, but they'd been felled to make way for housing estates like the Rothery and the relentless creep of the modern world. Now, it was less than a quarter of the size it had been fifty years ago, and even that was less than a quarter of what it had been when Damiola had created Glass Town back in the '20s. It was difficult to imagine just how much the city could change, even discounting the fact that six months ago a labyrinth of streets no one had walked upon for decades suddenly redrew the familiar maps of the city overnight. No one seemed willing to talk about them or how they'd suddenly appeared at the mouths of familiar alleyways and street corners after Josh destroyed the anchors securing Damiola's grand illusion.

A car backfired somewhere off beyond the trees, which startled an unkindness of ravens into the sky. The black birds banked across the thick clouds and wheeled away, their caws carrying all the way back to the grave. It wasn't exactly a twenty-one gun salute.

Julie watched the birds take flight, but didn't really think about what he was seeing.

He just wanted to get out of there.

Alex squeezed his hand, mistaking his restlessness for grief.

The priest closed his bible, and lowered his head, leading them in one final prayer for Taff's soul, before Mel and Sara came forward to drop roses on the coffin lid. Julie threw a handful of dirt into the grave. There was plenty of symbolism in the gesture, despite the ritualistic nature of it.

He turned his back on the grave and walked back toward the car.

"We're going back to the Green Man to raise a glass for Taff," Tenaka said, coming up behind him.

"I'm not in the mood," Julie told him.

"Do you think we are?"

"Point taken."

"Then we'll see you there?"

"I'll catch up with you."

He unlocked the driver's side door and climbed in. Alex got into the seat opposite. He fired up the engine, but didn't pull away until the other cars had all left the small graveled parking lot. Instead, he put the radio on, catching the last few lines of Martin Stephenson and the Daintees "Even the Night" as it morphed into "Wholly Humble Heart." They were the songs of his youth, and on another day might have put a smile on Julie's face. It was getting dark, so he turned the headlights on. Spring flowers were in full bloom along the dry-stone wall cordoning off the holy ground. They were a riot of color against the gray.

"How are you holding up?" Alex asked. "It can't be easy . . ."

The one peculiarity of their relationship was that despite the fact that Taff, the Lockwoods, and Glass Town had brought them together, even tangentially, they never actually talked about what had happened to him. The past was embargoed. Nothing from back there could find its way here. It was for the best.

"I'll be fine," he said.

"I know you will, but that's not what I asked."

The last car left the church, taking the left-hand turn that would lead them back toward the Rothery, skirting the limits of Coldfall Wood, and driving down the slope of Cane Hill toward the Rothery and the Green Man.

Julie followed. The song changed. He drove without thinking. It was one of the few escapes left to him where he didn't have to worry about what the recovery of Taff's body meant for him. After all, he was the man whose partner hadn't just been killed, he'd been dissolved down to a couple of bones by a prime suspect who himself had disappeared right around the same time. It didn't matter that Julie knew that Seth Lockwood wasn't coming back, or why his body would never turn up in the concrete stanchions of some flyover. He couldn't tell anyone, and not talking was eating him up inside.

He didn't see the man until it was too late. He was a blur of pale flesh as he dashed out from between the rows of dark trees into the road, and in front of them. With Alex's screams filling the car, Julie hit the brakes and wrestled with the wheel, trying desperately to change direction of their sudden slide even though the momentum was against him. Caught in the headlights at the moment of impact, the man went up over the bonnet of the car and sprawled, broken, in the road.

The sound of bones breaking and steel crumpling was sickening.

With the engine still idling, Julie reached for the door handle, but before he could open the door, the man rose up into the full beam of the bright headlights and turned his head to stare at them.

He was naked, long dark hair cascading down across his shoulders, and even crouched down it was obvious that he was considerably taller than Julie. That wasn't what stopped Julie from opening the door. The naked man wore some sort of antlered headdress, only the glare of the headlights made it look as though the horns grew out of his scalp.

The moment was broken by the sound of another car coming up the road.

The horned man rose to his full height, turned, and in a blur of motion ran back toward the dark trees at the heart of Coldfall Wood. It had to be a trick of the light and dark, but in the last few strides, the man's pale skin seemed to shift, shimmering as he transformed into a majestic white stag that bounded off through the trees without looking back.

Julie stared at the trees, haunted by the visceral recollection of another accident on another street not so far from here. Everything about that first accident was as sharp in his memory as it had been the moment it happened. And understandably so. It had been his first glimpse into the wonders and horrors of Glass Town.

"What just happened?"

History repeated itself, he thought, but he wasn't about to say it aloud, because saying it made it real. And he wasn't ready for that.

2

It started with a single shocking act of violence. It wasn't random. It wasn't senseless, at least not to the kid holding the knife. It was about honor. Ollie Underwood died on the pavement outside the fried chicken fast-food place on the High Street, his blood slipping down between the cracks. It looked like paint in the too-bright glow of the restaurant's lights. "I hope she was worth it," were the last six words he ever heard. "Always," the last one he said. He even managed a smirk.

Jamshid Kirmani hated him body and soul.

He deserved to die for what he'd done. It wasn't romantic. No one would write a musical about his one-night stand with Aisha Kahn, which didn't last even close to a night or make it as far as a bed. Poets wouldn't be inspired by their jeans around the ankles— hands against the wall of this very restaurant—grunting not-so-sweet nothings.

Jam stood over the body, knife in hand; Ollie's blood on his jeans, honor only partially satisfied. There was still the matter of Aisha.

In that moment he was the poster boy for Broken Britain.

He had become everything the bigots hated and feared.

Jam saw himself reflected in the window, wiping the knife on his jeans, and inside himself, the frozen faces of two teenage girls beneath their hijabs: Darya trapped midbite unable to look away from him, Hajara holding her mobile phone. She stared at its screen, seeing him through it as she filmed the whole thing. He knew both of them from school. That recognition went both ways. They knew him.

The first scream came from behind him.

It broke the weird spell that had trapped the street in that moment, letting dread and panic and all of those mixed emotions that came with reality hit him with the shock of defibrillator paddles. Jam looked down, saw the consequences of his anger sprawled out one arm across his chest where Ollie had tried to stem the flow of blood, the other dragging its knuckles in the road, and he doubted himself.

Another scream made it real.

He started to run.

He didn't know where.

He wasn't thinking that far ahead.

He heard sirens in the distance, but surely they couldn't be for him already?

He didn't look back. Let them yell at him. Let them chase him.

He just needed to get out of there before the girls could name him, but then what?

Aisha.

It had always been about Aisha.

It wasn't just about honor or shame, it was more than that.

She was *everything* to him.

And she had betrayed him.

That hurt in ways he couldn't put words to.

He'd been stupid to think that what they had would last forever. He didn't understand her twisted version of love. How could he? He had nothing to compare it to or contrast it against. The only thing he knew for sure was that it shouldn't have been like this.

Jam reached the corner. Behind him, the screams became another instrument in the soundtrack of the city.

He dodged around an old woman struggling with overflowing shopping bags, the plastic stretched to the limit, and pushed between student lovers in their uniforms of torn jeans and T-shirts with the faded faces of long-dead musicians, breaking through their clasped hands. Thou shalt not worship false idols unless they died with heroin in their veins or choked on their own vomit in the name of their art.

He crossed the road without looking either way and kept on running. An endless line of cars of every shape, color, and size lined the curb, making it impossible to get to the other side.

He kept on running, feeling the adrenaline burn in his muscles and the fear trickle down his inside leg. His route took him out of the bright lights of the High Street into the garbage-lined avenues of grubby lace curtains and dirt-smeared windows that made up the façade of a city used to turning blind eyes when people were in trouble. Every window harbored a secret, every door some dark desire. None of them could be saved.

Street after street, each indistinguishable from the last, until he crossed into the Rothery. The first landmark he passed was the burned-out shell of The Hunter's Horns. Black scorch marks on the red bricks told their own story. The place had been abandoned for six months, ever since the fire had killed Gideon Lockwood, the old guy who'd owned it. He crossed the street again, well and truly in the estate now. Up ahead, crossing the road like it had every right to be there, he saw a majestic white stag with huge antlers. The great beast's hooves clipped on the asphalt road. It ignored him and walked on.

The lights were on in Sal's.

Faded bill posters filled with thick black block capital names—Eubank, Lewis, Haye, Hamed, Benn, Bruno, Froch, and Fury—covered the windows. Sometimes those familiar names were low down the bill, beneath the names of fighters no one remembered now, as if that offered Sal's some sort of authenticity if you ignored the fact that they could be picked up for a couple of quid on eBay.

He pushed open the door.

Sal's was an old sweat-and-sawdust gym.

It stank of every musk and pheromone; reeked of sweat and blood.

He knew she'd be here. She was always here. According to her, the old man had offered her salvation and she'd taken it with two clenched fists.

Two fighters sparred in the ring, one with flat parrying gloves in front of his face while the other wailed on him, repeating the left-left-right jab-jab cross pattern of blows over and over twenty times in the short time it took Jam to walk down the ramp into the main gym. "Again! Again! Good, chin down, guard up! Again!"

Aisha was on the speedball, her bandaged fists going to town on the pigskin. She was relentless. There were patterns to the punches, rhythms. Some dirty grunge rock with gravelly vocals offered a musical counterpoint to the endless punches. She was playing the tune, matching it riff for riff on the ball.

Her black hair was tied up in a ponytail. Sweat glistened on the skin at the nape of her neck and trickled down the bare curve of her spine beneath her training top. She pushed herself harder as the beat quickened. It was a dance. A brutal, violent dance.

The constant motion gave illusion of flight to the hummingbird tattoo on her shoulder. Jam hated that damned thing. She'd been buzzing with excitement as she peeled off her shirt and teasing away the gauze to expose the angry red skin beneath. It had been their first real fight. The beginning of the end. Aisha just refused to accept that she'd changed Allah's creation and what that meant. She didn't care. She was a modern woman. She wasn't bound by rules made up by some long-dead prophet who couldn't know the life she was going to live. He tried to argue with her, but she countered everything he could think of saying with the truth that women in Iran had more rights in the '70s than girls like her did now. It was burned in his brain. He didn't know how to argue with her. That hummingbird was more than just ink; it was the fundamental difference between them.

She didn't take her eye off the ball.

Maybe she was imagining his face in place of the leather?

There were four other men in the gym. Two well-defined muscle boys hovering over the weights, another wiry lightweight toweling himself down as he watched the guys spar in the ring. The fourth, a brute of a man with no neck and a serious case of roid rage was working the heavy bag. The sounds of his fists slapping the punch bag and the dance of the chain anchoring it to the ceiling filled the momentary silence between tracks. Sal's specter was all over the gym despite the fact the old man had been dead three years. There were no lights on in the office overlooking the training floor. They were never on these days. No one went up there.

Jam made it all the way to the speedball without anyone noticing him.

Aisha missed her punch, blowing the rhythm.

The ball cannoned off the backboard and swung violently on its spring.

"What are you doing here, Jam?" she said, and then she saw the blood and the knife in his hand. He had run all this way without letting go of it. "What have you done?"

Even with the world reduced to a point where it was just the two of them he couldn't find the words.

He wanted to tell Aisha he'd protected her honor. He wanted her to understand that he'd done it for her. But nothing would come out of his mouth.

He felt stupid.

"I'm fucked."

"What did you do, Jam?"

She looked down at his hands.

"You're frightening me, Jam. What did you do? Look at me." She reached out for him, to touch his cheek, but he backed away a step, keeping the distance between them.

He was shaking. He held his hands out, the knife and blood like an offering. "I did it for you."

"What? What did you do?" She sounded frightened. Properly scared. She should. She had no idea what he was capable of. He'd only just found out himself.

Jam said his name, "Ollie. He had to pay for what he did to you."

"He didn't *do* anything *to* me. We did it *together,* Jam. I'm not a victim."

"You didn't know what you were doing."

"I did."

"Stop it. Stop talking like that, Aye. Tell me what to do. Just tell me."

"Everything all right, Eye?"

Eye. That was what they called her here. Eye. Eye of the Tiger. Not Aye like him. They thought they were being clever. She turned slightly, showing him the wing tips of that hummingbird on her shoulder. Flaunting her imperfection.

"It's all good," she told the brute. He'd stepped away from the heavy bag. The fighters sparring in the ring had dropped their guard, too. It wasn't good. It was far from good. So far from good it could never be good again. He wanted to scream. The edge of the bandage around her right fist had worked itself free. She tucked it back into the wrap. "Isn't it, Jam?" And when he still didn't say anything she said, "Why don't you give me the knife? Just put it down. We can talk."

He nodded, but that was the last thing he wanted to do.

He looked into her eyes. Once upon a time they'd been every happy ending he could have dreamed for himself. Now they were dead to him. Or he was dead to them. Maybe that was it?

"I think you should go, mate. Get yourself cleaned up."

He nodded again, but he wasn't listening to a word they said.

"It's none of your business, *mate,*" he spat out the last word, making it perfectly obvious they were anything but. "So why don't you just fuck the fuck off."

"Watch your mouth, kid."

He stopped listening to them. He could hear something else. Another sound, like the gentle susurration of wind through fallen leaves. He couldn't focus on it, but it demanded his attention.

Hwaet! Áríseaþ!

She hadn't said that. He'd been watching her lips the entire time. She hadn't said a word.

"Did you hear that?"

"Hear what?"

"The voice? The whisper. Like the wind. Did you hear it?"

"You're really beginning to scare me, Jam. What's wrong with you?"

"You," he said, as though she was the answer to everything. "You broke me."

"You really should go," the Brute said again, always interrupting him, stopping him from saying what he wanted to say, from explaining. He felt the Brute's hand on his shoulder and couldn't help himself—Jam reacted to the touch instinctively, lashing out.

The knife cut across Aye's throat, opening up a second smile.

She didn't scream.

She clutched her hands to the wound like she thought she could somehow hold the blood back. Maybe she wasn't that smart after all. The arterial spray bled out across the spit-and-sawdust floor as her legs buckled.

"What the fuck have you done?" The Brute half-yelled.

The knife fell from Jam's hand.

He lurched away from the Brute's grasp.

Come to me.

He heard it again, louder this time.

"I'm sorry. I'm sorry. I'm sorry," he said, over and over; the prayer for forgiveness losing all meaning.

He ran.

And he didn't stop running.

3

They stood outside of the huge old house on Holly Lane.

"Are you sure there's no one in there?" Rupert Brooke asked. He didn't like it. He didn't like the climbers clinging to the weeping bricks, the little pitted holes where they dug into the grouting, or the broken glass set into the cement along the top of the walls; he didn't like the skeletal limbs of the trees or the rustle of the wind through those disfigured boughs; he didn't like the way the city felt like it didn't exist here, that it was just them and the house, hidden away from the world. The windows that hadn't been bricked up were thick with the accumulated filth of a century's pollution. A plaque with a leafy face spewing vegetation dominated the lintel above the front door, grinning down at them. The inscription above the face read *DIO VRIDI SCANCTO*. He had no idea what that meant.

"You're really starting to piss me off, Ru."

"What about the lights?"

Stephen Blackmoore hawked and spat a wad of phlegm onto the gravel. The logo on his T-shirt was as bright—and feral—as his grin. "On timers. I'm not an idiot. I know what I'm doing. I've watched this place for weeks. The lights come on about an hour before it gets dark now because they forgot that the clocks changed last weekend. No one's reset them. Trust me, no one's home. There's no alarm, either, it's a dummy box."

They watched the empty windows for a couple of minutes.

"So, what's the plan?"

Blackmoore held out a stone the size of his fist. "Why make things more complicated than they need to be?" The quiet went both ways; if they couldn't hear the city out there the city couldn't hear them in here. And with that, Blackmoore crunched off across the gravel. His black leather jacket and black jeans rendered him nigh on invisible. Ru didn't follow him. Not at first. Not until he heard the sound of breaking glass.

Blackmoore punched the stone through the small stained-glass window inset in the heavy old door, shattering another leafy face, and reached through to open it from the inside. It was as easy as that.

Ru pulled down his balaclava and followed him inside.

The first thing he noticed was the sea of takeaway menus and unopened bills and final demands on the doormat. There must have been six months' worth of them. More. The second thing he noticed was the music coming from upstairs. It had an ethereal raspy quality to it, a woman's soulful voice above the crackle and hiss of old vinyl. The words were spellbinding. He stood there in the hallway listening to the singer belt out a challenge to the sinners trying to hide from their fate come Judgment Day like she was judgment and wrath rolled into one.

Ru shook his head, ready to turn tail and bolt, but Blackmoore stopped him.

He gestured toward the open door of the front room.

Ru began to shake his head again as Blackmoore turned a look of withering disdain on him, making no attempt to mask his utter contempt. "Just fucking grow a pair," his friend said and set off deeper into the house looking for cash convertibles: jewelry, money under the mattress, that kind of thing.

Ru went into the lounge. The room was a time capsule to the '70s with garish wallpaper and too-bright fabrics that were worn threadbare. It was bigger than his entire flat. The bay window that looked out over the gravel courtyard was big enough to screen a movie on. There were dead flowers in the vase on the coffee table. The water in the vase was a black sludge that smelled rank.

There was a bowl of red-striped mints on top of the piano and an oil painting of forest creatures, woodland nymphs, and fae folk frolicking in a leafy glen. They each had weirdly human expressions that gave him the creeps. More so when he noticed the details hidden in the shadows, another figure hinted at by the leaves, lurking there just out of sight. Beside it were two solemn clowns that could not have looked more different if they tried with their angular faces and sad eyes. They were both signed with the same name. Ru didn't know much about art, but he couldn't imagine anyone paying more than a few quid for the clowns, and the woodland scene was far too unwieldy to be worth the effort.

There was a tobacco tin on the table and a packet of cigarette papers resting on top of a newspaper that offered a headline from the best part of a year ago. There were tacky brass ornaments on the mantelpiece, none of them worth more than a fiver secondhand. There were a pair of slippers beside the open hearth, and burned-out white coals still banked up in the pit.

The only big bit of furniture that could conceivably have been hiding treasures was a mahogany dresser with glass doors and hundreds of little shot glasses, fragile glass ballerinas, and other oddments inside; things collected over a lifetime and filled with meaning and memories, but of precious little real value. He turned the three drawers out onto the floor; they were filled with Kodak-yellow paper wallets stuffed with photographs and pens of every color and size imaginable, notepads, lottery ticket stubs, and other nonsense.

He turned his back on the mess.

The music stopped as he reached the door. His heart hitched a beat as the silence dragged out for a moment, only to be broken by the sound of the mechanical arm dropping the needle back at the beginning of the record. The crackles of the lead-in lasted a couple of seconds before the first haunting strain of piano filled the house.

Blackmoore emerged from the kitchen, looking pissed off.

He pointed up the stairs. Ru really didn't want to go up there. While there was music they could move about down here unheard, but going up increased the likelihood of things getting messy. Blackmoore didn't hang about, he took the stairs two and three at a time. Ru had no choice but to follow him.

The music came from one of six rooms on the landing. It was the only one with the door open. A low yellow light burned beyond the threshold.

Blackmoore stood in the doorway.

He didn't move for the longest time.

The singer's voice wove a spell around them both, holding everything in the house absolutely still.

It couldn't last, but even so Ru didn't take the final step from the staircase onto the landing until Blackmoore breathed out a barely audible, "Fuck me."

There was a strange smell in the air. It wasn't just the rancid water in a couple of vases. Up here it was all-pervading. Sickness. Rot. It was everywhere—in everything.

He stepped into the room.

One entire wall was taken up with bookcases, another with records, sleeve after sleeve after sleeve crammed in so tightly they all seemed to blend into one. There was another woodland painting, too. This one darker: the shadowy creature more obvious in the brushstrokes, hinting at the emergence of an antlered man. There was a red velvet love seat and another low table with the fixings of a pipe spilled out across the top of it.

Ru didn't see any of this. He only had eyes for the mummified corpse sitting in the floral-patterned armchair beside the still-playing gramophone. The old man was long dead. Not days or weeks. Not even months. He'd been alone in his chair for almost a year, shriveling down to a withered husk that barely resembled the man he had been. Ru stared at him, unable to look away. His skin was blackened and leathery, stretched taut around a perpetual scream. There had been no graceful journey into death. The old guy had died in agony.

Ru heard the dead man's voice speaking right into his mind.

He was sure it was him; not part of the song.

He stared at the corpse as, without moving his lips the dead man said to him:

Hwaet! Áríseaþ!

He had no idea what it meant; only that he must answer the call.

4

Charlie Mann was alone in the world.

Once upon a time that simple statement hurt—like being doused in petrol and set alight pain—but in the six years since he'd lost everything, the hurt had dulled. Now, whenever he thought about it, the pain was less visceral, more like the tip of a blade pressing up against his cheek. While he may never heal, he could at least hope that in a few years' time he'd barely register it. There would always be days like today though that brought it back.

He walked the damp streets back to the group home, the rain on his face serving as tears.

Today was always going to be a bad day. Every birthday was. But this one started the countdown on his last year in Herla House. He had twelve months to find a job—any job, it didn't matter how shitty, and get some money behind him so he could move out on his eighteenth. It was all about twelve months from now. The long game. The escape.

He kicked a stone along the street. It bounced off the metal base of a lamppost and rolled away into the road.

Being told he wasn't good enough to answer the phones for a free newspaper was just the icing on the cake he didn't have.

The test call had been absolute bollocks. He'd gone through the canned response written on the sheet, introducing himself, asking how he could help, and the guy on the other end of the line had said, "I've got a punch bag to sell." He'd sounded completely normal. "Hardly used." Charlie dutifully wrote down the description, not really listening to what he was being told. "Five five, a little chubby, really fucking grating personality, never shuts up, always moaning, and can't cook for shit, but she can take a hell of a beating." He laughed. What else was he supposed to do? It couldn't be real. It was stupid. So he'd laughed. And they'd said they didn't think he was suited for the job. They'd been nice enough about it, but that was that. They'd suggested he think about going back to college, maybe try and get some practical skills, maybe plumbing or building or something. There was no point arguing with them. He thanked them for their time and left, feeling like shit.

The familiar iron gates were closed. He could see the silhouette of the old house between the iron bars. There were lights on in more than half of the windows, leaving the dark windows looking like some gap-toothed smile. It was a huge Regency place; the kind of building developers stripped and turned into half a dozen flats to turn a tidy profit. There was a buzzer on the side and a security camera mounted on the brickwork above it. Climbing plants dug into the layers of cement, covering more than half the perimeter wall. There was a smaller wooden door set into the wall like the entrance to some secret garden that the residents used to come and go. They all had keys, but the door was never locked.

He crunched his way across the loop of gravel driveway, and down the short flight of six steps to the basement door. He never used the main door. That meant walking past the office and having to make small talk with whoever was on duty. He wasn't into small talk. He wasn't that much of a fan of big talk, either.

Penny was in the kitchen, blitzing a witch's brew of fruit, yogurt, and multigrains and God alone knew what else into a purple smoothie. It didn't look delicious. It looked purple; that was about the best he could say for it. "Evening, Birthday Boy," she said, seeing him with the eyes she obviously had in the back of her head. She didn't look up or turn around. She was the sportiest of the kids who called Herla House home, more at peace in the gym or on the track running herself into the ground with her dreams of Olympic glory. She was good. Better than good. She was special. She had what it took to go all the way; everyone knew it. It was all down to how much she wanted it, and Penny Grainger *wanted* it. Fresh out of the shower, her hair scraped back in its usual ponytail, she wore her sweats and a plain white Nike T-shirt. She was three months older than Charlie, meaning three months closer to leaving Herla House for the big wide world. She was comfortably a decade more grown up and street smart than he was though, in that way girls have of just knowing more about life and leaving you feeling insecure about everything you want to say or do.

He wasn't looking forward to those three months without her around. She'd always said they'd go together, maybe share a flat in Camden, by the lock, and hit the clubs every weekend dancing until the sun came up. It was a good dream. Penny had been here the day he arrived, along with Zoe Fenn, who made up the third corner of their triangle. There were plenty of nights Zoe had put up with his tears and anger at being dumped on by the world while Penny always offered more practical solutions that involved getting drunk or getting laid. That was always her answer. They were his best friends. The sisters he'd inherited. He couldn't imagine his life without them. It went beyond blood; he was hopelessly in love with the pair of them.

"It is," he agreed.

"Funny boy. Bracken's on the warpath."

Bracken, *mein kommondant* to the group home's Auschwitz, ran the place with a bitter, bald fist. It wasn't exactly iron, but there was no getting around the fact he could be a right bastard if he set his mind to it. Charlie had heard all sorts of rumors when he first moved in, including one about Bracken's hand straying a little too close to a couple of the kids in his care up in the pool room in the attic. Little jokes like teaching them how to handle their balls, that kind of thing. He didn't know if it was true: the kids in question, Stephen

Blackmoore and Rupert Brooke, had left a couple of months before Charlie arrived, but there was no denying there was something a bit creepy about the guy at the best of times. And then there were the vague memories of kindnesses that, looking back on them, might just have been more, Bracken trying to groom him for whatever he had in mind, and his unhealthy interest in Charlie's sex life, telling him how he should get in there with Penny, how that kind of girl was pure filth. That kind of fake-matey talk made Charlie deeply uncomfortable, so more often than not he just stayed out of the old paedo's way.

"What am I supposed to have done now?" Charlie asked, but then answered the question himself before Penny could. "'It's your fault, *boy,* it's *always* your fault, haven't we established that already?'" he said, doing a passable impression of the bitter Scotsman.

She laughed.

He liked making her laugh.

It was a good feeling.

"Well, I'm going sit in my room and listen to suicide-inducing music for a while to get in the mood for the party later."

"You do that," Penny said. "And maybe think about a shower," she said sweetly. "You don't smell so good."

He did just that, enjoying the ten minutes under the piping hot water before he changed into his armor of ripped jeans and a faded Joy Division T-shirt, then he sat on the bed with his headphones on listening to *Closer* as loudly as the tiny cans would take without distorting. The music was rich with someone else's pain, and knowing Ian Curtis's story only made that aching sadness all the more real. His lyrics were all about coldness, pressure, darkness, crisis, failure, collapse, the loss of control, all of the things that echoed in the turmoil of Charlie's life. People didn't understand the importance of music when it came to knowing yourself. People might wear different T-shirts with different band names or clever logos in their uniforms of nonconformity, but the reality was they all wore them just the same, transforming them into a teenage army of fashion-driven drones. Different fashions, different darknesses and lights, but they all echoed the same basic desire to belong *somewhere,* to be part of *something*. He wasn't the only seventeen-year-old kid to find comfort in Joy Division. He was as big a cliché as the girls who fawned over One Direction and Justins Bieber and Timberlake.

He put a black shirt on over the top of his T-shirt to hide the cuts on his left arm. They were his life carved out on his flesh. He was a cutter. One scar for every problem as it reached the point where it became overwhelming, like some crazy old physician bleeding his patient to get the demons out. Four of those cuts had arrived on other birthdays. It was always a bad day. It was one of two days you were supposed to spend with your family, and all these particular anniversaries did was underscore the fact that he was and always would be alone.

As he was fastening his cuffs the door opened. It was Penny carrying a cupcake with a single candle in its frosting and singing "Happy Birthday." He pushed his headphones down so they hung around his neck and grinning, took the cake off her. He blew the candle out. "I'm not telling you what I wished for."

"Good. I don't want to know," she said. "Now come on, I'm taking you out for a milkshake. Every Birthday Boy needs a bit of brain freeze."

He took the candle out of the frosting then took a bite that was half the size of the cake and made a show of scoffing it down while she shook her head.

"You're such a pig."

"And you love me for it," Charlie said, pushing the last bite of cake into his mouth and licking his fingers as he hopped off the bed. "Okay, I'm in. Anything to piss off Bracken," he said with a grin, and then the two of them crept down the stairs to the back door and out into the yard without closing it behind them.

It was never about milkshake.

They walked around the fringes of the Rothery into the more affluent streets around the shithole they called home, looking for a suitable birthday mobile, something smooth enough to turn a few jealous heads but not so desirable as to be locked down by some high-tech incapacitating alarm. "This one's too hot," Penny said, looking at a

Porsche 911 Cabriolet. "And this one's too cold," she said, her eyes moving on to a battered Ford Mondeo.

"But this one's just right," Charlie finished for her, smiling at the sight of a flame red sports car parked up in the driveway that was just begging to go for a joyride.

It took Penny less than ten seconds to pop the lock and open the door.

Another thirty seconds had the ignition overridden and the engine purring.

Charlie clambered into the passenger seat and then they were off, tearing through the night streets toward the ring road.

Penny wound the windows down, putting her foot to the floor and weaving in and out of slow-moving traffic as she raced from main street to side street to backstreet and back again, the still-light shop windows becoming a blur as they tore through the city. The rain intensified as she drove, lending a surreal aspect to the scene. They didn't talk much. Most of the ride was taken up with laughing and shouts of "Left!" and "Right!" as corners came up almost too quickly to take.

They crossed the river.

Seen like this, the lights of the city were all the birthday present he could have ever asked for.

He sank back into the seat enjoying the spectacle of his windswept, rain-drenched city through the windscreen as Penny turned the radio on, then drove one handed whilst fiddling with the dial until she found a tune she liked. The tune was backed by the dopplering siren of a police car behind them.

"About time," she said. This was what the game was all about, cat and mouse. She slowed enough to let the flashing light close the gap between them, then put her foot down, somehow finding more speed under the bonnet. The city lights looked like dying stars tonight, torn apart by the driving rain sluicing beneath the windscreen wipers. A red double-decker with its sign promising a destination that sounded almost exotic cut across the two lanes of traffic on the bridge, kicking up a spray. Their headlights did the dance of the streets.

Penny focused intensely on the road ahead, changing through the gears and manipulating the pedals with unerring skill. Street racing wasn't exactly a talent that went on a CV, but it was part of what growing up on the Rothery meant. She cut up the Rover between them and the bus, then broke every traffic law on the books, overtaking the bus on the inside in a maneuver that had the passenger side door scraping up against the safety rails before they emerged on the other side of the suicidal charge amid a blare of horns.

She was still laughing when a red light on the far side of the bridge nearly killed them both, but managed to throw the car into a series of evasive twists and turns that put four lanes of cross-traffic between them and the police. She gave the chasing cops the finger through the rearview mirror, doubled down, and whipped the car through a series of ridiculously right turns and double-backs before reaching the arches down beside the river. The husk of a burned-out car was abandoned beneath the railway bridge. There wasn't a single flake of paint left on the warped metal, and all of the upholstery and soft fittings had fused into an amorphous mess of plastic and faux leather. Broken bricks lay scattered across the hard-packed earth around the car, an inner-city re-creation of Stonehenge's pagan altar. The wall inside the arch of the railway bridge had been daubed with a stylized rendition of the horned forest god, only he had no forests to watch over, only tower blocks with names like sycamore, oak, and elm.

They abandoned the car and ran away whooping and hollering as the siren haunted the near distance, still searching hopelessly for them. They split up; both taking a different route back toward the Rothery, guaranteeing that even if the law did spot them, there was no chance both of them would be hauled in. As it was, the sirens rolled on for another five minutes or so, going in circles, and then gave up.

Charlie made it back to the green in the heart of the Rothery first, and spent a good ten minutes sitting with his back up against the lightning-split tree in front of the burned-out shell of The Hunter's Horns waiting for Penny to catch up. A flicker of movement caught his eye—a majestic beast utterly out of place in this shithole—a huge white stag with a crown of antlers walked across the green, seeming to bow to the lightning-struck tree before it walked on. It was utterly mesmerizing. He watched it until it walked away up Cane Hill and disappeared from sight.

When Penny finally appeared, she was dancing in the street, arms flung out wide as she spun round and around, and tossed her head back, howling with laughter between butchered song lyrics, making him smile and forget about the stag as he enjoyed watching her dance and loving her just a little bit more.

Hwaet! Áríseaþ!

"You what?" Penny called out as she reached the grass.

"I didn't say anything," Charlie said.

"Well, it wasn't me," Penny said. There was no one else out on the green, no one in the streets around them. "It sounded like it came from here. A man's voice. You sure it wasn't you, Birthday Boy? You trying to freak me out?"

Charlie shook his head as he pushed himself to his feet.

"Weird."

Penny reached out to steady herself against the tree and as her hand came into contact with the bark everything changed. She understood what she had to do. What *they* had to do.

"Time to go back and face Bracken and death by seventeen candles," Charlie offered a lopsided smile. "And cake. Cake is good."

"Not yet," Penny told him. "There's somewhere we need to be. Can't you feel it?"

He shook his head again.

Penny held out her hand for Charlie to take.

This time he could feel it through her, the ancient tree providing the connection back to the land. His mind filled with images of what had once been a green and pleasant place. The landmarks—the natural ones—were all the same, all familiar, but they had been built on and bled dry over and over until all that remained was the lifeless brick and tile of the Rothery. He was seeing a glimpse of what this place had been like before, and it was beautiful. Unrecognizable, but undeniably beautiful.

He saw the white stag again as a voice filled his head.

Þes sy eorðcyning . . .

This is my land . . .

I am her king . . .

Charlie pulled his hand free from Penny's. With the contact broken, the voice fell silent. Penny looked as though she was in the throes of some intense religious experience, all thoughts of cake banished.

5

Julie Gennaro had dropped Alex off at the hospital an hour ago. Neither of them had touched a drop at Taff's wake. He'd picked Ellie Taylor up from the station and now the pair of them sat watching a giant unload the white-paneled van outside the charity shop on the High Street. The guy was a skinhead. Even from this distance, it was obviously down to standard male pattern baldness rather than some sort of fashion or political statement. He was big. Easily six three, six four, and built like the proverbial brick shithouse, his muscles like over-inflated balloons. He dragged a couple of black garbage bags to the side of the road and bundled them up against the wall. *Clothes,* Julie thought, seeing a white cuff poking through a tear in the plastic. Next out was an odd-looking metal-legged chair with a padded seat.

The guy set it down beside the door.

It took Julie a moment to realize why it looked so peculiar: it was a commode.

He put a standard light with carpet for a lampshade down beside it as though setting it up for the owner to take a break curbside and enjoy the evening air as he read a book and relieved himself. Then he put a balalaika down on the seat. It was one of the strangest juxtapositions of life he could remember seeing, a commode and a balalaika, but of course all lives were like that when they were gathered together in one place, no rhyme or reason to how the clutter of everyday was accumulated. These were a dead man's things, he realized. The last few remnants of a house clearance. Julie couldn't help but wonder if the deceased had played the instrument, or if his carer had, and now that he was gone had no need of it? That set his thoughts wandering down a strange avenue that culminated in a melancholic question: *What was the last song from those strings? Was it something silly or poignant? A good-bye, maybe?*

He realized he was staring but couldn't help himself.

So much had happened in the last six months, some of it even good.

Julie was a different man. He'd been given a second chance by Josh Raines and taken it with both hands. Even so, there wasn't a shift that went by without him thinking about Taff, the Hollywood succubus in the white dress, and the horrors they'd lived through. It was hard to believe the Lockwoods were gone, but there was no mistaking the power vacuum around the Rothery their deaths had left behind. As hard to believe as it was, the place was worse now than it had been last summer. The place was a pressure cooker waiting to blow, all of that anger and frustration simmering away beneath the surface. It was only ever going to take one thing, one spark, for the whole place to burn.

It was in the air.

And right up until that pale-skinned man with his headdress of antlers had stepped in front of his car, all of the crazy things he'd been a part of with Josh felt less and less real, fading in the way of a dream. But he'd seen the impossible again, the man metamorphosing into a powerful white stag, and no matter what else happened, he was never going to forget.

He moved from the flat above the shops to another flat, this one a newer build, trading his view of takeaway restaurants and their neon signs for one of trees. The new place overlooked the outskirts of Coldfall Wood, not too far from the cemetery where they'd just buried the last of Taff. The wood was one of the few surviving patches of the ancient Doomsday woodlands of London. It was a primary wood, meaning they thought that the trees had been there all the way back in prehistoric times.

Sometimes he looked out of his window and just let *time* sink in.

The biggest change, though, was the most unexpected one of all. Alex.

He'd found love, or at least the beginnings of something that was certainly heading that way. Only her brother called her Lexy, she insisted, and she hated Sandi or Sandii, Sandie or Sandra, had no time for Lex—which made her sound like a supervillain—Alexa, or any other less masculine variant, and who was he to argue?

He didn't see much of Josh these days—they didn't do family dinners or go to Orient games together, nothing like that, but what he did see was enough to know his transformation had been every bit as radical his own. Josh spent most of his days walking endlessly around the city looking for something that he was never going to find. There was an air of sadness about him now that was thoroughly depressing, like he'd lost himself along with everything else. With nothing to keep him there, he'd moved out of Boone's old place on the Rothery to the shrine to Eleanor Raines in Rotherhithe, the one good thing he'd inherited through his family's obsession.

Alex and Josh couldn't have been more different despite being carved from the same genetic building blocks. Josh was rootless, restless, still looking for the man he was destined to be, but Alex knew exactly what kind of woman she was. The first thing she'd asked Julie, no more than five minutes into their first date, was if he was a feminist. His answer, without even having to think about it for a second, was, "Isn't everyone?"

"Only the people worth knowing," she said, then told him to stay put for two minutes while she went to put some money into the jukebox. Her selections were anything but girl powered. She might be an awesome woman in so many ways, but she had seriously poor taste in music.

Just thinking about the songs put a smile on his face.

The delivery guy dragged another couple of bags out of the van, then emerged with an old black woolen greatcoat, like something out of coldest scenes of *Doctor Zhivago*.

His new partner turned to him and said, "Wait here."

She left the car door open as she clambered out.

"Sir? Excuse me?"

The big guy turned to look at her, puzzled, then saw the uniform and became immediately defensive. "What?" Not: *What can I do for you, officer?* Just: *What?*

"That instrument? How much do you want for it?"

"You want it? Have it. Better it goes to a good home, I guess."

"Let me give you something for it."

The guy shook his head. "Ain't mine to sell, I just emptied the place. The old guy died. Family didn't want the stuff. Knock yourself out."

She took it.

The guy ignored her as he continued to unload the last few things from the back of his van.

That was it, the sum of a life laid out on the street outside a charity shop.

It didn't amount to much.

She opened the back door and laid the balalaika on the back seat, then clambered back into the passenger seat.

"Didn't have you pegged for a Russian music aficionado?"

"I'm a woman of many talents," Ellie Taylor said, offering a lopsided grin. That she was. And as partners went she had one big thing in her favor: she wasn't Taff Carter. He could forgive her pretty much anything because of that, and all things being equal a love of the balalaika wasn't the worst secret she could have kept from him.

The call came through before she could close the door. The dispatcher's voice crackled over the airwaves. There was trouble on High Street, a stabbing. The culprit had been sighted making his way on foot, heading south from the scene, toward the Rothery.

That was the spark.

He knew it even as he heard the words. Six months of steadily mounting tensions were about to boil over and there was nothing he could do about it.

Ellie picked up the radio to respond to the call as he slammed the car into gear and peeled away from the curb at speed. She still hadn't buckled up by the time the white van was a distant gleam in the mirror.

It was less than three minutes to the scene.

Julie saw two teenage girls in the street, a few steps removed from the crowd that had gathered around the body. He fired up the siren, making sure everyone knew they were coming.

The girls met them at the car as they pulled over.

"What happened?" Ellie asked, already out of the car before it had stopped moving.

He left her to deal with the girls and hurried over to the milling crowd. This had to be done right. No second chances. Even the slightest screwup and it was all going to hell. "Let me through," he said, and like magic words, the crowd parted. He hunkered down beside the boy, checking his pulse and airways first, but it was obvious there was nothing he could do. There was blood everywhere. It had seeped down between the cracks in the pavement. It puddled in the road, partially obscuring the double yellow lines. "Step back, please. Give me some room. Step back." He could have repeated it until he was blue in the face, no one was moving. Death was a magnet, holding them locked in place.

All the training in the world could never prepare you for something like this.

His instinct was to take his coat off and cover the kid's face to give him some sort of dignity in death, but that was the man thinking, not the policeman. Everything he did now had to be about preserving the crime scene.

He lifted his face to stare up at a couple of men wearing the gravy-and-batter-stained uniforms of the takeaway restaurant, and said, "You two, make some space, we need to get the paramedics through and we'll have to start taping off the area so people don't trample all over the evidence." That seemed to get through to them, and adding their own shouts of, "All right, everyone, move back, give him some space, come on," to Julie's, they gradually cleared a little breathing space for him.

It didn't last long.

Ellie hunkered down beside him, holding one of the girls' mobile phones.

"Take a look at this," she said, showing him the video Hajara had filmed of the murder. The picture was clear, even with the glare of the restaurant's lights reflected in the glass window between them. He watched the silent exchange wishing the mic could have picked up the words that passed between them as the knife was driven home with brutal force. That wasn't the worst of it; it was the detached way with which the kid turned to look at the camera, wiping the knife off on his jeans, before he turned to run.

"His name's Jamshid Kirmani. The victim's Ollie Underwood. They are in the sixth form at Albion Grange."

"Do the girls know what it was about?"

"Another one of their classmates, Aisha Kahn."

"Okay we need to find her, priority one, make sure she's safe. As long as Kirmani is out there there's room for this to get so much worse than it already is," Julie said. Still kneeling over Ollie's body, he unclipped the radio from his lapel and called it in. "Dispatch, this is Gennaro. We've got one fatality here. The attacker's name is Jamshid Kirmani. A sixth former at Albion Grange. Eyewitnesses captured the whole thing on video. Looks like it is some sort of honor killing. There's a girl, one of their classmates, Aisha Kahn. She needs protecting until we bring Kirmani in."

"Too late for that," the dispatcher said. "Banks and Sykes just responded to a call over at Sal's Gym. She's been stabbed. Paramedics are on the way, but it doesn't look good."

"Shit. Just shit. And Kirmani?"

"Taken flight."

He looked around him. There were already maybe 150 people in the street, gawkers mainly, but there were others among the crowd looking for confirmation of what they thought had happened, not just ready but eager to take the law into their own hands.

"We're going to need more bodies on the street."

"That's the last thing we want," Julie said, the two of them meaning completely different things.

6

Tommy Summers and Daniel Ash sat side by side on the park bench; empty lager cans spread out in a circle around their feet. They were angry. They'd been on the High Street watching Ollie Underwood's body being hauled into an ambulance, not that there was anything the paramedics could do but zip him up in a body bag. That shit Kirmani had gutted him like a fish. That kind of disrespect couldn't be allowed to go unanswered. There needed to be a reckoning. A good old-fashioned eye for biblical eye. Justice. Because who in this fucked-up city looked out for the good kids like Ollie Underwood?

Well, tonight, they did.

They watched the game.

It wasn't much more than a kickabout, but a few of the lads were going for it. The coach's voice barking out commands that made no sense to either of the boys accompanied energetic claps and flurries of movement on the training ground. It wasn't quite jumpers for goalposts, but it was close, with four bright orange traffic cones arranged as makeshift goals at either end of a pitch at what was mostly mud. The kids were oblivious to the rain even as it went from a few fat drops to a genuine downpour, and slid about making rash challenges and risking broken legs.

They were watching one kid in particular, Musa Dajani. He had the world at his feet. That's what everyone said whenever his name came up. It was obvious he was special, even to a couple of no marks like Tom and Danny who had never kicked a ball in their lives. The ball seemed to be glued to his foot, he'd twist and turn and somehow find a pass, threading it through a tangle of legs and mud with perfect weighting, and always seemed to have space and time to do whatever he wanted even though everyone else was busy being kicked and sliding around caked in mud. Musa was just better than the rest; it was as simple as that.

Which made him perfect for what they had in mind.

One of the dads on the touchline crouched down beside his two-year-old son, talking to him all the while as he changed him from a smart little suit jacket into his Batman jumper. "It's like Bruce Wayne becoming Batman," he said to the delighted boy, then seeing Tom and Daniel watching him, offered a wink.

"Fantastic," Danny said, smiling right back.

It was a nice moment. A proper dad moment. The kind of thing he'd like to do if he ever had kids.

The little lad walked side by side with his dad, his tiny hand in the bigger man's light grip, beaming with pride. In that moment he really was Batman and it wasn't just make-believe.

Tom took a deep swig from the gold can in his hand, draining it, then crumpled the aluminum and dumped it on the grass with the rest of their discards.

A whistle blew in the center of the park and then half of the boys made a show of rubbing their celebrations in the faces of the other half before they filed off toward the changing rooms.

They'd managed to down the rest of their lagers before Musa emerged, showered, with his kit bag slung over his shoulder. His trainers were painfully white. Brand new. He had his headphones on and walked past them lost in the music. He didn't acknowledge the two boys, but he did walk just a little bit faster as he passed them.

"Time to make our presence felt, I think," Tom said.

He pushed himself to his feet and followed the young footballer.

Danny was a couple of steps behind him, and had to hustle to catch up.

A stray dog barked in the distance. That wasn't something you heard so much anymore, he thought, a bit like the white dog shit that used to be everywhere when he was small. Now it was all rich brown and healthy crap. He chuckled to himself. Tom gave him a weird look, as if wondering how he could find anything funny in what they were about to do. He scratched at the tattoo of the spider's web on the side of his neck, the fat vein there pulsing hard as his breathing quickened.

Musa glanced back over his shoulder, sensing them behind him.

They didn't break their stride.

The dog stopped barking before they reached the edge of the park. Weirdly, there were no other sounds to replace it. The night was eerily quiet. It was as though a protective vacuum had gone up around the park, sealing it away from the city.

Musa looked back again, his footsteps quickening again.

The boys kept their steady pace, falling into step beside each other as they marched from one puddle of streetlight to the next. Twenty feet closer to the gate, Musa started to run.

Tom and Danny took off after him, their longer legs eating the distance between them in seconds. Tom slammed his hands into the boy's kit bag, sending him sprawling across the ground.

There was blood on the chips of stone from where they'd cut through his trousers and opened the meat of his knee. It wasn't a lot, but once spilled it couldn't be taken back. The effect it had on Tom was primal, as though the smell of it tripped a mental switch that woke some dormant gene, transforming him into a feral animal. He launched kick after kick into Musa's back, lifting the boy bodily off the ground with the sheer ferocity of his attack.

The boy tried to curl up into a protective ball even as another vicious kick dug into his kidneys.

Danny heard him choking on his tongue and realized he was in trouble.

But Tom wasn't stopping.

Again and again he delivered crippling blows, then, not content with the damage he'd done, dropped onto his hands and knees, sitting across Musa's body, and punched him over and over until his knuckles were raw and bloody. "Fucking terrorist cunt, this is for

Ollie Underwood. Remember that name. Ollie fucking Underwood. He was worth ten of you ragheads."

"That's enough, Tommy," Danny said, but Tom wasn't listening. Another savage blow had the boy gargling blood. He wasn't coughing it up, it just dribbled out of his mouth. His eyes rolled up into his head. And still Tommy didn't stop wailing on him, his fists beating out a savage tattoo. "Jesus Christ, Tommy, you're *killing* him," Danny half screamed, and this time when his friend didn't stop, Danny dragged him off Musa and crouched down over the kid protectively, not thinking about what he was doing as he put his fingers down the kid's throat and tried to fish out his tongue. Musa convulsed beneath him, and then, even as Tommy hammered his fist into the side of Danny's head yelling, *"Let the fucking shit die!"* managed to hook his finger beneath the meat his tongue and cleared the boy's airway. It wasn't much, but it was enough to save his life for a few minutes more.

Hwaet! Áríseaþ!

"What the fuck did you just say? Speak English you fucking cunt. You can, can't you, you ignorant fuck?" Tommy raged, but it wasn't the kid talking. The voice came from far away and yet all around them at the same time, seeming to whisper with the rustle of the leaves and linger in the drumming of the rain.

"It wasn't him," Danny said, still disorientated from the shock of the blow to the head. He felt a surge of sickness swell deep in his stomach and come clawing its way up his throat desperate to get out. He fell forward on his hands and knees, puking his guts up.

Tommy stood over him.

"You know what that was?" Without waiting for an answer, he howled again and again and again in quick succession, each one rawer than the last. "That was a fucking call to arms, mate. This is our time. Can't you feel it? These bastards are going to bleed." He held up his hands. "This is *my* land," he said, echoing the voice heard by Charlie and Penny half a dozen streets away. "And I am the king."

Tommy turned and walked away, following the voice toward the trees on the far side of the park.

He left Danny kneeling a few feet away from his unmoving victim.

Danny crawled on his hands and knees to Musa's side, willing the kid to be alive as he fumbled in his pocket for his mobile phone intending to call for help.

A hundred yards away Tommy stopped walking. He tilted his head to the side as though listening to a voice only he could hear, then turned to shout, "We're going to need that piece of shit, bring him with you when you finally get your shit together."

7

The lightning-struck tree was a prison.

The world lurched around him, his horizon veering away alarmingly.

Charlie Mann reached out to steady himself, his right hand catching a low-hanging branch. In that moment, as skin and bark came into contact, Charlie's mind flooded with images of the great woods, towering trees and their lichen-smeared trunks, of moss-covered broken stones, of King Stag, the majestic white-antlered Lord of the Great Hunt he had seen only moments ago crossing the Rothery. And in that moment they were one, he was the Monarch of the Wild Hunt and the Monarch of the Wild Hunt was a boy on his seventeenth birthday. The image was fleeting; the shadow-burn of the Summer King lingering long after the last leaf had fallen away. He heard voices, chants, a stampede, rushing, rushing, rushing through his mind.

And then he saw fire.

He knew what he had to do.

He left Penny at the tree outside of The Hunter's Horns, running along the side of the road sniffing the air like he was trying to root out truffles. He moved from car to car, crouching down to inhale the filth of the underside, then pushed himself up and ran on to the next until he found the leak he was looking for.

Charlie dropped to his knees, reaching into his back pocket for the penknife digging into his ass, and flicked the blade out. Gripping onto the rusted bumper with his left hand, he leaned in beneath the car to the dripping fuel tank and jammed the tip of the blade into the rusted metal, turning the drip into a trickle into a steady stream as he worked it wider. Charlie cupped his hands beneath the hole, filling them with petrol. When he was sure he had enough, he crawled out from under the car and smeared it all over his coat, covering the material in black handprints.

Carrying the petrol-soaked jacket back to the grass square and the lightning-struck tree, Charlie wedged it into the vee where the wood had divided, and put a match to it.

It took a few seconds for the material to burn, wisps of black smoke curling off the sleeve where the match touched the stain. His fingertips burned before the coat did. Charlie struck a second match and dropped it onto the coat and stepped back.

This time it burned.

Penny stood beside him, watching the flames slowly rise, charring the tree trunk and slowly eating through the bark to get at the dried-out pulp of the wood itself.

It took five minutes to really burn, but when it did, it *burned*.

Charlie watched the flames dance, seeing shapes inside them.

Beside him, Penny breathed heavily, hypnotized by the sight.

The flames lit the planes of their faces, making it look as though they were in the grip of a rapture.

"Look. Can you see it?"

"I can see him," Charlie said, looking beyond the flames to the green where the white stag stood behind the tree, watching them.

"His horns . . . He is . . . *beautiful*."

The flames shrouded the tree, spreading out from branch to branch, crackling and snapping as it burned. Smoke thickened around the trunk, billowing away with the wind that rose up around them. Charlie felt a peculiar chill against his skin that defied the heat of the burning tree. The sight was intensely beautiful, beautiful in ways that he couldn't begin to describe. A gust rippled through the middle of the flames, conjuring a weird moment of visual trickery where the flames appeared to part, and through the smoke he could see the white stag walking slowly toward them.

"Look at him," Penny breathed, beside Charlie. "He is incredible."

And that he was.

"The Horned God," Charlie said.

8

Alex Raines looked through the dirty old window at the street below. The '80s anthem on the radio could have been narrating her life save for the fact that the synthesizer was ridiculously perky. She didn't feel the least bit perky, but then she had just spent the afternoon at the funeral of her boyfriend's partner, so every ounce of bone-deep tiredness was understandable. She'd forgotten about the coffee cup on the table, and now coffee had solidified into something that would amuse paleontologists for years to come.

She scraped a fingernail across a broken blister of white paint in the wainscoting.

Alex was too tired to sleep, but not awake enough to function. She was trapped in that weird half existence between the waking and sleeping world. So, she stood there, watching the boats on the river and the bright lights that lured the tourists in, waiting for the first crisis of the night to hit. There was no such thing as a quiet night. Something always happened.

It didn't take long—and it was the last thing she'd ever have imagined happening. No drunks, no stabbings, no cardiac events, car crashes, hit-and-runs, or broken bones.

The break room door opened and a doctor stuck his head around the corner.

"I need you," Aaron Rosenberg said. He was one of the good guys. "She's awake."

She didn't need to ask who. There was only one sleeper on her files. Emmaline Barnes. Age unknown, a Holloway woman. Major head trauma had left her in what was supposed to be a PVS—persistent vegetative state—the old woman had been on Alex's ward as long as Alex had been a nurse, and for years and years before. They talked regularly about freeing the bed up, moving her on to hospice care, because she wasn't supposed to wake up. Not now. Not ever.

Alex had honestly given up hope the old woman would ever open her eyes. She'd sat night after night, the only person sitting a lonely vigil, wondering if there was anyone in the city who mourned the old woman who wasn't dead yet, and tried to find the words to say it was over, that she should let go, without actually saying that.

Walking through the corridors, she amused herself with a much more immediate problem: What was she going to say to Emmaline? Those first few words? After all, it wasn't every day you got to introduce yourself to someone you'd been looking after for five years for the first time.

They all sounded like the kind of stilted dialogue that ruined those old black-and-white movies her brother was obsessed with.

The hospital was daunting, with all the menace of a Victorian asylum built into its labyrinthine corridors. Alex swept through the warren of wards to the bank of elevators—so old they had iron grills for doors—and up to what some of the staff referred to as the vegetable patch, the extended care unit. There were no more than seven patients at any given time. Today there were three. Emmaline Barnes had a room to herself. She had never met the mysterious benefactor who paid for the private room. The closest she'd come to that was seeing his name on the itemized bill: *R. Viridius*. The nurses had done their best to make it feel homey, but no matter how it was dressed up it would always feel like a hospital room. There was no escaping the antiseptic quality that permeated those four walls.

Rosenberg was at the old woman's bedside.

She was awake, sitting up in bed.

"Okay, Emmaline, there's someone I'd like you to meet," Rosenberg said, seeing her enter the room. "This is Alex, she's been looking after you."

The woman didn't say anything.

Her eyes were open, but she was absolutely still.

"Hey, Emmaline," she said. "It's good to finally meet you. How are you feeling?"

Nothing.

"She's not said a word since opening her eyes," Rosenberg explained.

"Responsive?"

Alex looked deep into the woman's eyes. The pupils darted up and down, taking in everything there was to be seen. She was aware. She was in there.

"Can you move your lips for me, Emmaline? Maybe a little smile?"

Nothing.

"How about something small, a finger?" She looked at the woman's liver-spotted hands, which both lay flat on the crisp white linen of the bedsheet.

Nothing. Not so much as a twitch.

"Okay, don't worry, Emmaline. These things take time. I want you to do something for me, if you can understand what I'm saying, can you blink? Does that work?"

It did.

The old woman's eyelids fluttered closed and open again.

"That's fantastic, Emmaline. Believe me. That's brilliant."

To check that it wasn't a fluke, Alex asked a couple of simple yes/no questions. One blink for yes, two for no. "Are you thirsty?" One blink: yes. She filled a plastic cup with water from the jug on the bedside cabinet, and held it to Emmaline's lips, but the old woman couldn't open her mouth to swallow. "Okay, give me a second," Alex said. She stuck her head through the doorway, calling to reception for a pack of the little pieces of blue foam they usually used to keep cancer patients' lips moist in their final hours, and a moment later was dabbing the swab across the old woman's parched lips. "That better?" One blink. Yes. "Do you know where you are, Emmaline?" Two blinks: no. "Okay. You're in hospital. You've been here a long time. I don't want you to be scared when you see yourself in a mirror. You've been asleep for a very, very long time. It's going to be hard when you see yourself. Do you remember what happened to you?" Two blinks again: no. "You were in an accident. I don't know what happened. It was before my time. I didn't think you were going to come back to us, Emmaline. It's so good to talk to you." And so it went, simple questions, one-blink, two-blink answers for the best part of ten minutes before they were interrupted by a knock at the door.

Rosenberg opened it.

Alex didn't recognize the nurse, but she knew what she was carrying: a communication board. They were set up fairly simply: look up, yes; look down, no; right, I don't understand; left, please repeat. This one was fairly simple: an alphabet in the middle with those four options on the compass points. Along with flashcards they were used to communicate with locked-in patients like Emmaline.

Locked in. It was a horrible phrase.

"Hi, Emmaline, I'm Nana," the newcomer introduced herself. "It's Greek. It means grace," she offered a slight smile. There was a hint of silver at her temples and the occasional strand of gray. Alex appreciated the fact Nana Katsani was growing old as gracefully as her name deserved. No cheap dyes, nips, or tucks. Just the gray hairs and laughter lines of a life well lived. "My job here at the hospital is to help people who can't express themselves for one reason or another. I've got some things here that should make it easier for you to talk to people." She sat down on the edge of the bed. "First, we've got these," she showed the old woman a set of cards specifically tailored to her needs. "All you have to do is blink when you see one you want. Let's try, shall we?" She held up one that showed a glass of water and another that showed a hamburger. She flipped through the cards slowly so that Emmaline could become familiar with them. She blinked as the picture of a toilet came up. "That's good, that's really good, Emmaline."

"You don't need to hold it in," Alex said from behind her. "You've got a tube in so you just relax and let it go."

The old woman's expression didn't change, but Alex fancied she saw a flicker of distaste in her eyes as she used the catheter.

Nana gave her a moment before she held up the communication board. The letters were grouped in clusters in each corner: six in the top corners, six in the bottom right, eight in the bottom left. "Now, how this works is you spell out the words you want to say one letter at a time, so if you want to say hello, you'll look up and to your right, that's where the H is, and then you blink twice because it's the second letter in that cluster. Then you look to the top left where the E is and blink five times because it is the fifth letter in the cluster, and so on. Look up for a new word, look down if I get the wrong letter. Do you understand?"

Emmaline blinked once.

"Great. Okay, let's start with something simple: How are you feeling?"

The woman's eyes darted to the bottom right corner with the STUV-WXYZ cluster. She blinked twice. T. Top right, two blinks. H. Top left, five slow blinks. THE. She looked up.

Nana wrote each letter down carefully in a journal.

Alex read over her shoulder as the sentence slowly took form.

The Horned God is awake.

The old woman repeated the same sentence again and again, blinking out each letter painstakingly slowly. The pattern never changed. *The Horned God is awake.*

"What the hell is that supposed to mean?" the speech therapist asked.

Alex had no idea.

9

Erin Chiedozie saw patterns where no one else did. She was the only person in the country in a position to see this particular pattern take shape. The emergency services dispatcher saw a statistical improbability that verged on impossibility: in the last eleven minutes their department had logged four calls for teenagers in distress, all unresponsive, exhibiting comalike symptoms. Four. At any given time there were no more than 100 coma patients in the entire country, out of a population of 64 million people, and those spanned all age ranges and walks of life. Four kids, the youngest thirteen, the eldest fifteen, all in the Greater London area, all at the same time. There were only 3.5 million kids in that age band, a little over 1.75 million girls. Four girls, all basically the same age, all within a couple of miles radius of each other went beyond statistical anomaly.

She pushed back her chair and rubbed at the base of her neck. She needed to wash her hair. The control room was an airless, soulless concrete bunker filled with the heat of hundreds of servers, screens, and machines that was in a constant battle with the cooling units. The lack of windows and natural light played havoc with her circadian rhythms. The wall above her was filled with giant screens that tracked every single emergency services vehicle across the entire 607 square miles of Greater London, covering ten ambulance trusts, A&E support ambulances, fast response cars, motorcycle response units, cycle response units, Helicopter Emergency Medical Services, trauma response cars, and physician response units, and in extreme situations, Hazardous Area Response Teams and Specialist Operations. This was the hub for 4,500 staff, 900 ambulances, 100 rapid response units, another 195 patient transfer units, all of them highlighted by different color codes on the huge interactive map of the city.

It was never still.

Erin could watch it for hours. It was like a virus under a microscope constantly replicating, growing, shifting, and in it a whole world of Rorschach blots took shape and dissolved, their meaning very much dependent upon the mood of the streets.

The dispatcher in the chair beside her was working a call, she put a hand over the mouthpiece of the microphone, and she mouthed, "Number five," entering the details into the central computer.

All of the calls were recorded, all of them scarily similar. She'd listened back to three of them after she'd sat in on the fourth, and there was no getting around the similarities. They were linked. She didn't know how, but they were.

"Maybe there's something in the water," she muttered to herself, trying to focus on the protocols that would guide her through this.

They were going to have to turn this over to the police with as much information as possible, so first they were going to have to contact the five admitting hospitals and talk to the medical staff who worked on the girls, comparing the cases. Any similarities, no matter how seemingly insignificant, any of them could be important. The police would work with eyewitnesses and parents, gathering the rest of the picture. If, worst case, they were looking at some sort of mass poisoning they were going to need to be on top of the investigation right from patient zero.

Erin ran a batch process on the day's emergency calls, narrowing the search by various parameters to hone in on patient names, addresses, where the calls had originated, and the hospitals they were taken to. She printed out everything they had on the five identical cases and downloaded digital versions of the calls. Then, because once you broke the barrier of statistical anomaly anything was possible, ran a second process to sweep up any similar cases that had been reported anywhere across the country in the last forty-eight hours.

The computer-aided dispatch system was more than just a log. It was a diagnostic tool, too, allowing the ambulance crews to arrive on the scene with a proper understanding of what was waiting for them, even a mapping tool that plotted a route from their current location to the patient and on to the nearest facilities, taking into account traffic reports, roadworks, congestion, and such. It was as close to a god hiding away inside the machine as possible, considering those seconds shaved off by automated processes were the difference between life and death dozens of times a week. The CAD system was networked with every other dispatch office in the UK, offering up a wealth of information, but stopped short of allowing access to patient records.

"Have you ever seen anything like this?" Erin asked, gathering the printouts from the printer tray.

Headshakes all around the room.

"Which means it has to be *something*, doesn't it? We're not just jumping at shadows?"

"Only one way to find out."

There were five of them on duty, due for a shift change in an hour. If this had happened even half an hour earlier, the calls would have been split across two shifts and the chances of anyone noticing would have been greatly reduced.

"Okay, let's make the calls. Clockwise around the room, starting with me: I'll take number one on the list; you take the second name," she inclined her head toward the woman at the adjacent desk, "and so on. Rachel, monitor dispatch. If it gets busy, pull one of us off this." The dispatcher nodded. "We're looking for points of similarity, symptoms, anything we can give to the police when we hand it over."

She sat down at her own desk to make the first call.

The name on the sheet was Kate Jenkins. Admitting doctor, Aaron Rosenberg.

She made the call.

It took her five minutes to get through to the right department, where she was put on hold and made to sit through another fifteen minutes of bland Muzak that wouldn't have been out of place on a 1980s computer game. Finally, he came on the line. "Rosenberg."

"This is Erin over at the hub, I need to ask you a couple of questions about a patient that was brought in today."

"Go ahead."

"Kate Jenkins, aged fourteen, admitted this evening in a non-responsive state."

"Yes," he sounded cagey, like he didn't really want to discuss this particular patient anymore.

"This is going to sound a little peculiar," Erin said, working her way toward the more off-the-wall questions she had in mind. "But did you notice anything odd about her condition?"

"Why do you ask?"

"We've had six identical calls so far tonight, all girls, all unresponsive, no physical trauma to account for the coma symptoms. Six girls in an hour. I don't need to tell you the statistical improbability of that."

"No," Rosenberg said.

"Anything you can tell us that might help other doctors looking at a similar situation? Any test results that might suggest some sort of environmental poisoning? Anything at all, really?"

"She said something," he said.

"You mean she woke up?"

"Not quite."

"Parasomnia?"

"She died—"

"Shit," Erin said, biting her tongue.

Rosenberg carried on talking despite her interruption. "—for almost six minutes. I pronounced time of death and left the nurses to clean her up. Somehow she came back. I don't know how. I don't know why. But I'm not in the habit of turning my nose up to a miracle."

"I can understand that."

"She hasn't regained consciousness, but when she revived she said one thing, just mumbled it over and over again until it lost all meaning."

"Could you make out what she was saying?"

"Yes, but don't expect it to make any sense."

"Try me."

"The Horned God is awake."

She wrote the line out on the scratch pad in front of her. "Are you sure?"

"Believe me, it's not a line I'd forget in a hurry." Before she could ask why, Rosenberg went on, "Another one of my patients, a lock-in, communicated with us for the first time in years today. She spelled out the same message with a communication board. The Horned God is awake."

"I'm not sure what I'm supposed to do with that, to be honest."

"Well, you did ask," Rosenberg said.

"That I did. Nothing else?"

"I think that's more than enough, don't you?"

"Yeah. Hard to argue with that, Doc."

Across the room Allie Roberts held up a piece of paper. She'd written the words THE HORNED GOD IS AWAKE on it in thick black marker pen. She saw Poppy Leeworthy staring at the message obviously struggling to understand how Allie had plucked those very words out of her mind. She held up her own notepad. The same five words were the only thing written on it.

"So, what would you say if I told you two other patients had said the exact same thing?"

"Three," Lacey Crooke said from across the room, holding up the same sentence scrawled across a sheet of yellow paper.

"Three," Erin amended.

"I'd hang up and pretend you'd never called," Rosenberg said.

The line went dead before she could answer.

"Seriously? You just hung up on me?"

"Four," Margot said, making it a clean sweep. Four calls, four identical messages. They'd have to confirm with the last one, but Erin knew exactly what they'd say.

The Horned God is awake.

The odds were way past the improbable—but what the hell was she supposed to tell the police when she turned the files over? Five teenage girls have simultaneously fallen into a comatose state, and they're all sleep-talking the same crazy chant about gods waking up? Yeah, that'd go down like a lead balloon.

10

It was the Time Between Times as the lost tribes of Albion used to call the hours between dusk and dawn. Charlie struggled to keep up with Penny as she chased the insubstantial figure up the steep incline of Cane Hill. The animal had led them a merry dance through the streets of the Rothery, moving unerringly toward the distant woods. Charlie's lungs burned from a short lifetime of nicotine and smoke abuse. After five minutes he was doubled over, hands on his knees, gasping. He looked up to see the girl racing away from him. He couldn't see the white stag anymore. The shadowy shape had passed into illusion, melding with the outlines of the trees and hanging branches it rushed toward.

Charlie forced himself to run on.

His legs were leaden, his lungs shriveled to the size of his clenched fist, but he wasn't letting the stag get away from him. He couldn't. He needed to be there. He needed to follow. The imperative burned bright in his mind, every bit as hungry as the flames that had consumed the lightning-struck tree.

He'd known these streets all of his life. He'd grown up around the desperation of those old red bricks and the shopping trolleys rusting in the stream, garbage clinging to their frames like seaweed. There was nothing romantic about the place, but unlike the concrete, glass, and steel of the high-rises across the river it still had a soul. He felt like he was seeing the place through new eyes.

Charlie's last glimpse of the white stag as it disappeared into the old woodland was another trick of the light as the creature rose up onto its hind legs, seeming to shift into the silhouette of a naked man. The leaves coalesced to form a cloak around his shoulders.

And then he was gone, at one with the forest.

Charlie felt the wrench in his heart as he lost sight of the Horned God.

The loss of separation was as powerful as any grief he'd ever experienced. He needed to catch up, to walk in the Lord of the Forest's shadow.

Ahead of him, faster and fitter, Penny plunged into the woods, pushing brambles and scrub aside as she followed the antlered man into the forest.

Penny was fifty yards ahead of Charlie, moving so much easier than he was as he labored to catch up.

A well-worn footpath carved a route through the great wood, rising up the steep rise of Cane Hill ahead of him, the barbed wire limits of the old cemetery on the left, a steep chalk cliff waiting straight ahead, but Penny had strayed from those well-walked routes, trampling down thick tangles of thorns to follow a greener path of moss and lichen that clung to the dirt and stones. After a dozen paces, he felt a change in the ground beneath his feet, as the hard-packed earth was replaced by an ancient causeway of neatly laid cobbles leading deeper into the heart of the wood.

In all the years he'd played around these woods he'd never noticed the stone path.

A shadow ghosted through the trees beside him, but as he turned to try and see who was there, it disappeared beyond the periphery of his vision into the nowhere hidden behind the undergrowth.

Penny ran ahead, darting between the trees as they wove a path he struggled to follow.

Around him, the old trees were rotten through to the core, their trunks split, splinters of black wood clawing their way out. Deadfall gathered on the ground. Towering trees lay uprooted, the dirt clinging to the bulb of their root system where it had been torn free of the earth. All manner of fungi grew on the rotting bark. The hollowed-out husks of last year's wasp's nests formed ladders up the trunks of the silver birches lining the causeway.

He'd never noticed it before, but the old wood was sick.

The undergrowth rustled around him approvingly.

He could sense eyes watching him, but wherever he looked he couldn't see anyone.

Charlie slowed to a walk, listening to the woodland around him. He heard the chatter of birds. The rustle of the leaves gave the wind a voice.

Penny disappeared from view, the trees closing around her.

Moonlight scattered like silver coins across the path ahead. The darkness was oppressive. Claustrophobic. Without the streetlights of the city to offer warmth everything felt so cold. The landscape became one of shades of gray and eventually black until the trees opened again, letting the moonlight stream in through the canopy of leaves up above.

He saw the Horned God properly for the first time.

The man stood in the middle of a shallow brook, the water swirling around his cloak of leaves and lichen. The layers of foliage gave the figure undeniable substance, but it was the eighteen points of antlers curving wickedly away from his temples that transformed him into the stuff of nightmares. In his left hand he held an elaborately carved staff, the bulbous head hollowed out to resemble his antlers. In the shadows it was impossible to see where his arm ended and the staff began. There was no flesh, only leaves. In his right hand he held a tangle of Penny's hair. The girl was on her knees in the water. The pair were surrounded by a mat of pondweed that choked the surface of the water.

The Horned God forced her head down beneath the surface, holding her there as she struggled against drowning. The bubbles came fast, rising to the surface in a desperate froth, more and more of them, and then less and less.

Then none as she stopped fighting him.

It was all done in silence.

He couldn't move.

"Why?" he tried to say, but the wind stole away the word.

He could only stare at Penny Grainger's body, facedown in the stream, her ponytail undone and her hair spread out on the surface around her like a dark halo.

The antlered man bowed his head, lowering the antlers as though in deference to his friend's sacrifice. The trees whispered primitive prayers; the rustling leaves calling out to the old gods of the earth and sky, their will be done.

Charlie couldn't move.

It was as though the ancient roots had clawed up out of the ground to tangle around his ankles and hold him firmly in place. The antlers curved upward viciously. He could imagine the elemental being locking horns with all comers, dominating them like the true monarch of the woods he was.

He looked up.

Charlie saw the most beautiful face he had ever seen, ethereal and yet masculine, haunted and yet filled with strength, the wind swept the locks of hair away from his brow as it blew others across his cheeks and into his mouth. The Horned God's powerful chest rose and fell, rose and fell, in time with the stream lapping around his waist. He planted his staff in the soft alluvial bed, then lowered himself into the water, his right hand still tangled in the dead girl's hair. He turned her over in the water so that those empty eyes could gaze up at him.

Charlie wanted to scream.

He managed a step. Just the one. Lurching from one foot to the other.

He was too far away to make out Penny's face for the shadows. That was some small mercy, at least.

He could smell something, the fragrance rising in the air around him. Roses. And beneath it, rot. Roses and rot.

He managed another step.

The Horned God hauled the dead girl up to her feet. Pondweed clung to her empty smile, giving her the appearance of green teeth. She looked so frail, broken, in the stranger's grasp. His grip was the only thing that stopped her head from lolling sideways on her neck.

And then he kissed her, breathing life back into her brittle bones.

Penny Grainger opened her eyes.

Her smile opened wider.

Her eyes were dead, but that couldn't silence her. When she spoke it was with the voice of the stream. "I will rise," she promised, answering that very first demand the waking god had placed in her mind. It was the same for all of them, but Penny was special. Penny was no longer herself. She was born again. Reborn. She was his creature.

Charlie couldn't look at her.

It was her eyes. Looking into them stole something from him.

In the legends of the old country, Jenny Greenteeth was the scourge that came crawling out of the brackish waters just far enough to reach out and drag you down. She was the hag with a pondweed smile. She haunted the old waterways of the great woods where the stream ran into the rivers and the rivers ran into the sea. There wasn't anywhere she couldn't swim with her pondweed smile. This was who—what—she had become.

Free of his grasp, Penny lowered herself beneath the scum floating on the surface and swam away, the ripples the only sign of her passage.

11

Danny Ash did as he was told.

That would be his epitaph, those six words carved in the granite headstone: *He did as he was told.*

Musa Dajani's body weighed heavily in his arms. How much did the kid's life weigh? He had no idea, but with every passing street as they struggled through the Rothery he felt heavier and heavier until every ounce of Musa Dajani's life—way beyond the weight of bone and meat—burned away the last of Danny's resolve.

He shouldn't be doing this.

There was blood on his hands, literally and metaphorically.

The kid reeked of urine and shit where he'd soiled himself during Tommy's beating. Danny could feel it on his arms where he cradled the boy close to his chest. He didn't want to think about it. It was tough not to. Each step he just kept focusing on the simple stuff, the act of putting one foot in front of another and not letting his body sag and drop Musa. For a while at least that was enough. It distracted him from what mindlessly following Tommy Summers into the woods meant.

He shouldn't just go along with this. It had stopped being about Ollie Underwood a long time ago. Now it was about something inside Tommy that was broken. There was right and there was wrong. It really was as black and white as that. Then there was this, which existed on an entirely different electromagnetic spectrum.

Danny looked around, knowing they'd walked beneath a hundred street cameras since leaving the park. London was the most-surveilled city in the world. There were cameras everywhere. Think about it long enough and you realize there isn't much in the way of places that aren't overlooked. The rats in the sewers—one for every person living in the world above—were the only ones with any privacy in the city. The police would be able to track them every step of the way, right up to the first line of trees. After that, though, they would vanish into one of the few blind spots in the city. The ancient woodland had remained unchanged for centuries. But they'd have to come out at some point, and the second they did they'd step right back out in front of the cameras—without Musa Dajani's body. As evidence went it was pretty damning, right up there with the kid who got kidnapped from the shopping center and beaten to death on the railway tracks years ago. The courts didn't need to see the killing to know exactly what had happened.

Even so, he followed Tommy into the woods.

Every time he'd told himself he wasn't a bad guy, every time he'd told himself he was going to be the hero of at least one life story, was undone with that first step. He wasn't a good guy. He wasn't the hero. He was Tommy's creature.

He didn't look down at the boy in his arms.

He couldn't, because that made a lie of everything.

Even as he felt him stirring, trying to come back from unconsciousness, he kept his gaze focused on Tommy's back.

"Where are we going?" he called for what felt like the hundredth time.

Tommy didn't turn around. He made no move to answer. He walked on with the confidence of a man answering to a higher purpose.

He knew where he was going.

Deadfall crunched under Danny's feet. A month ago there had still been snow on the ground. Maybe there was something to that whole global warming thing.

The woods were cold and dark.

He caught a fleeting glimpse of something out of the corner of his eye, a blur of movement, a shadow-shape, but as he turned to try and see better what it was, it was gone, disappeared deeper into the undergrowth all around them. He didn't *feel* alone, even though it was impossible to see more than a few feet ahead. The forest lost its depth in favor of darkness.

"Come on, Tommy, let's just dump the kid and go."

"No," he said, or maybe it was the forest itself that spoke to him, the harsh rejection some natural phenomenon that wanted Musa Dajani dead?

It was getting out of hand.

They were just supposed to give the kid a beating, screw with his legs to send a message to his people. His kind. That was the plan.

He concentrated on the sound of his footsteps. There was a rhythm to them, albeit an erratic one.

As the trees parted around them to let moonlight into some kind of grove, Tommy turned to face him. Danny could just make out a circle of gray stones. He knew where he was. The fairy ring. The wood felt so much bigger today than it ever had in all of the years he'd played here growing up. Sometimes it felt like everything in the world was different, and becoming more so every day, but some parts were immune to change. The fairy ring was one of them. Thirteen stones, each the size of his head, were arranged in a rough circle. The grass in the middle of the ring was higher, and greener, and the blades thick enough to make whistles, unlike the trodden-down scrub on the outside, which looked more like mud than lawn. That added a strange magic to the place, like the center of the ring was somehow removed from this reality and really was a portal to the fairy realms like they used to pretend as kids. And thinking about that made him think about the girls they'd grown up with back at Herla House. They'd loved this place. He remembered one night Zoe Fenn had even managed to convince that bastard Bracken to let her sleep here one midsummer, making a pillow of wildflowers, in the hopes that she would dream up the face of her true love. She never did tell him who she'd dreamed of, only that it wasn't him. It was never him.

"They need to be taught a lesson," Tommy said, spreading his arms wide. His voice spiked, the anger no longer beneath the surface. "They can't get away doing what they did to Ollie. We need to send a message."

"That's what we were doing," Danny said, tired beyond words. Ever since they'd entered Coldfall Wood he'd felt his resolve dwindle, and his strength along with it. The boy in his arms was a dead weight.

"Bring him into the circle."

One step.

Two steps.

Again, he caught that fleeting blur of motion, as though someone was running around the perimeter of the trees, ghosting in and out of sight as they did. He turned his head, trying to catch a glimpse of them, whoever they were, but all he saw were rustling leaves. The effect was dizzying. He turned and turned about, watching the rippling effect of the leaves as whoever it was out there raced around the glade, completing the circle once, twice, three times.

He heard a voice in the susurrus. Deep, rich, eternal. He couldn't understand a word it said, but there was no denying the power of it or how deep-rooted it was in the land. He felt, as much as heard it, the timbre vibrating within his bones.

As Danny Ash's foot broke the circle of the stones, stepping into the fairy ring, he finally saw the antlered man. The stranger towered over them, easily seven feet tall, eight with the curve of his horns. In the moonlight, his skin was the same shade as the leaves that cloaked his powerful frame.

Tommy knelt in the dirt, a look of pure adoration on his face. "Here. Bring him here."

Danny laid the boy down in front of his friend.

Hwaet! Áríseaþ!

Hark! Rise up!

"I will rise," Tommy promised the Horned God.

Danny knew what he meant now. The words made perfect sense to him. It was as though he'd always known them. He felt the compulsion to echo his friend's words, but didn't know if he had it in him to follow Tommy where he was going.

"This is *our* land," Tommy said, like a prayer. "This is our home. This is England." He looked down at the broken boy Danny had delivered to him. "And your kind aren't welcome here." There was a deadness in his voice, as though the words were coming through the veil from the great beyond. "There must be sacrifice. This is war. Your blood will open the dimgate."

He closed his eyes as Tommy brought the rock down in the middle of Musa Dajani's face over and over again until there was nothing of the boy left.

When Danny opened them again the sounds of the attack were over, replaced by Tommy's panting breath.

He watched his friend daub the dead boy's blood in streaks down his cheeks like war paint.

"Come here," Tommy said, holding out a hand.

Danny crawled toward him on his hands and knees.

I'm not the hero, he thought as Tommy pressed his palm against his left cheek, letting the blood smear beneath his fingers, then did the same to his right. *I'm the monster.*

"The gift is offered," Tommy said, sounding nothing like himself. "Blood is given. Blood is received."

The pair of them knelt over the dead boy, Tommy's strange words weaving a spell around them.

The Horned God watched impassively.

Danny didn't dare move for fear of breaking it.

The moment he moved, the real world would come rushing into the fairy ring, and the reality of the murder they'd just committed would be overwhelming.

Tommy raised his head to look at the Horned God.

"The dimgate is open," Tommy said.

Guard the way with your life, Gatekeeper.

12

Jamshid Kirmani stopped running.

He was lost in more ways than one.

His world had crumbled around him. No, that wasn't right, crumbling gave the impression of some gradual erosion, a slow disintegration, of it coming apart piece by piece over time. It wasn't like that at all. It was brutal. Violent. Everything torn out from beneath him in a single knife slash. All he could see now was blood, Aye's life ended with a single brutal cut that opened the veins of her throat.

He'd killed her. The one person he'd truly loved. He'd killed her.

Jam leaned forward, hands on his knees, and vomited.

He gagged on strings of puke, the stink making him retch all over again.

He wiped the back of his hand across his mouth.

He had hated Ollie Underwood enough to kill him. He'd meant to do that. He'd left the house that evening with the sole purpose of ending his life. But Aisha? He'd never meant to hurt her. He couldn't explain what had happened. He'd heard that voice, then seen that hummingbird tattoo and lost it.

When had he become this person?

He looked down at the dried blood on his jeans.

There was no honor in what he had done.

The headache pounded in his temples, like a bomb had been planted beneath the skin and was set to explode.

He looked at his surroundings, not recognizing any of the land-marks.

The night changed things, even buildings he passed every day, transforming the landscape into something both haunting and alien. Fear and adrenaline amplified those sensations. Together they had Jam turning in circles desperate to see anything even remotely fa-miliar, and turning again when he couldn't.

He heard it again, that voice, urging him on.

Come to me, it beckoned.

But where? His hands went up to his head, fingers digging into the temples. The blood pounded through his skull. He wanted to scream. He didn't know where he needed to be.

The voice existed in the rhythm of the blood. *Come to me. Come to me.* He wanted to howl at it, *"Get out of my head!"* but it wasn't going anywhere. Was this what it was like to lose your mind? To lose all sense of self? He couldn't think about anything. There was no *room.* There was only the voice demanding: *Come to me.*

He was moving again before he realized that was what he was doing, running from street corner to street corner in search of the owner of the voice, desperate to obey the command rooted in his brain before the pressure inside his head finally blew the plates of bone apart.

Come to me.

Up ahead, he saw the gates of the cemetery, the mausoleums and endless rows of gravestones marking out the lives spent on London, and beyond them the rise of Cane Hill and the oaks of Coldfall Wood.

Come to me, the trees seemed to call to him.

He answered the call the only way he could, by putting one foot in front of the other, helpless to do anything other than obey the imperative.

The closer he came to the forest the worse the pain inside his skull became, until it was blinding.

"What do you want from me?" he begged, trying to understand.

The path to the woods was lined with the bloated bodies of

black slugs and the shells of snails, their sticky tracks silver in the moonlight. He had never seen as many slugs in one place in his life. He placed his feet carefully at first, trying not to stand on any of them, but the closer he came to the trees the deeper the pall their shadows cast across his path, hiding them. He felt the first couple rupture beneath his feet and tried not to think about it as he walked on.

A stile divided the footpath in two, the branches of two silver birches intertwining to form an archway around the metal-filigreed gateway. The words *Coldfall Wood* were barely visible through the foliage, which tangled around the letters. He must have walked beneath that archway a hundred times, but it was the first time he'd noticed the red berries inside the O. The lights lining the pathway went out at nine thirty, leaving the wood pitch black for nine months of the year.

Jam followed the path as it wove its way up a series of switch-backs climbing the hill.

A bat flitted across his line of sight; its peculiar swooping flight drawing his attention away from the distant carousel wheel of the London Eye. As he followed the bat he caught sight of another indistinct shape in the shadows. At first he mistook it for a man, but it was something else entirely. It wore the darkness, blending in perfectly with the foliage around it, its cloak of leaves rustling in the breeze. It was only as it moved, ghosting away through the trees that Jam saw the darker outline of antlers protruding from its skull. It wore them like a crown, lowering its head like a stag in challenge to Jam's presence in its wood. He didn't move. Couldn't.

The Horned God prowled the forest around him, moving from tree to tree to tree, watching him all the while.

Come to me.

"I'm here," Jam told it, no idea why he was talking to the shadows.

Come to me.

He followed it as it moved away from the path, taking a winding route up to the top of Cane Hill and down the other side. The forest was alive with all of the sounds of its nocturnal wildlife, the scuttle of squirrels moving from branch to skeletal branch, the shuffle of hedgehogs in the undergrowth, rats and field mice, badgers, voles, and foxes. There was never a single moment of absolute stillness. The place was alive.

"What do you want from me?" Jam asked the shadows, not expecting an answer. He didn't understand what was happening here. His first instinct was to run, but stronger was the urge to obey the voice, to deliver himself up to the speaker.

The Horned God emerged from the trees up ahead of him, raising its right hand, commanding him to stop. He had no choice but to. His legs refused to obey him now that his mind screamed *flee*.

The undergrowth around him rustled. At first insubstantial, a whisper of sound that gathered substance fast, becoming the rush of footsteps, and beyond that more noises joined with it, creaks and groans followed by the harsh splintering of dry wood. Jam saw more movement in the shadows.

"Hello? Hello?"

The only answer was the sharp crack of twigs breaking beneath unseen footsteps.

His skin crawled. Despite the chill, sweat trickled down the nape of his neck. Jam felt the creep of an insect working its way around his neck. Unable to look away from the Horned God he reached back to slap it to death as it fed on him.

The slap of his hand was met by an almighty tearing as the roots of one of the mighty oaks ripped out of the ground, the huge tree toppling, almost as though the Horned God was punishing him for the murder of one of its creatures. He wanted to laugh at the absurdity of that thought, even as he stumbled back a couple of panicked steps. Then he did laugh as he tripped on one of the bloated white roots and couldn't stop himself from falling. The play of light fooled him into thinking the roots writhed in response to the antlered man's hand as though the Horned God conducted the roots, making them dance to his primordial lament.

The laughter died on Jam's lips as the ground rippled around him. Dirt spilled away from more roots as they broke the surface. He hadn't realized how much deadfall there was here. Every inch of dirt seemed to be covered with twisted spars and broken branches, and thicker pieces of bark that had stripped from the ancient boles like snakes shedding skin. Leaves mulched beneath the scattered wood. He pushed himself back up to his feet and carried on walking, deeper into Coldfall Wood. Every footstep threatened to turn his ankle or trip him. The ancient forest was carpeted in year-upon-years' worth of deadfall. Huge trunks of old timber were opened up, rot and woodworm devouring them from the inside out.

Another tree fell, this one tearing a path through the canopy of leaves and opening a wound all the way through to the sky.

He saw the moon, and across it the silhouette of wings.

He had no idea where he was in relation to the outside world. He could so easily have stepped back fifteen hundred years in time across the last fifteen hundred yards of his journey.

"What do you want from me?" Jam called out to the distant figure.

His question was greeted by silence.

He didn't repeat it.

The Horned God took a step toward him, then another.

The moonlight transformed its skin to a sickly green pallor, making it impossible to tell where his beard ended and his cloak of leaves and moss began. Even at this distance he cut an imposing figure, broad, powerful shoulders, the leaf cloak draped over corded muscles.

Jam reached out, looking for something to defend himself against the antlered man. His left hand closed around a piece of deadfall. He pushed himself to his feet, the weight of the wooden branch in his hand giving him the lie of confidence. He could do this, just like he'd done Ollie Underwood.

He was not the weak one here. "You don't want to fuck with me," he said.

The mocking whisper of the woodland answered him.

The entire forest appeared to move in the moonlight as the breeze stirred the branches.

Jam shifted his weight from his front to back foot and moved to transfer the makeshift weapon to his right hand, but he couldn't let go of it.

He swung it wildly in front of him, slashing uselessly at the air. "I'll fucking have you," he growled, slashing again. He sounded like the child he was.

Áríseaþ!

Rise up! The command reverberated through the plates of his skull.

The blood pounded through his temples, the pressure building up inside his head, excruciating.

Áríseaþ!

The wind answered his call, churning through the trees. All around him nature keened.

Jam slashed at the air again and again, blinded by the black agony raging inside his head.

He fell to his knees, one hand clutching at his head, the other unable to relinquish its grip on the wood. He swayed in place, the world constantly in motion around him. He struggled to focus on the antlered figure as its cloak billowed in the wind. He needed both hands to brace himself as he toppled forward onto his hands and knees. His right hand closed around a piece of wood that felt as though nature had shaped it purely for that purpose.

Again, he couldn't let go of it.

Twigs and leaves blew across the ground, piling slowly up around his knees as looked desperately around.

The wind howled through the treetops.

Bark skittered across the ground. Leaves swirled. All around him the wind rose.

He was at the eye of the storm.

The cold wind howled. The deadfall whipped up, churning around him, more and more of the forest's decayed heart battered his body.

He felt every blow.

He felt the splintered edges dig into his skin where he raised his hands to protect his face.

He felt the jagged barbs tear into his jeans, through his shirt, into his flesh.

He wanted to scream, but as he opened his mouth a sodden mulch of ripening leaves hit his face and stuck to his skin, swarming to fill his mouth so that he couldn't breathe.

More leaves plugged his nose and covered his eyes.

He was going to die here.

Or maybe he had already died and this was just his descent?

He deserved to be in Hell.

The deadfall continued to batter his body, clinging to him like a second skin, forming something so much bigger than Jamshid Kirmani had ever been in life. Pulp of every shade from the blackest rot to brittle white dust clung to his face. His body formed the bridge of the great beast's snout. He wanted so desperately to scream as the Horned God clad his corpse in more and more of the forest's debris until it was impossible to see him inside the carapace of wood as he became a great elemental beast, fashioned from the stuff of the ancient forest itself. The old wood reshaped itself, alive. It glistened with dew. It formed the curves of an enormous rib cage and the grand sweeping lines of the beast's huge wooden skull. By root and branch it grew until it could grow no more.

Jam was in there somewhere, his mind lost to the ancient anger of the old wood.

"I will rise!" he said; the voice nothing like his own. It echoed in the deep woods. It resounded through the rotten pulp of the fallen trees. It rustled through the canopy of leaves that sheltered the creatures of the forest in its shade. It sang in the blood of the land.

He had become a creature of legend.

An avatar of the Horned God.

He had become the Knucker.

The Knucker flexed its new limbs, clawing the air with those massive timbers as it rose onto its hind legs.

The wood groaned, taking the strain as his driftwood body rose, the gyring winds not faltering as they churned up more and more deadfall to flesh out the creature's impossible body.

The leaves parted around the mighty wooden warrior as he answered the Horned God's call.

13

The night didn't get any better for Julie Gennaro and his new partner.

After the stress of crowd control and the reality that they were first responders at what had become a double murder, they still had four hours of what felt like an endless shift to survive. Dispatch put through a call that on any other day would have been routine, but today felt like another strand in the elaborate cosmic joke history was happily repeating for Julie: a suspected breaking and entering over on Holly Lane. Another burglary, another repetition. He took the call.

They pulled up outside the house. A high wall with thick climbing vegetation and a wooden gate hid it away from the rest of world. The lights were on upstairs. He radioed through to dispatch, letting them know they were at the scene, then got out of the car, Ellie a couple of steps behind him as he pushed open the wooden gate, not sure what waited on the other side for him. This was always the worst part of the job, those few seconds of knowing something was wrong but not knowing what, or how bad it might well turn out to be. He unclipped the baton from his hip and extended it as he walked along the garden path.

Crossing the threshold, he heard music.

He called out.

No one answered.

Lights were on in every room.

He gestured for Ellie to check out the downstairs while he followed the music. She nodded.

He walked slowly up the stairs. The tension had his muscles taut. Halfway up, the music stopped. "This is the police," Julie called out. "Make yourself known." The silence was broken by the crackle of the record starting up again. Still no one answered him.

On the landing, he was confronted by a number of doors, only one of them open, so he went inside.

The room was filled with the bric-a-brac of life, but none of that was what had him shouting for Ellie to get up there and join him. Julie stared at the mummified corpse fused to the armchair. Julie thumbed down his radio and called through to dispatch, "We're going to need an ambulance to pick up a body," he said without pre-amble.

"Another murder? What the hell's in the water?"

"I don't think so," he explained. Checking the date on the news-paper on the table, he said, "Looks like he died a year ago."

"And no one's missed him?"

"Old guy, living alone, shit happens."

"Okay, the owner is listed as one Robert Viridius, aged ninety-two last birthday."

"We'll need the coroner, but I can't see any obvious reason to suspect foul play. Looks like the old guy just died in his chair."

"Okay, you guys sit tight, we'll get someone out to you to collect the body, and have forensics check the place out just to be sure."

"We're not going anywhere," Julie said, sitting in the chair op-posite the dead man as the music started another rotation, the nee-dle dropping into the groove and crackling away.

Ellie joined him.

"This place gives me the creeps," she said, looking at the oppres-sive oil painting dominating the only wall not lined with books. The small brass plate on the frame named it: *The Oak King and the Holly King*. With time to kill, she started checking out the titles, reading them off one by one. They all appeared to be about the mythology of the Isles. Maybe the dead man had been a scholar, Julie reasoned. It would explain plenty.

Death rooms were unique and yet perversely the same; maybe it

was something to do with the presence of the departed, some
gering trace of the restless dead, or maybe it was in his head?

"I don't know about you," Ellie said, turning her back on
daunting painting, "but there's only so many times I can stand listening to the same song. You mind?"

There was a gilt-painted glass on the table beside the dead man.
The pattern was some kind of elaborate crown of autumnal foliage
with three crimson dots of berries within the golden leaves. There
was a finger of Scotch left at the bottom of the glass. The old guy
had died without finishing his last drink.

"Knock yourself out."

Ellie crossed the rug to the old turntable. She thumbed down the
STOP button and a moment later the arm rose, lifting the needle from
the well-worn grooves.

A moment later the turntable stopped its endless revolutions and
the armature nestled back into the cradle. The silence was anything
but absolute. The single-glazed sash windows let more than just the
draft in.

That was when he noticed the peculiar smell; it took him a moment to place it because it wasn't rot or decay or anything else he
would have associated with the musty locked-in quality of a house
that had served as a coffin for a year. It was absolutely, incredibly,
natural: freshly mown grass.

He kept that to himself, fearing a stroke or some kind of brain
hemorrhage. That could cause sensory hallucinations, couldn't it?

"Okay, that's weird," Ellie said. It took him a moment to realize
what she was referring to. He'd mistakenly assumed the old guy's
skin was leathery with the mummification process, but it wasn't
leather at all. The deep grooves and hollows were more like the carapace of a wooden cocoon.

She couldn't stop herself from reaching forward to touch the dead
man's cheek.

The bark—because that's what it was—flaked off in her fingers.
More crumbled to dust as she brushed it aside. The skin exposed
beneath was surprisingly youthful and unblemished, as though the

bark hadn't merely protected it from the process of decomposition, but was instead revitalizing it. She quickly peeled away the rest of the death mask and stepped back to look at the man's plain but handsome face.

Julie saw something protruding through his blue lips. The tip of a leaf? He gripped the man's jaw and prized it open.

"Should you be doing that?"

"No," Julie said, but that didn't stop him from reaching in with a couple of fingers to tease the leaves out of the dead man's mouth. It wasn't just one or two that had been crammed in there, he realized, as more and more leaves spewed out and it became obvious someone had shoved a sapling down the man's throat, suffocating him. The sapling was the length of Julie's arm by the time the last of it cleared the dead man's teeth. He put it down on the coffee table. Bile clung to the still-supple wood.

"Gangland killing?"

Before he could answer, the dead man's eyes opened and his entire body arched against the back of the armchair. Airways clear, he drew in a deep hitching breath, nearly choking on the first air his body had tasted in seasons. More of the shroud of bark broke away as his body bucked in the seat. Life wasn't returning easily. Fingers curled around the armrests, digging deep into the fabric of the chair as the man writhed in obvious agony.

"Jesus Christ," Ellie said, behind him. She repeated the name over and over, like it somehow had the power to weave a holy barrier around her that would protect her from the dead man.

The dead man's hazel eyes fixed on Julie as he reached out with a hand still encased in bark to take Julie's hand. Julie pulled back, but only for those impossibly strong fingers to close around his wrist. Nails of bark sink into his skin. Julie felt a surge of electricity so strong the shock was enough to make him flinch back, recoiling forcefully enough to wrench his arm free of the dead man's grasp. Tears ran down Robert Viridius's too young, too smooth cheeks. More of the peculiar wooden carapace flaked away from his neck, revealing the raw pink hollow of his throat and still more fell away as he contorted in the seat.

"The dimgate is open," Viridius rasped. Every word visibly hurt him, but he refused to be silenced.

Julie couldn't look away.

"*We* have to close the way before he can return."

The smell of freshly cut grass was overwhelming. It was so real he could have sworn he could make out the tang of morning dew.

"Who? I don't understand. How are you even . . . ? You can't be . . ." Which really meant: *I don't want to understand. I don't want to be part of this. I don't want to still be trapped in a world I don't understand.*

"My father," Viridius said. "We have sacrificed too much of ourselves to ensure his banishment, and lost too much of who we were in the process. Look at me, I have become undone," he held up his hands, offering the brittle remains of the cocoon flaking away from his rejuvenated skin as evidence of just how much he had given. "He cannot be allowed to return. We are not strong enough to fight him again, not now, not here, like this. Every brick diminishes us, every road, every factory and shopping center, they strip away what little magic remains in the land and leave us husks of who we had been." There was a tear glistening on his cheek as he said, "Mother is lost. My brother does not know himself. I am like a child. This place has forgotten everything. The old ways are no more. There is no time for wonder. You know this broken country with its philosophy of me, me, me, look out of the window and tell me how can we ever find a belief in each other that is strong enough to stand in his way?"

He tried to stand on atrophied legs and stumbled forward into Julie's arms.

"Let me help you," Julie said, taking his weight as best he could. The old man was surprisingly heavy given the withered state of his limbs.

"No," the other man said, pushing himself away from Julie's embrace.

"At least let us take you to the hospital, get you checked out."

Viridius shook his head. "They could not help me, even if they wanted to. I am running out of time," but the way he slumped again into Julie's arms belied the words. "What month is it?"

"April," Ellie said, behind him.

The old man nodded. "So little time. The solstice approaches, and with it a shift in the balance of nature."

"I don't even know what to say to that," Julie said, struggling with the idea that somehow living long enough to see the sun rise on some arbitrary day could somehow heal anyone. It was patently absurd.

Like banishing Seth Lockwood into some mirror world within a mausoleum.

"Then don't say anything," the man said. "Actions make the man; words, like prayers, are useless. Help me," he didn't mean to stand, that much was obvious.

"What can I do?"

"The dimgate is open, the way is clear. We haven't faced this threat in three hundred years, since the last of the dimgates were closed. For it to stand open now is no accident. The world is changing. We stand on a tipping point. Things cannot remain as they are. Either the last of the old earth magic dies out forever, leaving our home a husk," he shook off more flakes of bark, emphasizing his point. Several pieces appeared to skitter across the rug like beetles. "Or somehow we return to how it was before, raw elemental energy surging along the ancient leys and spreading out through leaf and tree into every home and hearth, tearing down the walls that separate us from the land so that we might once more be one with our surroundings."

"And that's what will happen if the gate remains open?"

"It will be the end of this place," Viridius said patiently. "Everything that has been gained will be lost. The progress of generations will be undone as we step back into the Dark Ages. He must be stopped."

Again, all Julie could ask was, "Who?"

"He has many names, but only the single nature. He is King Stag; he is Lord of the Wild Things; he is the antlered man; he is the Lord of the Underworld; to some he is Cernunnos, to others he is Kernunno; He is the Horned God. He is Arawn, Lord of the Annwyn, but to me he will always be Father," the old man said. Julie's mind immediately flashed back to the sight of the antlered man on his knees inside the full beam of his headlights. "This place has forgotten him. But it will not be allowed to forget forever," Viridius said, ignoring his question. "He will force it to remember. I cannot allow that to happen. But this is not your fight. You should go. Perhaps he will spare you."

"I have seen him," Julie said.

"Then he has marked you."

"What does that mean?"

"That you are part of this," Viridius said. "You cannot walk away."

Behind him, Ellie made a cuckoo sign with her right hand, and interceded. "We really should get you to the hospital," Ellie said, proving the point as she put herself between the two men. "Get you thoroughly checked out; just to be on the safe side." Which of course meant he became someone else's problem, and no need to think about the miraculous resurrection they'd witnessed. She hadn't seen the antlered man as he somehow transformed into a white stag and bounded away into the forest, or any of the other wonders and horrors he'd witnessed since he'd answered that call to Albion Close with Taff six months ago. So, for her this was just the first weirdness; something she could shuck off onto someone else's desk and be done with it.

Gently, she steered the old man toward the stairs and the waiting car outside.

Julie took another couple of seconds before he followed, looking at the painting of the Oak King and the Holly King over the fire grate. It took him a moment to realize he could only make out a single leaf-cloaked shadowy figure in the painting no matter how much he stared at it. It was as though the man was supposed to represent the duality of Nature and was both the Oak King and the Holly King depending upon the viewer's perspective. He wondered which aspect he saw in the heavy oils, and what that said about him.

14

Julie and Ellie took the old man to the emergency room, and while he sat with Viridius watching the walking wounded come and go, she made her excuses and went over to the nurses' station to explain that the old guy needed a psych evaluation. She nodded a couple of times as the ward sister gesticulated her own kind of semaphore. He wondered for a moment if she'd confess to his miraculous resurrection, but the ward sister didn't appear to be summoning down the men with the white jackets for Ellie, so probably not.

Nurses came and went, numbers were called, treatments dispensed, until eventually it was their turn. He rose to follow the old man toward the curtained-off bed waiting for him down the corridor, but the nurse promised him, "We've got it from here, Officer."

Julie nodded his thanks.

Looking at the clock on the wall, Ellie said, "You get yourself home, I'll keep an eye on things here."

He wasn't about to argue. He was bone tired, but that wasn't why. After everything that had happened he wanted to see Alex. He'd promised to tell her everything at the wake, but with Banks, Sykes, and Tenaka there they could hardly have the kind of conversation they needed to have. She was about fifty yards above his head, give or take a concrete floor or two so he decided to swing by the ward, and if she had a few minutes to spare, put that right. That was one thing about being in a committed relationship that would take a bit of getting used to. In the past it had been all about him, about his needs, and when it came right down to it, his gain. But now his first instinct was to run to Alex. That was new. He smiled to himself as he walked the familiar corridors up to her domain.

The hand sanitizer on the wall outside the ward was empty. He nodded to a couple of the nurses at the station who recognized him, "She's in with Sleeping Beauty," one offered as he approached the desk. He nodded a thanks and followed the labyrinthine corridors toward Emmaline Barnes's private room. She had a view of the river. There were three people around the old woman's bed. Alex was one of them, Rosenberg another. He didn't recognize the third.

He knocked softly on the door. Alex saw him and smiled. She said something to the others then came over to the door. He realized why she was smiling. The old woman was awake. He couldn't help but smile right back. He knew how important she was to Alex.

"Hey, you," she said, opening the door.

"Hey, you back," he said, smooth. "I was just downstairs, had to bring an old guy in who wasn't doing too good, so I figured I'd see if you were busy."

"We're always busy," she said with an affectionate smile.

Alex checked with the others. Rosenberg promised to page her if there were any changes with Emmaline. A couple of minutes later they were sharing pod coffees and gazing out over the cityscape. There was an easy companionship that came with familiarity, knowing each other's silences. "I assume this is the bit where you confess the terrible things you and my brother got up to last summer?" Alex asked, still half a cup of froth left in her cup.

Looking at her slight smile, he realized this was neither the time nor the place for this conversation. He shook his head. "Not yet. But I will. I promise."

"So, what's on your mind? You look like you're carrying the woes of the world on your shoulders."

"It's been a bad night."

"Does it have anything to do with that naked man we hit in the car?"

He shook his head again, opting to unburden himself of the more mundane tragedies of the night. "A kid was killed on the High Street tonight. Stabbed. Some sort of honor killing."

"Oh, Jesus, that's awful."

"It gets worse. Before we could stop him, the boyfriend ran into the Rothery, found his girlfriend working out, and slashed her throat."

"What the fuck is wrong with people?"

He didn't have an answer for that. "I just wanted to see you," he shrugged. "You know, a little bit of normality in an otherwise mad world. Let's talk about something more cheerful. Emmaline. I take it she's awake?"

Alex took another sip and nodded around the steam. "Yep. I'd given up hope, to be honest. Then, no warning, she just opens her eyes. You want to talk about weird, we've been trying to communicate with her all night, but the only thing she's said makes absolutely no sense."

"Try me," Julie said, "I'm good with things that don't make sense. It's my superpower."

"You'll love this. So, she's said the same five words over and over again. The Horned God is awake."

The words hit him like a brick to the side of the face. They were so close to Viridius's message it couldn't be coincidence. One thing meeting Josh and the old magician Damiola had taught him was that there was no such thing.

"And that's not the *weirdest* part of it. Maybe an hour ago a kid comes in: unresponsive, no obvious trauma. She flatlines. Rosenberg pronounces time of death."

"Ah, shit, sorry."

"She was dead. And then she wasn't. She wakes up mumbling—"

"The Horned God is awake," Julie finished for her.

"Spooky, it's almost as though you were there. It freaked Rosenberg out. He came straight back up to Emmaline's room to confirm he wasn't losing his mind."

"Which he wasn't."

"Which he wasn't," she echoed. "And we're *still* not at the weirdest part of it."

"I dread to ask?"

"Not long before you guys showed up Rosenberg took a call from the hub. So, get this, they've had *five* identical calls tonight; girls brought in unconscious, no obvious cause, flatlining, failing to be resuscitated despite everyone's best efforts only to come back five or six minutes later, after the doctors have called time of death. They're

72

not really back, not properly. They're all locked-in, though they all said the same thing about the Horned God before falling silent. It's creepy as fuck."

It was exactly that. First the antlered man trapped in their headlights, then Viridius's uncomfortably weird rambling about the horned gods of the Underworld, and now this. He crossed to the window, not that he could see out through the glass because of the glaring reflection of the fluorescent striplights, which created an identical break room inside the window, complete with mirror images of him and Alex. "I don't know what the hell is going on, Alex. I'm lost. After Taff . . . Josh . . . everything," he didn't finish that sentence. She didn't know the half of what he'd been through, but everything that had happened with Josh and the Lockwoods had fundamentally changed the way he looked at the world. For one thing, he was a lot less eager to brand something as impossible now, even this. Especially this. Antlered men and mythical forest gods waking up? Men transforming into stags? Why not? That made as much sense as a prison trapped one hundred years out of time, and he'd seen *that* happen firsthand, so the world as most people saw it wasn't anything he was about to take for granted.

Part of Julie wanted to focus on the case at hand—and honor killings were much more his remit than ancient gods—but the bigger part of him knew that he couldn't just walk away. Maybe once upon a time, but now that he was in the kingdom of second chances, he wasn't about to screw his up. So, he told her about Viridius and what had happened at the house on Holly Lane, but left out the part about pulling a huge sapling out of the dead man's mouth and him somehow, miraculously, coming back to life. The rest of the truth was hard enough to swallow without that.

She listened.

She didn't interrupt him once.

He could see her trying to piece it together with what had happened in the hospital, and as he told her about the old man's promise that they were marked because the antlered man had seen them, he could see the fear take shape behind her eyes. He wanted to reassure her, to say that just because the old guy said it didn't make it real, but the risk in playing it down was that she'd let her guard down and walk into whatever trouble was waiting outside. Better to be frightened and because of it cautious than to live in ignorance and die the same way, he thought, remembering all too brutally Taff's final few minutes of rapture in the old Latimer Road cinema as the succubus consumed him.

Long before he was finished, Julie realized there was only one person who *might* have an inkling as to the true nature of the resurrected man, how a naked man could transform into a stag, and locked-in girls could leave messages of Horned Gods, but even that was a stretch.

He hadn't talked to the old magician in six months, and if he was being honest with himself, he would have happily go another six without seeking him out, and another six after that, but there was no escaping the fact that when the world went weird he was the closest thing they had to an expert. After all, he'd made a prison out of mirrors in an abandoned mausoleum, and banished Seth Lockwood to a time out of time. If anyone had a hope of understanding Viridius's ramblings and everything else that had happened, it was Cadmus Damiola.

15

Ru Brooke stood at the top of Cane Hill and looked down upon the whole of creation, at least it felt that way to him with the winds whipping up a storm.

Rain might be the only thing that could prevent the inevitable, but that was far from a given. He could feel the pent-up violence simmering on those streets down there. Everywhere he looked, they were coming out, first in twos and threes and then in real numbers, looking for justice for Ollie Underwood and Aisha Kahn, for retribution. It was going to get ugly. Once upon a time it might have taken a day, two, for the outrage to spiral; now it could spike in a matter of minutes as social media spread the anger.

Stephen Blackmoore was on his hands and knees behind him, digging in the dirt.

They stood in the middle of one of the chalk men's penis. The fertility symbols were among the oldest in the country, unlike the Cerne Abbas Giant, which could only legitimately trace its existence back to the seventeenth century, the Cane Hill Men dated all the way back to the Doomsday Book. From above, they looked curiously deformed, as though their duty as guardian of this great city weighed down on their shoulders so heavily their spines had buckled beneath the strain. The locals called the Cane Hill Men "Gogmagot the Albion" and "Corenius the Britain." The giants were the Guardians of London. Even now they were on the banners carried during the Lord Mayor's yearly march, along with wicker mascots carried by the revelers. Over the years people had come to confuse their origins, because there were two figures in the chalk, and because of Gogmagot's name, with Gog and Magog, the biblical characters that would rise up in the battle for humanity at the end-times.

Blackmoore scooped up a handful of chalk and smeared it across his cheeks. "Come on, get over here," he said, urging Ru to hunker down so that he could daub his face with the same white stripes of battle like they were party to some ancient ritual. "No fucking about, Bro. We're in this together. You and me. Brothers."

He nodded.

"Always, man. Always."

Ru knelt down beside him, feeling like a fool as Blackmoore painted his face with the chalk of the giant. Two fingers, two stripes on each cheek, one slash across his forehead.

He didn't know what he was doing here.

He'd heard the voice, and knew he had to answer the call. He'd known he had to come here, to Gogmagot and Corenius, but beyond that he was lost.

He'd begged Blackmoore to just go, leave the dead man's house empty-handed, but Blackmoore was adamant he wasn't leaving without getting what he'd come for.

In just a few minutes his life had gone to Hell.

He didn't know what he was going to do—for one thing their prints were all over that house. It was supposed to be an easy job, in and out, grab a few easily sellable pieces: pocket watches, chains, nothing fancy. And they had that, and more. Blackmoore had filled his pockets. But a dead body changed everything. Someone would find the old man. That would bring the police to secure the scene and relatives to pick over the corpse. They'd realize things were missing when they started arguing over their inheritances and that would bring questions—and enough scrutiny to screw with them once forensics started checking the place for prints. He wanted to believe they weren't deep enough in the shit for words like murder to be bandied about in the interrogation room but Blackmoore wasn't exactly a stranger to the cops. There were enough bent bastards out there no matter how clean the Met liked to pretend it was, someone on the take could see them as the ideal opportunity to help out some shithead looking to make a name for themselves. The Lockwoods might be gone, but the city would never be free of their kind. They were like those mythical snakes; chop their heads off, they went and grew another one.

The wind carried the faint strains of music with it.

He recognized it without ever having heard it before. The Song of Albion.

It sang through his flesh. It fired his blood.

Down in the forest below he saw a stirring, a rustle in the canopy of leaves that spread out from a single point—where two trees fell one after the other. The song rose in the air. He turned and turned about, tears streaming down his cheeks. Blackmoore was lost in his own rapture. He gripped both hands together in prayer, doubling up as though punched in the gut, and rocking back and forth. If he was praying, it was to no deity Ru had ever heard named. Agitated ripples rolled out through the treetops, churning the leaves up like a roiling sea of green. Something was happening down there. In the sixty seconds he stared down at Coldfall Wood the ripples became ever more violent, the trees shaking like their roots were trying to tear free of the ground. The fallen trees stood at the epicenter of the gathering storm.

From within that dark eye, a huge ungainly shape began to move through the trees. At first it looked as though the forest itself was rising up in answer to the Horned God's call, but as the wooden warrior surged through the trees from glade to grove toward the fairy ring, more and more of its grotesque form became visible. Ru's mind wrestled with what he was seeing, trying to make sense of the impossible. He watched as the Knucker breached the tree line. Its massive body defied everything natural. The huge living champion of Coldfall Wood, an elemental warrior of the wood itself, surged on through the trees, pushing branches and thicker limbs aside. Blackmoore's mumbled prayer provided an uncanny backdrop. It was incredible to behold. And terrifying.

The song soared as the Knucker pushed its way up the rise toward them, the forest rippling against its presence. The song flourished as the great wooden warrior climbed the hill, looking down over the city.

"Can you see that thing?" Ru let out a breath he had no idea he'd been holding, the words whispering out of his mouth in an awed rush.

Blackmoore didn't answer him.

Ru saw why immediately. He had fallen forward, onto his hands and knees. Or more accurately elbows and knees—his hands had sunk into the chalky outline of Corenius's manhood, and he was still sinking, being drawn down inch by inch into the chalk hill. In a matter of moments his chin was pressed against the chalky soil. He was smiling. Like he *wanted* it. He didn't struggle against it; Cane still had him. Blackmoore looked up at him then, wild-eyed but frightened. A rabid hunger for what was to come burned in his "This is why it wanted us to come here. This is what it was all being here, now, ready." His smile was full of religious fervor.

Blackmoore welcomed it, throwing back his head, even as the ground beneath him lost any semblance of solidity. The chalky white mud welcomed his body.

And then he was gone.

Ru felt the ground beneath him lurch alarmingly even as a shadow-shape ghosted across his vision, moving fast, all but impossible to focus on: he saw a blur of movement, rustling leaves in all shades of decay, and the deceptive impression of antlers dipping down in challenge, like a rutting stag.

Áríseaþ!

Rise up! The command reverberated through his body, carried through his blood by the song.

Áríseaþ!

Rise up, for Albion, for this once great land of ours.

Rise up, fight for what has been lost. Remember all that has been forgotten.

Rise up; reclaim the fields and the forests, the rivers and streams, the hilltops and the valleys.

Rise up, champion. Rise up, giant. Rise up, brothers mine. Rise up, my sons.

Rise.

And so it echoed in his mind, the chorus as simple and irresistible as:

Rise up!

Rise up!

Rise up!

"I will rise," Ru Brooke promised as the chalk ground welcomed his body. He sank lower, to the knees, to the waist, and resisted every instinct to fight what was happening. He braced his hands on the grass that grew on either side of the white outline. It didn't feel real beneath his fingers. Fear thrilled through his body as he sank deeper. It wasn't enough to silence the panic in his mind as the chalk filled his mouth, choking the air out of his lungs as it spilled down his throat.

And then the land closed over his head, burying him alive, side by side with his brother in crime.

Áríseaþ!

The song commanded.

Áríseaþ!

He became the land.

He tried not to fight it, but basic survival instinct took hold as the chalk began to suffocate him. He lashed out at the ever-constricting liquefied rock all around him, wriggling and writhing desperately in the precious few seconds before he ceased to be. He felt the remorseless crushing weight on his ribs, the first sharp crack of bone as his sternum collapsed, and still it bore down on him, solidifying around him. It cocooned his body—setting across his eyes, nose and mouth sealing his airways off—even as it became his corpse.

Rupert Brooke was buried in a tomb of chalk.

A minute, an hour, a year, time lost all meaning in limbo. He was painfully aware that he was dead. He had always imagined there would be no consciousness in death, and caught himself panicking at the prospect of an eternity of awareness trapped in his chalk grave, unable to move, not needing the basics like sustenance, water, air, and unable to turn his mind off and stop thinking. It was in every way imaginable, Hell.

He felt rather than heard the song as it continued all around him, carried by the stones.

He saw in his mind's eye two giants, twins white as chalk towering over the trees, clubs in their hands ready to give their lives once more in defense of the land they loved. The Song of Albion swelled to fill his mind, within it a single recognizable word: *Gogmagot.*

If this was death, it was a strange one.

Áríseaþ! The voice demanded. His body responded, the bones pushing back against the crushing weight of the rock, the cracks this time from chalk shards sheering away from the base rock.

"I will rise!" he screamed, the chalk in his throat absorbing any attempt at sound, carrying it from the outline of one giant to the outline of its twin where Corenius the Britain's cry of "I will rise!" answered him.

The rock above his head cracked, a fissure opening up. Through it he saw the silver of the moon.

The fissure widened as he strained against it. He felt pain for the first time in minutes—it had only been minutes, hadn't it?—as he pitted his body against the land, and won, inch by precious inch, opening the fissure wide. Cold air rushed in to fill the cracks between the broken stones. It felt delicious against his skin, so full of life. He felt vital. Alive. But different. Changed. Like he was being born again. A butterfly. A moth. A creature forced to claw its way back to life out of a chalk cocoon. White stone crumbled beneath his fingertips as he clawed at it, tearing his nails off in a desperate scramble to be free. To live.

He twisted his body to free his hands, earning the precious freedom to reach up, over the edge where chalk met sky, and found the grass with his hands.

He tilted his head back, swallowing down a huge lungful of air and choking on it as he tried to suck it down past the chalk still clogging his throat.

It demanded every ounce of strength he had to claw his way out of the chalk tomb.

Across the curve of Cane Hill he saw Stephen Blackmoore climbing out of his own grave, moonlight shining down on him with artificial intensity. It wasn't Blackmoore anymore than he was still Ru. His skin was as white as chalk, his body so much taller than it had been only moments ago, stretched thin like the chalk man carved into the side of the hill, his frame awkwardly twisted, shoulders burdened.

It was Corenius clawing his way out of the earth.

And he was Gogmagot.

The champions of the hill: born again to the chorus of Albion's need.

The song soared inside him. It fueled his blood. It was the magic in his veins. This land: his home. This land: his protectorate.

"I will rise!" the giant bellowed, beating his chest.

Corenius matched him blow for blow, then set off down the hill toward the city below.

Gogmagot followed him down.

16

Danny Ash wasn't like his friend.

He wasn't the Gatekeeper. He was something else.

He stood there with a joyous idiot smile on his face, free to discover exactly who he was. Everything around him looked different now. Or maybe it was just the way he saw it that had changed; after all the Rothery was still the Rothery and the old wood was just that, the same place they'd played as kids when they'd been together in Herla House. Everything was the same as it had been an hour ago. He was the only thing that had changed. Danny caught himself whistling the snatch of a familiar melody and for a moment thought it was an old tune, something from a forgotten movie, but it was more essential than that. The music owned a place inside his soul. It was rooted deep down in the darkness of his primitive hindbrain where instincts learned by ancestors long forgotten dwelt. Instincts like fear that were taken for granted by modern men, but had to be learned once upon a time.

It was the Song of Albion.

The music of the land itself.

The tune of Mother London calling out to her children.

The nurturing harmonies of her soul.

Danny let the music fill him body and soul, and let his own song fill the night as the rain fell, drumming on every surface around him. His song and the counterpoint drumming of the rain on the canopy of leaves made for a bittersweet symphony.

It felt like he was home for the first time in his life.

All around him the foliage encroached on the clearing, choking out the moonlight but at the same time sheltering him from the growing storm. The nature of the song changed. Now it sounded as though he was listening to a haunting strain of panpipes. The melody was ephemeral, each note fleeting.

He caught a glimpse of a figure moving through the trees. It was almost impossible to focus on it as it blundered through the endless layers of leaves, blending in with the natural world so absolutely with armor of bark and branch. He saw a few red berries within the holly over its chest as the Knucker in turn watched him.

It wasn't alone. There were others. Smaller, fleet of foot, moving lightly from tree to tree through the ancient wildwood, watching him. Danny only ever managed glimpses of their strange childlike silhouettes, seeing the trailing leaves of their clothes as they slipped tantalizingly out of sight before he could see them properly for what they were.

The nature of the song changed.

He hadn't realized it at first, but where there had been the haunting woodwind strains of pipes now the trees were filled a more demanding sound, wood on wood like drums.

Tendrils of fog spilled out from the fairy ring toward the circle of trees around him. Tommy didn't move. He had the same idiot-rapture grin on his face. The effect was most peculiar; it seemed to be roiling out through an open doorway, but there was no door, no arch, no keystone, and try as he might all Danny Ash could see out there was an ever-thickening mist.

The dark figure of a man began to take shape within the mist. Only he was like no man he had ever seen before. His frame was stunted, and there was something wrong about the way his legs were jointed, almost as though they bent backward. Wraiths of fog curled around the dark man as he advanced.

"Cume, Godbearn, se foldweg biþ gerúmed."

He couldn't see the speaker. The words, though utterly alien to him mind, echoed back to him through ancestral memories. *Come, child of god, the path is cleared.*

The drums, he realized, originated on the other side of the mist, not from within the impenetrable darkness of the trees.

Danny saw the towering figure of an antlered man on the edge of the clearing, beckoning the dark man to join him.

"Se foldweg biþ gerúmed," the Horned God repeated, though this time the same words resounded with an entirely different meaning in his mind. *The doorway is open.*

Danny tried to get an angle to better see what was happening, only for a childlike figure to step out into the path ahead of him. The girl had a crown of daisies tangled in her hair and a smile to melt his heart as she dropped into a deep curtsy, but that was the full extent of the softness. When he looked up, Danny saw that the girl's skin bore the same natural tones as the forest she called home, a subtle shift of hues from deepest greens to golden browns, textured like the fading sun. Her eyes were ancient. It wasn't about color or depth. They had seen the world age through a millennium that defied her small childlike form.

A scar ran down the girl's right cheek, from just beneath her eye all the way down her throat, disappearing beneath her dress of leaves.

"Brother," she said, her voice faltering as she reached out a hand, beckoning Danny toward her.

Two more of the curious children stepped out into the glade behind him, meaning he was effectively surrounded. He heard a rush of footsteps in the undergrowth, crashing through the bracken, and caught sight of a great black dog, twice the size of a Rottweiler, but with the same incredible physicality. The animal was fast. It rushed toward the antlered figure, responding to his call. It turned, looking at Danny with eyes that burned brimstone-bright and for just a moment he was paralyzed. Rooted to the spot. A second black dog circled the sacred grove in the opposite direction. The thing was *huge*. It moved with pantherlike grace, powerful muscles bunching and releasing, bunching and releasing, as it prowled around the enclosure. He watched the pair of them circle the fairy ring three times each in opposite directions. At the end of the third circuit, closest to him, one of the pair stopped to sniff at the air, isolating his scent. The beast had four wickedly sharp incisors, saber-toothed, that were too big for its mouth to contain.

Danny didn't dare move.

He wasn't sure he even could.

Tommy grinned his idiot grin, the mist curling around his legs. He watched Danny and the Children of the Forest do their dance.

The fear fell away as they ran up to hug him, tiny voices babbling excitedly, the only words he could easily make out being "You are home, Brother," despite the fact that those weren't the words the children of the wildwood used. The voice was honeyed. And that was exactly how it felt as Danny fell into their embrace.

He felt their lips on his as they pulled him down by the hair to cover him in kisses, each one gentle but hungry at the same time. It was innocent in one breath, and oh-so-knowing in the next.

The first children dragged him down to the ground.

Their appetite was insatiable.

Danny felt their hands all over him, pulling at his jeans, tugging at the buckle of his belt, at his boxers, lowering them even as more kisses smothered his face. The kisses reached his neck, and as they tore at the buttons of his shirt, down the flat planes of his stomach, not stopping as they traced the tight lines of muscle down to his cock. Tiny hands stroked him even as their lips closed on his mouth and more hands covered his eyes.

It was heaven.

And it was hell.

Balanced.

He could hear the dogs prowling around the fairy ring, the rasp of their breath, the heavy footfalls of their passage around the stones. Blind, he had to focus on his other senses, willing them to come alive. He could smell the heady fragrance of the grass, all of the grass— the thin reeds, the long blades, the scrub, each type with its own unique signature. There was a loamy richness, more than just the soil, and a freshness to the air that was unlike anything he'd breathed in the city. He could taste the lack of choking pollutants pumped into it. Danny lost himself to the sensory overload, falling into memories of the land as he tried to concentrate on each individual caress even as their sense of urgency became undeniable.

He knew he should be frightened.

Everything that was happening to him was wrong.

But the song calmed him, swept away his fears, whispering to him just how right it was.

Finally, the Horned God commanded, *"Cume."*

Come.

The demand had a double meaning.

Danny tried to open his eyes, but all he could see was the darkness of the palms of the hands cupped across them.

He tried to speak, but there were no words.

"Open yourself up," he heard. Simple words, but they might as well have been riddled in tongues, as he had no idea how to satisfy their request.

The song rose in the air around him, and in it Danny heard so many memories of the land, and of her first children. He tried to focus on them, holding on to just one, but even as he did, it slipped away to be replaced by another and another. There was so much he needed to know, but it was so far beyond his understanding. The hands roamed all over his body, finding his most intimate places, and their explorations brought pleasure he had never imagined possible. And still the hands worked his body even as his fingers dug deep into the earth, connecting Danny body and soul with the land as the powerful release swept over him.

"Don't be afraid to die," a voice whispered in his ear.

The dark man.

It had to be.

The voice curled around him. Insidious.

Before he could react, Danny felt a weight on his chest as the dark man straddled him. The children of the wildwood pinned him down, pulling his arms and legs painfully wide to accommodate the dark man. Now the hands on him were threatening in their ministrations. There was nothing sensual about the touch. Nothing tender. Danny felt fingers dig into his chest: a sharp stab of pain accompanying the breaking of his skin as the dark man's wickedly sharp nails parted the muscle to get at the bone.

The music swept and swooned all around him, consuming him.

He was lost to it for the longest time, carried away. He saw colors in the music, the world around him losing shape and form in favor of a sort of watercolor wash, shades of green fading into brown into blue, and sunbursts of red where the Gatekeeper still hunkered down beside the door into the other place.

Danny opened his eyes to see the cruel face of the dark man glaring down at him.

"You are mine, child, promised to me by my lord. Let me in." Only he didn't say "lord"; the word he used was *dryhten*. Danny knew it, like so many of the strange words he'd heard since the call reached his ears. He had always known it. It was the language of Albion. The true tongue. Danny didn't have the luxury of time to dwell on what his understanding meant. He felt the man's clawed fingers tear at his heaving chest, his panicked breathing multiplying the agony a thousandfold. He twisted his head left and right, trying desperately to wriggle out from beneath the man's weight, but there was no escape. The man drove his hand into Danny's chest, burrowing deeper even as he leaned forward to run his rough tongue over his lips. It wasn't a kiss. He was *tasting* him. His touch was vile. Invasive. There was no pleasure to it, unlike the children who had prepared him for this violation.

Danny's grip on consciousness swam away from him.

"Hush now," the man commanded; masculine, powerful. His voice resonated in every leaf and tree around them. "Surrender yourself. Become who you were always meant to be. Say your name. Taste it on your lips, know it to be true. Remember who you were and who you will always be. Tell me, who are you? Say it."

Names have power.

Names are the key to the soul.

All he had to do was say his name—the name he wanted them to share in some fused body, parasite and host.

"Say it," the man demanded. "Just one word. Let it live in your mouth."

Danny bucked against his weight, refusing to give in to him. The movement offered a glimpse of his legs. The man suffered from some weird deformity, his legs bent back the wrong way, the joints in his knees backward. He wore some sort of fur trousers—no, that was a lie; Danny's mind was trying to rationalize the sight of the fawn's hind legs and cloven hooves. The creature's cock was red and angry, raging, but not through any sort of sexual gratification or promise of release. He was simply reveling at being *alive,* being *here,* not trapped in his prison on the other side of the mist. "Rise up, Púcel," he demanded, bucking back against Danny's naked belly. He gyrated his hips, rubbing his tip against the muscles of Danny's stomach. His touch left a snaillike trail across the contours of skin.

Danny gave in to him, and said it, recognizing as he did it so many other names this creature had been called once upon a time: Puck. Pan. Bucca. Hob. Akercock. Woodwose. Green Man. Devil. All of them were true in their own way, but none of them were his true name, the one that gave power to his magic.

"Not *that* one. That would be too easy. Say my real name," the fawn demanded. "You know it. I know you do. I can see it in the front of your mind, just waiting for your tongue to curl around it. Do it. Say it. Let me inside you."

Danny named him again, a different one this time. He whispered the name that felt right, that belonged to this trickster and this trickster alone: "Robin Goodfellow. The Holly King."

In his mind's eye, it was Danny who had the cloven hooves and a fawn's legs.

He owned the name.

Something was happening to him. He saw the wisps of fog curl back away from the gate into the Annwyn. That he knew the true name of his Otherworld prison—the Ande-Dubnos—was proof enough that by naming him the god-borne creature was one with him now.

With that acceptance of what he was becoming the pain faded.

Danny raised his hands to his face, not trying to push his attacker away, simply to weep with joy at having found a way back here after all this time.

They were russet colored now with the dirt of the forest floor smeared into them.

The Song of Albion swelled, accentuated by the incredible cathedral acoustics of the wildwood. He felt its harmonies in his blood. He knew every note instinctively. The panpipes fused seamlessly with the melody of the forest creating something at once beautiful, haunting, and greater than the sum of its parts.

He became the song and the song became him.

Long is the day and long is the night, and long is the waiting of Arawn.

Arawn, the Lord of the Underworld hell he had just escaped. Arawn, the antlered man. Arawn, the Horned God. He knew things he couldn't possibly know. He understood. Tommy had said the dimgate was open. It was the way for the children of the Wild Hunt to return, and marked Arawn as the Once and Future King, with his curse to protect the land, to stand at the moment of her greatest need.

"My life for yours," Danny breathed, understanding that he would be no more; that he was becoming the host to the ancient trickster pressing down upon his chest. There was no Danny Ash anymore. He felt those words reverberate deep within him, calling out to him. "I will rise," Robin Goodfellow promised the Horned God, becoming in that breath the last of his champions.

His promise, his pledge, that Albion would recapture its lost beauty. It was that or leave her to wither and die, and with her the last of the earth magic that had dwindled to virtually nothing in the years since Arawn and his champions had last stridden this green and pleasant land. He looked at it now, in the stolen memories of Danny Ash, and saw the monstrosity that their land had become with the choking concrete and suffocating steel where there had been ancient wildwoods nourishing the earth magic. He made another vow: those towers would fall. They would be swept away before the Wild Hunt. All those man-made markers of civilization would fall so that the natural beauty of the land could flourish. It was the only way Arawn's champions could bring forth fresh magic from the land. There needed to be an end for there to be a beginning. As with the night, so with the day. Seasons end. It was time to usher in the Kingdom of Summer.

Robin stood slowly, rearranging the scraps of his torn shirt, and pulled up his jeans in an attempt at modesty he didn't really feel; it was a last lingering leftover from the young man he had been.

The children bowed down to him, falling to their hands and knees in worship, pressing their temples to the earth, echoes of the great song in the chant they offered the coming dawn. Behind them the Gatekeeper matched their benedictions, his own voice adding to the Song of Albion.

Robin raised his hand, causing them to fall quiet.

There was only the music now and the sound of the rain falling down through the leaves.

The Knucker lumbered into the grove; its immense bulk dwarfing the fairy ring as it cast its long shadow.

"Come to me. Brothers, Sisters, mine," Robin said, "Our wait is over. The time is upon us. This land, our land, needs us."

"We shall rise," the children said as one, answering the call.

He smiled as the first blush of dawn touched the sky, bringing an end to the Time Between Times.

"We shall rise," he agreed.

PART 2

Albions mountains run with blood, the cries of war &
  of tumult
Resound into the unbounded night, every Human
  perfection
Of mountain & river & city, are small & wither'd &
  darken'd

—WILLIAM BLAKE, *JERUSALEM*

17

Julie found the old man exactly where he'd last left him, sitting on the bench outside Ravenshill Cemetery. It was easy to imagine that Damiola had been in the same spot for six months without fail—sunrise to sunset, sunset to sunrise, and all the times between—because he wasn't a normal man.

Julie walked toward the wrought-iron gates with their rusted raven's wings. He'd been thinking about what he was going to say all the way here, and still didn't know how he was supposed to ask for help, never mind the kind of reception he'd get from the old man.

Damiola dipped grubby fingers into the newspaper wrapper to pluck out a cold chip and stuffed it into his mouth. To anyone who happened to walk down this narrow street in this quiet part of the city he would have looked like any of the city's eight thousand homeless people with his fingerless gloves and layer upon layer of torn and frayed coats swaddling his skeletal frame. Damiola's unkempt beard offered a home to remnants of dinners scavenged and consumed and his body odor was fierce enough to put up a physical barrier between him and the rest of the world. But looks could be deceiving and that was the essential misdirection of the magician's art.

Julie nodded in greeting as the old man recognized him. He didn't move to make room on the bench, forcing Julie to remain standing.

"I didn't expect to see you again," Cadmus Damiola said.

"I could say the same," Julie agreed.

He noticed a telltale flicker of movement in his eyes, an involuntary twitch that had him look toward the cemetery.

"Whatever it is you think I can help you with, Officer Gennaro, I can't. Whatever it is you think you want to know, you don't. Believe me, the world is better that way. You shouldn't be here." His voice, speech patterns, and comportment made a lie of his derelict frame. "It would be better for both of us if you just moved along and left me here to rot, if I even can."

"It would be," Julie agreed. "But we both know that's not going to happen."

"We can dream," the old man said, almost wistfully.

Julie laughed; he couldn't help himself. "I could say I'd missed you, old man, but that'd make a liar out of me."

"And given you've come cap in hand, that's not a good thing."

"One question, then I'll go."

"One answer is all you'll get."

"Sounds fair to me. So, my question: Does the phrase 'The Horned God is awake' mean anything to you?"

"Should it?"

"That's not an answer."

"Did they teach you nothing at school?"

"For argument's sake let's say they didn't."

"Cernunnos. Kernunno. Karnayna. Janicot. The antlered man. Herne the Hunter. Lord of the Wild Things. He has many names, but a singular nature. Potent. Virile. The Horned God is born in winter, impregnates the Earth Mother during the heady months of spring, is Lord of the Summer, then dies during the autumn and winter months only to be reborn, birthed by the goddess at Yule, completing the cycle. His aspects can be divided into different deities at different times of the year, including the Oak King and the Holly King, among others. He is among the eldest of the gods still worshiped in some form today, known to his adherents as the Lord of Death. He rules the Summerland where souls reside as they await rebirth. In the old faith that place was sometimes known as the Annwyn, and its master was given the name Arawn. He is the Lord of the Wild Hunt, and his horns may well be where we draw our Christian impressions of the devil from. Consider that today's lesson, and your one answer."

"The devil?"

"The devil," the old man repeated, picking at a bit of gristle that had stuck between his teeth.

"I don't know what I'm supposed to do with that."

"Why do anything?"

"Because five kids have been mumbling that phrase over and over since dusk yesterday. An old woman woke up in a hospital bed after years in a coma, offering the same portentous warning; an old man with his throat full of tree came back to life in front of my own eyes; and I hit a naked man with antlers in my car last night. That's why."

"One answer, Officer Gennaro. Now one piece of advice, given freely: walk away. This is not your fight."

"Five kids," Julie repeated, because that had to mean something, even to an old man like Damiola. "They're locked inside themselves; they can't express anything beyond the warning that the Horned God is awake. If you know anything that might help us, you've got to share it. You bent time, for fuck's sake. You made a prison out of a tomb and locked Lockwood out of time. I can't think of another person better placed to understand what is going on here."

The old man inclined his head slightly, tilting it to the right as he studied Julie. "It wasn't that simple," he said, which wasn't an answer to the question Julie had posed—but then he'd only promised one answer, hadn't he? "I didn't *bend* time. No one has that kind of power. And Lockwood isn't out of time, that's just a convenient way of thinking about what happened."

"Okay, and this is relevant to the Horned God how?"

"The Underworld. The Annwyn. Glass Town. They're aspects of the same thing."

"Are you trying to tell me you trapped Seth Lockwood in Hell?"

"If you believe in Hell."

"Who—or what—the hell are you? Jesus Christ, you talk about this stuff like it's *normal*."

This time it was the old man's turn to chuckle, but he didn't answer, at least not directly. "Perhaps it is normal where I come from," he offered, as Julie realized what he'd said.

"So, what are we talking about really, if not Hell and Heaven. Parallel worlds? Is that it?"

"It's not as simple as that, at least not in my case. It's not worlds, just world, singular. The Annwyn. Though it has many other names, the Underworld, the Otherworld, the Summerland, the Netherworld, Tartarus, limbo, purgatory, the Inferno, the Kingdom of the Dead. And like its master, it has a singular nature. Do you understand the concept of Newton's Laws?"

"You mean gravity and stuff?"

"Action and reaction," the old man said.

"For every action there is an equal and opposite reaction," Julie said, remembering the phrase without remembering where he'd first heard it.

"Think of it in terms of our world and the Annwyn, and the nature of contact interactions. Whenever these two worlds interact with each other they exert forces on each other—in Newtonian terms, action and reaction. When I sit on this bench I exert a downward force upon it, but simultaneously it's exerting an upward force on my backside. It's all about pairs. Two objects interact, two forces act. Take that bird," he pointed at the starling walking along the iron railing beside them. "Its wings push the air downward, but because of mutual interaction, the air is pushing the bird upward, making it possible to fly."

"Okay," Julie said. The concept wasn't a complicated one, but the implications were. "So, what you are saying is we did this? By opening a doorway into the other world to banish Lockwood we opened a door out of there, too?"

"And the Horned God stepped through. One for one. Equal and opposite."

Julie remembered where he'd seen the words *one for one* before. They were burned into the floorboards of Josh's flat in Rotherhithe, the place Josh had inherited from his grandfather with its walls of crazy, including one dedicated to the old ways, an incredible tree that he'd seen echoed on the door of Damiola's workshop. *One for one.* Boone had worked it out. He knew what it meant, and the implications of what they'd done.

"You said five children have taken up the chant?"

"Yes."

"Then he is looking to bring through five of his champions. Equal and opposite. Five souls find themselves drawn into the Annwyn so that five others may leave. As foretold, at the time of the land's greatest need he will return. Arawn is here. That is what it means. The Horned God is awake. And it is all my fault."

"How do we fight him?"

"We don't."

"There has to be *something* we can do. We can't just sit here and watch the world burn. Equal and opposite, right? What if we free Lockwood?"

"Arawn is already here. It would do no good. The interaction has already happened, the forces played out. We can't just take it back. I never should have indulged Joshua in his vengeance. It was stupid. And now look where it has led us." He seemed to think of something then. "You are right, equal and opposite," the old man said, as though it explained everything. "As long as Lockwood is alive in there—or whatever passes for life in the Underworld—there is a link between the pair. That is the only answer you need to take from this meeting, Officer Gennaro. Equal and opposite. Five for five. While the champions live, the children are lost to that other place. To bring them back, the link has to be broken."

"The champions must die?"

"Or if you look at it from the other side of the Newtonian equation, for the champions to live here in our world without fear of being dragged back to the Annwyn the children must die," Cadmus Damiola said. "They are in grave danger."

Julie finally understood the lesson the old man had been trying to teach him. "How do you know this stuff?"

"It is why I am still here," he said, again, not offering much in the way of an answer. Did he mean why he was here, outside the cemetery, watching, or why he was here in London, now, waiting? He was too intimately familiar with this stuff not to be a part of it, somehow. But before Julie could press him, the old man said, "Now, tell me about this resurrected man?"

Julie told him all there was to tell, about the call out and the weird carapace of bark that seemed to be some sort of cocoon around the dead man's body, and how when Ellie had accidentally touched it the bark had begun to flake away, exposing far-too-young skin for a man who was supposed to be in his nineties. How he'd found the leaf between his lips and pulled the sapling out of his throat, allowing the man to breathe again. He repeated as much of the man's words as he could remember, though to be honest he was vague on most of them, and fixated on the threat that the returning deity had marked him and just what that might mean. "We took Viridius to the hospital to get him checked out. Ellie insisted on a full psychiatric work up. I didn't have the heart to tell her the old guy was sane; it is the world that's fucked up," Julie said, earning a chuckle from the old magician.

"His name was Viridius? Who else but the god of spring should be born again by pulling a branch in bloom from his throat?"

"A god?"

"Well, he was worshiped once, so what would you call him?"

Julie shook his head.

"And he is returned?"

Julie nodded.

"Well, that is something, at least. Perhaps we have an ally in this?"

"If they let him out of the psychiatric ward."

"I warned young Joshua that there would be consequences," Damiola said. "Now we must face them."

18

There was a scar in the Rothery where Gideon Lockwood's pub The Hunter's Horns had burned to the ground. Corrugated iron fences had been erected around it, covered with posters for concerts that had happened months ago, and layers of inventive graffiti. The police station was less than three hundred yards away.

Julie parked in the underground garage and trudged up the ill-lit stairs to the station. The concrete stairwell reeked of piss. It was vile. Astringent. Someone had snuck into the garage and left a message for the constabulary. Julie took some small comfort from knowing that if he was ever on fire, there was at least one local who would do the right thing.

Smiling tiredly, he punched in his four-digit code and when the lock clicked in response, pushed open the security door.

"Evening, handsome," WPC Melissa Banks said, seeing him from across the room. "The boss is looking for you."

"Which *can't* be good," he said, changing direction midstride.

"You might be surprised."

"Will I be?"

"Nope."

"Didn't think so. Cheers, Mel." He pushed through the fire doors to the backstairs. So much for five minutes in and out, and then off home to bed. He climbed two at a time, meeting the Chief Inspector halfway, meaning she'd called up to let Tenaka know he was on his way up. Traitor. He caught himself smiling as he looked up at the boss. It was a power play. Tenaka was only five foot six inches, so he liked to catch officers on the stairs where he could talk down to them.

"Gennaro, just the man I was looking for." The man's voice was like grinding stones.

"Sir?"

"Underwood and Kahn, bad business. Any closer to finding the Kirmani boy? It'd be good to get this thing wrapped up before things turn ugly."

"There hasn't been a single sighting of Jamshid Kirmani since he fled the boxing club," Julie admitted. It bugged him. The kid wasn't smart enough to simply disappear. In this day and age it took serious nous to cover every track, and until a few hours ago Jamshid Kirmani was an ordinary kid, not Ronnie Biggs.

"Known associates? School friends? Anyone who might harbor him?"

"We're running down leads at the moment. Our best bet's the

family. We've got them under surveillance. We're hoping that Kirmani will reach out to them for help. He can't run forever. He's just a kid, and he's running scared."

"We can but hope," Tenaka said, none too convinced. "In the meantime, we've had a report of a missing persons case that has me concerned."

"How long are we talking?"

"The boy didn't return from football training this evening."

"So, what, seven or eight hours?"

"Long enough."

"Checked in with friends? Maybe they went to catch a late movie or something and he ended up crashing at a mate's and forgot to let Mum and Dad know?"

"His phone was active. We triangulated the signal and traced it to the park where he'd been playing football. Uniform found it under a bench."

"Kids lose phones all of the time."

"That they do. But there was blood at the scene, which SOCOs are checking. The lad goes to the same school as Underwood and Kahn. He's in the year below and by all accounts is something of a rising star. Lots of articles about him being offered terms with several of the Premier League clubs in the area."

"Well known and popular, and I'm going to assume Muslim?"

"Musa Dajani," Tenaka said, as though a name by itself was enough to racially profile the kid.

Julie followed his gaffer's train of thought to the inevitable conclusion, "Which makes him a perfect target for retaliation against an honor killing."

"That it does. You know what it's like out there, Gennaro. The anger and fear are festering. There's a rotten core to it, Gennaro. Our patch is breaking apart. It only takes one idiot to think an eye for an eye is an answer to turn the Rothery into a battlefield, which cannot be allowed to happen. We're going to increase our visibility over the next few days: more patrols, community outreach, get officers into the schools to talk to the kids."

"Better than kettling them," Julie said, only half-joking. "I assume we've checked with the local hospitals?"

"No admissions matching Dajani's description," Tenaka confirmed.

"You want me to talk to the boy's parents?"

"They're downstairs waiting for you."

"Okay, leave it with me." His bed was a long way away. He checked his watch. Ten past five. Those poor people must be going out of their minds. The likelihood, if not the absolute reality, was if he wasn't home now he wasn't coming home. He couldn't imagine what they were going through. Packing your kid's lunch box in the morning, checking he's got his kit for training before you ship him off out of the door, only for him never to come home again. Julie caught himself on the word *never*. He couldn't go in there thinking like that; the boy's parents would pick up on it. They were frightened; they weren't idiots.

"I knew I could count on you, Gennaro," Tenaka turned around and walked back up the stairs, leaving Julie to do the same, in reverse.

Instead of going straight into the interrogation room where the Dajanis were waiting, he stopped by the break room to grab a treacle black coffee. He was still wrestling with the paper filter when Sara Sykes, Melissa's partner, came in. "Have you seen this?" She held up her mobile phone. He recognized the Twitter app running, but was too far away to read the newsfeed she was watching.

"#ollieunderwood, #rotherystabbing, #justice4ollie, #aishainourhearts, #nohonour, and how about this for a nicely fucked up sentiment? #strikebackLondon."

He knew the basics about how hashtags worked, creating an index where all of the tweets under the same banner could be aggregated for easy reading by anyone with a computer or mobile phone. It changed the nature of communication. Information spread like wildfire. A single #strikebackLondon tweet could be seen by half a million teenagers in half an hour if the right person retweeted it; after that it would take on a life of its own. It would mutate, different exhortations would follow, everyone weighing in on what a bastard Jamshid Kirmani was, how Ollie was no angel, or how Aisha got what was coming to her, and every opinion in between. Opinions being like arseholes. Anyone looking up Ollie's or Aisha's names on the social network would find all of the tweets conveniently arranged to tell the story of the last nine hours.

They had been lucky in that it was raining and London had to sleep. Those two factors had stopped things from exploding all over the internet last night.

But that was yesterday. Today, as the saying went, was another day.

The rain had eased off at dawn, now the sun was coming up and the streets were wet, but the morning was fresh and cool, the air filled with that heady rush that always accompanied the scouring clean of the streets. He'd sensed the tension on the High Street last night, and that was before they knew about Aisha's death. Both sides were just waiting for the tipping point. And that tipping point was a kid who went to football practice and never came home. When that got out things were going to turn ugly, fast.

"Do I want to know what they are saying?"

"Fuck."

She pushed the phone toward his face. The latest tweet painted a target squarely on the back of Kirmani: *Jamshid Kirmani murdered #ollieunderwood & #aishakahn. Find Kirmani. Time to #strikeback-London. Demand #justice4ollie. #nohonour #riseup!*

"Fuck," Julie agreed. It was the only fitting sentiment.

Within the next minute or so Kirmani's name was retweeted a dozen times. The thirteenth tweet linked to his Facebook profile and put his face out there for the world to see. It was the butterfly that flapped its wings in the social media forest and started the perfect storm.

"This changes everything," Julie said.

"No kidding. We've got to find the kid before the mob do. And they've got a lot more eyes out there than we have," which was no word of a lie. If it turned into a witch hunt, there was only ever going to be one outcome. The last thing any of them needed was to get the call that Jamshid Kirmani had been lynched from one of the lampposts in the Rothery, making a martyr of the little shit. "We'll circulate his picture through the Boroughs, put everyone on alert. Hope we get a hit. Someone somewhere *has* to have seen him after he fled the boxing club. Techs are already going over footage from the surveillance cameras in the area. If there's anything to be gleaned from them, they'll find it."

"And in the meantime, we need to bring Kirmani's parents in. Sweat them. He's out there and we need to find him before anyone else does. If they know anything, we've got to get it out of them. It's their kid, he's up for murder; they aren't going to want to turn on him, so don't hold back."

"I'll get Mel to bring them in. You've got to wonder what the hell is going on inside his head right now? How do you get to a place where killing the girl you love is ever an answer?"

"Don't ask me. I'm not one the with a degree in deviant psychology, that's Ellie."

"I wonder if we can manipulate him into reaching out to the family to hurry it along, rather than just wait?"

"Put Mum and Dad on TV saying 'Just want him to come home,' that kind of thing?"

"Maybe not exactly those words, but yeah, appeal to the lost kid in him."

"That's assuming he'll see anything we do."

"I'll run it by Tenaka. Can't be any worse than doing nothing. Assuming the family will get on board."

"Check with them."

Julie nodded.

He gave up his struggle with the coffee filter and headed off to find Musa Dajani's parents in the interview room. They looked up at him so hopefully as he opened the door it broke his heart. He took the seat across from them, waving them to sit as they started to stand. He shook hands with both of them, introducing himself. "Mr. and Mrs. Dajani? I'm Julius Gennaro. I'm the officer looking into your son's disappearance. Anything you can tell me—anything at all—that might help us find him, would be a tremendous help. Let's start by talking about his routines. Have you noticed anything different about Musa over the last few days?"

Both Mum and Dad couldn't shake their heads quickly enough: eager to please, desperate to help, and terrified that they had nothing of use to tell him.

Julie nodded a couple of times, "Have you talked to his coach or friends from football?"

"The last time anyone remembers seeing him was at nine o'clock, walking back through the park," the boy's father said.

"Which is where they found his phone," Mother Dajani added. She choked out a small sob with her next breath, then straightened her back and looked him in the eye. She had her hands clasped, ready to say a prayer. "It's not good, is it?"

Julie might not have been God, but at least he was listening. He thought about lying; it would have been easy to just say that kids lose their phones all the time and they shouldn't jump to conclusions, but the seeds of false hope were worse than no hope at all. It wouldn't be fair to them. "No," Julie admitted. "It's not good." Kids were glued to their mobile phones. Their entire lives were on them. They didn't willingly leave them behind. So no, it wasn't good. He debated telling them about the blood, and almost didn't, but he needed them to trust him so he had to give them a reason to and that meant being straight with them. "My main concern right now is that we found traces of blood at the scene."

"Oh, God," Father Dajani said, his mind leaping to the worst-case scenario.

Mum was a little slower to react. "You think it's his, don't you?"

"I really don't want to speculate."

"Which means you do."

"It's a possibility we have to consider," he said. "Because it changes how we go about things. Right now we're checking hospital admissions for anyone matching your son's description. We've got people combing through surveillance footage from cameras on the park gates to see if we can see when Musa left and if he left alone. Right now we are in a good place, as good as we can hope in situations like this, as strange as that may seem. The first forty-eight hours are vital in a missing persons case. We've got good procedures laid out to help us find your son, and a lot of experience to draw on, but I'm not sure we can treat this as a normal disappearance."

"Because of the stabbings last night?" Mother Dajani asked.

He could hardly deny it, so he nodded.

"You think the two things are related?"

"I think there's a strong possibility," Julie admitted. "And to complicate matters someone has leaked the name of the killer, which is only going to muddy the waters. If we send uniforms out door to door to see if anyone saw anything, they're going to make the same connection."

"People will take matters into their own hands," Father Dajani said, something close to approval in his voice.

"But not turning over every stone decreases the chance of Musa coming home," Mum said, understanding the dilemma. "So you have to do it. You have to go out there and hammer on every door. You *have* to."

She was right; he knew she was right, even if it meant bringing hell to the Kirmanis' front door.

19

The old man sat in the chair by the window. It wasn't comfortable. Nothing about this place was comfortable. It reeked of sickness and death. The sun rose slowly above the rain-slick slates of the rooftops of the city. It was going to be a glorious day, he knew. The only pity was that he wouldn't be around to enjoy it. He was dying. Again. Life came in cycles; that could not be denied. They'd woken him too early from his restorative sleep. The rot was still within him. There was nothing he could do except accept it.

But that didn't mean Viridius had to like it.

He played with the bracelet the hospital staff had fastened to his wrist. His name was written on it in blue ink. All he had to do was rub his finger across the plastic for the ink to smudge. There was no permanence in anything. That was curiously appropriate. They'd asked him a thousand well-meaning questions, and he'd told them the truth in every answer, so of course they thought he was insane. That was the only logical conclusion for them to make, so he didn't disabuse them of the notion but rather let them think whatever they wanted to think. The truth would be hard to deny soon enough.

He held out his right hand, palm raised to the sun, and with the tip of the index finger on his left slowly traced a circle, round and around, like the kid's game, and in his mind pictured a single seed and willed it to shoot. Round and around, until the white shoot pushed against his skin, forcing its way through. Round and around, as the seed flourished, drawing nourishment from his body and the sun at the same time.

There was a knock at the door.

He closed his fingers around the half-inch long shoot, hiding it from the light as the nurse stuck her head around the door.

"Everything all right in here?"

He nodded.

"Anything I can get you?"

He shook his head, but then changed his mind. "Yes, actually," he said. "The officers who brought me in?" She nodded. "Is there any way you could reach out to them? I would like to thank them."

"Of course. I can pass your thanks along, that's no problem."

"Actually, if it isn't too much trouble I should like to thank them in person?"

"Okay, well leave it with me and I'll see what I can do. Can't promise anything, but you never know."

"I appreciate it."

"No juice or anything?"

"I'm fine."

"Okay, if you need anything, I'm just outside. They'll be around with breakfast in an hour."

He nodded and she closed the door.

Viridius opened his palm and held the seedling up to the light. In the few seconds that they'd been talking it had sprouted three small green leaves and grown another half-inch in the process. He smiled, gently running the tip of his finger in another circle and watching the seedling grow.

Over the next hour he nourished the seed into bloom, putting all of himself into it, only for the seedling to wither and die in his hand. He brought forth more than a dozen leaves, making them flourish for a few seconds only to die one by one, browning and curling. They couldn't hope to survive the rot inside him, and he lacked the strength to transform that sickness into another sapling within his craw. Without realizing what they were doing, the detectives had doomed this cycle of the Eternal's life before it had even begun. He carried in him all the sickness of the season, desperate for the rebirth of summer and its vitality, but it wasn't to be. Perhaps if he could convince them to return to his house and retrieve the branch so that he might consume it again, and in the process channel all of the rot consuming his vital organs into the stuff of the sapling, he would have a chance of making it to the other side of the equinox?

He almost crushed the withering plant in his fist from sheer frustration, because he knew the truth of the matter was that nature was undeniable. It was the Oak King's place to fall and the Holly King's to rise. He must die another death so that his brother could wake. That was his nature as the Eternal. But his brother had been nowhere to be found for a century, and every death left this place unguarded for half of the year. And now, with their father returned, it needed them more than ever. The plant was one last desperate attempt to change things, but he couldn't keep even that little of his magic alive in this damned place.

It was all he could do to watch as the leaves fell away from the stem to rest on his upturned palm.

He placed the leaves on the windowsill, in full view of the sun, and crossed the small room to the wardrobe where they'd hung his clothes. The old man took a tobacco tin from the inside pocket of his coat and from it, the papers he needed to roll a cigarette. Instead of using the tobacco in the tin, he stuffed the paper with the leaves from his palm, then licked the edges of the paper and rolled it into a straggling little runt of a cigarette. He put it in the tin, and had just put the tin back into his coat pocket as the door opened on a different face.

It was the female officer who'd brought him in. She smiled at him, "Mind if I come in?"

"You are very welcome," he said, indicating the room's only chair. "Please excuse my unsightly attire, I promise to do my best with regards to turning my back to you and exposing you to horrors that can never be unseen."

Ellie Taylor laughed at that. There was genuine warmth in the sound. "How are you feeling?"

"I've been better," he said truthfully. "I'm dying, after all." She didn't say anything to that. No *I'm sorry* or *Don't be silly*. No *How can you know?* She just looked at the old man and waited for him to explain. "Rather than feel sorry for me, I wanted to thank you, and thought perhaps you might indulge me; help me get out of here, so I can die with the sun on my face? No one deserves to die in a place like this."

"I'm not sure," Ellie said.

"What can it hurt? We sneak up to the roof, maybe smoke a last cigarette, and watch the sun come up over London one last time for me at least. And if I don't die, then you bring me back down here and we let the quacks shrink my head all day?"

She smiled again. "Why do I get the feeling that I'm going to get into trouble for this?"

"Because you're a smart woman," Viridius said, earning another chuckle.

"Come on then, sunshine, get your glad rags on."

While he dressed, the police officer went out to the nurses' station to check if it would be okay if she took him for a little walk. Then together they rode the elevator to the top floor. Across from them as they emerged, they saw a door marked *Helipad* beside a second bank of elevators. It wasn't locked. They climbed a short flight of stairs, and walked out onto a concrete division—on one side there was a cultured rooftop garden, on the other a bright red helicopter waited idly.

"Can't have you trying to make a break for it," Ellie said, steering him toward the garden pews on the other side of the divide. The potted plants were green, but there was barely a bud on them and no flowers. They sat. From their vantage point the most famous skyline in the world looked like a watercolor postcard with the red a little too rich over the water as it rippled toward morning. Even in the city, with so little of the natural world to see, the sounds of the dawn chorus were mesmerizing, with every starling, pigeon, sparrow, blackbird, and magpie lent their voices to the song. This was life and he would miss it so very, very much. He felt the tear break and roll slowly down the smooth plane of his cheek, and resisted the temptation to wipe it away.

"It really is quite beautiful, isn't it?" Viridius offered, just happy to feel the sun on his skin. He didn't look to see if she agreed with him. There were different kinds of beauty and there was no denying that Sir Christopher Wren, Sir Charles Barry, and John Nash had built an incredible city. Even the new additions, the Shard and the Gherkin were things of beauty in their own right, their intrusion brutal against the skyline. *If there had to be a last view, this wasn't such a bad one,* he thought to himself. He could feel himself failing fast. He knew the sensations that accompanied death far too intimately, although every time he suffered them they came as a fresh surprise. "Do you mind?" he reached into his pocket for the tobacco tin and that special cigarette. Despite the rising sun it was cold enough that he was glad of the coat.

"Knock yourself out," Ellie said. "Look, I didn't come here to hear you say thanks. I'm trying to understand what happened back at your house. You were dead—"

He cut her short, "Merely sleeping, though it is more akin to hibernation than forty winks."

"But that thing, that branch . . . how? Julie pulled it out of your mouth. Who did that to you?"

"No one," Viridius said, knowing he could never explain it. Instead, he offered her the cigarette. She took it from him, and put it to her lips as he took the lighter from his pocket to light it. He almost felt sorry for her, for what he was about to do to her, but reminded himself that the other one—he couldn't remember than man's name—was already marked. He had seen the Horned God, but more importantly, the Horned God had seen him. "There is more to this life than you can possibly hope to understand, dear lady," he said as she inhaled her first breath of him. "Few can. Fewer still would want to."

"Is this where you ruin everything by telling me about stag kings and dimgates again? We were doing so well." The cigarette tip flared redly as she sucked in another lungful of his essential being. Soon enough her perceptions would start to shift; like a junkie getting high.

"I wouldn't dream of it, dear. This is where I apologize for ruining your life."

"That's a bit of an exaggeration," she said, smiling as she watched a couple of starlings bicker over a tasty morsel. She inhaled another breath of him.

All that remained was to wake the magic within her; then he could go and put an end to his pain.

"Tell me," Viridius said, as though the thought had just occurred to him, "of all the things that you do for this city, what do you consider to be the most important?"

The cigarette tip flared red again as more of his leaves smoldered to ash, their smoke filling her lungs. When she exhaled, the smoke drifted up in front of her face. "We keep the peace," she started to say; then stopped herself. "But that's just an aspect of what we do. The most important thing? We help those who can't help themselves. Like yesterday, just before we found you, we were on the High Street where a young man had been stabbed to death because he'd fallen in love with the wrong girl. A few minutes later we found out that the girl had been killed as well. Someone needs to remember them. Someone needs to stand up and be a speaker for the dead. That's what we do. We stop the world from simply forgetting the victims."

Viridius smiled, "The Speaker for the Dead," he said, breathing the last of his life into the words. "How very true. And just what this world needs now."

Ellie didn't notice the slight shift in emphasis as he named her; indeed, she didn't notice him slump in his chair as the life left him. "I like to think so," she agreed. "It's important someone is there for the victims in all of this. We're in such a rush for justice and retribution, but when it doesn't come easily there are always so many more victims to fight for that some inevitably get forgotten. That isn't right. We shouldn't just forget. Not someone's life. Not something so important."

"You are more right than you could ever know," Viridius said, thinking of all the injustices that had been forgotten, the lives and sacrifices paved over and built upon to fashion the skyline before him now. "Someone must speak for the ghosts of London. I think you are the perfect choice for the role." Viridius held out a hand. She helped him rise unsteadily, and together they walked right up to the waist-high wall that enclosed the rooftop terrace, and looked out over the edge, all the way down the dizzying drop to the Thames below.

She snuffed the last of the cigarette out on the stone wall and flicked it over the side.

"Well, we really should get you back down to your room, you'll catch your death out here, and I need to go home and get some sleep before the rat race begins all over again."

She turned her back on the city, and in the process saw the old man's body still slumped in the pew where he'd died a few minutes earlier.

"I am so very, very sorry," the old man's ghost told her.

"I don't . . ."

"I am out of time, but at least I can leave this place knowing that it is defended."

Viridius walked away from her, and long before he reached the pew his body faded into the rising sunlight and was no more.

The potted plants were in full bloom.

20

Sykes and her partner, Melissa Banks, drove to the Kirmanis despite the fact it was less than five minutes' walk from the station.

They couldn't get to the house on Fisher Row. The crowds were already gathering. There must have been 150 people outside the Kirmanis' red-brick terrace. The curtains were drawn so no one could see in or out. There was a local television broadcast truck blocking half the street. They were in the process of setting up the camera unit for a report to feed the beast that was the twenty-four-hour rolling news cycle. Even when there was nothing to say they were more than prepared to fill the silence saying it. "This isn't good," Mel said. She had a gift for stating the obvious. Sara leaned closer to the wheel to flick the switch so the siren announced their arrival. The crowd parted reluctantly, giving them room to drive slowly down the white line in the middle of the road.

They could hear the vile racist chants without rolling down their windows.

Sara opened the door.

The hatred amplified a hundredfold.

She closed her eyes—counted to three to steady herself—then clambered out of the car to face the mob. The worst of it was that they looked so utterly normal but for the hate in their eyes. They could have been bank tellers, shop clerks, baristas, and sheet metal workers. All walks of life were there, and that was anything but comforting. "Okay, folks. I'm going to ask you nicely to go home. There's nothing to see here. These people have done nothing wrong."

"Scum!" someone shouted.

"Bastards!" came the answer, followed by the inevitable, "Fucking Pakis!"

Mel climbed out of the car.

"Look, this is a bad situation, but what you need to realize is that you're making it worse. We are looking for Jamshid Kirmani. He's not in there. His parents are. His baby sister is. I get it, you're angry, but not at them. This isn't helping things. Please, I'm going to ask you again, don't give this lot," she gestured dismissively toward the camera, "an excuse to plaster your faces all over the six o'clock news. Be smarter than that. Trust us. We all want justice for Ollie and Aisha."

"Like fuck you do," someone shouted from the back of the crowd. The voice was strident, full of bitterness and pent-up frustration. "Ollie and Aisha were our kids, they grew up here; we all *knew* them," the crowd parted so Sara could see the speaker. It was an elderly woman, in her seventies if she was a day, with blue fingers in fingerless mittens and nylon pop socks rolled down around the varicose veins of her ankles. She wore soft-soled slippers on her feet. She was the last person in the world Sara would have expected to swear with such vitriol, but that was the Rothery. "That worthless piece of shit killed my grandson. So, don't expect me to just sit down in front of my television and wait for my turn to die. That piece of scum," she pointed a trembling—accusing—finger at the Kirmanis' front door, "better hope you find him before we do." Her promise was greeted by applause and shouts of agreement from the crowd.

"Look, I get it," Sara said, trying to be heard over the noise. "I really do. And my heart goes out to you, but all you are doing is terrorizing a family in there. Please. Go home." She was aware of the camera on her and didn't want to give them their sound bite, either.

They moved away, grudgingly. Mutters of discontent followed them down the garden path.

They didn't need to knock on the door; it opened a crack before they reached it. Sara could make out the gold links of the security chain that wouldn't have kept them safe from an irate toddler.

"Mrs. Kirmani?" The chain rattled against the hasp and fell free and the door opened wider to a roar of anger from the other side of the hedge.

"Come in," the voice was timid against the backdrop of anger.

Sara and Mel disappeared inside. The woman locked the door quickly behind them, sliding the security chain back into place as though it were the ultimate defense against a pitchfork-wielding mob. "Go through to the lounge, please."

The rest of the Kirmani clan had gathered in the small room. There were no free seats so they stood in the middle of the off-white carpet looking at the ring of faces. "Is it really true?" a girl of maybe fifteen asked. She had long raven-black hair and eyes to match. "What they're saying about Jam? Did he really kill Ollie and Aye?" She used both names with familiarity, and obviously knew both victims.

Sara nodded. "I'm afraid so. The assault was captured on video by a couple of girls in their class."

"My foolish boy," the woman who'd let them into the house moaned and seemed to sink into herself; slumping against the doorframe. She needed it to keep her from falling. "What have you done?" The question went out to the one person who wasn't there to answer for himself.

"I know this is hard," Sara said, "but I need you to think. Is there anywhere Jamshid might have gone? Friends or family who would hide him? You can see what it's like out there. It's important we find him before anyone else does. If there's anything you can think of, a place we can start looking, now is the time to tell us."

"He's got cousins in Watford and Bedford, but he hasn't seen them since he was ten or eleven."

"His best friend went to Uni up in Newcastle," the girl suggested.

"Are they still in regular contact?" Mel asked.

The girl shrugged. "Facebook, Twitter, that kind of thing. They don't send love letters—"

"Neysa!"

"It's okay," Sara said, before it could turn into something. "Do you remember his name?"

"Marcus French. He's doing Business Studies."

"That's great, thank you." Before she could ask anything else the huge bay window shattered in a spray of glass. There were screams as a chunk of brick hit the side of an elderly woman's face, opening a deep gash as she fell out of her seat. The others were up on their feet, screaming and yelling as chaos broke out inside the room. A bitter chorus of hate spilled in through the broken window. The net curtain flapped in the breeze. Shards of glass ground underfoot as people ran to help the fallen woman.

Sara radioed the attack in, calling for backup to the Rothery hoping to stave off what felt like the inevitable escalation. "Stay here," she told her partner, and went back outside to yell at the crowd, one voice against the mob. "Enough! There are children in there. That brick just hit an old lady in the head. I hope you're proud of yourselves." She leveled a finger at Ollie Underwood's grandmother. "You need to stop this now."

"No, I don't," the old woman said. "They're scum. Their kid deserves everything that's coming to him."

Before she could argue, someone at the back of the crowd called out, "They've found a body in the woods! Look."

"It's that kid," someone else said, looking down at their own phone. "The footballer who went missing last night."

"Musa," someone gave him a name.

Her radio cracked to life, the call from the dispatcher directing officers to respond to an incident up at Coldfall Wood. Sara was already looking at the too-vivid photograph of Musa Dajani's broken body that scrolled by under the hashtags #justice4ollie, #strikeback-London, #aishainourhearts. The missing boy had been stripped naked and strung up from the iron letters that spelled out the forest's name. His young body, stretched thin by the crucifixion pose—wrists bound by vines to the first and last O—had taken a battering before he'd died. It was a pitiful sight.

Sara felt sick to her core, and so much worse as the old woman leaned in to get a good look at the picture, a vindictive smile cracking across her weather-worn face.

"It's a start," the old woman said. "But it doesn't change anything. It doesn't bring Ollie back. My grandson is still dead."

"And now someone else's grandson is, too," Sara snapped, unable to stop herself. "*You* did this. This boy is dead because of *you*. He's the only innocent person in this whole fucking mess. So you tell me, who's the scum here?" She had to stop herself from saying more, but the anger was there for all to hear, including the mics on the cameras. She turned her back on the old woman, shaking her head in disgust, and walked back down the short garden path.

A second brick sailed over her head, missing her by a couple of inches. It powdered against the wall, leaving a red stain against the side of the Kirmanis' house.

Sara Sykes spun around on her heel, glaring at the crowd as she growled, "Which moron threw that?"

The camera had caught it all, and the camera never lied.

21

Julie found Joshua Raines sitting by himself in a café on the South Bank, watching a tugboat wrestle with a deep-sea vessel. He had changed. He was a shadow of the man Julie had helped trap Seth Lockwood. Lockwood might have been in a prison where one year passed like a hundred, but Josh was the one aging that way. There was an empty espresso cup on the table beside him. A coffee-colored scum of espresso thickened around the white rim. A garishly illustrated paperback book picked up from the market stall beneath the bridge, lay open beside the cup, its spine cracked so that it lay flat on the wooden surface.

Josh had his eyes closed, lost in thought.

Julie Gennaro dragged back the second chair and joined him.

"Julie," Josh said, without opening his eyes.

"Josh," Julie said, all very polite. Their relationship had never been exactly normal, given how they'd first met. If ever a first impression was going to define a relationship, it was that one with Josh seeming to step out of a tear in the world, right in front of Julie's squad car. Julie caught the waitress's eye and pointed at the empty espresso cup, signaling two. He settled back into the uncomfortable chair. "You're a hard man to find."

"Not really, I only go to three of four places these days, and none of them are exactly far from home." Home, though, wasn't the house on the Rothery he'd shared with his mum and grandfather; it was the secret flat he'd inherited from Boone Raines along with the mystery of Eleanor's disappearance. He'd cleaned out the walls of crazy, taking down the newspaper cuttings and the old headshots and dismantled the crisscross of red threads, so the only reminder of Glass Town that remained was the map scorched into the floorboards, along with those three little words. Everything else was gone, if not forgotten. "Not to be rude, but what do you want?"

Julie said, "World peace."

"Better get used to disappointment, mate."

"Indeed. Sadly, this isn't a social visit."

"What am I supposed to have done?"

"You remember when the old man said there would be consequences to banishing Seth?"

"It's not a day I'm likely to forget."

"Well, looks like it's time to pay up. The way the old man explained it, it's a two-way door, we opened a gateway to some sort of Hell when we banished Lockwood. He went in through the door, but something else came *out* while we were busy congratulating ourselves. *One for one*, that's how Damiola said it." That had Josh's attention. He could see the fear ripple across the surface of Josh's eyes. Josh knew those words; he lived with them underfoot every day.

Julie was thinking about Myrna Shepherd, or the thing that had clothed itself in her glossy cinematic likeness. Julie knew it was Shepherd, because it was always Shepherd. He saw the actress's face every single night in the darkest hours, when he woke sweating in a tangle of sheets. He couldn't escape the memory of her devouring Taff. He didn't know what memories haunted Josh. It was enough to know that they had a shared vision of Hell that began and ended with Glass Town.

"It can't be happening again," Josh shook his head. "It's over. We won."

"We did. At a price."

"I can't do it again," he reached instinctively for the empty espresso cup and stared into it before setting it aside uselessly. "Please don't ask me to get involved. I don't think I can."

"I saw the old man this morning. What we did, it's affecting others now. Kids. They're going to die if we don't do something. I know you, Josh. You're not going to sit there looking at the river sipping your coffee while kids are dying. Not when you know it's your fault."

"Fuck you, Julie. I didn't ask for any of this. Look at me. What do you see?" Before he could answer Josh had his own answer. "I'll tell you what you see, a broken man. I had to sit with her while she died, Julie. I was right there, trying to be strong for Eleanor, trying to see the beauty in one final sunrise. And now you're telling me we fucked up. That we opened some door and freed something worse than Seth? Eleanor's dead. Boone's dead. My mum. Dead. You see a pattern here? Seth took everyone I've ever cared about from me. He left me with *nothing*. Now you're trying to tell me that wasn't enough?"

"I need your help, Josh."

"I'm done helping."

"That's what he said you'd say," another voice said behind them. Alex Raines pulled up a third chair from a neighboring table and joined them. "I didn't believe him. Not my brother." She put a crumpled five-pound note on the table and pushed it toward Julie. He pocketed it.

"You make a lovely couple," Josh said as the waitress delivered two delicate espresso cups, the white porcelain advertising some unpronounceable heritage for the coffee it contained. Josh pushed his toward his sister. "Knock yourself out."

Alex didn't need telling twice, she downed the coffee in a single swallow. "We're going to take a walk," she said, like a mobster making an offer her brother couldn't refuse.

"You're not going to change my mind," Josh said.

22

Julie left them to go back to work. He wouldn't say what had happened, only that he had to go in because all hell was about to break loose. He hadn't slept in twenty-four hours and was barely functioning. She knew him better than he knew himself. Alex kissed him and told him to be safe. He promised he would. It was a stupid lover's promise taunting a world he couldn't possibly control. He knew that better than anyone, but he still made it just the same.

Alex wasn't big on romance, not in the holding-hands-walking-in-the-rain kind of romcom definition of it, anyway. She was big on simple thoughtfulness, and trying to make the day a little bit better for someone you love. So, less bunches of flowers and more aluminum trays filled with piping-hot Indian takeout after you come home from a grueling shift.

She smiled at the thought, making herself hungry.

The walk along the river took fifteen minutes.

On another day, under different circumstances, it would have been nice. Brother and sister taking a stroll down by the waterside, tourists moving all around them, dozens of languages in their ears at once so the noise lost all meaning and all that remained was the excitement of being here, now. The gray skies and shrinking puddles couldn't dampen their enthusiasm for the city. A funfair had grown around the enormous stanchions of the London Eye. There were carousels and shooting galleries, bumper cars and duck shoots and kids having the time of their lives. The metal braces anchoring the wheel to the riverside were the size of a small terraced house, each bolt bigger than a person. The wires between the braces and the wheel itself were so thick a gaggle of schoolkids could have held hands one by one for a game of Ring a Ring o' Roses without the last pair being able to join hands to close the circle. They were that huge. But everything was, even the hot dogs the kids ate and the giant bars of chocolate they carried away as their prizes.

Alex hadn't seen much of her brother since their mum's funeral. She'd wanted to, but Josh had retreated into himself.

She'd made the mistake of giving him time, thinking that eventually he'd have to come back to her, but instead he'd disappeared into himself. He hadn't set foot in the family home in months, spending his nights in that flat down in Rotherhithe. They'd put the place on Albion Close up for sale, but there were no buyers. The place had a reputation; after all it was the murder house.

She looked at him as they walked. He looked tired. Bone deep. His skin had a waxy tinge to it, and he needed a decent shave. There were spots of blood on his neck where the dull blade had cut him yesterday or the day before. He wasn't taking care of himself.

"How are you?" Alex said, letting him have the room to be honest if he wanted to, or to just say he was fine and let them walk the last couple of hundred yards to the hospital in awkward silence.

"Been better," Josh said. "Coping. Most days, anyway. Some days it's a struggle to get to grips with complex stuff like putting my trousers on the right way around," he tried to make light of the situation, but it was painfully obvious he was struggling. Depression was a killer, even with very real, very obvious reasons for it. Ignoring it was as dangerous as leaving cancer to metastasize whilst putting all your faith in some ancient Chinese herbal remedy. You *could* do it, but it wasn't wise.

"Are you talking to anyone?"

"You," he said.

"Funny. You know what I mean."

"What am I supposed to tell them? You know what happened. How do you put something like that into words? How do you explain so that someone who hasn't been through it—hasn't seen someone live a hundred years without aging a day—can understand and not immediately think you've lost your mind?" She didn't have an easy answer for that, in no small part because she hadn't lived it, not like Josh. She'd only had to cope with the fallout, the loss, and that was hard enough. She didn't try to offer platitudes. They were beyond that. "There's magic in the world, Lexy. Real magic. People don't want to believe that; they might say they do, but the reality is they want a world with boundaries that makes sense. Something they can understand. When something that doesn't fit into their understanding of the world it doesn't make them excited, it makes them *frightened*. Look at the television, the newspapers; they use fear to kill our minds and stop us thinking for ourselves. Frightened people do what they're told. Or most of them do, at least. The others react badly . . ." Josh lapsed into silence, looking down at the cracks in the pavement as he walked. He placed his feet carefully, altering his stride pattern to avoid stepping on them.

As they rounded the long curve in the embankment and the hospital came into sight he tried to explain himself. "It's different now. I don't feel like I belong here. I don't want to believe anymore. I don't want to live in a world with magic. I want to go back to the days after Boone died, give the letter to Seth, and be done with it. Forget Eleanor Raines and the obsession that destroyed my family. I just want to be *normal*. I'd kill for one day just being myself again. I sat beside a woman and watched her *slowly* crumble into dust, terrified and yet somehow strong, and I *never* want to live through anything like that again. And now your boyfriend turns up and tells me it was for nothing? That I created new nightmares? I can't give it room in my head."

"I know," she said. "I do. But—"

"Please don't say anything after that, no but-you-have-tos."

"You have to," she said.

They reached the hospital.

"Just come in, see for yourself. If you really feel like you can't do this, I can't make you, Josh. But I can't imagine a world in which you'll walk away, either."

"Maybe I'll surprise you," he said, following her in. "Do you remember Boone's funeral?"

"Hard to forget," she said.

He nodded. "You heard Seth mocking us, all of that stuff about Boone's father being in and out of the asylum. If I try and tell people about the magic I've seen, about what he put me through, that's my fate. You know that. That's what Seth's eulogy was all about. It wasn't a good-bye to the last good man in London, or whatever he said; it was a warning of what would happen to *me* if I opened my mouth." He was beginning to sound like one of those homeless guys who lived down by the river and claimed to have been probed by aliens because they knew The Truth, but it was hard to argue against his point.

Alex led Josh up to Emmaline's room.

Before they went inside she told him, "Okay, Brother. You don't have to do this, not if you don't want to. I understand. I do. This is it, your get-out-of-jail-free card. If you want to go, just turn around and head back to the elevators. I won't hold it against you."

Josh started to turn around, but then offered his sister a crooked half smile. "Like I could walk away."

"I told you I knew you," she said, but she wasn't smiling this time.

The old woman was alone in the room. Her eyes were closed and the television set was on providing background noise. She looked so delicate with her hair spread out across the banked-up pillows, her skin bone-china pale and waxy.

She opened her eyes, sensing their presence.

"Hey, Emmaline, I want you to meet my brother, Josh."

Josh drew one of the empty chairs toward the bedside, and offered a slight smile to the helpless woman. He picked up the communication board, studying the layout of the letters. The old woman blinked rapidly, trying to say something. Her eyes darted upper left, lower right, blink, blink, blink, some drawn out, others barely a flicker, so fast it was difficult to count them.

"Slow down," Alex said, sitting on the edge of the bed. "Start from the beginning. I've never done this before, okay?"

The woman kept on blinking. Frantic now.

Josh held up the board, trying to count out the letters.

Finally, Alex saw a pattern in them. Emmaline was spelling out the same words over and over, like before, but this time her message was more personal, or at least seemed to be: *He is here. One for one. He is here. One for one. He is here.*

"It's okay, Emmaline. I get it, I'm with you," Alex said, trying to calm the old woman down, but she wasn't about to be soothed, and neither was Josh. Something about that six-word message on endless repeat had spooked him. "What is it? What's wrong?"

"It's a setup, isn't it? Julie told you what to say. Bastard."

Alex shook her head. "I have no idea what you're talking about. Cross my heart."

"*One for one.* Julie put those words into your mouth, didn't he? That's not what her eyes meant at all, you're playing me."

"Look at me, Josh. Look *at* me. I'm telling you the truth. He asked for my help convincing you. That's it."

"Then he must have told the old dear, planted the seed in her mind so she blinked it out. It's a con. You can admit it. Right now, tell the truth, and I promise I won't get mad."

"I'm not lying, Josh."

"Then how did she know to say *one for one*? It's what Julie said when we were at the café. Word for word. One for one. He said we opened a doorway when we banished Seth, and this is our reward. We let something into our world from . . ." he bit his tongue, finally saying, "That place," rather than naming it.

"It's not the only time since she's woken up that Emmaline's said something that someone else has said," Alex told him. "Her first words were 'The Horned God is awake,' which is not exactly the kind of thing you hear every day. Last night, five kids were brought into hospitals around London. They were all in a near-catatonic state, mumbling the same phrase over and over. 'The Horned God is awake.' Five different kids, Josh. It's all linked. Any way you look at it, that's not right. You said there's magic in the world. This is it. I don't know what its purpose is, or how it works, but this is magic. And it's not good."

"She's trying to say something else; grab a pen, quick." She started to call out the letters one after the other, spelling out the terrifyingly short message that could only ever have been meant for Joshua Raines.

"This is a trick. You're making it up. It's got to be."

Alex tore the top page from the legal pad, crumpling it up into a ball, and hurled it uselessly at her brother's back as he walked away. She didn't need it. The three short words she'd carefully scratched out were burned into her brain.

You are his.

23

"There's more," George Tenaka said.

There's more meant this nightmare went beyond Ollie Underwood, Aisha Kahn, and Musa Dajani.

Julie sat across the table from his Chief Inspector, looking down at the pile of missing persons reports Tenaka had gathered. They were all dated yesterday.

He took the one off the top.

Charlie Mann.

It took him a moment, but he recognized the kid.

Placing him took a little longer. He'd seen him recently. In the last day. He'd been on the High Street, Julie realized. He'd stood out from the crowd because he was walking away from Ollie Underwood's corpse, not trying to get a better view. Not that he was oblivious, just that he wasn't interested. He'd been well dressed, or as well as you expected a seventeen-year-old to dress; a cheap polyester suit that didn't quite fit and a tie that looked like it was strangling him.

"Resident of Herla House Group Home. Safe to say he's a troubled soul. One of two kids the home reported missing last night."

He checked the next page, which listed Penny Grainger's home address as Herla House.

He looked at the picture of Penny paperclipped to the upper-right corner. She was attractive. Young. Fresh-faced.

"Any chance the two of them met up to celebrate Charlie's birthday?" Julie asked, after seeing the date of birth on her file, and checking Charlie's. "Next year they're both eighteen, so this is last one they get to celebrate before their little family of inconvenience scatters to the four winds. Maybe they had a good night and slept it off somewhere?"

Tenaka made a face. "Normally I'd be inclined to agree. Charlie and Penny match the descriptions of two joyriders we chased last night, but given this," he held out a second sheet with the Crown Prosecution Service letterhead, "I'm thinking no."

Julie skimmed the page and realized it was an ongoing investigation into historic cases of child abuse at Herla House, and linked in with the Yewtree operation. It made grim reading.

"Thirty complaints dating back to the seventies. And these are just the ones we know about. It's not looking good."

"Jesus Christ."

"Has very little to do with London these days."

"Well, that changes everything. No way of getting around the fact these kids are at risk. They could be runners. Last year together before they're cast out. Those bonds are tight. Maybe they decided to mark Charlie's birthday with new lives for everyone."

"That's the Harry Potter version of the story where kids who live in cupboards under the stairs get a happy ending," his CI said. "Since when have you known life to be happy?"

The next two papers belonged to Stephen Blackmoore and Rupert Brooke. They were two years older than the others, and didn't fit in with any obvious pattern laid out by the other kids, although both, Julie noted, were ex-residents of Herla House. In Blackmoore's case he had a rap sheet as long as Julie's arm. He wasn't a good kid. On the spectrum he'd be diametrically opposed to Charlie Mann. Rupert Brooke wasn't as bad, but he was far from an angel with three counts of breaking and entering, one of criminal damage, and one grievous bodily harm charge that had earned him an Anti-Social

Behavior Order twelve months ago. There was nothing since then. So, maybe the ASBO had done the trick and young Rupert was a reformed character. That, or he'd become better at avoiding getting caught, which was far more likely than a slap on the wrist working like some sort of magic wand.

The final names on the table were well known to Julie. Tom Summers and Danny Ash. Again, he noted the Herla House link. Both boys had served their time. They'd left eighteen months ago. Nasty pieces of work; the pair of them: poster boys for Britain First and that whole right-wing extremist crap that seemed to be gripping the nation.

Six names.

He'd come into the room expecting to hear that five kids had been reported missing; *one for one,* as Damiola had promised.

Six, though. Eight if you counted Musa Dajani and Jamshid Kirmani. More if you added the dead. Either Damiola was wrong, or at least one of these names didn't belong. What was more likely? He spread the reports out across the table, arranging them in different orders, shuffling them left and right as though that made an actual difference to how they fit together. Four names stood out as different. Blackmoore, Brooke, Summers, and Ash. They didn't fit the victim mold. They were everything that was wrong with the youth of today.

"The question is: What, if anything, have these kids got in common besides Herla House?"

"Why discount it?"

"I'm not."

"Good, because the most obvious answer is that they're all vulnerable, and Herla House just highlights that," Julie said. "It's the thread that binds them all. My gut instinct says yes. We're talking about kids in high-risk situations. We don't know what happened to them in that place. But we can assume it was nothing good. Systemic abuse dating back decades. This is a mess. And it's what links all of them. They're linked. They have to be."

"Find out."

"I'm on it."

24

"Ah, but you lot are a sight for sore eyes," Robin breathed in deeply, savoring the slow burn of the air in his lungs for the first time in what felt like forever. He had missed this place, but even as the thought crossed his mind he realized it was *different* now. Wrong. Crouching, he dug his fingers into the soil, lifting up a handful of dirt to his lips. He tasted it, shaking his head in sad disbelief, and then smeared it across his face—left cheek, right cheek—breathing in what little remained of the life of the land. He should have been able to feel the echoes of the great Song of Albion in it, but there was nothing. It was just dirt. Robin scooped up another handful of soil. It should have been alive with the rich potency of earth magic. That was how he remembered these woods, as being so very, very *alive*. Not like that other place. He couldn't help but glance back toward the gate, the curls of mist still rolling out through it, and shivering.

From the other side he heard the elegiac sounds of battle, steel clashing, the cries of the damned, their moans haunting the mist.

It was enough to drive a man mad.

He smiled at that.

There were worse things than madness: most of them made their home in the mist.

Robin turned his back on the gate.

A lone hawthorn stood to the side of the ring of stones. Somehow it had survived the hatchets, axes, and saws of humanity, and stood still, proud and strong. He knew it. It was one of the first trees of the wildwood. Now huge mushroomlike growths made a ladder out of its trunk. Like so much else in this place, the old tree was sick, but it was still here, clinging stubbornly to life.

Oh, how he loathed these children of stone—and that was precisely what they were, greedy little children, all take, take, take.

Consume. Devour. They had so much, more than any of his kind ever had, and as harrowing as it was to contemplate, humanity had been blessed with the ultimate gift, and were capable of feeding magic *into* the land. But for every precious spark of beautiful energy Mother encountered, there were a thousand dark and hungry souls gathered around it looking to feed off the raw magic until there was nothing left.

It had always been that way, ever since the first of them drew breath into their lungs and let it out as a scream. The sense of entitlement was staggering—even as they watched the fields sour and the earth turn into dead dirt, it meant *nothing*. They fed on Mother all the more voraciously. Their appetites were insatiable. They should have listened to Arawn when he shared his visions of the future these children offered. They were a blight on the land, and now Mother was suffering.

This time Robin Goodfellow held onto the breath until it burned inside him.

"I don't mind admitting it's good to be back, even if the old wood is barely recognizable," Jenny Greenteeth said, flashing a mossy grin at the gathered wild things.

"Feels like my bollocks have been slammed between a couple of rocks," one of the brothers said, scratching at his cock with filthy fingers. "Which isn't as pleasant as it sounds."

He sniffed them.

That earned a chuckle from the others crowded around the fairy ring's spiral of mossy stones. Corenius and Gogmagot, the chalk giants; Jenny Greenteeth, and more of the children of the wildwood, woken—the dryad, the nixie with their hungry faces—and of course the Gatekeeper who had offered the blood sacrifice to the broken stones that opened the way for their return. Even the Knucker was there, lurking at the rear of the leafy enclave. All gathered to answer the call; all pledged to rise up in this time of need, to fight for their father.

He just had to pray that it wasn't too little too late for the land.

In the shadows, the object of his devotion, his everything: the

Lord of the Hunt, the antlered man, King Stag. The Horned God. Arawn looked on silently.

"You know, I've honestly missed your way with words, Corenius," Robin said.

"Of course you have, Rob. I make life interesting."

"Well your tongue certainly does," he said, offering a leering grin as he skittered out of range before the chalk giant could slap his backside. Robin clambered lithely up the rotten trunk of the dying hawthorn to a vantage point in the silvered branches overhead. *This is the life,* he thought. *Right here, this place, these people. This is where I was always meant to be. Who I was always meant to be.* The thoughts, as comforting as they were, didn't belong to him. They were the last lingering echoes of the body he had possessed. There wasn't much of Danny Ash left inside this meat suit, only the occasional flashes of unconnected memory and the pains associated with them; themselves no more substantial than ghosts, but those memories offered glimpses of a world he couldn't hope to understand. Robin allowed the boy these few last lingering moments before silencing him forever, and in doing so felt a surge of gratitude and then he was gone.

From here Robin could look down upon all of his friends with their unfamiliar faces. Faces didn't matter. They came; they went. With owners as old as them, only the souls remained the same. A man could do a lot of things, but he could not change his soul. He smiled at the thought of the chalk brothers having anything as pure as a soul. They were of the earth. They were dirt. They were worms and grubs and broken flints. They were loyal, unbending. And strong. Most of all they were strong.

"Can't say I've missed this shithole, mind," Corenius muttered, making sure everyone heard him. Robin saw his hand hovering over his chest and remembered the wound that had killed the chalk giant the last time they walked this wildwood. It was worse for his brother, that damned sword had taken his head from his shoulders. Truth told, it wasn't a happy memory for any of them. *But then death seldom is when you're on the receiving end of it,* he thought and had to stifle another chuckle. "All of those damned Blight Priests trying to bend what little of Mother's magic was left to their will. The sheer bloody temerity of it. Shit stains on the landscape, all of them. Thinking they're so fucking *special,* and crapping over everything wonderful in their lust to break it."

"Rather those priests than their bloody soldiers with their swords," his brother put in helpfully. "Those were the real bastards. Nothing worse than iron. It all started to go wrong when they found iron."

"Yeah, that's one discovery I could have happily lived without," the chalk giant's lips twisted into something approximating a grin at that, but Robin saw the way his fingers lingered over his third and fourth rib, touching the way to his heart. It wasn't a smile; it was remembered pain.

"I don't remember you being this funny last time," Robin observed, shifting the conversation.

"I've had years with an audience of one to amuse," he said. There was an undertone to his flippancy, an echo of the prison they'd escaped, which offered a glimpse of the real pain their deaths had led to. That self-deprecating line came with memories of the mist, of wandering endlessly through the Annwyn, crying out, lost, alone, save for the occasional echoes out there in the shadows. And always, the sounds of battle and dying all around them, close. Robin had no idea how long he had been alone in there; time lost all meaning in that place. But in all of his searching he never found any of the four dark towers: Murias in the north, Findias to the south, Gorias in the east, Falias in the west. The names stopped making sense. They became myths among the dead. A promise of home for the ghosts of Albion.

The place was Hell. Nothing more. Nothing less.

He was in no hurry to go back there.

Robin Goodfellow hunkered down, deftly balanced with his toes curled around the thick branch and one hand resting on the trunk, and said, "This place is dying. I can smell the rot. It's *all* I can smell."

They thought about it, breathing the corruption in and struggling to remember what it had been like before. It was hard to remember that far back, to make adjustments for the flesh, but it was undeniable that things *had* changed, and not for the better.

"Aye, it is," the chalk giant Gogmagot agreed, somberly.

Robin saw the crusted blood where his rebirth had been hard. The streaks had dried in like slashes of war paint across his cheeks and down his neck. On a different face they might have looked like tears of blood.

"The river's tainted, too," Jenny Greenteeth said. "There's so much shit in it the fish are dead."

"There's more to it than that, this place is *sour*."

That was a phrase he'd almost managed to forget, but along with it came the images of the Blight Priests chanting, their elegiac voices spiraling into the moonlit sky as they drew the last dregs of richness from the soil to nourish the crops for one last season, leaving soured fields in their wake.

"We did this," the voice came from the trees.

There was no arguing with it.

The forest should have been the most natural place in the world. The only aromas here should have been filled with the loam of life and the mulch of nature's constant evolution. Instead, all Robin could smell was the sour death and rot of a land bled dry. It had nothing left to give.

"And it falls to us to make it right. This is *our* land."

"Mother needs us more than ever," Robin agreed, casting a look toward the tree line where the shadow of the Horned God watched. More than anything, he wanted to please their father.

"It makes me want to puke," Corenius offered thoughtfully. "Keep things simple, Robin, tell me who to kill to make this right." He cracked the bones in his neck and reached down for a huge branch he intended to use as a club. The chalk giant hefted it, slapping the wood against the meat of his huge hand.

That brought a smile to the trickster's face. "Your simplemindedness is a beautiful thing, Brother. You are right, if we are going to linger here there is killing to be done. One for one," he said. The others nodded slowly, grasping the implications of the ancient promise.

There was a brief rustle of movement as Jenny scampered into the center of the stone circle, and crouched, running her fingers through the deadfall of autumn past. She scooped up a handful of leaves, her touch bringing back their color. It was a small magic. Her delicate fingers folded the leaves, and one by one she threaded them onto a vine, fashioning a makeshift crown from them. Robin watched her, fascinated by the simplicity of it. It reminded him of the May Queen. And that thought sent a shiver soul deep. That was one soul he prayed she would never see again.

"Pretty," Robin said.

"Practical," Jenny contradicted him.

"Oh, yes?"

"*Oooh,* yes."

"Am I going to have to drag it out of you?"

Jenny Greenteeth danced up to the feet of the giant Corenius and bade him lower his head. He looked anything but happy at the prospect, but Robin nodded. "Humor her."

Corenius bent to one knee and leaned forward as Jenny placed the crown of leaves on his head.

"Pretty," Robin said again.

"Shut your *pretty* mouth," the chalk giant said, but for all the bite in his tone his eyes twinkled with mirth. "Unless you want me to shut it for you?" He was a strange one, Corenius. All those years in the Annwyn had changed him, but of all of the wild things he had the purest heart. He would die before he let anyone hurt Mother.

"Consider it shut," Robin said, straightening the dirty folds creased into his torn shirt.

"Let the leaves be your guide" Jenny said. "They will keep you grounded, linked to the old wildwood as you move through the dead city. They are your tie to Mother. Follow their lead. Let her show you to your soul's twin, on the other side of the gate, and then do what you have to do. They will wither and die the closer they get to the source, until, finally, in the presence of the one who must die for you to remain, the leaves will crumble to dust."

"I will take no joy in the killing," he assured them.

"And neither should you," Jenny assured the big man. "But Mother needs you to be strong, my brother."

"The rest? Are we all meant to take our own, or does it fall to me and ugly here to do the dirty work for the rest of you?" Gogmagot said.

"I'll shoulder the burden," Corenius promised the others. "No need for you to stain your souls."

"But where's the fun in that?" asked Robin.

Across the ring of stones Gogmagot coughed. He raised an eyebrow as they turned his way. "Not being funny, but if he's got one, I want one." He tapped his temple. "It's only fair." That earned a joyous peel of laughter from Jenny Greenteeth. "I'm serious."

"Of course you are," Robin agreed.

Jenny gathered up another handful of dead leaves and breathed life into them. The wild things watched as one by one she threaded the verdant green leaves onto a few twigs and proceeded to entangle them, making a second crown. She offered it up to Gogmagot. The big man lowered his head, taking the knee somberly. "Yours is different, sweet Gogmagot," she told him.

"In what way?" the giant asked suspiciously.

"It will lead you to the five, but the leaves will not desiccate. Not until they are in the presence of the May Queen herself."

"That bitch is here?"

"She's here," the voice belonged to Arawn.

"I'm not sure I want this thing anymore," the chalk giant said, reaching up for the crown. He couldn't take it off. Thorns had burrowed into his scalp, and the more he pulled at it the more stubbornly they clung on, digging deeper and deeper until blood ran through his fingers. He gave up. "Seriously? Her? Isn't there another way?"

Robin shook his head. He'd known it from the moment he woke. "She must be sacrificed."

"You say that like she's some delicate fucking flower."

"Careful what you say about our lord and master's immortal beloved, Brother," Corenius said, grinning. "He's not exactly the forgiving kind."

Gogmagot sniffed and sighed. "One question," he turned back Jenny. "The crown crumbles to nothing when we find the Sleepers that make up the soul bridge, but what if we don't kill them?"

"Then the dimgate remains open."

"I get that, but what does it mean in practical terms?"

The Horned God emerged finally from the shadows of the trees. He planted the base of his staff into the loam, causing worms to squirm up from the dirt. "It means that they can banish us, and this time there will be no escape from that barren place," Arawn said, his voice the rustle of the leaves as the wind stirred the wildwood.

"Well then, when you put it like that," Corenius said. "Come on, Brother, we better get on with the killing, because I've got no intention of going back *there*." He cast a glance back toward the gateway and the roiling mist still spilling out through it. "I'd rather chop my nut sack off."

"And her? What about the May Queen?"

"You heard your brother," Arawn said, no hint of love on his face, despite the fact his words were condemning the woman who had owned his heart every year for the last two thousand summers and more. "She is the sacrifice. Without her, it is all for nothing. She must die for us to live."

"That's what you get for being the kind-hearted one," Corenius told his brother. "They just tell *me* to go and kill five children."

"Aren't you the lucky one?"

25

"This isn't going to be easy," Ellie Taylor told the only two people in the world who knew just exactly how difficult it was going to be to look when that sheet was peeled back. "Do you need a minute?"

Father Dajani shook his head. He'd aged twenty years in the last twenty-four hours. He was a shell of a man. He gripped his wife's hand for strength. There was despair just below his skin. He knew the words were coming, and it didn't matter that they were two of the simplest words in the English language, once they were out of his mouth life as the Dajani family knew it could never be the same again.

"No. I'll never be ready, no matter how long we wait," he said, unable to look at her. "I need to do this. Before I can't."

Ellie nodded. "I understand," she said, but of course she couldn't possibly understand what the man was going through. The words were just words. Meaningless. "There's no good way to do this, but what's going to happen is: we'll go in, the nurse will pull back the sheet so you can see the face, and I'll ask you if you recognize the body. All you have to do is say yes or no, and then she'll cover him up again. He's been prepared for viewing, but even so he's going to look different. I'll be right beside you all the time."

Dajani said nothing.

Taking that as her cue, Ellie opened the door. It was such a small thing, the most mundane of all actions she could imagine, but life-changing just the same.

She followed him into the cold room.

Ellie crossed the linoleum floor to the side of the gurney, nodding to the nurse who already had one hand on the sheet ready for the reveal. It was the worst magic trick imaginable. She drew back the sheet as far as the shallow bay beneath the dead boy's Adam's apple. The blue skin didn't look real; it looked as though it had been shaped out of Play-Doh stretched out too thinly.

Time in the room divided; for her the few seconds of silence were no more than that, but for Father Dajani they were endless. He looked down at his son's face willing there to have been some sort of mistake, for it to be anyone other than Musa on the slab. He reached out to rest a trembling hand against his boy's cheek. That was when Ellie noticed the too-lush smell again, just like it had been back at the old man's house, and again up on the rooftop garden when Virid-ius had died.

"Help me."

The words lit up inside her mind, crystal clear. A male voice. Young. Not Father Dajani's. Not the nurse's.

"Please. I . . . I don't know where I am . . ."

Ellie backed away from the gurney, her eyes darting all around the room, looking for the source of the voice, for the trick, and cursing the old man and his insincere apology. He hadn't been lying when he said he'd ruined her life. She didn't know how, or why, but she knew exactly *what* Viridius had done to her.

"I can hear voices . . ."

So can I, she thought hysterically.

"I can hear the crying . . .

"They're lost."

"It's him," Dajani said, utterly broken.

Ellie put her hand on his shoulder, ignoring the voice that refused to get out of her head.

"Cover him up," she told the nurse.

"Not yet. Can I have a minute with him?" He still hadn't taken his hand from his son's cheek.

"Of course. Take all the time you need."

Even as she reached for the door the dead boy's frightened tears filled her mind. She wanted to scream, "*Leave me alone!*" his baleful moans haunted her. The dead boy refused to be silenced. He sounded absolutely terrified as he cried: "They're out there . . . in the mist . . . all around me . . . I can hear them moving about . . . but I can't see them. I don't want to be here. I want to go home . . . Help me go home . . . Please . . ."

Ellie closed her eyes, willing Musa Dajani gone. "Please," she said, and the nurse mistook her meaning, nodding in response and following her toward the door.

"It's cold here . . . So cold . . ."

She looked back at the body on the slab as she opened the door, and shook her head, refusing to listen.

"Help me . . ."

They left Dajani alone in the room with his boy, closing the door on them. With the door closed, the voice inside her head was silenced. She saw Julie looking at her, and realized that Mother Dajani was waiting for the world to come tumbling down. "I'm so, so sorry," Ellie said, and for a moment the woman didn't seem to register what she'd heard, but then she collapsed in on herself, falling forward. Julie didn't let her fall. Mother Dajani curled up into his embrace, her face pressed into his shirt. Even muffled, the woman's wails were wretched. She kept choking on the sobs she couldn't get out of her body; her chest heaving, the sounds emerging from her mouth ragged, raw, desperate, and broken.

Father Dajani didn't leave the room for another quarter of an hour.

Fifteen minutes wasn't enough for the bereaved woman to compose herself. She looked up at him when he finally emerged, her face blotchy and raw with grief, willing him to tell her there had been some terrible mistake, that it wasn't her son in there on that slab.

He couldn't look at her.

He just held out his hand and said, "I need to get out of here."

"Of course. We'll take you home."

Dajani shook his head. "No need," the man said. "We brought the car. I want to be on my own."

"I can appreciate that, but you're in no condition to drive, either of you. Let us take you home."

The fight went out of him. He shrugged and allowed Julie to lead him and his wife back toward the elevators. Ellie was slow to follow. Instead, she went back into the mortuary to look at the boy on the slab, pulling back the thin cotton sheet so she could look at him.

She glanced back over her shoulder to be sure the door was closed. The last thing she wanted to do was upset the dead boy's parents. "I'm here. I'm listening."

She touched his cheek, just as his father had, and in that moment felt a surge of electricity so strong the shock was enough to make her flinch back, recoiling from the contact. The room filled with the fragrance of freshly cut grass damp with morning dew. The contact lasted no longer than the cavernous silence between heartbeats, but the aroma lingered, as did the screams of the damned that had swarmed into her head in that moment. Ellie Taylor looked down at her hand, not trusting herself to touch the dead boy again; not after that.

"Can you hear me?" she asked, feeling stupid, but not knowing what else to do.

He didn't talk to her this time.

"How am I supposed to help you? Jesus Christ, listen to me . . . I'm talking to a dead kid."

She shook her head, and left the dead boy on the slab, determined that she would help him the only way she knew how: she would find his killer.

26

The Horned God heard the agitation in the voices all around him; they knew he was listening. They cried out to him, begging to be heard, pleading for him to take up their fight, to save them; not realizing they were beyond saving. He didn't care. He craved their desperation.

She was here.

His queen.

It had been so long since they had stood side by side, since his sacrifice.

He searched for her, wandering through the battlefields of his memory until he found the May Queen, on her knees, hands clasped around the bleeding warrior's wrists as she refused to let him fall. She turned her eyes on Arawn, seeing him walk toward her through the curling mists. "I thought I recognized the smell," she said, the slight smile undercutting the harshness of her words. "Here to relive the glory of your youth?" He shook his head. "This is down to you, Arawn. All of it. Take a look around you. Breathe it in: the blood, the piss, the shit. The essence of life lost. It's on *you*."

He remembered this place, and with good reason.

This was where he gave himself to death, but it hadn't been like this.

The ground beneath his feet was slick with mud. Carrion birds had already begun to gather, and there were rats picking at the corpses of three men who wouldn't be going home tonight. His men. Arms lay across chests and flung out in the mud, legs twisted impossibly, eyes stared blindly.

This was all wrong.

She hadn't been some beneficent healer offering a moment of peace to the dying. She had been there, yes, but she had demanded her sacrifice. His sacrifice and like her damned birds she had settled on the corpses to feed on their final moments, drawing their dreams out in those last precious seconds, partaking in a feast of what-might-have-beens.

A sword had been driven into the earth, the hilt looking like a funeral cross. It was his weapon. Two black winged birds fought savagely over a loop of gray entrails from the guts of the body beneath it, each trying to steal the food from the other's mouth even with so much to go around. He watched them for a moment. The choreography of their dance was brutal. It took no more than a minute for one to emerge victorious, the other left to bleed. Even among the dead there was more killing to be done, he realized.

"Savage little bastards, aren't they?" she said, following the direction of his gaze.

"Like us," he agreed.

She smiled at that, seemingly enjoying the inference.

He wasn't wrong, of course. It was just their nature. But, whatever she said, how could this be his doing?

He looked around him. He knew this place. It was burned into his mind. This was where he had taken the knee, and bowed his head, accepting his beloved's knife to the jugular. The dead were his. His own corpse was in their number somewhere; lost to the rot. In a hundred years the bones would be gone, in their place a field of wildflowers. In two hundred years there would be a settlement of sorts, the dying these fields had seen forgotten. In three hundred it would be a town, in four hundred years there would be a city, strange-sounding street names all that remained of the killing fields.

Bones grew out of the ground like unholy vegetation; fingers stripped clean of meat by the carrion crows, eyes hollowed out, skin bloated and feeding fungal growths. There was nothing holy or sacrosanct about this death.

"You don't belong here," she said. "Not this version of you, my love."

It was hard to disagree.

He turned to face the May Queen, remembering in that moment how very much he had loved her. She looked at him, something akin to pity in her eyes. He looked from her to the warrior kneeling glassy-eyed in front of her. He barely recognized himself. He certainly didn't remember this moment, but he could feel her fingers on his own wrists, even though there was still some distance between them, both literal and metaphysical. Her grip was tight, stemming the flow of blood that would leave Arawn as another corpse for the birds to feed on soon enough.

"This is your curse, my sweet," she told the supplicant warrior. "You died here once, giving yourself and the magic of your blood to the land to buy her time, and you will die again for her soon enough, but now you understand that death is not the end for you. Your entire being is bound forever to our beloved land, and when her need is greatest you will find a way back to her. I name you Mother's protector, my love. You and your wildlings will wander the mists of the Otherworld, denied eternal rest. Yours will be an eternity of consciousness, trapped in a hell of your own making, where time lacks meaning, and the only thing that can liberate you will be Mother's pain."

"Why?" he asked her.

"Who else would sacrifice so much for her? It has to be you. It was always you. Nations will rise, civilizations fall, but you will remain locked out of time, waiting for the moment when she at last cries out for you to rise up, when the last of her magic is spent, when there is nothing left, and you will answer her, giving your blood for her once more to drive away the evil that tears apart her heartland. That is my promise to you," she cursed him, and he welcomed it. How could he not? He had willingly bent the knee and bowed his head when she promised him his blood sacrifice would be the difference between life and death for Mother. The May Queen had woven a spell around his soul, denying him the end that must come to all things, and in return he had given every ounce of the magic that flowed through his veins, as king of this place, last of his line, and done so willingly.

She was wrong in blaming him. He had done everything she had asked of him. If she had failed and their world had gone to hell, it was *her* fault, not his. Everything that followed his death was on her: the blood, the tears of a land torn apart, all of it. He was merely a pawn in a greater game.

Behind her, tendrils of mist writhed, snaking toward where she knelt. He hadn't noticed it before. His first thought was that the mists had come for him, that he would never be free of them, but he didn't trust his mind anymore.

Arawn moved to take another step when he saw dark shadows slowly coalesce within the fog. It took no more than a few heartbeats for them to gather substance and form, resolving into the silhouettes of four men.

No, there were women among them.

They were hardly warriors. They were battered, broken. He didn't recognize any of them.

This wasn't right.

This wasn't what had happened.

They hadn't been in this place.

But as he watched the leader emerge from the bank of fog, his face gone, Arawn knew it didn't matter. The faceless man was here now, proving that death held no dominion over his kind. There was gristle and bleached bone where there should have been a grimace, there was a deep wound where his nose should have been. In his hand he held a great blade. The sword was right; it was Manannan's cursed weapon, engraved with a spell that bound it to the heart of Albion. But this wasn't Manannan. He had no shield. Behind him two more figures took shape: one lacking a jaw, the other with his guts sliced open. Blue flame flickered across the fingertips of the older man, marking him as a druid. The last figure, a woman, remained in the mist, her ethereal form solid enough for the twin bolts she fired to burn as they struck, one burying itself high in his right shoulder, turning him violently as the other struck level with the first. His entire body convulsed as the metal pierced Arawn's cloak of leaves to bite into the soft meat of his chest.

He staggered beneath the onslaught, clenching his teeth against the pain and wrongness of it.

A distant voice trapped in his mind screamed. *This wasn't what had happened here.* These four with their bolts and blades hadn't finished him. But that didn't stop the sword slamming up into his gut, doubling him up even as his would-be killer opened him up.

Blood gurgled around the sword's hilt as he closed a trembling fist around its blade. He pulled it slowly out and cast it aside, turning to face the others even as the mist threatened to overwhelm his vision, turning the world to black.

"Why are you doing this?" he said, or tried to. The words lacked any clarity. They had no shape to them. He was dying. Again. Differently.

"Because, dear heart, you don't belong here; not now. Mother needs you," the May Queen told him, her voice carrying back to him all the way across the mists of time to where he stood back in Coldfall Wood.

The leader stepped forward, and with three vicious hacks took his head not so cleanly from his shoulders.

He saw it all, detached, seemingly from the view of the towering oak, no longer one with his body. He saw the whole thing like some horrible play being acted out for his own punishment.

May Queen turned her gaze upward, as though she saw him up there: his soul still shining brightly, unable to let go.

"We will see each other again, my love," she promised.

27

Cadmus Damiola was dying.

He had known it for a long time.

Maybe it was punishment for what he'd done to Eleanor, or more likely something utterly prosaic like cancer. It didn't matter much to him either way. He could *feel* the disease inside him. It had begun as a pain in his shoulder, such an innocuous thing, and had progressed to become a throat that felt like it was lined with razor blades, which made it impossible to swallow. It was just a matter of time, but if one man in London understood just how unimportant time actually was, it was Damiola.

The wooden slats of the old park bench dug into the base of his spine like some flagellant's punishment. He wasn't twisted; there was no comfort in pain. He didn't *enjoy* it. The bottle didn't help much, either. He took another swallow and wiped his lips with the back of a grubby hand. No amount of cheap whiskey was going to shift the burden of guilt he felt for what was happening to them. He should have known better. He looked through the cemetery's iron gateway. Not many people got to see their own grave. It was a humbling experience. The old stones would be around long after he was gone. They'd already stood against the elements for the best part of ninety years. The sharp edges were weathered smooth and pitted where the frosts had worn away at them, but they would easily stand for another ninety or more, even if they were abandoned to nature.

He had known something would come through; that was why he had taken up his lonely vigil. He had just assumed it would emerge here, through the weakness he had made in the veil, not somewhere else. He was nothing more than a foolish old man with a little knowledge—and as the saying went, that was a dangerous thing.

Damiola had spent the longest part of the night, through three o'clock—he'd once heard about how more people died at that hour than any other, which with the moon silver on the rooftops around him, was a disconcerting thought—wondering how it had come this far, how things could have got so out of control. It was more than just cause and effect, or the notion of balance. Seth, Eleanor, Josh, him, they were the instruments of something so much bigger than that.

He saw a crow watching him from the iron gateway. The bird's head inclined slightly as it ruffled its feathers and adjusted its perch. Those beady black eyes darted left and right, never settling for more than half a second on any one place in the old street. The crow gave the old man the creeps.

Damiola needed somewhere peaceful where he wouldn't be disturbed. What better place could there be than his own final resting place? He pushed himself unsteadily to his feet and shuffled toward the gate, causing the bird to fly. It moved off into the cemetery, settling on one of the stones.

If he was right, the Horned God—or whatever the thing that had come through from the Annwyn really was—was gathering the creatures of the Wild Hunt to his side. What would happen to the city when they were all gathered? He shivered, looking at his mausoleum and knowing that no goose had walked across his grave. If he understood the mythology correctly—and it was always hard to separate truth from legend—the wildlings were more akin to forces of nature than living breathing heroes, but that was how the collective myth functioned. It created realities we could understand from our limited point of view, shaping the stories handed down from generation to generation into something fantastic where giants climbed up beanstalks and wolves dressed in granny's shawl. To Damiola's mind they represented the sheer destructive force of the world at its most catastrophic. They were a cataclysmic force waiting to be unleashed.

How did you stand against that?

You don't, he thought bitterly. *You hide and wait for the world to end.*

But he couldn't do that anymore than he could run.

Damiola had dared to hope they might have been lucky. It was naïve of him. Nature always sought out balance. Julie's visit, trying to guilt him into helping, had done nothing more than put the lives of those five children on him. There was no escaping the fact that they weighed heavily. They were as good as lost if he didn't at least try to save them, but short of going toe-to-toe with Arawn's wildlings he didn't know what he could do.

Stop lying to yourself, old man. You know exactly what you've got to do, and you know exactly what will happen when you try and do it, which is why you're putting it off.

He walked among the gravestones, trailing his fingertips across the rough surfaces of a few of the closest, not thinking about what they represented.

He reached his own mausoleum.

The crow moved four times during his sad parade through the dead, keeping him in sight every step of the way. He saw a battered sign declaring no loitering, no ball games, and couldn't imagine what sort of kid would willingly hang around a place like this. The crow cawed and rose up above him like some kind of omen. He did his best to ignore it.

The ironwork around his final resting place had seen better days; it was choked with weeds and climbers, colorful blossoms just beginning to flower on the vines offering a brilliant counterpoint to the rust. He pushed the gate aside and entered. Instead of taking the few short steps down to the doorway, he lay on his back in the grass and looked up at the sky. The world was never less than strange from this perspective. The clouds gathered, foreshortening his view of eternity.

Damiola pushed all of the thoughts of Arawn and the wildlings from his mind, banishing the face of Seth Lockwood and the memory of his rage as they cornered him.

He needed to be in the moment.

Clear.

Calm.

The crow watched him intently.

It was impossible to pretend it wasn't there, so instead he used it, concentrating on the minutia of its feathers, the tiny imperfections as its wings beat a steady rhythm against the air, rising and falling, drifting, rising and falling, as it circled overhead. The bird's oily black feathers glistened slickly in the moon. Damiola concentrated on his breathing, with each inhalation imagining he drew the universe and time into his body, and with each breath that slipped out between his lips he let his soul out to merge with the source of all things, sending it back whence it came. He'd learned the trick from a fakir almost a century ago. He tried to remember the man's name . . . it sounded like a foreign land or maybe a mountain. *Alkeran*. That was it. It was the only thing about the fakir that he did remember. There were no details to the man's face when he tried to bring it to mind, but that was memory for you. He hung the clothes of recollection on sensory triggers, smells, funny little ticks or gestures, and more often than not forgot to fill out the skeleton with simple things like names or faces. What he did remember was the story of how the fakir claimed to have come by the sacred knowledge whilst on pilgrimage to some remote corner of Tibet's perilous mountains. A guide had taken him north—a month's walk through thin air and ice—into shadows of the highest peaks to pay homage to a holy man who they claimed had taken up residence beyond the snow line. The man, they said, had lived a thousand years and more, and possessed wisdom from the oldest of the mystical texts. They called him the Eternal. Alkeran spun a good yarn, and his fractured English hid the fact that he had been born into a life of relative privilege in the Raj, not forced to work the tea plantations until his fingers bled, and the more obvious lie that no man could live for a thousand years. But no one was interested in the reality of it; they only wanted the showmanship. That was the secret to selling the illusion. Alkeran was on the same touring circuit as Damiola, more often than not a day or two ahead of him at smaller venues, no more than a week ahead at the major theaters, lifting the red curtain to offer the good, ordinary people of England a glimpse at the mysteries of the subcontinent where men could live an eternity.

Damiola had been sure he was a faker as well as a fakir.

He'd been wrong, of course.

The man had a gift, and the Eternal, far from being some exotic Tibetan wise man, was every bit as British as the land itself. Rather than live at the top of some unconquerable mountain, the old man made his home in the ancient wildwood on the outskirts of London. His name was Viridius. It was funny how things moved in circles. He was back at that name again. Viridius, the god of spring.

His own act might have been little more than smoke and mirrors in the early days, but Alkeran offered him his first glimpse of what could only be called true magic, the greatest of which allowed him the grace to leave his body and soul walk a short way.

Alkeran had needed to ingest some sort of root to divide body and soul. When chewed, the root possessed hallucinogenic qualities, but when left to dissolve slowly on the tongue it seeped into the bloodstream and allowed the fakir to leave his flesh behind, if only for a short while.

That was what Damiola needed to do now, but without the aid of the hallucinogenic root.

All he had was his faith and desperation.

He needed to believe that the gods of every season were listening now, and cared.

He saw the face of the divine slowly begin to take shape in the pattern of feathers, ignoring the fact that he couldn't possibly see anything in that kind of detail from where he was, and concentrated on it and only it, until he felt himself drifting and realized he was no longer looking up at the crow but down at his own body unmoving on the grass below, seeing the world through the eyes of the black bird.

A silver umbilicus glittered a trail down to his body.

His eyes were open, staring blindly into the great cosmos, whilst Damiola stared back the other way.

It was a dizzying dislocation.

There was no one moment when his spirit began to soar. No silence between heartbeats when his spirit slowly separated from his flesh, no ghostly transition where he rose up, up, and away to fuse with the consciousness of the bird. Damiola felt himself drift farther away from his body, the cemetery falling away vertiginously beneath him until his body was a speck, a smudge of black on the ground, and the canyons of the city streets began to take on shape and form around him. The rooftops did little to hide the poverty to the left of him against the glittering glass wealth of the offices to the right. One hundred feet, two hundred, four, five hundred, up and up, spiraling ever higher. He banked to the left, gliding on a warm current of air.

Damiola's breathing turned ragged, coming in short, sharp gasps despite the fact that the last thing he needed to do was breathe; it was all an illusion, a memory of the spirit. He was free of the burden of the flesh.

He looked out across the rooftops of the city, following the zigzag of tiles and flashing as they moved street by street down toward the water. He didn't know exactly what he was looking for, only that there had to be some hint, something that marked the gateway that had allowed the wildlings into this world. He needed to find it, and he needed to close it before more of them could come through. He envisioned the Wild Hunt coming: first the champions, then behind them the dancing dead, the chorus of myth and legend, the ethereal figures riding out of the mist and onto the streets of London intent on razing the place to the ground. That way lay madness.

He willed himself toward the river, imagining the slow beating of wings to carry him south. The streets rolled by beneath him as the glittering umbilicus stretched out ever thinner.

He could *feel* it, he realized.

The other side. The Annwyn.

It was like a black hole trying to draw him in.

Its pull on his spirit was relentless. Instinctively, he pushed back against it, and had to stop himself fleeing as fear threatened to overwhelm him. It was the bird's influence on his personality. He had to fight it to fly on. He'd been naïve enough to expect to see some bright, burning wrongness blazing through the streets, a glowing silver arch lighting up the sky to mark the gateway, something like that. But of course it was never going to be so obvious, why would it be?

He saw the trees of Coldfall Wood and the rise of Cane Hill in the distance; the natural beauty of the world was laid bare by the deep wounds in the concrete that allowed them to shine through. And they were *glorious*.

Mother, the thought bled into his mind. He had no idea where it had originated, but it felt right.

Damiola willed himself to move, struggling with the dizzying sensation of the riverbank rushing along below. All of the people scurried around like ants beneath him, oblivious to his soul. He knew the city, or had known it, but things had changed beyond all recognition since his grand illusion had opened Glass Town.

He changed his angle of flight, banking and soaring.

He imagined he could feel the wind on his face, but of course he couldn't.

The silver line shimmered all the way back to the graveyard, stretched thin. Fissures had already begun to appear in the umbilicus. The black lines shot through the silver rope of his soul. The farther he ventured from his flesh, the more tenuous the link would become. Venture too far from the body and the likelihood of returning to a corpse was virtually assured; the autonomic memories controlling the breathing and heartbeat wouldn't go on functioning indefinitely. They would slowly begin to fail without the proximity of the soul to keep the organs vital and then he would be cast adrift. Those black lines were the first hints of necrosis stealing in.

Damiola had never pushed it more than a couple of minutes before, but he had to ignore the cracks slowly opening in the tether and focus on the cityscape beneath him, understanding as he did that he didn't need to see the gateway to find it, all he had to do was surrender to its tidal pull—and with that realization the streets sped away beneath him, all those lives racing by as old industrial red-brick chimneys reared up before the magician only to disappear in his wake as he was drawn over the water and on toward Coldfall Wood.

Where are you?

The Rothery looked like Hell from above; everything broken, everything in the grips of decay, weeds growing in vibrant green through the cracks in the pavement, shopping trolleys abandoned in the stream to rust and along with the detritus of everyday, carrier bags, the frame of a bike, the wheel rims stripped of rubber so the spokes jutted out, snagging wrappers from candy bars and a fluttering of black fabric that might have been panties or a bra once upon a time, before all of that innocence was lost.

He looked away from the stream, toward the trees, and realized how majestic the old wood must have been before the city came. Even in the years he'd fast-forwarded through, the forest had shrunk in half and half again with the houses encroaching on its heart.

Damiola saw the light through the dense undergrowth of the ancient wood; at first it appeared to be a scattering of coins on the ground, the silver glow filtered through the leaves, but as his spirit neared, Damiola saw the first curls of mist and knew what he was seeing. The silver glow emanated from the dimgate.

Something stirred down in the foliage.

He needed a different angle to better see into the clearing, so banked and rolled, angling his flight to skim along the canopy of leaves. They rustled in his wake, more agitated than they had any right to be from his passage. The movement rippled outward from the circle of the fairy stones, and the wooden warrior that in turn circled the stones.

It was a magnificent creature, unlike anything he had ever imagined even in his darkest nightmares—and it was absolutely a creature of those dark places, capable of instilling fear bone deep in all who set eyes upon it's twisted grace. The wooden boughs of its rib cage bowed as the beast breathed, alive. The desiccated leaves still clinging to those boughs rustled, a thousand tiny voices filled with the fears of the great wood going back generations.

The Horned God stood beside his pet, looking up at Damiola. The Knucker crouched beside the antlered man, a boy kneeling at his feet. Arawn held a rowan staff in one hand, while the other rested on the boy's chest, over his heart. He felt the intensity of Arawn's loathing all the way back to his bones where they lay in the old cemetery.

It was the first time he had set eyes upon a god—and there was no doubting that whatever the antlered man was, he wasn't merely flesh and blood, he was something very much more than that—and it reduced him, stripping away the years of experience and knowledge to leave an infantilized caricature in the magician's place.

Damiola was afraid.

He wasn't thinking about flapping his stolen wings anymore; all he could think about was bolting, getting as far away as fast as humanly possible, as Arawn's voice sounded in his mind:

I see you . . .

The words chilled the blood in his borrowed body. He couldn't fight against them. The air around Damiola chilled as it filled with a weird static charge that thrilled at the promise of the Horned God's magic. He recognized it as the precursor of real magic; his own spells had a unique signature scent that made it easy for other practitioners to recognize the caster. In his case it was cinnamon. A sweet smell. He'd met others who smelled of freshly baked bread, of vanilla, of grass, and darker fragrances, oil and petrol and smoke. But Arawn's magic was an ancient one, its signature the heady scent of the forest itself.

It was overpowering.

Dizzying.

Damiola felt his grip on the bird's mind slipping.

In that moment—trapped in the heart of the Horned God's earth magic—he saw the ghostly white stag seem to leap through Arawn's flesh to meet his challenge head on. The stag charged through the clearing, negotiating the broken stones on the ground, and launched itself up to meet Damiola's crow.

The symbolism was as old as time itself, the white stag and the black crow, and fundamental to the battle for Albion.

He should have known better than to meddle in the matter of men and gods.

Damiola couldn't flee.

The white stag charged into the air, its ethereal hooves sparking with crackles of blue-tinged electricity as they struck the nothing beneath them, rising effortlessly. This was Arawn's second skin; the form he took at the head of the Wild Hunt. He was King Stag. The ghostly creature broke through the cover of the trees, charging head down to meet Damiola in the sky.

Ic béo wacende þé, the voice sounded in his mind, and with it came images of a distant battlefield where the Carrion King picked over the remains of the dead, moving from corpse to corpse, no respecter of sides, of right or wrong, as he feasted upon the soft sweet meats of the dead. *I know you. I see you.* Or, more sinister in its overtones, *I am watching you.*

Damiola shook his head, trying to banish the image, to tell the Horned God he was mistaken, that he had never seen that killing field in this life or any other, but he recognized the contours of the land for what they were: the ground beneath them. He was seeing—*Being shown? Remembering?*—killings that had happened in this very place, and beyond it. It was a glimpse of the real tragedy of this place. This was where King Stag, the Horned God, Arawn—all of the names he owned meant little across time—had been cursed. This was his doom. Where he and his kind had been Albion's doom, tearing the green grass apart in war. The Horned God was doomed to be her savior now. It all crystallized in Damiola's mind. He understood the great tragedy for what it was. King Stag was the source of all of the myths around the once and future king.

The ghostly stag and the stolen crow clashed in a battle of antlers and feathers.

There could only ever be one winner in the mismatched fight.

Damiola felt the feathers of his borrowed body mat together, slick with blood as the stag came at him again. A blazing white light burned off the god, the crow's flesh blistering beneath its onslaught.

Damiola couldn't fight a god.

No one could.

Cadmus Damiola was dying.

28

Charlie Mann didn't meet their eyes.

He was shit scared.

He was sure they could smell the urine that had trickled down his inner thigh. The denim clung stickily to his skin. His heart hammered. He blinked. He clenched his fist. He concentrated on the pain his nails caused, digging into his palm. Fear was going to betray him. There was no way he was walking away from the wood.

He kept his head down.

The dirt had never been so fascinating. He stared at the browned, curled leaves from last year's fall that had turned to mulch in the mud. A few more good rainstorms and they'd be gone, to dirt returned.

He wasn't like the others.

Somehow he was still *himself.*

He didn't know how it had happened—what had protected him, not ignorance despite the fact that he hadn't grasped what was happening until it was too late; he'd thought it was all some sort of game Penny was playing for his birthday and been happy to go along with it, running behind her, laughing and whooping as he barreled into the ancient forest. And then everything had changed.

By the time he'd realized it wasn't a game it was too late; Penny was dead. And then she wasn't.

Charlie was fucked.

Utterly. Completely. Totally. Fucked.

He wanted to go home. To hide in his room. Pull the blankets up over his head.

But he couldn't.

He couldn't move a muscle. Not while there was a war being fought inside his body. It wasn't pretty. Despair was winning hands down; hope didn't stand a chance.

Charlie couldn't begin to understand what had happened to his friend. It didn't make sense. None of it did. The only thing he was remotely sure of was that it had all gone to shit after she'd touched the lightning-struck tree outside the old pub. But how it had gone from that to Penny stumbling into the stream and the guy in the weird antlers pushing her down beneath the surface until she stopped fighting him?

Charlie ground his teeth, chewing on his lower lip until he tasted blood. He couldn't get the memory of how her hair had fanned out around her lifeless body from his mind. The way the bubbles died along with Penny Grainger would haunt him for the rest of his life—however long or short that ended up being.

Charlie had felt the pull of something then, impelling his feet forward one agonizing step after another as the sweeping echoes of the great song threatened to overwhelm him, and in that moment he almost lost himself, finally. He *wanted* to. He just wanted it to be over. But when he looked at Penny now, there was no second truth, the filth of the stream clung to her body, and try as he desperately might he couldn't convince himself that she still had somehow miraculously returned.

Whatever that thing inside her skin was, it wasn't *her*.

Some basic survival instinct stopped him from running. Instead, he faked it, walking side by side with her as she followed the antlered man in his robe of rotten leaves to the stone circle back in the clearing they called the fairy ring. Danny Ash was there: his knees covered in dirt, his shirt torn; but he was smiling, happy. His face betrayed no flicker of recognition when he saw Charlie. Danny was one of them. Whatever *they* were. Tommy Summers was there, too. He looked like death. And there were others who'd lived with them at the group home, too. Stephen Blackmoore and Rupert Brooke.

They started calling each other weird names, and talking like they'd known each other forever about stuff that made zero sense. Rather than risk betraying his difference, Charlie kept his head down. He tried not to listen to what they were saying, but it was hard to ignore talk of murdering kids. He watched Penny make crowns of flowers. She seemed so innocent and childish next to the others as she put the flowers on their bowed heads and promised they'd lead them to the children that needed to die.

Those two ran off, tasked with the actual killing. Blackmoore and Brooke.

Charlie watched them go.

For a moment, he dared to believe he might actually get away with hiding in plain sight.

The antlered man prowled around the clearing, sniffing the air, turning and turning again.

Behind the man, the dimgate shimmered, a trail of mist snaking out around the stones at its foot.

Charlie saw shadows moving about in there. What those insubstantial wraiths were didn't bear thinking about.

A frigid breeze blew through the gateway.

The Horned God stopped moving, tossing his head back and throwing his arms wide. In that moment Charlie Mann knew that he was screwed. He knew he should run, but he couldn't move. Lank black hair fell across the man's face as he brought his head forward. Vegetation was matted in the wet locks. As his hair fell away from the root where the horns embedded into the plates of his skull Charlie realized the man wasn't wearing some weird crown of bone; the horns protruded from his skull.

Charlie's feet shuffled in the dirt, barely a scuff but enough to draw the full intensity of the antlered man's hateful gaze.

Charlie was face-to-face with the devil himself, and the devil knew he was a cuckoo in this particular nest.

The antlered man leveled the bulbous head of his staff at him and spoke, and as with everything else that had come from his mouth, Charlie hadn't got a clue what was being said. There was no natural instinctive understanding for him, no connection buried deep in the primeval part of his hindbrain. He wasn't one of *them*. He didn't belong here. To his ear, the words were nothing more than deep guttural sounds, grunts barked out. But they didn't need to make sense for Charlie to grasp the menace within them.

The antlered man approached, reaching out a cadaverous hand for Charlie. The Knucker followed loyally at his side. The boy fell to his knees, unable to look away. Black fingernails rested on his chest, right above his heart. He stared down at the hand, feeling his gut rebel as the man began slowly to apply pressure and the nails dug in painfully, and kept on digging as though he intended to force them between blood and bone to close around the vital organ.

Charlie was sure in that moment that he was going to die—not at some distant point in time where immortality would eventually wear out, but right here, right now. Before he could, the antlers whipped around, the Horned God's gaze turning skyward as he barked out a challenge to some unseen threat.

Charlie followed the direction of the blackened fingernail and saw the dark smudge set against the bank of clouds: a solitary black bird.

The antlered man barked out more guttural commands, and delivered a punch to the air above his head. There was something wrong about his clenched fist; it appeared to stretch, not beholden to skin and bone, elongating like a streak of lightning that burned bright in the sky as the jagged end of the bolt mutated into antlers and the body of the stag became obvious as it rose to meet the crow head on.

The two clashed.

Charlie didn't stick around to watch the fight.

He ran.

He didn't look back. He raced across the clearing, head down, arms and legs pumping furiously to drive him on, and burst through the shield of trees, hurdling deadfall as he bounced from tree trunk to tree trunk, staggering as he pushed himself on. There was no beaten track to follow. He plunged on into the undergrowth, snapping branches that whipped back to slash at his face. The new buds stung where they struck.

Ancient trees roots protruded from the earth, each one reaching up to try and snag him as he ran. The sharp edges of broken stones made the ground treacherous. There was nowhere he could safely put a foot as he raced on. Charlie breathed hard, fear a cold fist around his lungs, squeezing them tight.

He could hear them crashing through the undergrowth behind him, taunting him. They called out in that guttural language he didn't understand. He wanted to scream. They wouldn't go away. He couldn't lose them. There was nowhere to hide. They dogged his passage every step of the way.

Charlie didn't slow down. He couldn't. To slow down was to surrender himself to the monsters he'd heard plot to kill a bunch of kids. He was under no illusion what they'd do to him.

He crashed through a tangle of brambles ignoring the pain as they tore at his arms as he wrestled them aside.

Wild roses tangled with creepers to form a wall.

He had no choice but to push on through it.

Charlie cried out as a thorn opened a deep cut on his cheek.

The sounds of pursuit seemed to come from all sides.

He scanned the trees, his eyes drawn to any and every movement.

To the left he saw a loosely built cairn of rocks. It wasn't high, but would offer some cover at least, so he changed direction, angling toward the pile of stones. He ran along the wall of tightly entwined vegetation. The light was barely strong enough to pierce it. It had a curious effect on sound: wrapping him in the crunch of his own feet, the rasp of his own heavy breathing, and the susurrus of displaced leaves as he ran. Beyond it lay a shallow declivity lined with a stone wall that supported one side of the gully. There was no obvious path alongside the crack in the ground. A trodden path ran down into it, a hollow way, the hard-packed earth worn smooth. Without thinking Charlie took the trodden path, following it down to an almost-dry streambed. He ran on, following the meandering curve, the beginnings of a stream trickled around, splashing on, always running, always forward because back was where they were—plotters, child killers, monsters.

The stones of the gully's man-made wall were furred with fungal growths.

The air reeked with the sour stink of spoiled water.

Charlie slipped on the slick surface of a wet stone, turning his ankle. He went over, landing hard on his hands and knees. Looking up he saw a shallow cavelike opening beneath the huge root system of a giant tree that grew out of the gully's wall, its roots all the way down into the brackish water. He pushed himself up to his feet only for his ankle to give away beneath him before he'd managed a couple of steps. He looked back. He immediately wished he hadn't. *Always forward.*

There was movement in the trees. Closing in.

He tested his ankle. He managed to hobble three tentative steps before a flare of pain had him reaching out for the wall for support. The fungus was wet beneath his hand. He heard something. A voice. A girl's voice; calling to him from the darkness of the tree. His mind was playing tricks on him. It had to be. But in that moment it sounded like Penny. It had to be a trick. Something they were doing to fuck with him.

But he listened to her.

Hide, she whispered. *Here,* she promised.

He stumbled toward the deep dark cave beneath the root system and not knowing what else to do, splashed forward on his hands and knees, and crawled inside. The ripening leaves of the trailing branches fell across the cave mouth, a living veil between hunter and hunted.

It was small, smaller than he'd imagined from outside, the roots forming a cocoon around him. The dirt was wet, but there was a ledge at the back of the wooden cave that promised dryness.

Charlie pulled himself up onto the ledge and curled up against the cold dirt wall of his hiding place, drawing his knees up to his chin and wrapping his arms around his legs. The opening in the earth wasn't deep. It barely offered enough shadow to hide in now he was inside it.

He stared through the veil of vegetation, looking for a glimpse of his Hunters moving around out there.

He could still hear them, and if he could hear them they could hear him.

Charlie gripped his knees tighter, pressing up against the hard-packed soil at his back.

Still your breathing, Penny whispered. *You're safe,* she promised.

He didn't believe her.

He didn't think he'd ever feel safe again.

His heart hammered against his rib cage. It felt like it was trying to beat its way out.

Close your eyes. Rest. Sleep. You are safe. That is my promise to your friend. My thank-you. She gave everything so that I might return. Keeping you safe is the least I can do. No harm will come to you; you have my word.

He heard footfalls in the shallow stream. Pebbles grinding under heavy feet. He was sleepy. He hadn't been, but suddenly his eyelids weighed a ton. It was all he could do not to close them as he felt the roots swaddle him, offering shelter. *Sleep, my dear sweet friend.* No, he promised himself. Not while they were still out there. Not until he was safe.

He heard sniffing from beyond the veil of vegetation. Breathing. Loud, shallow, excited. They had his scent. Charlie rocked in place. There was nothing therapeutic or healing about it. He was going out of his mind. The sweat dripped down the ladder of his spine, betraying him with each fragrant bead of perspiration. He wasn't getting out of this hole alive.

The roots curled protectively around him, cocooning him. He felt them moving like snakes around him. And still he heard the others out there, prowling around the gully, sniffing at the air for any lingering trace of him. He couldn't move. There was nowhere to go. He rested his chin on his knees. Outside he heard the splash of water. They were moving away.

Let the forest cradle you. Let Mother shelter you. I will wake you when it is safe. Sleep.

And despite everything, that was exactly what he did: he fell asleep, safe in the embrace of Jenny Greenteeth's sanctuary.

29

The call came into the station an hour before shift change.

Someone in an office block on the far side of town had seen a body in a cemetery. Normally there was nothing remarkable about that; bodies and cemeteries were a natural fit. This particular body hadn't been buried. The officer worker reported seeing an old man walk through the tombstones, arrange his layers of coats as though making himself comfortable, and lie down. Then he hadn't got up. The officer worker had thought nothing of it, but the old man had been there for most of the day, so he'd called it in hoping someone would check it out. Ellie volunteered. She was already on that side of the city so it wasn't out of her way. Even so, with traffic building up and the rush hour getting a head start on the day, it still took her twenty minutes to get there, and another five to park up and negotiate the graves.

She stood outside railings of the derelict mausoleum where Cadmus Damiola had been laid to rest.

Twice.

The gate was open, hanging precariously on a rusted hinge. The fretwork was incredibly detailed. It took her a moment to realize she was looking at the wings of a bird wrought in iron. She saw the old man lying on the ground. She recalled the office worker's description of the old man taking his time to arrange his coats before he settled down, as though he'd picked this place, this moment, to die. He looked peaceful. *There were worse ways to go,* she thought. Going through the motions, she checked his throat for a pulse that wasn't there.

She radioed in to the station, explaining what she'd found and requesting the coroner; she then settled in to wait. It took a while. These things always did. More traffic, more time. What had been twenty minutes for her would be thirty or forty for the coroner's team. She wasn't going anywhere in a hurry. It felt wrong sitting on a tombstone, so she walked over to the rusted iron railings and sat with her back to them. Alone, she had too much time to think. And thinking meant remembering what had happened on at the hospital and again in the morgue.

"Can you hear me?"

She didn't need to look at the corpse to know the dead man was speaking to her. It was beginning to become a habit.

Ellie crossed herself reflexively, the last refuge of the lapsed Catholic, and went to check him again for a pulse she knew wasn't there. As she rested two fingers against his neck, she heard him. Distant words. Nothing she could make out. She saw a migrainelike jagged line of rainbow colors cut across her vision: soul light.

"You *can* hear me, can't you?"

She was losing her mind. She had to be.

The dead didn't talk.

She looked up. She was no longer alone.

"Listen. Listen. This is important. Really important." She started to stand, her fingers drifting from his cold neck. "No, no, don't break the contact." Ellie froze, caught in an uncomfortable crouch, looking up at shimmering blue ghost light of Cadmus Damiola's soul. Pale. Translucent. Standing there in the shadow of his own mausoleum looking at her in desperation. "I need you to do something for me, girl. I need you to find Joshua. And Officer Gennaro. Talk to them. Tell them you have seen me. They will understand. *One for one.* Remember that. He's here. Arawn is here. He's stronger than we ever could have imagined, and he's gathering an army to his side. The Wild Hunt. It's going to take to the streets if they don't stop him. And then God help you all. You've got to get the message to them. They've got to cross over, go to the other side. The Annwyn. And I can't help. Not anymore. There's nothing I can do. I'm done. I'm dead. My part in this is over. I made a mistake. I got too close. He saw me. They've got to help the children. It's all about the children now. They are depending on them. Do you understand? It's all about the children. He's bringing his accursed kin through the dimgate in Coldfall Wood. It's the only way."

None of it made any sense.

How could it?

"How? How do I help you?" she asked. "I don't understand what's going on. What's happening to me? This is new. This," she waved her free hand from the corpse at her feet to its shade before her.

The ghost spoke slowly, laboring over every word. "Find Julius Gennaro. Tell him . . . tell him that Damiola is dead. That Arawn is here. Everything he feared is happening. Now. Here. Tell him he is going up against an army intent on tearing this place down. And if he doesn't move soon, there will be nothing he can do to prevent the Great Beast of Albion from waking. He's got to cross to the other side. Tell him I'm sorry. I got it wrong. And now I'm paying for my mistake."

She felt cold, but she was supposed to wasn't she? That was how it worked, surrounded by the dead. Their cold rubbed off on you. She looked at him. Both of him: from ghost to body and back.

"What's happening to me?"

"The dead need to be heard. You are the one who listens. You can give them a voice. You can help them find some kind of justice; help them find meaning for one last time. You can help me." His words grew weaker the more he tried to speak, as though it was harder for him to stay, harder for him to interact with her, to make himself understood. More than anything Ellie just wanted the old ghost to go.

30

The hammer was heavy in Josh's hand, metaphorically as well as physically. He knew that to anyone watching he must have looked unhinged, walking fast through the streets with the silver-headed hammer banging against his thigh as he muttered to himself. A couple of kids in superhero T-shirts sat on a low wall, kicking their heels and smoking cigarettes as he walked by. The girl said something to the boy beside her, a half-assed witticism that went over his head. Josh didn't bother turning around to teach her a lesson in manners; with the hammer in his hand any engagement would have been blown out of all proportion. Better to just walk on, focused on the gates of the cemetery at the far end of the street. The ironwork really did look like wings from a distance.

The bench where Cadmus Damiola so often held his vigil was empty. It was unlike the old man to abandon his post.

Had he not been so wrapped up in his own thoughts he might have noticed how weird the atmosphere in the city had become. There was a raw elemental *charge* there: permeating every nook and crack in the pavement, seeping into the hearts and minds of her residents. It was in the ranks of the disaffected youth where it was most pronounced; the way they looked at the older Londoners around them. It wasn't distrust; it was dislike. The millennials saw all that was wrong with the world, Arawn's war cry resonating within them, and laid the blame squarely at the feet of the Gen Xers and baby boomers who'd come before them with their greed and their me-me-me existence.

The first fists had already flown, a group of teens beating a forty-something suit on his way to a nameless bank inside the Square Mile. That had been followed by six preteens savagely tearing into a day trader on her way to the Stock Exchange. More reports were coming in by the hour, each detailing more and more brutality, all of it at the hands of the teenagers of the city. No longer were they content to be the voiceless generation. Those first few reports all made reference to a weird ululating chant the teens made as they waded in with fists and feet, though none of the victims knew what it meant.

Halfway down the street, Josh saw a group of schoolkids in their striped blazers—they had been red and navy, but the red had faded with age to a soft pink—and ties gathered in a circle, shouting and jeering.

"On your knees!" one of them barked. "Get on your knees like a fucking dog!"

It took Josh a moment to see the woman in her pencil skirt and business suit; she'd been pinballing between them as they shoved her around the circle. Now she stood in the middle of the group, gasping like she was choking on the air she needed to breathe. The heel of her shoe had snapped off and lay on the pavement a few feet away. Long bangs of hair fell over her face as she slumped into a schoolboy's fist. "I said get down!"

It went from nothing to Josh raising the hammer above his head and roaring what amounted to a battle cry in a couple of seconds. He raced toward them, not sure what he was going to do until he reached them. He just knew he couldn't stand by and watch whatever they were about to do. He scattered the circle with half a dozen wild swings back and forth, lurching violently from side to side to make sure no one knew where the next swing might land. The schoolkids, none older then fifteen or sixteen, a few much younger, backed away from the mad man. That didn't stop them from mocking him.

"You'll get yours, fuckhead," the smallest, with a basin haircut and big ears, screamed up at him, spittle flying from his lips. The kid's entire body *shivered,* straining with pent-up rage bursting to get loose.

"You're fucking dead, man, dead," one of the older boys howled, shaking his head like he couldn't believe anyone could be so stupid as to come between them and their prize. The pits of acne scarred his face.

The woman was on her knees.

Josh looked at her to check she was all right. The fear had reshaped the muscles and bones of her face. She was far from all right. She was a mess. Her knees were bloodied and her neck flushed red as the tears stung her cheeks, and she'd have a spectacular black eye before too long. The skin around her right cheek still bore the angry imprint of her attacker's knuckles.

"Get away from her," Josh yelled, locking eyes with the boy he took to be the ringleader. He kept telling himself he was just a kid, but there was something really wrong with the way the boy stared back at him, like he was broken inside. He was taller than Josh by a couple of inches, whippet-thin and probably anemic given his pallor. Josh whipped the hammer around in a vicious arc, knowing that the absolute last thing he wanted to do was make any sort of contact. Brutality would only escalate the situation. He needed to defuse it.

The kid watched the hammer and laughed at him. In his face.

Josh's heart tripped.

"That's enough," Josh said. He we breathing so heavily the words barely made it out of his mouth.

"Give it up, you bag of shit. Just back the fuck off and let us have her. It's that or we do the pair of you. That what you want, old man?"

Josh leaned into another backhanded swing, the hammer head missing the kid's jaw by less than an inch as he stood his ground. The kid didn't so much as flinch. A smile curled at the corner of his mouth.

There were nine of them in the circle. Impossible odds, even if they were just kids.

Josh used the hammer to create a perimeter, giving the woman room to get back to her feet.

"Wrong choice," the oldest kid said, shaking his head sadly. "Want to try again?"

She stood beside him.

"Back off," Josh barked, swinging wildly. "Back. Get back." The hammer arced silver between them.

The kid didn't budge.

Josh swept the hammer around again and again, each pass a little looser, wilder, than the last. It was getting harder and harder not to hit them.

The fury of exertion began to tell as Josh's muscles burned.

He kept on swinging.

It was a fight he couldn't win. There were too many of them. If they came for him at once there was nothing he could do beyond hurt a couple, maybe crack a skull or a jaw before they took him down.

They closed the circle around the pair of them.

Josh stopped swinging.

Instead, he held the hammer out straight in front of him, keeping the schoolkids at arm's length.

"Everyone needs to just calm down," Josh said, trying to appeal to reason. Any other day on any other street he'd have described them as decent kids; that was how they looked with their posh school blazers and trendy haircuts that spoke of wealthy parents and nice houses in good school catchment areas. The disconnect between their public schoolboy image and the brutality of their actions was vast. "You don't have to do this," Josh said, trying to catch his breath. He was breathing hard. His heart hammered. "Walk away. We're not going to chase you."

After a cackle of laughter, they answered him as one, their voices coming together in an adolescent chorus. He couldn't understand a word of what they were saying. It was more of a chant than argument, the words given a hypnotic rhythm that just made it eerier.

Josh risked a sideways glance at the woman beside him who was none the wiser.

The clamor of noise mocked him, escalating quickly.

Their voices bayed.

"Shut up! Quiet!"

But the cries just spiraled, louder and louder, until they could be heard streets away.

One of them broke the rhythm of the weird ululating chant to quote a line Josh hadn't heard since he was fifteen, *"Kill the pig, kill the pig . . ."* and he knew he'd just been cast in the role of the unfortunate porker.

He pushed the hammer out, stabbing it toward the nearest kid in the circle.

A trickle of sweat beaded and broke on his brow, running down the side of his face.

It was the middle of the morning, in bright daylight, in the middle of the city. It wasn't like they'd wandered into gang territory in downtown LA, the street on the division between Bloods and Crips territories. It was a couple of minutes' walk from the pound store and a row of equally depressing charity shops. "We don't want any trouble," he said. The words sounded thin and frightened in his own ears.

The kids said nothing.

The silence was worse than all of their chanting combined.

The way they looked at him, the mix of hunger and madness in their eyes, turned his stomach. It was purely animalistic. The fine hairs along his arms bristled as the air around them filled with the charge of danger.

"Let's all just calm down, shall we? Nice and easy, boys. Don't do anything stupid."

One step, they came closer, closing in the circle.

Two steps, they came closer still, just out of reach.

Three steps, it became painfully obvious words weren't working.

Josh lashed out with the hammer.

He didn't connect.

And then in the distance some unseen lookout yelled "Scatter!" and the boys broke rank, half-turning, then racing away.

Their laughter echoed the length of the street.

Josh's arm went limp. The hammer fell against his leg. He watched them go, not quite believing it was over, not quite understanding how it had begun in the first place. He felt his entire body slump as the adrenaline fled his system. His knees buckled. He shrank an inch, but didn't fall. There was a moment when the one who'd spoken that line from *Lord of the Flies* looked back over his shoulder, grinning so fiercely it looked like a razor had sliced his smile, and drew a finger across his throat before bursting out into fits of laughter as he sprinted away. It was the most blood-chilling moment of the whole terrifying scene. Josh wanted to turn tail and run in the opposite direction, but before he could the woman broke the silence between them.

"I don't know how to thank you. You didn't have to . . . I mean so many people wouldn't have put themselves at risk like that . . . but you stepped in. I just . . ." she shook her head, struggling to find adequate words. "Oh, God. Oh, God . . ." she broke off amid desperate gulps, choking back the realization of what would have happened to her if Josh hadn't turned up. She leaned forward. Josh thought for a moment that she was going to go over, but she braced herself with her hands on her knees and gasped and coughed and gagged on the air she tried to breathe.

"It's okay," Josh said, uselessly. "It's okay. They're gone. You're fine. You're okay."

All he could do was give her time to gather herself. He didn't even know her name. That gave him something to say. "I'm Josh."

"Roz. Rosamund," she managed after a second. "I don't know what I would have done if you hadn't stepped in . . ."

Josh just shrugged. It wasn't the most eloquent gesture, but it spoke volumes. He had no idea why he'd put himself in the middle of that circle, only that he hadn't thought; he'd just done it.

"What happened?"

"You saw as much as I did," Roz said. She wasn't angry, just lost. This wasn't her world. He realized she probably walked this street twice a day without anything like this happening to her. Would she ever feel safe again here? Properly safe? Or had that been stolen away from her by a group of kids?

"I mean how did it start? What made them turn on you?"

This time it was her turn to shrug.

"I've got no idea. I was just walking to work. I turned down the street, my bus stop's a couple of streets over that way," she gestured back in the direction of Aldwych, "when I saw them walking toward me. I didn't think anything of it." She shook her head, still trying to make sense of it. "I mean I pass groups of kids every day. There are three schools less than ten minutes' walk in either direction. They're everywhere. They're just kids. Good kids. But it's strange today. You can feel it, can't you?" Josh caught himself looking around as though for some physical manifestation of the strangeness she was talking about. The street was just a street, same as it ever was, houses that had seen better days, patches of front garden that had run to seed or been converted into off-road parking. It could have been any of a thousand streets in a hundred identical neighborhoods. But he knew what she meant. Josh had lived through riots in Notting Hill as a kid, and more recently Tottenham and Clapham as an adult. There was *something* in the air now; same as there had been *something* in the air back then. The entire city was on edge, holding its breath as it waited for the incredible pressure that had been building up and up since the first murders finally vented. When that happened things were going to turn nasty.

"Are you going to be okay?" he asked. It was a stupid question. It wasn't as though they were going to become best friends because he'd done something unthinkingly stupid to protect her. She'd go her way, he'd go his, and that'd be that.

She nodded.

"I'll be fine. Can I ask you something?"

He nodded in return.

She looked down at the hammer in his hand. "What are you doing with a hammer in the middle of London?"

He laughed at that, a sharp burst of nervous energy amplified by the release of tension in his body. "I'm off to rack up a lifetime's worth of bad luck." She had no idea what he meant, but that was fine by him.

It had been a long time since he'd set foot inside the cemetery grounds, but nowhere near long enough. He never wanted to go back, not after what they'd done. Walking the last quarter mile down the road was harder than it had any right to be. He kept looking back over his shoulder every few yards for the boys, but there was nothing to suggest they were coming back. It was just one foot in front of another, but it felt like he was carrying all the weight of the world on his back—or more accurately, all the weight of London and what was happening to it, so not the *whole* world, just his part of it. The phrase *one for one* kept circling around in his mind. Over and over. *One for one.*

There was something about it that had been nagging at him since the old man had first used it.

Something they were missing.

It was obvious. Right there in front of his mind, just waiting for him to give voice to it. But for the moment he couldn't. Instead, as he walked beneath the familiar arch with its wrought-iron words, he turned his mind to what happened next. Because, like it or not, they were right; Alex, Julie, even the old man, Damiola. What was happening to those kids *was* his fault. He'd fucked up. He should have just killed Seth and been done with it, but that hadn't been *enough* for him. He'd been determined to make the man suffer for everything he'd done to Eleanor and Josh's family that he had damned them all.

He was the only one who could do anything about it, and that was exactly what he intended to do. He was going to set Seth free. He'd smash every mirror they'd used to trap Lockwood in that other place, giving the bastard a way back, and do what he should have done the first time, end it. He hit the head of the hammer against his thigh. The impact numbed the muscle where it hit. That was where his plan fell apart, because after that he had nothing. What was he supposed to do? Pray that the same *one-for-one* logic applied in reverse? That he could somehow put everything right with a hammer?

He walked through the winged gates, and followed the path through the uneven tombstones with their weathered memorials to the daunting dead house where they'd trapped Seth.

He wasn't alone in the cemetery.

He saw a woman—no, a police officer, he realized as he got close enough to make out the uniform—standing inside the iron cage that fenced off the magician's final resting place. He was about to call out to her, to tell her about what had happened outside the cemetery and get her to radio in a report for others to be on the lookout for that gang of *Lord of the Flies*-loving schoolkids when he saw the shape at her feet.

Even at this distance he recognized the layers of the old man's grubby coats as they spread out around his body.

He wasn't moving.

"Get away from him!"

The officer turned slightly, looking up to meet his challenge.

"Get away from him!" Josh yelled again, running full pelt across the grass between them, the hammer raised above his head. "What have you done?" He didn't care what he looked like.

The female officer held up her hands, palms out, "It's okay, it's okay," she said, trying to placate him before he could launch himself at her. "Put down the hammer, Josh. Just drop it on the ground by your feet." She talked at him, her words coming thick and fast, but Josh couldn't focus on them. She knew him?

How?

He'd never seen her in his life.

Common sense still controlled his muscles. The hammer fell from his hand. He stopped a few feet shy of the old man and stared down at him. There was no mistaking the deathly pallor. Josh let loose a desperate, keening cry that tore out his heart and fell to his knees.

He saw the officer's hand on Damiola's chest, and heard her voice still talking to him—level, calm—asking questions Josh couldn't focus on.

"Get your hands off him."

She shook her head. "I can't. He needs to talk to you."

Josh lost it.

He couldn't think.

Couldn't breathe.

Everything crushed in around him, his world coming undone.

He struggled, sinking beneath it all.

He couldn't find a way up for air.

Her tone was an anchor for him, linked with heavy chains that led all the way back to this place, this time, and his dead friend. And because of that he didn't want to grab that chain just yet. Instead, he took hold of the old man's dirt-ingrained hand with its black fingernails and gripped it tight, willing Damiola to open his eyes and grin that damned grin of his one last time.

"He's gone," she said. But that couldn't be right. He'd thought the old man would live forever. He'd already lived more lifetimes than anyone had a right to. Why would he leave them now, like this, when they needed him the most? "If I break contact, I lose him.

There's no guarantee I can get him back. He's desperate to talk to you. He won't shut up."

Josh refused to believe it.

He leaned in, shaking the old man by the shoulders as though he could force him to open his eyes if he just shook him hard enough.

He was so very, very cold.

There was nothing of the old man left in there. It didn't matter how vigorously Josh shook him; he wasn't opening his eyes. Josh felt his stomach contract, and had barely scrambled a couple of feet away before he gagged, spitting up bile, and gagged again, the vomit sticking to his lips as his gut emptied.

He stayed on his knees, hands planted either side of the stinking puddle of vomit.

He couldn't move.

He could hear her voice. She was still talking, but not to him, he realized, as he craned his neck to look at her. She in turn was looking in the direction of the mausoleum, or more accurately the shadows within it.

Pieces of a nightmarish puzzle began to drop into place, their edges barely fitting.

He didn't want to believe he was right, but couldn't shake the feeling as he watched her looking again to the shadows for guidance.

He'd come here to finish this, to smash the mirrors and set Seth free, bring him back so they could drive Damiola's Horned God back to where it belonged. Who else but Seth could have done this? Which meant she'd set him free, didn't it? That was who she was talking to in the shadows. Had she lured Damiola away from his bench, betraying him to Seth?

If she had, he'd turn the hammer on her.

"What have you done?" he demanded, starting to push himself to his feet. As he leaned forward he planted his hand in the puke. He didn't care. He shook it off. "Where's that bastard? Where's Seth?"

"He wants to talk to you."

"I'm not talking to that bastard. I've come here to kill him." He realized that was a stupid thing to say to a cop, but it was too late to take it back.

"Stop laughing at him," she said, not to Josh, to the man hidden away in the shadows. She turned back to him. "He said not to be so stupid, you're wasting time. He's not Seth. He told me to remind you the last time you saw him you cut your finger off and lied about it. Does that make sense? He thinks it's enough to convince you he's dead and talking to you at the same time." Josh stared at her, remembering the last time he'd seen the old man. "You've got to listen. I don't know how long we've got." She looked toward the shadows again, seeking encouragement from within them. "Damiola wants me to tell you that Arawn is here. He saw him. He wants you to know he got it wrong, but you aren't to waste time mourning him. Everything he feared is happening. Now. Here." She looked away from Josh, back toward the shadows, "Slow down, I can't keep up. You've got to slow down." And then turned back to Josh. "I'm sorry, he's frantic. There's so much he's trying to communicate; I think he's frightened he won't have time to tell you it all before he goes."

"Tell him I'm sorry," Josh said."

"I don't need to, you did," the Speaker for the Dead said, smiling gently. "He says yes, yes, of course you are, but there's no time for that."

Despite himself, Josh smiled at that. It was so absolutely Damiola. It couldn't have been anyone else.

"They want to tear this place apart, Josh. They won't stop until they've pulled down every building and given the land back to their goddess, the Earth Mother. If you don't find a way to send Arawn back, no one will be able to stand against the Great Beast of Albion as it wakes. I have no fucking clue what any of that means, but there you go."

Josh looked at her, trying to make sense of what she was saying. It was a *lot* to take in. She kept looking from the shadows to the corpse and back to the shadows again.

"You're talking to him right now, aren't you?"

She nodded.

"What do I do? How do I stop this?"

"You've got to go to Coldfall Wood . . ." she said, nodding as she listened to the voice he couldn't hear. "There's a weakness there, a dimgate. He says you'll know what he means, that it's like Glass Town, a way through to the Annwyn. That's what he calls it." Josh nodded, staring at the shadows, willing Damiola's ghost to show itself. "There's a stone circle at the end of an ancient hollow way, a causeway; within it, Arawn's opened a gateway. It's guarded by creatures of the Wild Hunt. They are more powerful than they seem. Your eyes will see schoolkids," he found himself thinking of the pack he'd just encountered, "but they're just the vessels, the Hunters are parasites that have taken up residence in their flesh. Whatever they look like, they aren't kids anymore. They want the Sleepers dead so they can stay here. This land used to be theirs. They believe that by following Arawn they are fulfilling an ancient curse that doomed them to protect this place. They see us, humanity, as the greatest threat to the land. You need to cross to the other side. That's the only way you can save the Sleepers."

"Okay," Josh said, though it was anything but.

"There's something else."

"Tell me."

"You aren't going to want to hear it."

"Tell me anyway."

"He says this is your fault. Now you have to stand up. Make things right. Everything that has happened, everything that is going to happen is because of what you did."

"If I smash the mirrors, if I bring Lockwood back, will that change things?"

"He doesn't think so."

31

The old man's ghost watched them take his body into his own mausoleum.

It wasn't an event Damiola had ever expected to bear witness to, but then how many people got to be visitors to their own funeral?

He'd lied to Josh, not through any sense of shame, not trying to shift the blame, but because Damiola needed him to step up. It wasn't his fault; none of it was. It went back further than that; all the way back to Seth and Eleanor. *One for one.* He'd created Glass Town, he'd fashioned the illusion and bonded those streets to the Annwyn. He'd banished them, not Josh. In all of this talk of *one for one,* they'd been ignoring the most obvious flaw in their thinking: Eleanor Raines.

If Arawn was here, now, in place of Seth, then that had to mean there was another of his kind in this place somewhere, a counterpart that balanced out Eleanor's banishment, and whoever it was had been here for a very, very long time. That was the nature of balance.

He hadn't always known how it worked, but as things became clearer, his understanding crystallized and it grew more obvious that everything that had happened—and was going to happen—lay at his door. He'd had a lot of time to mull things over on his bench watching over the cemetery. He had created Glass Town. He had trapped Eleanor and Seth in that hellish place. No one else.

So, *one for one,* he'd started this, and because of his own stupidity he wasn't going to be around to finish it.

That was why he'd lied to Josh.

He needed him motivated to fight, but no so guilt-ridden that he curled up into a ball and surrendered.

Damiola didn't know who had come through, or what role they would play in the coming days, if indeed they would play a part, but he was sure they were here, and had been for a long time. There was a cuckoo in the nest.

He followed them inside.

"Is he here with us?" Josh asked, the female officer.

Ellie Taylor nodded.

The pair of them struggled with his bulk. The narrow corridor that led into the chamber of mirrors they'd set up to snare Seth wasn't exactly made for carrying a dead body down, which was ironic given the purpose of the building they were in.

"What do you want us to do with your body?"

Damiola hadn't thought about it. How many people did? Maybe those facing down their last days, putting their house in order. But normal people still laboring under the misapprehension they'd live forever? Not so many, he'd wager. He looked at the pathetic bag of bones and those rags it was clad in. There wasn't enough meat on it to feed the worms. "I don't care," he told the Speaker for the Dead. "Tell him to prop me up in the corridor with a sign around my neck saying *Abandon Hope All Ye Who Enter Here*." The ghost chuckled at that. She didn't look quite so amused by the notion.

"He says he doesn't care."

Diplomatic.

They stopped at the last door.

It was obvious that Josh didn't want to open it. He knew what was on the other side.

"Tell him to get a move on, some of us haven't got all day."

"Do you remember the last thing I said to you in here?" Josh asked the ghost.

He did.

He'd told him he wouldn't live forever, that one day he'd come back to break the glass and finish Seth once and for all. The threat was chillingly prophetic.

Josh reached up to rest his hand on the lintel, contact breaking the seal Damiola had put in place in a scintillating cascade of purple sparks that trailed like the corona of a fast-burning firework. A fine curtain of Northern Lights colors rippled across the doorway as Josh opened the door.

Ellie Taylor held her Maglite torch between her teeth, shining the way forward. The beam caught in and reflected off the array of mirrors set up inside the musty confines of the burial chamber.

One of the first mirrors they reached had a web of cracks spidering through its silvered glass. Damiola remembered exactly how the mirror had broken.

A single candle flame burned in the center of the room.

Unlike any normal candle its light was eternal. It would burn and burn, and as long as it did the enchantment holding Seth in Hell would hold.

They set his body down.

Josh crouched down beside it, placing both hands flat on the stone just as Damiola had done when he'd sealed the tomb. The ghost remembered the words of the chant, but couldn't bring himself to say them just in case they might actually work from the afterlife. He didn't need to. Contact with Josh's hands conjured filaments of bluish light from the cold stone. The light *smoked* as it chased along each and every crack back into his hands, undoing the latticework of raw energy that had trapped Seth Lockwood.

The mirrors behind Josh began to move, sliding back to reveal Seth's prison.

Josh lifted his hands from the stone and turned to look at the glass.

Breaking contact, the energy dissipated, the crackling electricity behind Damiola's illusion fading away to nothing as the magic found its way back into the earth.

Josh looked up at him through the mirror, and seemed finally to see him. He had aged a decade in as many minutes.

Josh banged on the glass with the side of his fist, but it remained empty. Again, more insistently this time, trying to summon Seth Lockwood's leering face to the fore.

"Where are you? Seth?" Josh raised the hammer, resting the ball head against the glass of the mirror prison. "All I've got to do is hit it once. Just once and you're free. Where are you?" Where before there had been an infinite array of doppelgangers trapped within the glass, now there was nothing. The only glimpse of infinity was emptiness.

Whatever mirror world existed behind the glass, Seth's rage-twisted face wasn't part of it. "I'm talking to you! Come here and face me!" He hammered on the mirror again, causing the glass to bow beneath each impact.

But Seth didn't oblige.

He didn't stop pounding on the glass until the Speaker for the Dead echoed Cadmus Damiola's one word back to him. "Enough."

It had the desired effect, leeching all of the fight out of Josh.

He let the hammer fall from his hand, and stepped away from the mirror, pressing his back up against the wall as he slid slowly down it until he sat on the floor. He drew his knees up under his chin and wrapped his arms around his legs, making himself as small as he could possibly be.

"I don't know what to do . . . I don't know how to win . . ." Josh looked up at the ghost, not seeing him there.

"Neither do I," said the ghost. "But it was never going to be as easy as breaking a few mirrors."

The Speaker didn't relay that message, instead she sat herself down beside Josh and wrapped an arm around his shoulder, drawing him in to a protective embrace.

"Come on," she said. "Let's get out of here."

When they finally left, the ghost didn't follow them out.

It still had business here.

32

The chalk brothers, Gogmagot and Corenius, walked through London oblivious to the way that other people looked at them and their leafy crowns. This wasn't the land they remembered. This wilderness of concrete and filth wasn't the land they'd given their lives fighting for or come back to save. It was choked. Dying. Once upon a life, they'd walked this same way, able to see for miles across rolling hills down into the river basin, and it had been *beautiful*.

It smelled wrong, too. The subtle fragrances of the wilderness, the pollen and the lush grass, the syrupy flavor of the sap, living aromas that should have been everywhere were replaced by dead smells that pretended at life. Nothing of the world they'd left behind existed anymore.

Men in drab suits hurried by in a parade of uniformity, each one looking like a carbon copy of the man before him. Steel-tipped toes and canes danced to a downtrodden tune. Their march had the order of a battlefield about it, while the random motion of the tourists moving around them with their overflowing plastic bags played the role of the routed enemy.

They followed the path their leafy crowns mapped out for them, taking turns from street to backstreet and back again as the edges of the first couple of leaves began to curl and brown. It wasn't the most accurate form of map, more like playing out a game of hot and cold where the leaves withered and died the closer they got to their prey, but gradually they worked their way closer and closer to the center of the web of streets that eventually led them across the river into a land of towering office blocks and windows high in the sky that reflected the sun across the rooftops below. Two men in high-visibility vests wrestled plastic sacks into the trash compactor of their garbage truck while a third attacked a stack of flattened cardboard boxes with his boots before feeding them in behind the sacks. The compactor ground its way through the rubbish. The reek coming out of the back of the garbage truck was the most natural thing they'd smelled since leaving the forest.

"You get a whiff of that?"

"Ambrosia," Gogmagot said with a wry grin.

"It's making me hungry," his brother agreed.

They stood beneath a stone archway, ahead of them a huge Victorian red-brick building, behind them a row of cheap hotels. The white stones of the hotels were caked with soot and filth of exhaust fumes. The patina was so thick it looked as though they had suffered serious fire damage not so long ago. Almost all of the leaves on Corenius's crown had browned and shriveled up, meaning they were close. The leaves had led them this far, he trusted them to lead them all the way to their first victim. He took no joy in hurting people, but didn't question Arawn's wisdom. If Father said that these five needed to die for the greater good, then die they would, and the sooner the killing was over, the sooner they could go about breathing life back into their beloved Albion.

"We can eat when we've taken care of what we've come here to do. Come on."

He led his brother into the courtyard beyond the arch. Beside him Corenius sniffed the air, his huge nostrils flaring again and again as he tried to isolate a single unique signature amid all of the scents clogging up the air around them.

"It's hard to smell anything with all of this sickness in the air."

"Inside," Gogmagot said, looking up at the black bars covering the rows of grimy windows. Climbing plants rooted deep into the weeping brickwork, suffocating many of the lower ones, tangling with the bars. It was as though nature was reclaiming the place. The whole thing gave the dilapidated old building an all-pervading air of hopelessness. It wasn't the kind of place you came to heal, he thought. It was the kind of place you came to die. Which was useful.

They went inside.

The foyer reeked of bleach and urine. An imposing grand marble staircase with the worn-down steps of generations of sick and their mourners shuffling feet dominated the vast space. A number of orderlies came and went, ignoring the brothers. There were other visitors sitting in the plastic seats of the waiting area. Corenius could smell the sickness beneath their skin. There was cancer in the room. With all of the other aromas crowding out every natural odor it was amazing anyone could smell anything in this day and age. But his nose was sharper than most. He could make out a dozen diseases, the imbalances in sweat glands and fungal infections in the patients, as well as the shit stains of the body in one of the nearby rooms waiting to be cleaned up.

There were only three leaves on his brother's crown that hadn't withered.

They were close.

The brothers climbed the stairs, beginning their search. They moved through the wards one corridor at a time, checking each room, watching the leaves as they prowled the long halls.

Nurses looked at them, but no one challenged the chalk brothers' right to be there.

A leaf fell.

He looked down at it on the tiled floor, then up at his own reflection in the doors at the end of the corridor.

They were getting closer.

"Can you smell her yet?" Corenius asked. He titled his head slightly, savoring the next breath he took.

Gogmagot sniffed at the air.

"I can't smell shit," he admitted. "Everything about this world fucking *stinks*. I don't know how people can live like this. Don't you miss the fresh air?"

"Not as much as I miss whoring," he offered with a grin. "Speaking of which, it's been too long since I felt like a man. When we're done here let's go and find something to fuck."

They pushed through the doors and entered another ward. This one was filled with side rooms and with beds curtained off from each other. The smell in this place was truly sickening. Nurses busied around a station at the far end, coming and going from behind the curtains with bedpans, while others doled out the next round of meds. A petite Asian nurse with the beaten-down eyes of an NHS veteran came out of the side room in front of them, and did a double take. Her gaze lingered on their hands. Gogmagot realized she was staring. He looked down at his own hands and saw the smears of mud and chalk that stained his fingers.

"Who are you visiting?" she asked, finally looking up at his face.

"My friend," he said.

"That's not much help."

He offered a shrug. What was he supposed to say? He didn't know his victim's name.

He touched his lips. "She cannot talk," he said, thinking about what he knew about the child he was looking for. This time he waved his hand across his face. "She is not . . . here."

The nurse struggled to grasp his meaning.

"The poor child—" the nurse heard all she needed to know in those three words and was ushering them out of the ward before he could finish his sentence.

"The PICU is two floors up," she said, and was already moving off to deal with the next crisis.

"Then that is where we need to go," he said to his brother.

The penultimate leaf fell as they rounded the landing onto the children's ward. Corenius ground it underfoot.

The ward formed a vee, the nurses' station serving as the axis. There was a playroom to the left, filled with brightly colored plastic building bricks, rag dolls, and toy cars. A television set played cartoons to the empty room. A second smaller waiting area was filled with the same mismatched collection of toys, its walls covered in a rainbow of colors, including an actual rainbow, along with a host of curious characters looking for its end. Instead of a pot of gold it was bubble pool filled to overflowing with plastic balls. A toddler drove a miniature car down the middle of the ward chased by two girls on kick bikes, laughing as they pretended to be police cars. It was chaotic. Full of life and energy, but when he breathed in deeply he could smell the undying sickness just beneath the surface of the kids' skin. Leukemia. It was rooted deep in their blood. None of them would see the year out, he realized. That's what he learned from their scent.

There were several adults in the ward, but no one challenged their right to be there, so the chalk brothers moved down the ward one private room at a time, pausing at the doors to look through the small wire-reinforced windows set in them at the patient inside. The rooms were all much the same with slight variations on the theme—beloved literary characters painted on the walls, posters of cartoonish heroes— and machines, room after room of life-saving machines.

The final leaf fell as they reached the sixth door.

"Here we are," he said.

"Looks like it," his brother agreed.

He opened the door.

They went inside.

The girl lay on the bed. The shallow rise and fall of the crisp white sheet tucked tightly into the mattress was the only proof that she wasn't a little china doll dressed to look like a child. Her cheeks were too pink. Her eyes were like glass. There was a tube taped into her mouth that fed back into the machine that was keeping her alive.

Gogmagot closed the door behind them and leaned back against it, making sure no one would unwittingly barge in on them in the act.

He watched the helpless girl. She held the key to their survival. He had to focus on that, but it was difficult. It took him a moment to realize the doubt belonged to his host. Rupert Brooke's thoughts were bleeding through into his own. He'd imagined possession would snuff out the kid once and for all, but he was still inside him, somewhere, or at least an echo was, and that echo lacked the stomach for what needed to be done.

He closed his eyes, pushing down the sickness he felt at the prospect of killing the girl.

When he opened them again, his host had fallen silent.

The respirator hissed on, breathing for the girl. The sound was hypnotic. He watched the shallow rise and fall of her chest as it matched the steady beeps coming from the cardiac monitor beside the bed.

"This is going to be easy," Corenius said.

"Shouldn't be though, should it," he said, moving around to the side of the bed. They'd gone from defenders of the city to murderers of children. He tried to banish the thought but there was a crack in his psyche and Rupert Brooke was haunting him through it. He reached up with his right hand, tangling his fingers in the muddy knots of his hair. He pulled down on the roots, focusing on the pain in the hopes that it would be enough to seal the fracture if only for a moment. "Look at her. She's no warrior. This ain't a fair fight." They weren't his words, but they were the truth. "This is the kind of thing that taints a soul, Brother."

"Got to be done, though," Corenius said, reasonably. "Just think about it in terms of them or us. And I ain't planning on going no-where. We're here to stay. This is our home. No one belongs here more than us."

Which Gogmagot knew was true, but looking down at the kid in the bed he realized how wrong he'd been to think he could be a part of snuffing the life out of a sleeping child.

Corenius took the killing out of his hands. His brother reached down for the tube and pulled it out of the girl's mouth. Blood bubbled up with it from where the tube had cut something in her windpipe on the way up. Corenius didn't care. He simply leaned forward and clamped one hand over the girl's mouth, while with the thumb and forefinger of his other hand he pinched her nostrils shut to the panicked alarm of the respirator.

It didn't take long. The girl's body bucked against the tight sheets as the death throes shook her; her body resisting, desperate to live.

"Let go," Corenius whispered. "Just let go. It's okay." And to Gogmagot, "Come over here, hold her steady."

He did as he was told, leaning forward to put his weight on her shoulders and pin her to the mattress.

She bucked against him.

The alarm seemed to grow louder, becoming more insistent with every spiraling tone.

And then she lay painfully still.

Even then, with the girl dead, he couldn't shake the expectancy that someone would come racing in to save her, some hero or villain drawn by the discordant beep of the machine.

His brother yanked the power cords out of the wall, silencing the machine. It was as easy to kill as she had been.

He leaned in close, part of him hoping to feel just the softest feather of breath against his neck, but there was nothing. It was done. One of them was here for good.

When he looked up from the dead girl he saw the smallest buds of leaves on his brother's crown had begun to open.

As they left the room the leaves were lush green, full of life that would in time kill another child just like this one.

33

Jenny Greenteeth remembered everything her body had been through in Herla House. All of it. His touch. The foul odor of his rancid breath as he leaned in close, drooling over this skin. All of it.

Bracken had no right. None whatsoever. This wasn't the world they had left. It was different here. The children weren't his possessions. He was not lord and master. He was meant to protect them. What he did was a violation. She closed her eyes, tapping into the fading memories. That girl had lived with so much pain from his hands. They all had. Even the boy she'd saved from the Hunt. Her heart quickened at the thought of betraying her own father.

She wanted to make it right. It felt important to her. This man, Bracken, should experience the same kind of pain.

Jenny Greenteeth smiled through a mouthful of jetsam, a cruel smile filled with the green teeth that gave the water witch her name.

Could he swim?

Sometimes the old ways were the best.

That pretty face of hers was nothing more than a mask over a dark soul.

She let the girl loose for a moment, allowing the memories bubble up to the surface. She knew these streets. Each turn was ingrained into her muscles. She only needed the flesh to remember for long enough to find the house, and then she would lure him out.

The house was so central to everything she didn't have to dig deep.

Jenny's nostrils flared as she inhaled.

Her eyes rolled up inside her head, showing the whites as her eyelids fluttered rapidly and her jaw fell open. Her entire body went completely rigid. Turgid water gargled deep in her throat, bubbling up and spilling out of her mouth until it seemed she might drown standing on dry land. When she opened them again her eyes were shot through with threads of blood where the smallest capillaries had ruptured. She knew where he would be.

She followed the stream out of the forest.

Taking those first faltering steps out of the sanctuary of the ancient wood left Jenny shaking, gripped by a physical withdrawal. Without Penny Grainger's pain to lead her down toward the streets waiting at the bottom of the hill, she might never have been able to make it. Even then, those first few steps on the dead tarmac of the road were like crossing over from life to death, and on the other side she felt utterly bereft, cut off from the vibrancy of the forest and the soul of Mother.

But she followed her through the warren of streets with red-brick houses and blacktopped roads like scars on the land. They acted as a barrier between her and her world. She was cut off from the residual magic of the Earth Mother, unable to tap even the thinnest vein of that vital energy. She had never felt so alone in her life, not even that day when it had all ended for her here the first time around. Still, she focused on what she had to do, and why, and drew strength from that as the city around her transformed into a downtrodden hell on earth. Decay was everywhere, despair entwined with it. She understood now what they were fighting for. And that she was prepared to die for a second time if needs be.

She stopped outside the high wall of Herla House.

The brickwork was topped by a budding clematis. More climbers dug into the render on the house itself, suffocating it. The iron gate was open. It led through to a secret garden that had been left to run wild. The weeds were already ankle high and would only get higher.

She waited, out of sight of the windows in the shadow of a tall tree. Resting her back against the trunk, Jenny Greenteeth began to sing a haunting melody. Her siren song brought faces to the windows, but the song was sung for one man and one man alone. Bracken. He appeared in the doorway a moment later, disheveled and confused, scratching at his scalp as he shuffled down the few short steps into the garden. Behind him the sign named the house. She couldn't help but wonder if he had any idea of its origins or its link to Arawn's Wild Hunt. It was wonderfully appropriate that the girl had dwelt under its roof.

"Who's there?" Bracken called out uncertainly. He looked left then right then left again, like he was practicing his Green Cross Code, then stepped out onto the cracked paving stones that led to the gate. "Come on, out with you, you funny fuckers. Stop pissing about."

Jenny's voice rose in a haunting sweep of emotion. There were no words to her song. She channeled deeply buried emotions, calling out to the primal instinct at the man's core, her tune one of seduction and promise that drew him two steps along the path, then two more, and two more until he was at the garden gate looking up and down the street for any sign of the singer.

She moved in the shadows, her footsteps silent on the damp grass, and projected her voice; her song seemed to come from everywhere and nowhere at once. Bracken stumbled out into the street, the door and the gate both left open behind him. She followed, her song rising and falling with a promise only Bracken could hear within its delicate harmonies. His feet shuffled on the paving slabs, the rubber toe of his slippers catching on the uneven edges of the flagstones.

She led him down to the water's edge, through businessmen and schoolkids who looked at him like he'd lost his mind; an Alzheimer's victim wandering the city, lost. But those who took the time to look at Bracken properly saw a look of bliss on his face that defied description. He was in the grip of the highest high.

He found the stone steps cut into the side of the riverbank and walked willingly down into the water. She watched Bracken from the embankment as he took his first faltering steps into the water as the Thames lapped at his slippers, sliding on the mud-slick pebbles as the river washed over them. The evangelical euphoria of his expression didn't change as he plunged into the river. The water swallowed him up to the waist, and then another step took it up to his neck as he went over the shelf. It was only then, in those last couple of seconds as the River Thames closed over his head, that Bracken knew fear but he was helpless to stop his body from dancing to Jenny Greenteeth's tune as she led him to a watery grave.

It would have been better if he had suffered, the water witch thought. He deserved to suffer for what he had done to the children in his care, but for now it was enough that he wouldn't abuse any more vulnerable souls. They were protected. She took some satisfaction in that. She had done a good thing here. In death she had saved so many more from suffering. In that realization she understood that the Horned God was right, in death they could save this broken land of theirs.

34

Julie wouldn't have seen the pattern if it wasn't for Alex talking about the locked-in kids.

He wouldn't have even known to look, never mind *where* to look.

He had ringed two names in red: Annie Cho, and Bethany Laws.

He put the phone down, and picked up the pen, bouncing it on its point half a dozen times, thinking.

The girls had too many things in common for their lives—and deaths—not to be linked. Even if taken individually, the events around their deaths weren't suspicious—strange, yes, but not suspicious—but collectively they should have been enough to raise more than just an eyebrow. Not least the fact that they'd all sleep-talked the same five words over and over: *The Horned God is awake.* Three of the girls who had been admitted to hospitals across Greater London as lock-ins in the last twenty-four hours had died in the last six, all seemingly of natural causes. Talking to their doctors, the general consensus was that their bodies had simply failed them. It was possible, of course, that whatever had caused them to shut down initially had taken too much out of them in the end, but for one thing, in two of the three hospitals nurses reported seeing a pair of disheveled youths milling around the wards in the time leading up to their deaths. Julie had emailed photographs of some of the missing children Tenaka had given him, and got a positive ID on Stephen Blackmoore and Rupert Brooke. In both cases, the witnesses were at pains to say that both boys appeared to have been sleeping rough for a long time and remarked upon their smell and that their faces were smeared with streaks of white chalk, like war paint.

Now he had a direct link between the disappearances and the locked-in kids, one he could file on a police report, even if he couldn't say what had caused him to look for one in the first place. There were several more connections he could never file, like the fact that he believed Blackmoore and Brooke were agents of the thing that had come into this world because of what he and Josh and Damiola had done to Seth, and that they were removing the anchors that allowed them to cross over from Hell so that they couldn't be banished. He bounced the ballpoint pen half a dozen times more, thinking back to that first call to the Rothery that had opened the door to this nightmare. He'd never hated Taff Carter more than he did now. If Taff had never taken Seth Lockwood's bloody money, none of this stuff would have been happening to him.

Julie put the pen down and sank back into his chair.

He needed a drink. Not that drinking would help.

Ellie Taylor stopped at his desk and looked over his shoulder as she put a cup of black coffee on his desk.

"Thanks," Julie said, without looking up.

"Three?"

He nodded. "And I got positive ID on Blackmoore and Brooke being seen inside two of the hospitals."

"What the hell's going on, Julie?"

"No idea," he lied.

"You've seen the other reports coming in this morning? Dozens of isolated incidents of gangs of schoolkids attacking people in the streets of South London."

He'd seen them.

"It's getting ugly," he agreed.

What he couldn't say was what he feared the most: that this, too, was linked to Arawn's return, and that the disaffected youth were being manipulated into fighting his battle for him. And that, in turn, was pretty much on Julie.

The coffee was still too hot to drink.

Tenaka appeared in the doorway. "Taylor, Gennaro," he curled a finger in their direction, "the incident room, now."

Julie left his coffee where it was and followed his chief inspector to the Major Incident Room that was being set up upstairs. An hour ago it had been a big empty space. Already, in the space of the half an hour since Julie had poked his head into the room, an array of computers, desks, chairs, and noticeboards had been installed, along with a large conference table where a map of the city had been laid out and locations were being marked in to match the incident reports coming in that morning. The left side of the incident board was taken up with faces; victims first: Oliver Underwood, Aisha Kahn, and Musa Dajani beneath them; then to the right, the row of missing kids: Charlie Mann and Penny Grainger, both current residents of Herla House, the ex-residents Stephen Blackmoore and Rupert Brooke; and last, the suspects column was filled with three pictures: Jamshid Kirmani, with a line linking him to Ollie Underwood and Aisha Kahn's photographs, and Daniel Ash and Tom Summers, with a line linking them back to Musa Dajani's photograph. All the details they knew: times, dates, locations, witness testimony, and such were linked to each case. Two words stood out: *HERLA HOUSE*.

One computer had been set up to monitor Twitter feeds for the relevant hashtags that had been trending since last night, looking for links to the reports of violence coming in this morning. Another monitored Facebook and a third Instagram. Correlations were being run against the Police National Computer, looking for cases of grievous and actual bodily harm linked to the owners of those accounts. It was all about trying to find the red thread that wound between them all; the one thing that tied the evidence together and proved it was all linked the way that Julie knew it was but wasn't able to explain.

Stills from security camera footage had been taped to the incident board.

Julie hadn't seen them before.

There were four in a line, and they showed Daniel Ash and Tom Summers dragging Musa Dajani out of the park. The angles weren't good and the images weren't clear. The CCTV cameras were from two locations. The first two captured the trio's passage for a couple of blink-and-you-missed-them seconds from shops close to the park. They were hard to make out in any sort of detail because they were in darkness. The two remaining stills, close to the gates of Coldfall Wood were taken closer to dawn, with lightness creeping into the image. They showed the two boys walking away alone. Julie knew that out of camera shot Musa Dajani's body had been strung up and crucified on the sign.

"What are you thinking?" Tenaka asked, behind him.

"The obvious motive here's revenge for Underwood. It's a racial thing. White kids hitting back at the Muslim, they lay in wait for Dajani after football practice, lure him away and kill him, tit for tat. I don't think they give a crap about the girl at this point, she doesn't fit their narrative, she brought it on herself, Ollie was just an innocent victim."

"Agreed. And?"

"And the board's not right." He moved the photographs of Stephen Blackmoore and Rupert Brooke from the *Missing* column to the line of *Suspects*. "Or at least it's only partially right. Blackmoore and Brooke aren't victims." Tenaka didn't say anything, but several of the officers working the incident room looked up from what they were doing to follow the exchange. This was new information. "We've just had visual confirmation in the last few minutes that both boys were seen in wards at both Guys and Kings this morning. By itself, it's noteworthy, the first two sightings of two of our missing kids, but two patients died within a few minutes of their sightings. And while it might be coincidental, I'm inclined to think it isn't."

"You think Blackmoore and Brooke killed them?"

Julie nodded. "Bear with me. Both patients had been admitted with a condition known as parasomnia." Tenaka looked at him like he was speaking Swahili. "Locked-in syndrome, you know, a waking coma."

"Jesus Christ," Tenaka shook his head. "So you think Blackmoore and Brooke hunted out these locked-in cases? Talk me through it. How do you see it fitting in? Big picture."

"It's not my case to make," Julie explained. "An emergency services dispatcher, Erin Chiedozie, noticed something weird was going on in London. In any given year there's no more than a handful of cases across the whole country. She started looking for points of similarity, anything that might link them: a single point of contagion if it was viral, something like that."

"Did she find anything?"

"She found a link, but I'm not sure it's something we can act on."

"Let me be the judge of that," Tenaka told him.

Julie took his notebook from his pocket and made a show of thumbing through the pages until he reached his notes on the short conversation he'd had with Chiedozie even though he didn't need to. The words were blazed on the back of his mind: "They all said the same thing; one line, that linked them all. 'The Horned God is awake.'"

No one said anything.

"Like I said, it's not exactly a tangible link."

"Some kind of cult thing, maybe? Like the Scientologists?" Ellie asked.

Julie nodded. "Something like that, I guess."

"So, they made some sort of pact? Drank poison like the Heaven's Gate mob, expecting a UFO to take them away to a better afterlife? In this case one with horned devil gods? It's no crazier than Xenu."

Julie shrugged. There were worse connections they could draw. "And Blackmoore and Brooke are tied into this?"

"It would explain the disappearances," Ellie said, putting two and two together and making something a long way from four, but which had her excited. It was something that made sense. Something they could work with.

"Okay," Tenaka mused, the side of his fist resting on his lips as he thought it through. "Maybe there's an angle there. Some sort of doomsday cult in the city we've not heard about poisoning a bunch of kids, then sending their most devoted out to finish them off when the drugs didn't do the job? Look into it, Ellie."

"You should know that there were five cases of parasomnia reported in hospitals across London yesterday," Julie said, letting that sink in before adding, "A third patient died at St. Thomas's this morning. If there's a link, if Blackmoore and Brooke are going after them, that means the other two are at risk. Twice might be a coincidence, but three times is a pattern."

"Get onto the hospitals," Tenaka agreed. "I want security on each ward. We're not losing any more kids to this pair." He looked back at the first face on the incident board.

"We've had a lot trouble on the Rothery this morning," Ellie noted. "Sykes and Banks were caught up in it. There have been a number of reports of assault by gangs of schoolkids all along the south of the city and into the East End, too, all almost certainly originating from anger toward the murder of Ollie Underwood."

"We need to put a lid on this."

Julie didn't need to be a mind reader to know his boss was thinking about the bad press that came with fighting on the streets. When you rose to the level George Tenaka had, you couldn't help but become a political animal. It wasn't about the police work. "Have we got any further chasing down Kirmani?"

"I've contacted his family in Watford and Bedford, but none of them have heard from the boy. We drew a blank with his friend up in Newcastle, too. If he ran in that way, he never made it." Ellie said.

"So, what's the thinking here? Blackmoore and Brooke caught up with him?" Tenaka asked, looking for the nice neat answer he could tie a bow around and present to the press conference in a couple of hours, telling the world not to worry: *Yes things had got nasty there for a while, but we're on top of it; no need to panic.* Those were the key words: *no need to panic.*

"Right now I'm not thinking anything, sir," Julie said. "Just going through what we know."

"But you think it's all linked?"

"I wouldn't go so far."

"Gut instinct, Gennaro?"

He looked down at his boss, "I'm worried they might be," he said, which was absolutely true.

Tenaka nodded.

He didn't say anything else for the longest time, looking straight out of the window across the rooftops of the city, lost in thought. When he finally came back, he nodded again. "Okay. Right. Yes. Taylor, I want you to head up the team here. Bring in whoever you think you need to get things done."

"If you don't mind me saying, sir," Ellie said, "it might be a good idea to make ourselves seen out there. People tend to feel safer when they see a police presence. Double foot patrols in the Rothery, for one thing, making sure uniforms are a visible presence."

Tenaka nodded, essentially ending the meeting.

He left.

Julie was halfway out of the door when a young PC, Nathan Mullins, called, "You should see this."

"I'll catch you up," he told Ellie, and crossed the room.

Mullins was looking at a suicide sheet.

"What am I looking at?"

"A body fished out of the river this morning." Four hundred people a year chose to end their lives in the Thames. Whatever their own personal tragedies, fishing a body out of the river was quite literally an everyday occurrence for the River Police. "I wouldn't have thought twice about it, but it came up during a connected search between the missing kids."

That had his attention. "Explain?"

The officer brought up a police profile, meaning the deceased had a record—or had at least been the subject of an investigation. "The body's been identified as James Bracken."

Julie didn't recognize the name.

"His day job was as warden of a children's home, Herla House."

"Tying him to the Grainger girl and Charlie Mann, right now, and historically to all of the kids up on the board apart from Kirmani and Kahn." Given what had happened with Blackmoore and Brooke hunting down the locked-in kids, the obvious assumption was that one or more of those kids up there were part of Arawn's army and that somehow Bracken's death was tied into it. "And he's in the PNC because?"

"Complaints of impropriety to Social Services. Five instances of historical abuse were investigated, two including allegations of sexual abuse against a minor in his care. Stephen Blackmoore. The complaints were dropped. Blackmoore was judged to be an unreliable witness even though there was plenty of circumstantial evidence, including witness testimony, but Bracken made a deal to give evidence against two of his coworkers that saw them put away for a long time, exposing the systematic abuse of kids in the care system."

"And he was allowed to stay in the job?"

The officer nodded. "I guess everything was swept under the rug. The file was sealed. I can't get at anything beyond that without a court order." Which of course meant it wasn't the end of it at all. "There's nothing else on him in the system." No way it could have played out like that, not after Yewtree, the Jimmy Savile scandal, and the horror stories of the Elm Guest House over by Barnes Common. Those records were sealed for a reason. Julie was well aware of the near constant rumors of a VIP pedophile ring at work in the city going all the way to the top. They all were, but there was never any evidence. It was just whispers. Shadows. High-level corruption in the corridors of power. The only reason a piece of shit like Bracken would be allowed to walk would be in the hopes of landing a bigger fish. Spyware in his computers, surveillance on the place, looking for the links between him and others of his predilection. And that being the case, there would be some very worried perverts in the city tonight as the news broke.

"Suicide seems like a confession to me," Julie said, but men like James Bracken didn't suddenly develop consciences or become wracked with guilt. Bracken had lived with his crimes for years. More importantly, in his mind he'd gotten away with them. That Bracken had taken it upon himself to end it all today of all days smacked of something else entirely. Penny and Charlie's disappearances coupled with Bracken's suicide felt like a settling of old scores, and wasn't that exactly what Arawn's return was all about? "Are we absolutely sure it's suicide?"

"We'll need it confirmed by the coroner's report, but yes."

"Okay, mark up the links on the incident board. I want you to get that file unlocked. I want to know exactly what's in there. Oh, what a tangled fucking web . . ."

35

It was Robin's favorite time of day: the time to make mischief.

He left the forest with no little trepidation, looking back over his shoulder at the abandoned safety of the trees every twenty or thirty steps. He imagined faces in the leaves, watching him go, willing him to be brave. Breathing deeply of the polluted air, Robin Goodfellow struck out, his eyes fixed on the tower blocks and office blocks in the distance. He heard the forlorn cry of a train's horn as it bellowed around a curve, warning the world it was coming. It sounded so similar to the cry of the Bain Shee, the ancient enemy, in the other place that he stopped for a moment, sure that the veil must have been pierced and the ancient enemy escaped. He looked every which way, high and low, for a glimpse of the fey creatures, but saw nothing but the endless sprawl of life where mankind had multiplied like rats. Satisfied he was alone, Robin skipped around the cold lifeless concrete of the paving stones that led away from the wood as far as he could, not willing to risk setting foot on them for fear of what might happen if he did. Without following the lines of the cracks and a balancing act of walking only on the cracks, that first step on the dead stones was inevitable, and it wasn't as painful as he had feared.

It was worse in so many other ways, though, not least the fact that it cut him off from Mother. Within a dozen faltering steps Robin was isolated from nature. He felt the thrill of earth magic, already so faint, falter and fizzle out between footfalls. It took all of his mental strength not to cry out in panic; he'd known it would be like this, but knowing and experiencing that moment where the cord was cut and he was cast off, utterly bereft, was harrowing. He fell to his knees and clawed at the ground, trying to worry his fingernails between the curbstone and the paving slabs where weeds grew. Tears glittered in his eyes. To anyone who might have been watching, he must have looked like a pathetic drunk on his hands and knees, searching desperately for his lost dignity.

It took every ounce of will that he had to force himself to stand on unsteady legs and walk on, but he did it, because they were counting on him. Without him, the Hunt would fail, and if those few seconds of true loneliness could teach him anything, it was that he could not afford to fail them. Mother needed him.

One step.

That was all it took.

One step.

And then another.

Nothing more difficult than that. Just one step. He concentrated on his feet. Closed his eyes. Took the step. And then another. And another. A slow smile reached his lips. He could do this. He wouldn't let them down.

When he opened his eyes again he saw a young girl, no older than five or six, looking at him from across the street. Robin waved at her, offering a broad smile. "What's your name?" He called.

"Rosie," the little girl called back.

"What a wonderful name," Robin told her. "I'm Robin. I used to live here, a long, long time ago, but I'm a bit lost at the moment. So much has changed."

"Mum says I'm not supposed to talk to strangers."

"Your mum is very smart, Rosie. You should listen to her."

"Are you frightened?" the little girl asked.

"Is it that obvious?" Robin said, surprised that Rosie crossed the street to hold his hand.

"It always makes me feel better," she said, squeezing his fingers.

"And it's making me feel better," Robin agreed.

"Where are you going?"

"I don't know. I'm looking for someone."

"Who?"

"I'll know when I find them," Robin assured her.

"Can I help you look?"

"Won't your mum worry about you?"

"As long as we don't go far it'll be okay. I can only go three streets from here. I'm not allowed to go farther than that."

"Well let's start by looking around here then, shall we?"

They walked the few streets Rosie was allowed to, together. The little girl was an incessant chatterer. She had something to say about *everything*. This street, that street, what had happened here, who lived there; it all came out in one big bubble of enthusiasm. It didn't take long for them to reach the edge of her territory. Rosie stopped at the curb but made no effort to cross even though Robin was already one step into the road. The sudden stop pulled Robin up short. He looked across quizzically. "I'm not allowed to cross this road," Rosie explained. "Three streets."

"Ah, right, and this is the fourth. Do you want to come with me?"

"Yes," Rosie told him, wrestling with the internal conflict that crossing the road entailed. "But I can't."

"What if I talked to your mum?"

"She wouldn't like it," Rosie said.

"We wouldn't want to upset her, but she's not going to know, is she? Not if you just take a few steps, then a few more? Maybe come with me for another street or two, then you can come back here?"

The girl looked down at the road like it was a raging river, too dangerous to cross.

A black cab slowed down as it passed them, checking if they wanted a ride. When they didn't stick out a thumb it accelerated away, its yellow light calling out for business.

Rosie shook her head.

"You're a good kid, Rosie," Robin told her, kneeling down in front of the little girl half-in half-out of the road. He brushed her blond bangs aside and planted a kiss on the girl's forehead. "That'll protect you from anything bad happening to you tonight. It's a magic kiss," he explained. "It tells the Hunters you're one of us." He smiled reassuringly.

Rosie looked at Robin; her young face serious for a moment. "Can I give the kiss to my mum?"

Robin shook his head. "It's only for the young. If you're too old, it won't work on you."

"So, what about Mum? Is she going to be safe?"

"You'll have to look after her the way you looked after me," Robin said, sadly. He knew there was no way a little girl could stand up to the creatures of the Wild Hunt if they decided they had a taste for her family, but he wasn't about to tell the child that. "Can you do that?"

Rosie nodded earnestly.

"Then it'll be fine."

"I hope you find them," Rosie said, letting go of his hand.

"So do I," Robin said, seeing a group of teenagers on the street corner. "In fact, I think I have."

That was as close as they came to saying good-bye. Rosie skipped away, back toward the safety of the three streets she was allowed to roam, and Robin crossed the road, plastering on his most charming smile as he did. He adjusted his host's torn shirt and brushed back his hair.

He held up a hand in greeting as he neared them, but was greeted by an aggressive, "Who do you think you're waving at?" from one of the girls in the group.

Robin Goodfellow chose to walk right into whatever was coming and blew the speaker a kiss.

His kisses were contagious. They worked magic. Their power was weaker than it might have been in the wide-open green spaces of nature, but they still had their charms.

The girl looked at him differently.

Children were cruel and only grew crueler as they grew up. His kiss, diluted by the city, diluted still by the polluted air between them as it flew to its mark promised a different kind of belonging. It promised her that there was a place for her in the Wild Hunt and the ride to come. It promised her that she'd never be on the outside of things again. There was a moment, the silence between heartbeats, when he thought she might try and shake it off, but her need to belong was stronger than that. She came running toward him and swept Robin up in a huge embrace, holding him tight and spinning him around where they stood. He laughed and laughed, completely carried away by the moment.

Her friends looked on, bewildered by the sudden change of events. Robin giggled as she set him down.

"This is Robin," she said breathlessly. "Robin, this is everyone! Everyone, Robin's brilliant. He's just . . . brilliant. You'll love him."

"I hope so," Robin said. "Because I've been looking for you."

"What the fuck's wrong with you, Zoe?"

Robin turned his attention on the boy and blew him a kiss, too.

"Fuck you," the kid said.

"You should be so lucky, sweetie," Robin said sweetly, and the others laughed as his kiss changed the atmosphere around them. "It'd be the ride of your life."

He knew them all. He looked at them one at a time, his scrutiny moving from wispy bum fluff to pitted acne craters to flawless porcelain skin, pathetic in their uniforms, a rage of hormones and hatreds clothed in the respectable face of youth. They were exactly the kind of small-minded foot soldiers Arawn needed to serve as sacrifices, feeding their blood back to Mother to nourish her dying soil. It was only fitting that they should become his warriors, spreading his message across the city that everyone who heard his words should listen and rise up.

He let them think that they were special.

He offered them sweet words and promises.

His promises were mostly lies. The only truth he offered them was that together they would change the world. They were young enough and prideful enough to believe that he was offering them their destiny, when really all he had to give them was a bloody violent death.

"If you wanted to make people take you seriously, what would you burn?" he asked, inviting their answers.

"The Pakis," the first suggested. "Bastard reported me to the cops for nicking a packet of fags."

"Think bigger," he told them.

"The new shopping mall they're finishing by the wharf. Topple the cranes. That'd make some fucking mess."

"Better," he said.

"The new bank tower they just opened by the river," another offered. "Dad says those fucking parasites put my nan on the street. It'd be sweet to sort *them* out."

"Good. Yes. I like that."

"What about the Tower?"

"How about Parliament," another suggested, grinning. "Gunpowder, Treason, and Plot."

"Good," he said. "Think big. Think of places people will see, that mean *something*, that send a message. Landmarks."

"The Olympic Stadium."

"The O2."

"The sign at Piccadilly Circus. Everyone knows that."

He nodded at each suggestion. It wasn't about his choosing one; none of the names meant anything to him. It was about firing up their blood, getting them thinking about destroying things. Making them malleable. Making violence seem *natural*.

"Do you want to have some fun?" he asked, knowing the answer would be yes. It always was. They nodded eagerly, lapping it up. His smile was the most sincere thing about Robin Goodfellow as he sent them on their way, each with a target in mind, streets to burn, buildings to bring down, pain to inflict, windows to shatter, and they were desperate to please him. "Then I want you to do *exactly* what I tell you. Can you do that?" More eager nods. "Spread the word. It's happening tonight. We're going to tear up the streets. We're going to burn the hellholes down. We're going to make a statement. This is our land. We're going to take it back."

"Yes!"

"Then go. Do what you must. Our time is now."

He watched them run, then went in search of his next audience. He had an idea: Why scour the streets looking for one or two sacrifices when he could go to their schools and address them as congregations? Robin had learned a lot from his host. He recognized the way they branded themselves according to color and dressed alike to show their belonging to their unique tribes. Time might have marched on, but the human need to belong hadn't changed in the slightest.

He heard voices—loud, laughing, riotous. The sheer joy of being young filled the air. It wouldn't last; it never did. He followed them, coming a few minutes later to a huge school playground with painted courts for basketball, five-a-side football, and hockey, along with other random-colored lines painted on the asphalt. Thirty kids were spread out in a line across the middle of the courts, their uniforms all somehow subtly different whilst being mostly the same, with rolled-up sleeves and backward ties, shiny leather shoes, and scuffed trainers. The same number again, both boys and girls and all in their teens, ran across the yard from end to end, heads down, heads back, arms and legs pumping furiously, spinning on their heels, twisting and turning while the ones in the middle tried to stop them from getting to the other side. The game expertly mimicked the failures of life as the slowest and weakest were picked off one after another.

He watched, working out who among their number were strong enough to lead and who would only ever follow. He then made his move, walking across the playground toward the pack leader. The fact that he looked like one of them meant that they didn't immediately stop their game to gather around. He laid a hand on the boy of his choice and whispered a word of encouragement only the boy could hear so that he turned directly into his kiss. The boy's eyes widened in surprise, surprise quickly replaced by need as he tried to draw a second lingering kiss before Robin could move on to his next victim. The boy reached out, his fingers fumbling at and failing to hold the threads of Robin's shirt. Grinning, Robin shook his head and placed a finger on his lips as though to ask: *What have I done?* There was feigned innocence in the expression that was betrayed by the knowing in his eyes and confusion in the boy's.

He dropped to one knee, bowing his head in deference.

"Get up, silly," Robin said lightly enough, but in the moments after that kiss his words became the boy's world. He lived to please. He sprung back up to his feet eagerly.

Robin reached out for the hand of a second boy, planting his kiss against the rough skin.

His lips spread a contagion between them that resulted in sixty faces looking eagerly for direction, boys and girls alike, all wanting to please him more than anything else in the world.

They lived for his approval.

All they had to do was listen and bleed.

They were more than capable of doing both.

"Gather around," Robin said, keeping his voice deliberately low so that the kids had to move in close to hear what he had to say. They did as they were told; all of their eager faces looking excitedly at him. He cupped a hand to his ear. "Did you hear that?"

"What?" the first recipient of his kiss asked.

"His call."

The boy shook his head and closed his eyes at the same time, straining to hear the voice that was no longer there to be heard. He shook his head again, more forcefully this time as tears broke. They dried halfway down his cheeks as he sniffed and drew the back of his hand up over his snotty nose.

Robin let him suffer a little while longer, before he tossed his head back and let loose the cry of the Wild Hunt, mimicking the Horned God's voice, *"Hwaet! Áríseaþ!"*

Recognition flickered across their faces.

"I heard it," one said.

"Me, too."

"I didn't understand it."

"Do you now?" he asked.

"I don't know. I think so." The boy looked down at his hands, making fists out of them, then looked back up at Robin.

"Now is the time; there is power in the air, old magic. This is our land. These streets distance us from what was and what will be, but tonight with the setting sun we shall run wild, surrendering to the Hunt. As the Time Between Times is upon the land we shall tear the walls asunder, we shall rive the stones of the Olympic Stadium, the shopping malls and department stores, the O2, the signs at Piccadilly," he said, his voice becoming more and more impassioned with each example that the kids had provided, feeding into their disaffection with images of violence. "And we won't stop until we reach Parliament," he concluded triumphantly. "Are you with me?"

"Yes," they chorused as one.

36

The Horned Man emerged from the trees.

The fight with the magus had been unexpected. He had believed this place entirely drained, the land soured, but it would seem there were some few still connected to ancient leys and sacred sites they connected, able to tap into what little magic remained of Mother. That was worth remembering, as it might make all the difference as the night played out. He wouldn't make the mistake of thinking he was the only one in touch with the old ways.

As the sun began its arc toward the horizon, a trail of sparks blew away from Arawn's staff, each one burning brightly for a fraction of a second before falling to the ground in his wake. They marked his passage through the ancient wildwood. With a single word he stirred them back to life, creating a wall of fireflies at his back. At first it was just one or two that rose again, then more, gyring up into the air until a hundred points of light lit the dark wood, then it was a thousand and a thousand more, each one emitting a discordant hum. The sight was dizzying, conjuring thousands of constantly shifting eddies in the shadows the fireflies cast. It was as though his presence was enough to ignite the stuff of the air, forming a curtain of fire behind him. His antlers were blacker than black against the flames.

Arawn walked barefoot across the black tarmac.

He let the warmth flood through the soles of his feet into his toes, and that warmth in turn bled into the tarmac softening it until the black became molasses, bubbling and sticky beneath his weight. The tarmac spread away from his feet, slowly parting around them to offer a glimpse of the scorched earth beneath. With a word he brought forth a root, the green shoot rising between his toes. With another word he brought forth two more green shoots that budded quickly into summer blossoms. All around him the roots buried deep beneath the road began to respond to his call, rising up. The paving slabs buckled, cracks between them opening wider as they were pushed apart. It was like a tidal wave surging beneath the surface, rushing away from him deeper into the city he was about to reclaim. On the verges, the grass grew wild; weeds, clovers, and foxtails sprouted up, flourishing in seconds as nature began the painstaking process of reclaiming the land for its own. The soft asphalt of the road itself split along the white line as huge roots forced their way out into the fading light.

The trees lining the roadside budded and blossomed, overflowing with the spiky shells of horse chestnuts that cracked open and spilled out the ripe brown conkers, while on the other side of the road cherry blossoms erupted into color and fell, blanketing the road in brilliant hues.

This was always my land, he thought, *and ever will be.*

He breathed deeply, hating the filth he tasted in the air, but knowing now that it was only a matter of time before it was clean again.

Vegetation tangled around the wheels of parked cars, weeds running wild as rose bushes grew up the sides of houses, thorns digging into the weeping grout between the bricks. Where there had been concrete and stone there was *life*.

With every step he took along the deserted road, more shoots of grass and shrub somehow found a way through its surface.

By the time Arawn had walked the distance to the first corner the forest had spilled out into the street, reclaiming it.

It was just one street, a few hundred yards of stone, but it marked the opening salvo in the war to come.

"Hwaet! Áríseaþ!" he bellowed, demanding they hear him now, demanding they rise up in answer.

He heard their whooping chorus in the distance. Robin Goodfellow had marshaled his army of innocence. Now to march them off to the slaughter. Their blood would spill through the cracks even as they tore the streets asunder, bringing down the man-made monoliths to vanity and greed with their bare hands. Their sacrifice would feed the land, their lives nourishing the dead earth until perhaps enough would finally seep into the earth to stir the magic of Mother and breathe life back into the Great Beast of Albion.

The time was now.

The Hunters were abroad.

With the fireflies trailing in his wake and the green shoots of a better tomorrow rising up around his feet, the Horned God walked resolutely toward the inescapable conflict; the most ruthless warrior the land had ever known taking up arms one final time.

It was his fate to restore Albion.

The May Queen had damned him with it. And saved him with it. That was the other side of the curse. It offered balance. Fate.

Let the scourge burn away, he thought grimly, as he traversed the road, reaching a narrow alleyway between houses, which he followed through to the heart of the Rothery and the lightning-struck tree on the green in front of The Hunter's Horns. The ancient tree called out to him. It should have died a long time ago, but like Arawn himself clung tenaciously to life. It wasn't ready to go. *I feel your pain,* he told the oak, reaching out his right hand to lay it upon the still raw wound in the trunk. He let the thrill of Mother's magic flow through him into the tree. Once, hundreds of years ago, it had stood at the center of things.

He had been here before—stood in this very spot—with his hand pressed against the trunk of the same tree. The memory was dim, the darker truths of it locked away from him.

I know you.

The thought wasn't his.

The voice sent shivers through his soul.

It was as old as time itself. It spoke to him in the language of suffering; all of the sins of mankind inflicted upon its source.

It was the voice of the old gods.

Albion spoke to him.

With its recognition, the veil drawn across the memories of betrayal fell away and he remembered:

They had been summoned by the May Queen. She had ensured their presence at the moot with the enigmatic message that the fate of the land was at stake. There was something disconcerting about the sacred grove and the world tree at its center. The old woman had invited Arawn to place his hand against its rough bark and feel it for himself, feel the souring.

He remembered.

He shivered as time marched across his grave.

This was the place where the essence of magic that fed the land had first failed.

He knew the tree for what it was.

This was the spot where Albion had first begun to die.

The Wild Hunt had gathered in the sacred grove, lighting the torches that would burn for the duration of the moot. Across the circle, the enemy sat cross-legged, studying them silently.

There were three of them: pale-skinned creatures of fae origin. Dwellers from beyond the mist. Arawn studied their albino complexions and delicate features, committing them to memory. The blue labyrinth of veins just beneath the surface painted a map across their skin. Their eyes were akin to lava pits that burned with their abhorrence of all things human. He knew them for what they were. He knew them for the fate they promised.

The Bain Shee.

They were her prisoners.

"I'm sorry," she said. "I *know* you will understand, my love, because in my place you would do the same. We exist for this place. For the land. Our land. We would do anything for Mother. Believe me when I say it is the only way. Don't make this any harder than it needs to be. Take the knee—bend your head and offer your necks— and pray that your blood is potent enough to save this place. Look at me, my love; see me, and know that this was always meant to be." The moonlight changed the shape of her face, stripping the mask of humanity away from the old woman's face and offering a glimpse of the pale-skinned creature that lurked beneath.

"I know you," Arawn gasped, disbelieving.

"I should hope so, my sweet. After all this time I'd be offended if you didn't recognize me. After all, you are pledged to me: body and soul. You are mine, Arawn. You always were and always will be."

The Badb, the warrior goddess, known by three aspects dependent upon the penitent's need: Macha; the Morrigu; and Anu, her tender earth maiden's face. He knew many of her names, but she owned many more: the Raven Queen; the Great Queen; the Queen of Phantoms; the Specter Queen; Fury; and in this place at least, the Summer Queen. Wherever there was war, wherever there was dying to be done, she could be found, feeding off the blood of the fallen. Her damned birds were ever present. They scoured the land for carrion to feed her sick appetites. She was a parasite, nothing more. A parasite with a thirst for blood. Whilst all those that came into the presence of the Badb spilled their guts and blood for her, she prevailed. She lived. And lived. She was a cuckoo in their nest. And yet, for so long she had succeeded in fooling them. "Now, I ask you again, will you die for me, my sweet, sweet man? It's the last time I will ask anything of you in this life. I *am* this place and it is *me*. And we both need you to die. Without your sacrifice there won't be the raw vitality in the land to withstand them. You are Mother's champion. To fight for her you must die."

He closed his eyes, content.

It was her.

It always had been.

It always would be.

He felt her presence as she came up behind him. Felt her hands move around him. Felt the touch of her lips on his neck. Felt the bite of her teeth as she tore into him. Felt the blood spill from the ragged wound, hot on his throat, even as it soaked into the dying earth.

"Bleed for me," she breathed in his ear.

They were the last words he ever heard. The rest—her curse—that came as his consciousness faded.

The Babd held him close as his body bucked against dying.

"This is your fate," she told him again, lips close to his ear. "Your curse. Your commitment. You die here. You have already experienced this moment, but now you understand that death is not the end for you. Your entire being is bound forever to this place, this land you saved once with your sacrifice, and now, when her need is greatest you have found your way back from death. You are Mother's protector, my love," she cursed him, and sounded almost sad as her words wove their spell around his soul. Finally, the May Queen let him fall, and he experienced his death all over again.

She had traded him for the land. His magic would sustain her for a while, but not long enough. Not for eternity. Their enemy would never be sated by a single death when there was a world of souls to feast upon; they both knew that.

This time he was aware of the sour land beneath him, and understood that he had fallen where the magic itself had first begun to die. His blood—the blood of a god—was never going to be enough to nourish the land, but it was enough to feed the May Queen and sustain the ancient oak through the decimation of the great wood, alive centuries beyond its natural span.

Arawn concentrated on drawing out the rot first, healing the black wood at the heart of the tree.

He took the poison into his own flesh.

Sickness threatened to overwhelm him, but he refused to break contact with the lightning-struck tree. The black rot attacked his blood. There was so much of it. It just kept coming and coming, oozing out of the wounded tree into him. He drew it up through roots that stretched far, far beyond the height of the tree itself, all the way under the green, under the cellar of the pub across the street, beneath the foundations of the houses built around it. This was the dying heart of the Rothery, but more than that, the rot tapped into the heart of Albion itself, the black tarlike poison dripping through the corpse of the great beast. He felt the splinters of wood begin to knit and reknit; slowly healing the broken limb. It would take more than his newly woken earth magic to restore the ancient tree to anything approaching bloom, but it would not die and that was more important than anything else.

He could feel her presence.

She was near.

Awake.

The May Queen. The Badb.

The *woruldgewinn* could not be stopped.

The earthly war.

37

They were drawn to the ancient wood.

They came in twos and threes, then in a steady stream: lines of youths filling the streets in hoodies and sweatshirts, denim jackets and fleeces, spring jackets and school uniforms. Whatever their walk of life, they came together to answer the call, responding to the voice only they could hear.

The voice went to the core of their being.

It was inside them.

It had always been there.

Dormant.

Waiting.

But he could never have imagined the world he would wake into.

Once upon a lifetime ago, the ancient wood had stretched from one end of the river to the other, across the rolling downs and into the vales between, acres upon acres upon acres of every tree imaginable. It had been the heart of the land, the land of the heart. Its roots spread everywhere, worming down deep into the soil of Albion, deeper into what had come before, all the way down to a time before man had set foot upon this green and pleasant land. The land had been alive in ways it wasn't now, choked and dying beneath endless concrete and steel. There was power in it. That power, that essence, was there to nourish us, to provide for us. And we were there to protect it. Only that relationship shifted. Where there had been rolling pastures and the great woods lush and full of their ancient magic, now there was concrete sprawl, urban decay, rot, and ruin. Ours had become a plastic world, manufactured, hot-molded, disposable. Out of our windows we look out over a throwaway landscape. The true essence of the land is lost to us, the nutrients that once upon a lifetime ago gave life to everything, suffocated by the greatest threat she had ever faced, us.

Where there was magic, now there is superstition, the vague memory of what it might have been like before us; new age mysticism, ley lines, and earth nodes along the old Roman roads, stone circles and chalk men and horses. They might have meant something once, but now they were more like stories than truths—the bean nighe who foretells the death of mortals, a visitor from the Otherworld, a washerwoman who cleans the bloody clothes of those fated to die; the black dogs of the fae who bark once as a warning, twice as a threat, and a third time to doom you; the Alp-luachra that crawls down your throat while you sleep to feast on your last meal; the Dearg-Due, once a beautiful woman who killed herself to escape an arranged marriage only to rise up after the funeral, crawling free of the grave to kill her family; the church grim, the ancient soul that guards holy land. The grim could wear many forms—a pig, a dog, even a small man who rings the bells late at night; the Nuckelavee, a twisted creature with the torso of a man sewn onto the back of a rotting horse, whose sole purpose is simply to hurt the living, bringing blight, disaster, floods; boggarts, brownies, corn dollies, ettins, green men, hag stones, and redcaps; Devil's Jumps and haunted gibbets; Black Annis and Jack o'Kent; Barghest and Jenny Greenteeth, witches and giant killers; drowning pools and the Wild Hunt, and most potent of all of them combined, the May Queen herself—but as with every story there was a grain of truth, an element of memory, that could not be denied.

He was that memory.

This was his land.

And still they came, answering his call, his children.

Word spread like fire, with the same destructive rage.

Hwaet! Áríseaþ!

Hark! Rise up!

He was the Summer King.

And he had returned.

38

Emmaline Barnes lay in her hospital bed. The name was a good one. It fit with who she thought she was, though the nurse insisted on shortening it to the more familiar Emma. She wasn't an Emma. Never had been and never would be, not in any of her lives.

Sweat matted the gray bangs of her hair and beaded in the deep crags and valleys of her face. She had no idea what that face looked like. No one had shown her a mirror since she'd woken up. There were no reflective surfaces for her to catch an unexpected glimpse of herself in. She had no idea when it was, or how long she'd been locked in the silences of her own mind, but she'd seen the slack skin of the backs of her hands, covered with liver spots, that looked like twigs in leather gloves; that was enough to know she'd slept the best part of a lifetime away in this body awaiting Arawn's return.

She had no real concept of time in this place.

The sun came up in the window; the sun went down in the same window, day after day after day, night after night after night. She had no way of knowing how many times that had happened since she'd last uttered a word. Thousands. She'd become accustomed to telling the time by the changing fragrances of the ward around her, with the astringent burn of the disinfectants stronger in the dark hours as the cleaners worked unseen, fading during the daylight hours as the sweat and urine and blood battled to regain some sort of olfactory supremacy. The aromas had filtered through her unconsciousness to that strange place she'd been trapped, waiting for his return to wake her from hibernation. As it was, her old bones ached, her muscles atrophied, and her skin was raw with sores and sticky with the grease of ointments and unctions meant to alleviate the pain not moving caused.

She *could* have changed it all, of course. It was in her power. All she had to do was give herself over to another facet of her trifold aspect; the innocent face of the maiden was her favorite for the subtle influences it wielded. Everyone loved a pretty face. There were things she was capable of in that guise that defied reason quite simply because men were so willingly stupid around her they forgot themselves; then there were the more womanly features of the mother, who had her own virtues when it came to manipulating the foolish sex, because every man at his core wanted to return to his mother, needing to be nourished with her love. But she chose the slack skin and brittle bones of the hag because they had suited her purpose. The world had a way of underestimating the elderly, it always had. And that was where true power lay, in being underestimated by your enemies.

No one had taken away the dead flowers in the vase at the foot of the bed.

The fragrance brought the flicker of sadness to her lips, but it didn't last.

She felt another one of them die. It was an acute stabbing pain that twisted in her gut as the thread binding them was severed. One by one the Sleepers were falling. It was only a matter of time now. Arawn was severing all ties with his Otherworld prison now that he was free of it, and there was nothing this old body of hers could do but wait for him to come for her. He would. They were bound in ways that went beyond the confines of the physical realm.

She'd always known it would come to this.

A crow settled on the sill outside the window. Within a minute it had been joined by a dozen more so that thirteen of the slick black birds jostled for place against the glass. Their beaks rata-tap-tapped against the window as they turned their beady eyes inward.

The May Queen watched her children, listening to their muted caws through the glass as they told her their stories, her eyes and ears in the world outside, reporting back everything they had seen and heard since the Knucker found his legs. They were linked in ways that didn't need words. Images of what they had seen out there flooded her mind; they were fractured and flighty, jumping from thought to thought like a bee pollinating a summer garden, but she was able to piece together a coherent whole: they had seen the Hunt abroad, the chalk twins doing the bidding of the trickster, Goodfellow. They were responsible for the deaths of the Sleepers and wouldn't stop until the last of the five were dead and she was isolated in this place, the last tie to the past.

The door opened.

Alex Raines took the seat beside the bed, and reached for the communication board before she said, "How are we today, Emma?"

Her eyes flicked across the letters, ignoring the question. She spelled out a name: *Annie Cho*.

Alex looked confused.

She spelled it out again. And again. Until she wrote it down.

"What are you trying to tell me?"

This time she spelled out a different name: *Bethany Laws*.

Alex wrote them both down. "I don't understand what you are trying to tell me, Emma. Talk to me. Help me understand what you mean."

Dead. Her eyes flicked across the message quickly. *Sleepers. Need to help the others. Keep them safe.*

Alex repeated the words back to her, as though she couldn't quite believe she'd interpreted the eye movements correctly. She spelled out one word. *Yes.*

"I'm not sure what I'm supposed to do, Emma."

Frustration bubbled over inside her head. She looked down at her hands, willing them to move, even just a finger, a twitch.

Come closer, she spelled out with her eyes, causing Alex to lean in, ever so slightly. *Closer,* she repeated until Alex's face was inches from hers, as though they were on the verge of that transition from friends to lovers with the first tentative kiss.

Fly, she thought, the thought greeted by a flurry of wings beating against the glass as the gathering of crows took flight. *Bring me back word of what is happening to the land, my children.* The sudden burst of noise made Alex turn toward the window. In that moment, the hag's cadaverous hands snaked out and grasped either side of her head, bones digging into her temples as she drew her close. There was nothing tender in this twisted embrace. Alex cried out, more in shock than in pain, at least at first, but the pain followed as her mind was flooded with all Emmaline had seen, all she feared, filling her head with images of Albion fallen, of the Wild Hunt, the chalk giants, Jenny Greenteeth, the mischievous Puck himself, and of course, at the heart of everything, Arawn. The myths and legends of an all but forgotten land flashed through Alex's mind; the truths of the Time Between Times, of the failed magic of the earth, all of it, and every time the picture she shared was worth so much more than a thousand words wasted trying to explain the importance or impact of what she was sharing. Emmaline shared the truth of the lightning-struck tree and the nature of the Bain Shee, the single darkest evil to face this and all other realms. They were the eaters of worlds. They were the darkness. And with the veil between their worlds tearing, the inevitability of death for all, promised oblivion as more of the pale warriors came through. Hidden away within the kaleidoscope of icons and images, the truth about the old woman on the bed and who she really was. The last thing Alex saw was a great sword sheathed in light. Runes chased down the sides of it. There were runnels carved deep into the blade to help the blood of the dead spill off it. She couldn't read the ancient script, but somehow she knew what it said: *Freagarthach*. The blade of Manannan, she knew, forged by the Mother Goddess of the Aos Shee, Danu. It blazed with a light strong enough to banish the darkness of their kin, the Bain Shee. The sword was a weapon fit to kill a God King. Through the ages of man it had owned many names, the Answerer, the Retaliator, but most fitting of all, the last it had ever answered to: Widowmaker. She saw it lying on the chest of a dead man, in a ruined temple.

She grasped the nature of balance and the war that was to come. She understood that the Bain Shee—or Banshee as the word formed in her mind—stood against all humanity, old gods and new, against the realm of the fae and the sons and daughters of the Aos Shee, or the fair folk as the stories had renamed them. In the struggle for life she saw the ultimate darkness of the Bain Shee and how it would need the amassed strengths of all the champions of light, no matter their differences, to come together against the coming dark or they would all perish. The Horned God and his Hunt, the Eternal, The Holly King and the Oak King, the May Queen, the Chalk Brothers, the trickster, all of them would have to stand beside her friends and loved ones, despite all of their differences, it was that or the end of everything.

The enemy they faced was not their enemy at all. Arawn was one of the purest champions of the Aos Shee, and everything he was doing here, to this place, now, was in his mind meant to make it stronger, to return the magic that mankind had so foolishly choked out of the Earth Mother.

He was cursed to return at the time of the land's greatest need—she saw it all and understood—the last hope. He would die for her. He already had.

Alex understood.

She saw the veil, though in her mind's eye it became a more metaphorical wall, the last barrier between the Annwyn and that nether-hell where the Bain Shee had been banished at the dawn of time. And she saw the fissures in it and knew that it was crumbling. The first evil, the essence of all the world's unmaking, was pounding against it, weakening it blow by blow.

It could not stand. Not forever. Not without the greatest sacrifice.

And that sacrifice fell on them.

Alex pulled away, breaking the bond between them. She gasped hard, trembling. Sweat beaded on her brow and streamed in a single tiny rivulet down her temple and cheek. Her eyes took on a haunted aspect. She had seen things that could never be unseen. She understood things that could never be forgotten.

"Understand?" the hag managed; one word in a dry rasp of voice that hadn't managed a word in longer than Alex Raines had been alive.

Alex shook her head, more in denial than confusion.

She understood.

"You must protect the others," those five words were all that her brittle vocal cords could muster before she broke down in a coughing fit that hacked away at the substance of her voice and made itself soundless even as it wracked her emaciated frame. She swallowed hard, struggling to muster the strength to finish the warning. "If they die . . ." she didn't need to say the rest. The woman understood.

Alex pushed herself back, lurching away from the bed. She dropped the communication board, which hit the bed frame and the floor with a thunderclap. She took two steps back. Another two. Half turned to look out of the window as the crows banked and turned in the sky, riding the wind away from their perch. "Danu?"

"The last hope," the hag said, not answering the question.

The wilted flowers in the vase began to slowly straighten, the browned petals finding their bright colors again, full of life.

Alex saw it, but didn't seem to grasp the fundamental importance of what otherwise might have been a parlor trick. At least not at first. But then the implanted memory of the triple aspect of the goddess surfaced in her mind, the maiden with the crown of flowers in her hair.

The King and Queen.

Now she understood. She was in the presence of the Horned God's wife.

"Go," the hag said, more strength in her new voice than she would have imagined possible even a few moments ago.

Alex couldn't resist the command.

She closed the door behind her, leaving Emmaline Barnes alone in the room. It took her a moment to gather herself before she forced her old bones to move, ignoring the pain and the weakness of atrophied muscles to stand. Her head spun as vertigo threatened to overwhelm her. She reached out for the bedstead for support, and shuffled a couple of faltering steps around the bed. This weakness would never do. She had waited too long.

Like an aged angel of death, the hag shuffled painfully out of her room and with one hand trailing down the wall to keep herself upright, followed the smell of sickness. Cancer had a unique aroma. She followed the stench to a room not far from her own. These were death rooms along this ward, she realized. Every single patient here was marked for death by the doctors and nurses tending them. These were nothing more than waiting rooms. She opened the door to the first room and shuffled inside, her bare feet scuffing on the linoleum floor.

The old man in the bed looked at her as she entered, and *knew*.

He nodded, like her arrival was the most welcome thing in the world and he was giving her permission to take him, and didn't flinch once as she leaned in low to place her teeth against his cold, cold skin and suckled, drawing the life and the blood out of him.

He kicked twice, his back arching as his spirit left the mortal realm, and collapsed back into the sweat-stained sheets.

She stopped feeding in that moment, not wanting to swallow dead blood. There was nothing to be gained from that. The hag straightened up, and wiped at her bloody lips with the back of her leathery hand.

It wasn't enough, but it was a start.

Thankfully there was a banquet of suffering outside this room, more than enough to give her the strength she needed to face her once and future love.

39

Dispatch forwarded Ellie's summons.

Joshua Raines was at Ravenshill Cemetery.

What the fuck was he doing back there?

Confronting his demons?

Starting the slow process of putting Humpty together again, even if he lacked all of the king's horses and men?

The only logical reason Julie could come up with for Josh being at the graveyard was that he'd gone looking for Damiola, just as he had, to ask how they were supposed to fight whatever it was they were up against?

What didn't make sense was Ellie's involvement.

She didn't have anything to do with this. Julie couldn't imagine Josh bringing her into the fold willingly—he wasn't big on sharing his own personal hell—which meant trouble was waiting for him down among the dead men.

Julie's driving skirted legality, running lights and cutting corners and up other drivers as he redlined it across London. All along the pavements, the pedestrians were like butterflies emerging from their cocoons of winter colors, greeting the sun with bright shirts and shorter skirts. They sat on rickety aluminum and wooden chairs chain-smoking and trading empty philosophies and celebrity gossip; who'd died, who looked good and didn't look good in the candid snaps of the Paparazzi, who'd put on weight or was losing the battle with anorexia, who had a drug problem or personality disorder or any of the many permutations being "normal" offered.

He heard the call for all cars to respond to disturbances along the High Street, the outskirts of the Rothery, and the shadow of Cane Hill and Coldfall Wood, and more calls going out from the Embankment, Canary Wharf, the city proper, and the tourist traps of the West End.

He ignored them all.

The nearest parking space he could find was still a couple of minutes' walk from the cemetery gates. That gave him time to run a hundred worst-case scenarios through his mind but none of those imagined things matched the pain of finding Josh with his head in his hands on Damiola's bench, discolored streaks of tears down his red cheeks. Ellie had her arm around him, trying to comfort Josh as another wave of grief threatened to overwhelm him.

"What happened?" Julie said, before he was close enough to be heard.

Ellie saw him coming.

She inclined her head toward the cemetery gates, but Julie couldn't see anything wrong as he peered through.

Josh tried to speak, but the words refused to come so Ellie filled him in.

He couldn't believe that Damiola was dead, or that Seth had somehow escaped his mirror prison, not if the glass was unbroken. The one person he would have wanted to ask wasn't talking.

"I need to tell you something, Julie. You're not going to believe me, but I'm not lying."

"You'll be surprised how much I'm willing to believe," he said, casting a glance toward the mausoleum in the distance.

"I can talk to him. I don't know for how much longer, but while he lingers I can still talk to him if there's something you need to say. To ask."

"I'm not following."

"The old man. I can talk to him."

"Damiola? You said he was dead."

"He is."

"I don't—"

"Neither do I. It started happening after we found the old man, Viridius. He did something to me."

"How can you—?"

"Talk to his ghost? Same way you're talking to me."

She didn't sound the least bit weirded out by the craziness of what she was saying, and he desperately wanted to believe her, so he followed his partner as she got up and walked through the graves to the magician's tomb. The ghost greeted them at the door, though only Ellie Taylor could see him. Without contact she couldn't hear a word he had to say. She led Julie through to where the dead man lay, and stood beside him with both hands on his chest. "What do you want to say to him?"

"What do we do? How do we fight this thing? I don't know . . . how are we supposed to *win*?"

She didn't look down at the body, he realized, she looked over to the right, toward the door where, he assumed, the ghost was lurking. He turned slightly to follow the direction of her gaze, but all he saw were shadows. There was nothing unnatural or *super*natural about any of them. She actually smiled before she answered him. "He said if he knew that, he wouldn't be dead. He sounded quite amused by that and said you needed to ask better questions."

"Tell him I'll do my best," Julie said.

She inclined her head, listening. Nodded once, in the direction of the doorway and interpreted the dead man for him. "He said he was wrong. Or right, but too focused on the one part of one for one, and forgot all about the fact that two were banished. If something came through in Seth's place, then something else came here for Eleanor. He doesn't know what, but he's sure they are here, and have been for a very long time."

He was right.

Of course he was.

One for one couldn't just apply to Seth. That wasn't how physical laws of the universe worked—they were *universal*.

"What do they want?"

It was a question the ghost couldn't answer. Instead, Ellie took her hands away from the dead man's chest and told him, "Arawn has dispatched Hunters into the city. They are wearing the bodies of normal kids—the missing kids we've been looking for, I think—but they're not themselves. They're just vessels for these ancient spirits that have come through since Arawn opened the gate. That's where he was when he died," her eyes darted toward the dead man on the slab. "Not here. He was spying on them when Arawn found him. He severed the link between the old man's soul and his body. That's why he's still here. He doesn't know how long it will be until he can no longer maintain any sort of grip on this plane, but he's trying desperately not to go because the fight is only just beginning. He said the gate is within an ancient stone circle called the fairy ring, in Coldfall Wood. It's still open and as long as it is, then other creatures from the Annwyn can come through the mists. There are worse things out there than the Horned God. Much worse. He has seen them. You've got to close the gate."

"How the fuck am I supposed to do that?"

Ellie Taylor laughed suddenly; a single sharp snark of laughter she almost choked on. She looked from Julie to the empty doorway and back again. "He said without getting yourself killed."

"That's helpful."

His phone rang.

40

To kill the king, you must become the king.

The thought belonged to the old woman, but it was there inside her head, telling her what they needed to do. Arawn was the king. She could see each point of his majestic crown of antlers in her mind's eye. The presence of these memories was overpowering. Alex was on the verge of losing herself, like a castaway clinging to the wreckage of a sinking ship. There was no way to sift through them and quieten those that weren't her own.

She staggered out of the hospital into the fresh air.

Sounds assailed her from every side; kids running toward the big wheel and the fairground beneath it; lovers walking and whispering arms entwined; tourists marveling at the historical buildings in sing-song back and forth that sounded like mynah birds; takeaway cartons being cast aside and cans rattling into the trash; the swish of fabric from suits rushing to the office and the clack of towering high heels on the paving stones tapping out their Morse code messages of despair; horns on the river, cars on the roads; the chorus of life that was the city closed in around her. She staggered out of the court-yard and across the cycle path to lean against the iron railings over-looking the river.

It was all in her head now. The grand plan.

Alex closed her eyes, trying to concentrate on nothing more than the next breath, on the simple in and out of it, filling her lungs with the pollutants that pretended at freshness.

The old woman had shared the past with her when she'd gripped Alex's head in her crow-clawlike fingers, forcing her to *see* it all. A burden shared was a burden doubled.

She felt like her head was going to explode. The plates of bone couldn't contain the sheer mass of memories forced into her mind. The blood thundered against them, a constant drumming, drum-ming, drumming that refused to be silenced.

Alex threw back her head and screamed back against it. She felt tiny. Irrelevant. That wasn't helped by the fact that her bansheelike wail didn't cause so much as a ripple on the water below.

No one even looked her way. Had a screaming woman become that common an occurrence in the city that it didn't even merit a second glance?

Her legs gave out. If she hadn't been holding onto the rail, she would have gone down in a heap.

The memories refused to be silenced. They bubbled up one after the other, offering her glimpses of lush green fields and towering ancient forests, of kings of the wildwood and queens of the May. They flooded her head with visions of druidic stone circles, of moon worshipers watching a red sunrise and all of the portents it promised, of the land beneath her feet souring and slowly dying. That was the hardest to take. Watching the Blight Priests spread their sickness twisted her gut.

Alex spent another forty minutes leaning against the railing—just staring out across the choppy water as she tried to come to terms with the staggering sense of loss the old woman had burdened her with.

How could the world have changed so much?

How could they care so little about it now? Humanity had a parasitic relationship with the land, like skin cancer.

A ripple of motion in the Thames caught her eye. Within it, Alex half-imagined she caught a fleeting glimpse of a face beneath the surface.

A girl.

But she was gone as soon as she was there.

The memory lingered, and in it she'd been called Jenny Greenteeth. A witch to some, a siren to others; she was a dark and vengeful water spirit. And she was here, returned.

Before Alex could turn away, a kindly old man came up beside her and asked if she was okay. She nodded. "I like to come here to watch the water," he told her. "It's got a way of making you feel so small. It just goes on about its journey, ripple after ripple racing toward the sea only to be swallowed up by it. Sometimes I think there's a life lesson in that, don't you? That we're all racing to some place where we can simply stop being us?"

Before she could agree an explosion rocked the horizon.

It was followed by two more in quick succession.

The old guy's mouth opened wide and his hand gripped the rail tighter.

It looked for all the world as though he was having a heart attack, but quickly became obvious that he was staring in appalled shock at the familiar view of St. Paul's and all of those unchanging rooftops, spires, and domes suddenly bathed in flame as arsonists struck building after building.

Alex knew what was happening.

The Wild Hunt was abroad, taking back the streets after a millennia's exile. The Hunters were ruthlessly efficient in the war they were waging on the city, aiming one brutal strike after another at iconic landmarks, and wouldn't be satisfied until they'd brought the whole place down around them.

That was their endgame. Their win.

They were here to tilt the balance of nature and bring the old world back, the ancient woods and their earth magic. She remembered the words of the old woman when she'd called Arawn the once and future king, condemning him to return to the land at the time of her greatest need, and Alex *understood*. The land had faced a million threats, but none so dangerous as the voracious appetite for progress and industry that had gripped the last few generations.

"You don't belong here," she told the memory, and turned her back on the landscape of the riot unfolding across the river just as a young woman—breathtaking in her simple innocence and beauty, a summer child if ever there had been one—emerged from the main door in a hospital gown. She looked at Alex. A flicker of recognition passed between them before the woman walked away.

It was in the eyes.

Even across the short distance of the cycle path, it was obvious that she was staring into the old, old eyes of the hibernating goddess she'd spent the last few years caring for. From within the shared memories, the bitter pain of transformation from mother to maiden, from maiden to hag, hag to mother, mother to hag came back to her. Each time, the toll the change exerted on the goddess's flesh was beyond imaging. It wasn't like she simply changed a mask, slipping from one identity into the next. Each time she was born again demanded fresh sacrifice.

With the earth's magic long since soured, the only vitality of creation lay in blood. She remembered the rituals of sacrifice that welcomed the Queen of the May, though in her mind they were more vampiric in nature than the jingling bells of Morris dancers and garland wreaths and maypoles could ever be. There was something so much more sinister about the dance that ended with youngest and most beautiful being offered up to the hag so that she might be born again.

Alex looked again at the woman's back as she walked away, at the gap in the surgical gown that exposed the curve of her spine and its ladder of bones, and the flawless skin there, and knew that she was looking at a rejuvenated Emmaline Barnes. Sacrifices had been made and the ancient goddess was born again.

Instinctively, Alex moved to follow her, but before she'd even let go of the railings she felt the phone vibrate in her pocket.

Julie's face looked up at her from the screen as she answered it.

"Hey, you," she said, still watching Emmaline Barnes.

"You busy?"

"Always. What's up?"

He took longer than she'd have liked to answer. A seed of doubt flourished, rooting in her belly.

"Josh is a mess. Damiola's dead."

That stopped her cold.

She didn't ask how.

Dozens of questions occurred to her, shock bringing them thick and fast. She only asked one, because it was the only one that mattered in that second.

"Where are you?"

"Just left the cemetery. We're heading toward the old wood behind the Rothery. I'll explain later." Julie gave her a rendezvous point on the south side of the river, on the outskirts of the estate. It was no more than twenty minutes' walk from where she was. Five in a cab.

"I'll be there. Look after him, Jules."

"You know I will."

"I know . . . But I'm asking anyway."

"Stick to the backstreets," he told her. "It's hell out here."

Alex walked out on her responsibilities at the hospital. As the crow flies, it would have been quicker to stick to the main roads, but with fires rising across the city, and the fact she couldn't transform into a black-winged bird, Alex had no choice but to take a convoluted path through backstreets and narrow alleyways. She kept on walking until she saw three people coming toward her in the opposite direction; Julie, Josh, and a woman she half-recognized but didn't know.

Her brother was a mess. He looked like a tramp buried beneath layers of coats. He was wearing Damiola's on top of Boone's. He must have been roasting beneath the weight of fabric. His face was red and puffy from where he'd been crying; though, there were no tears now, only steely determination.

He leaned on Julie.

"You look like crap," Alex said, her lips twitching into something that never quite became a smile.

"Love you, too," Josh said. "He told you?"

She nodded.

"I don't know what I'm supposed to say. I'm not good with stuff like this."

"Just say you'll help me finish this."

"You know I will. You and me against the world, Bro."

He laughed at that, and it was almost as much of a laugh as her smile had been a smile.

They walked and talked, not looking toward their final destination. There was a denial in the way they looked down or looked at each other as Alex filled in the gaps they didn't already know; how Emmaline Barnes, the old woman she'd been looking after forever, had finally broken her silence to call the locked-in kids *Sleepers,* and begged her to protect them. She didn't explain how she knew what they were. How was she supposed to explain that the May Queen had planted the images right there in her head as her fingernails dug into her temples? Alex told the others how when she'd rung around the hospitals, she heard the same thing every time: in less than twenty-four hours Annie Cho, Bethany Laws, and Kate Jenkins had all died, all of them in suspicious circumstances. There were only two Sleepers left. Two girls between Arawn and closing the gate to the Underworld. Both Ellie and Julie knew the names. As they crossed the litter-strewn streets of the Rothery, they offered the police perspective, sharing the mundane narrative from the incident room.

Alex finally looked toward the specter of Coldfall Wood, the ancient trees coming to life for her in a way that they never had before in a lifetime of living in their shadow. Julie told her that the working theory was that Stephen Blackmoore and Rupert Brooke were behind the deaths. Which was right, but so very, very wrong, as well. Alex struggled with how to frame the truth that she'd been caring for a hibernating deity—the mother, maiden, and crone deep-rooted in myth—and that Blackmoore and Brooke were no longer themselves, but Hunters doing the bidding of a reborn Stag King in severing the mortal ties that bound them still to the other place. She saw it all now, had glimpsed the grandeur of what was lost, seen the kingdoms unfurled before her, the bright beauty of the shires and rolling hills, the shimmering blue waters of the inland lakes and the stark-white cliffs that marked the edge of Albion. She had seen it all as it had once been, back before the first invasion of the Bain Shee and their Blight Priests and the souring of the land as mankind plundered Mother's heart for all of her riches. She felt sick drawing on the memory; conflicted. No one ever believed themselves the villains of the peace, but having glimpsed what lay beyond that wall, remembering the horrors of the vampiric creatures lurking there, she could almost understand why Arawn would lay waste to everything to stop them, such were the stakes in his mind. This wasn't his world, though; this wasn't the place the May Queen or the Horned God had left behind. It had moved on. Whatever essence of magic there might have been once was long gone, in the same way that the coal and oil reserves were being depleted. It was the way of all things. New forms of energy would be found, be it the sun, the moon, or the air. Things hadn't changed that much in the centuries since the land had yielded up its last dregs of magic. The land endured. No matter the hell it was put through, it endured.

She looked around them, at the red-brick Eden that was the Rothery, as man-made a canker on the corpse of the world as ever built, but she didn't see the rot; she saw homes, safe places, and despite everything, despite the grime and the decay and everything that had happened to her family here, for the first time in years she saw hope, too. That was just how close the bond was between the mythological, the monstrous, and the mundane. "But I know how we win."

"How?" Julie shook his head. "There are *four* of us. We don't have tanks or guns or bombs. There's nothing special about any of us." She didn't contradict him. "We don't have a prayer."

She wanted to tell him prayers were useless anyway. He was right; they wouldn't stand a chance going toe-to-toe with the old gods and their rioting faithful. But they didn't need to. That wasn't their win. "We need to look for the exhaust port in the Death Star."

Josh burst out laughing. He shook his head. "Trust you to nerd it up in the face of certain death."

"It's a gift," she agreed. "We didn't start this war, and the fighting on the streets are the first skirmishes of something much bigger. We can't allow Arawn to dictate the terms of this fight, because you're right, we can't beat him like that."

"It's about more than just him," She said. "He wants what we want, but is capable of acts that to us must seem incredibly evil simply because all he cares about is banishing the greater evil."

"Like the greater good?" Ellie said.

She nodded. "Exactly that."

"Then how do we beat him and his kind without the greater evil winning?" Ellie asked for all of them.

She thought of Aos Shee's weapon, Freagarthach, that the old woman had shown her, and the warrior's tomb where it lay waiting for a righteous soul to wield it once more. It offered hope. Light in the gathering darkness. "The greater evil, they're monsters of mythology. It is about balance. There are the Bain Shee—the evil—on one side; the Aos Shee—the good—on the other: light and dark. They are mythic creatures, creatures of the fae lands. Dökkálfar and Ljósálfar, the Norse called them, opposing sides in the eternal conflict of good and evil. It doesn't matter what we call them; they don't change. Names don't mean anything. They don't make a difference. Their nature remains the same. There is us, there is them. We need a weapon equally mythic in nature to fight them. A sword to kill a king. We won't find that here. We've lost the magic, whatever there once was, but we might, just might, find it over there. So, we do what we came here to do. We walk into the woods, find the gate we know is in there, and cross over to the other side," Alex almost said *to the Dark Side,* but caught herself before that slipped out. "And find that sword. Arawn wants the gate closed, we know that much, so we can't let that happen. Not on his terms. The Sleepers are in there. Their spirits. Souls. Whatever you want to call it. Kids are in there because of what you did." She looked at her brother as she leveled the accusation. He didn't deny it. "There may only be two left now, but that's still two innocent kids holding the way open. We need to do everything we can to find that sword, and if we can, bring those kids home."

She set off with purpose, marching toward the trees.

The ancient forest had begun to spill out into the streets of the council estate. Nature in all of her glorious color and vibrant life had begun to peer up through the cracks and make her presence felt. The trees themselves wore mosslike green beards. The east wind blew through the branches, stirring the leaves into a gentle rush of sound like urgent whispers spreading through the trees back to the Gatekeeper waiting by the archway into the Annwyn.

She didn't wait for the others to follow her into the woods.

Alex knew the path to take as the trail led up the winding slope through the woodland. She brushed aside trailing branches, and pushed through overgrown bushes and bracken until she could see the glow of the gateway in the fairy ring in front of her, and the teen standing between her and another world.

41

They watched him from the shelter of the trees.

The teen didn't move from his position. Julie whispered his name: "Tommy Summers." For the longest time Alex was convinced that whatever entity had been piloting him had gone, leaving him empty.

His stare was utterly vacuous. He saw nothing. He heard nothing. He simply waited.

For something.

He wasn't going anywhere.

The gate itself was a thing of otherworldly beauty: wholly natural, with curls of mist rippling around its foot. A trick of perspective made it look as though the branches of trees behind it formed the arch. The illusion meant that from where they were crouched the leaves of each tree appeared entangled. The moonglow cast the gateway in molten silver.

She didn't realize she was holding her breath until her lungs burned and she was forced to breathe.

Julie mimed making a rush at the gate, but that wasn't going to work.

They needed to think.

She shook her head.

Josh scratched at the rough patch of bristle growing through his cheek.

They weren't going to be able to get through the gate with the teenager blocking their way.

"We need a distraction," she whispered. "Something to draw him away from the gate."

Josh nodded.

He rooted around in his pockets, digging down beneath the layers of Damiola's coat to the pocket of Boone's greatcoat beneath it, and pulled out his grandfather's lighter and tobacco tin.

She thought for a moment he was planning on lighting up, but as he whispered the word, "Fire," she understood.

He had everything he needed to make a small blaze right there in that tin.

The trees were too green, and the forest itself was still damp from the rain of yesterday.

Josh peeled Damiola's coat off, and wadded it up in a heap on the ground. She watched him loosen the screw on the petrol lighter then splash the smallest flecks of lighter fluid onto the material. It seeped in through the weave. "Give me some space. He's going to come this way; you circle around, get through that gate."

"You?"

"I'll be right behind you."

They broke rank, running almost silently between the trees, coming around in a wide arc to rush the gate from the other side the moment the Gatekeeper moved.

Alex couldn't take her eyes off her brother as he thumbed the lighter's wheel. That one tiny motion conjured a small flame. Josh watched it for a second, mumbling some sort of prayer or promise over it, then touched the flame to the material.

For a long moment it looked like it wasn't going to burn, then she saw the vapors turn blue as the flame took hold. Seconds later it was burning. Josh backed away, moving off to the right, careful to keep the denser brush between him and the burning coat. The flame would do the trick; the erratic movement would draw the eye, and given his nature it was a safe bet the Gatekeeper, like the rest of his kin, was attuned to the forest in some way. Wood burns. Fire is the most natural threat to his ancient habitat. If anything was going to pose threat enough to draw him away from the gate, it stood to reason it would be fire.

They just had to make those few seconds of opportunity count.

Alex crouched and waited, every muscle tense, ready to bolt.

He didn't move.

He didn't blink.

"Come on," she urged. "Come on."

It worked.

The Gatekeeper hurried to investigate, curiosity turning into panic in a couple of seconds.

It was now or never.

Alex burst out of the cover of the trees and ran, head down, arms and legs pumping furiously, trying to force every millisecond and millimeter of speed out of her body before her legs buckled. Twenty feet from the gate she risked looking up and around. The gateway looked like a solid wall, a thick soup of impenetrable mist. The illusion of the branches as keystones holding the portal in place was betrayed by her angle of approach. There was nothing holding the gateway open or in place; not the stones around it, not the trees above and behind it. It simply stood there, a gateway to another world. To her left she could see Julie and Ellie running hell for leather toward her.

She couldn't see Josh.

Alex half-turned; the move costing her momentum as she tried to see her brother within the trees.

She heard him shout, "RUN!"

And did as she was told, still looking back over her shoulder as she stumbled into the mist.

She saw him then, trying to dodge around the brutish Gatekeeper, but before she could cry out, her momentum carried her into the mist and he was lost to her.

She felt something brush up against her face—not curls of the mist she had plunged into, something soft that beat at her face and eyes over and over, buffeting, battering, a ceaseless assault of black wings—crows. Guardians on the threshold, keeping watch between worlds. The birds churned around her, cawing and crying louder and louder, their voices becoming awful shrieks in her ears. It was impossible to tell how many of the birds assailed her as they became a vortex around Alex's body. She didn't fight them, even though every instinct screamed for her to put her hands up to her face to ward them off. Instead she tried to slow her breathing, to control the rising fear, and keep on walking into the mist one step at a time.

And then the birds were gone—if they had ever been there to begin with.

The shift left her disorientated. She pushed on as the ground beneath her feet lost its solidity. One heartbeat, it was there; the next. it was simply gone and she was falling forward with nothing to break her fall. She couldn't trust her own senses. Sensations assailed her. She could still feel the sting of the crows' wings, and the scratches of those black beaks against her cheek and chin, but everything was different now. Robbed of sight, the other senses amplified the intensity of the transition. The air against her skin turned cold, the chill of the mist a dozen degrees lower than the evening she'd stepped out of. Elegiac whispers wove around her, voices of the lost and damned begging her to save them. They were so much colder than the air. Her nostrils burned with the acrid sting of blood and carrion and days-old death.

Alex flailed out, grasping frantically for something to take hold of as she fell forward. And still the barrage of sounds, tastes, and foul smells assailed her senses, overwhelming her.

There was nothing to grab a hold of in this No Place. There was nothing of any *substance*. What there was were other noises that took focus to distinguish from one another; the clash of steel, ancient battles being fought out endlessly, the dead dying all over again and again in this land between lands, where time held no sway and the gods had long since forgotten. Bright spots of light danced across her blind eyes, flaring in the endless darkness like fireworks going off against her retinas. Finally, the whispers merged into a single voice welcoming her home in a tongue she knew she had never learned, but knew. The meaning of the words were rooted deep in the primitive part of her brain. The voice, too, was familiar: Emmaline Barnes. The Badb. Macha, the Morrigu, Anu. Whatever the name she went by, the voice belonged to Mother, just like the crows that had met her as she moved between worlds.

Suddenly she wasn't falling. The shift was jarring.

Alex stumbled a step, her knees buckling beneath the sudden resistance of the unseen ground, before she straightened up. She reached out blindly, calling out into the mist. There was no answer. The mist was no less claustrophobic, visibility no better, but the world at last felt as though it had a horizon, even if she couldn't see it, and that made all the difference.

The mist, she realized, wasn't a mist at all. It was the spirits of the dead, wisps of their life force still bound to this place, living between the cracks of our world and the next, unable to let go of the life that had already left them. The chill gripped her heart and, like the dead that instilled it, refused to relinquish its hold on her. She'd never been religious, despite her upbringing. She'd never had faith, not like her mother. She'd only ever gone to Sunday school to collect the stickers, and when she'd got fed up with trying to learn off by heart the little passages from the bible, those stickers had lost their appeal. With the realization of the mist's nature, faces began to form within it. They weren't familiar. They weren't her dead haunting her, though she had enough of those to last a lifetime thanks to Seth Lockwood. They were just faces—and more likely than not, just figments of her imagination; her mind seeing things that weren't there, like the kid's game where you tried to find shapes in the clouds.

Alex put one foot in front of another, taking a first step in this other place.

And another.

And with each successive step the mist seemed to thin, the faces dissolving, and through the wisps and smokelike tendrils, she began to recognize the features of an unspoiled landscape taking shape around her. Off in the distance to the left, she could just make out the silhouettes of the first trees of a great wood; to the right, rolling hills, and spread out before her, vast open fields.

Free of the cloying fog at last Alex stumbled and sank to her knees. She fell forward onto her hands.

She was alone. An endless landscape stretched out in front of her, no sign of humanity to mar the land. There was a flickering glow far, far in the distance: a beacon calling out to her. She yearned to push herself up to her feet and walk toward it, but something, some deep buried instinct like her gift with the language she'd never learned, warned her away from that light. No good could come of walking toward it.

They come, Mother said, her voice all around Alex.

She saw a low, dry stone wall marking off one side of the field. It was crumbling in places, uneven in others; the flat stones piled one on top of another. They gave her a detail to focus on as she tried to gather her wits.

She felt sick.

Her stomach churned. Nausea clawed up at her throat. Her head spun, her balance completely undone by the translocation. She felt as though she could no longer trust the proof of her own eyes, that the world as she knew it might suddenly veer away beneath her at any moment and leave her hanging. It was a momentary sensation. It didn't last.

There was no color in any of it though, she realized. The place was devoid of life, like the mist that clung to it. The great gray land of the Annwyn, home of the banished gods of our past. Thick cloud patterns swirled and churned overhead, moving faster than they had any right to, like time-lapse photography had been used to re-create the world around her.

Alex turned to look back the way she'd come, only to see the rising bank of a muddy hill, clumps of long grass spiking up in patches here and there, and no sign of the ancient forest. The gate was nowhere to be seen.

There was no moon in the sky, no sun, but then there was no night and no day here, only a gray grim world.

Ellie Taylor collapsed out of the ancient path they had traveled into the thin air in front of Alex's eyes. Julie was three steps behind her; hands over his face and eyes, as he struggled to keep the sights and sounds of the mist at bay. Ellie stumbled away from him, and doubled over, retching violently.

Julie knelt beside her, but she pushed him away.

A chill breeze blew across the hillside.

He saw Alex on her knees looking up at him and ran to her, sweeping her up in a fierce embrace.

"Where . . . I just . . . I don't . . ." He couldn't manage a full sentence. She couldn't blame him. She just . . . she didn't . . . either. "I saw him . . . Taff . . . I think . . . in there . . . But it couldn't be him . . . That blackness . . . I can't go back in there." He shook his head, a little at first, but every time it moved from right to left the shaking became more exaggerated and he couldn't stop it.

"You don't have to," she promised. It was a promise she knew she couldn't keep, not if he wanted to go home again. But with no gate in front of them, only those few receding tendrils of mist that had clung to Julie and Ellie as they'd stumbled out of the ancient pathway, there was no easy way home for them to take. "Where's Josh?"

"He was right behind us," Julie told her, looking back over his shoulder as though he expected to see Josh right there and not a world away. And as though summoned, Josh stumbled out of the rolling mist into the gray landscape of the Annwyn, Boone's greatcoat flapping around his legs as he caught his balance. He staggered forward, twisting around awkwardly as though fending off some unseen blow. A scream tore from his lips as he flapped ineffectually at his face.

Alex looked at her brother as he struggled to stay on his feet.

Something was wrong.

As he turned back toward her, she saw that his face was deathly pale.

"Josh?"

He slumped forward, clutching at his side. As the coat fell away from him she caught the glimpse of silver—steel—buried deep in his side.

Blood spilled between his fingers.

It took her a moment to realize he was trying to pull the knife out.

She yelled at him, "No!" and ran toward him.

He didn't listen.

He pulled the knife slowly out, screaming at the pain as it slid through the meat of his body, the serrated edge doing more damage on the way out than it had on the way in.

He didn't look up. He only had eyes for the knife. His hands pressed down against his blood-soaked shirt. There were three other tears in the fabric, each one bloody, and one long slash across his chest, which wasn't deep but looked the worst of them all. He looked back over his shoulder, fear written deep in his gray flesh, but there was no sign of pursuit.

She had no way of knowing that it was the same knife that had killed Musa Dajani to open the gateway. She couldn't see the symmetry involved in that same knife delivering the killing blow to her brother. The knife had been acting like a plug, stemming the loss of blood. Without it, the life was pumping out of Josh one heartbeat at a time. "I've got you. I've got you." Everything she said was coming in double sentences, the same imprecations repeated. "Look at me, Josh. Look at me. I'm here. I'm here." And again, "I've got you."

He didn't have the strength to argue.

He let go of the knife and sank forward, collapsing into his sister's arms. The knife fell at his feet.

"I'm not ready to go," he managed. His eyes were glassy, the light flickering and failing behind them. "I did this. I need to make it right."

"Shut up, stupid man. You're not going anywhere, Josh, you hear me? Because those are shit last words. You are *not* going to die on me."

PART 3

Albion goes to Eternal Death: In Me all Eternity.
Must pass thro' condemnation, and awake beyond the
  Grave!
No individual can keep these Laws, for they are death
To every energy of man, and forbid the springs of life;
Albion hath enterd the State Satan! Be permanent O
  State!
And be thou for ever accursed! that Albion may arise
  again.

—WILLIAM BLAKE, *JERUSALEM*

42

Josh lay on the muddy hill.

They gathered around him.

Silence hung heavy around the intruders.

Alex held her brother's hand, willing him to live.

"We can't stay here," Julie said. He had a flair for stating the obvious.

"We can't just leave him," Alex argued.

"I know."

"Then what do you suggest? We can't go back, there's no gate here. And it's not like we can carry him in his condition. It'll kill him."

"I know," he said again.

"Then do me a favor and shut the fuck up until you do know something," Alex snapped.

That shut him up for all of thirty seconds. He shook his head. He scanned the mist-wreathed horizon, eyes drawn toward the fire burning in the distance. It seemed to be closer than it had been just a moment ago. "Maybe someone there can help us?"

"No," Alex said, definitively. One syllable that brooked no argument.

He didn't push it.

"Look, I'll carry him. We can't just leave him here, and we can't just sit here waiting for him to die. We've got to do *something*."

She shook her head. "We can't move him. Not yet. I've got to get the bleeding under control."

"We can scout around," Ellie offered, meaning her and Julie. "Tell us what you need. See if we can't find something that will . . ." she was going to say *help*—that much was obvious—but without a miracle, nothing was going to help.

"Do that. I need to try and pack the wound. Stop the bleeding as best I can. I'm going to need a fire. Gather some wood, anything that will burn. We're going to need to get the metal of that knife *hot*." She was thinking aloud, but at least she was thinking. Boone's old lighter by itself wouldn't burn anywhere near hot enough to cauterize the wound, even temporarily, but the metal blade of the knife that had almost killed Josh might just be what would end up saving him. That is, if she could get it hot enough. "And look for bark, willow bark, that's good . . . hawthorns . . . the thin vines of willow, something like that we can use to bind the bark over the compress to keep pressure on the wound. Anything that'll buy even a little time." She was trying to think of anything the land might provide. Superglue would have been better, but it wasn't like that was something people carried around in their back pockets.

"On it."

"See if you can find something we can use to build a makeshift stretcher, while you're at it. Let's be positive. Because you're right. I know you're right. We can't stay here. So as soon as I've got the bleeding under control, we're moving out." She pressed down on the wound. Josh's skin felt cold and sticky through the cloth.

"We'll be fast," Julie promised. "Just keep him alive until we get back."

She nodded. "I plan on it."

She didn't watch them go.

She turned her attention to her brother. "Okay, Josh, stay with me, okay? I know you're in there, so listen to my voice. We're going to get through this, you and me. You aren't leaving me now."

He didn't answer her.

Working quickly, and trying not to think about what she was doing, Alex peeled away Josh's coat, using the knife to cut it off his shoulders and pull it out from beneath him. She wadded up part of the back tail to fashion a pillow for his head, and make him as comfortable as she could, then cut the shirt away in strips. She used the knife to make the wadding she would use to pack the wounds when the others got back. Scrunching one of the strips up, she used it to press down on the worst of the wounds and kept applying pressure while the cloth soaked up the blood.

Without water to clean the cuts up, and a needle and thread to suture it, anything she did was only ever going to be a temporary fix, but temporary was better than no fix at all.

She kept applying pressure, willing the others to return.

Every minute seemed to drag on forever.

She started filling the silence with anything and everything that occurred to her, starting with the fact she was really glad he wouldn't be wearing that ratty old coat of Boone's anymore, but even as she cursed the old man's fashion taste, she thanked God for the fact he smoked like a chimney right up until his dying day, because without that lighter of his, her brother would be joining him in the great working men's club in the sky.

Ellie was the first back; her arms filled with thin kindling, stuff small enough and brittle enough to get a fire going. Julie was a couple of minutes behind her, his arms overflowing with bark and thicker deadfall, even something that looked a little like hawthorn with those spiky needlelike thorns. "Will this do?" he asked dumping it all out on the floor.

She nodded. It would. Or more precisely, it would have to. That was a different thing.

"There's a lighter in the coat pocket. Use it to get the fire going."

"I flunked out of Boy Scouts," Julie said, trying to lighten the mood as he fumbled around in the ruined coat for the fixings of a fire whilst Ellie banked up the kindling and added a couple of the strips of cloth beneath to help get the blaze going.

It took a few minutes, and a couple of times it threatened to go out before it got started, but eventually they got a small fire burning, and began to add a couple of the bigger logs to it, so that it generated some proper heat.

"Put the knife in the fire. Only the blade. I've got to be able to hold it. I'm going to use it to cauterize the blood vessels before I pack the wound up."

"Jesus," Julie said. "Are you sure he can take that?"

Out loud the idea of burning the damaged vessels sounded barbaric, but she knew what she was doing. And it wasn't like they had a lot of choice in the matter.

"Next best thing. I'm sure that he *can't* live without it. The knife's got to be hot. Really hot. It's got to burn the center of the wound until the skin crusts over."

Julie nodded.

She kept on pressing down on the wound; desperately enough that she was surprised the bones beneath didn't crack.

Finally, Julie handed her the knife.

"This is going to hurt," Alex told her brother, even though he couldn't hear her. She pressed the blade down flat across the two-inch cut, charring the edges of the gash, and trying not to gag at the sweet reek of burning flesh that emanated from it. She didn't flinch even as Josh came back screaming as the pain seared through him. She kept on pressing the blade down, reheating it, and pressing it down again until it stopped bleeding and a thick black crust had formed across the wound. He blacked out somewhere around the fourth or fifth time, and for a moment she thought she'd killed him, but his pulse was there, thready, but there when she felt for it at his neck. The other wounds were still bleeding, but none of them were deep or particularly threatening so she left them.

Everything about the next couple of minutes was filled with urgency as she set about packing the wounds and binding them. Without tape to hold the layer of bark in place, she improvised, using the long thin vines that Julie had stripped from a willow tree and tying them off as best she could. They wouldn't hold up against any sort of exertion, but in terms of the difference between life and death they were definitely tilting the scale the right way.

None of it would do much good in the long-term. They needed to get Josh to a hospital, which meant they needed to get out of here one way or another.

Suddenly all thoughts of ancient swords and fabled towers were a million miles away. She didn't care about the Sleepers or the fate of the world she called home, because the only home she really had these days was right here in her arms clinging on to life.

When she looked up again the ghost light on the horizon was so much closer than it had been even a few minutes before.

She could just make out the silhouette of what looked like a flat-bottomed boat, and realized what she'd taken to be smooth rolling fields was actually becalmed water, and the light, a torch burning in the hand of the boatman guiding it toward their shore.

A flicker of movement off to the left caught her eye, but before Alex could focus on it, whatever it was, was gone. "Did you see that?" she asked.

"What?" Julie asked, meaning obviously he hadn't.

"I don't know. Something over in the trees." Even as she said it, Alex felt the peculiar creeping sensation of being watched. "There's someone over there."

"I don't see anyone," Ellie said, but she was up on her feet and walking toward the trees before either of them could stop her.

Alex heard a rustling in the trees, a rush of movement that pre-saged a huge dark muscular blur bursting out of cover. It took a moment to process what she was seeing, and refocus that blur into an enormous emerald-colored dog barreling toward Ellie at incredible speed. Huge didn't cut it; the dog was bigger than any beast Alex had ever seen, more like a panther than a hound as it ran at Ellie. The sheer power behind it was awe-inspiring. There was no mistaking it for any creature's prey. This was an alpha predator. Ellie saw it too late, and couldn't run. She had no way of getting out of its path as the beast's powerful gait devoured the distance between them in seconds.

At the last, its gait changed, the muscles of its hindquarters tensing, ready to spring, then launched itself at Ellie.

There was enough power behind its leap that the impact would have snapped Ellie's spine in two, but as the green dog launched itself at her, she hurled herself to the ground, and rolled as the beast's momentum carried it over her.

It hit the ground with the natural grace of a hunter and kept on running.

Julie snatched up a brand from the fire and rushed the dog, flailing around with the burning wood, sweeping it around in great wide arcs that had the flame guttering and threatening to blow out. He lunged toward the animal, using its momentum against it to steer it out wide, away from Ellie as she struggled to rise. It looked for one sickening second as though the beast was about to give up on him and set its sights on easier prey—the kneeling Alex and her brother in her arms—but Julie wasn't about to let that happen. He yelled, making enough noise to raise the dead, and charged the huge dog head-on, slashing the torch across its face again and again, driving it back toward the water's edge.

Alex hadn't realized how cold the air in this place was until that moment, with the beast only feet away. She saw something in the green dog's rage-filled eyes she couldn't explain. The fire burning in them went beyond cunning. It was recognition.

It *knew* her.

This wasn't some dumb animal. It had sought her out.

And now it had found her.

There was no wind. The air between them was absolutely still.

Julie drove the green dog back three paces, dancing forward and back like a fencer, the burning branch his rapier.

It gave ground reluctantly; its fear of the fire in his hand the only thing preventing it from tearing out his throat.

The beast growled deep in its belly. It was caught between rage, hate, and fear; its entire body absolutely still, heckles risen, jowls curled back. Julie slashed the burning branch through the air again, risking a step closer.

The animal didn't move.

Ellie raced across to the fire to grab a second burning branch while Julie kept the beast at bay.

Out on the flat gray sea the fire drew closer still.

Alex could make out the boatman's hood and the deep shadow obscuring his face. There were others in the boat, six women dressed in white. She could just make out their mumbled prayers as the boat drifted closer.

The beast on the shore wasn't giving ground.

Ellie stood side by side with Julie, the fire in their hands giving the great dog no avenue of escape.

Ellie stepped to the left and back half a pace, opening up an escape route for the animal even as Julie lunged forward again, jabbing the burning end of his branch into the beast's muzzle.

It snapped and snarled, nearly taking his hand off with its powerful jaws. The bite left ragged tears in the sleeve of his coat. Even from where she was, Alex could see blood on the dog's yellow teeth. It tensed to launch another savage attack on Julie, but Ellie stepped in, shrieking at the animal and slashing wildly at its face. The fire seared away a great swathe of fur along the side of its muzzle. The dog growled deep in its throat, and clawed at the ground, raking five deep gouges in the gray grass. Alex thought it was about to launch another ferocious attack on her friends, but with more fire approaching from the sea the beast knew when it was beaten—at least temporarily—and took the escape offered. It darted between Julie and Ellie, splashing along the skirt of the water. It left deep prints in the ground, the pad of each paw bigger than her hand, fingers outstretched. She watched it go, bounding away with a burst of speed they couldn't have matched if they had wanted to.

The dog disappeared into the trees.

Alex hadn't thought once about using the knife against it. She wasn't sure it would have had the slightest effect on the beast's thick emerald-colored hide, hot or not.

Julie reached down to put his hand there beside one of the prints, and pressed his fingers down into the soft ground, and like grains of sand it parted around them to accommodate him.

Ellie Taylor was the first to say anything. "What the fuck was that?"

"A devil dog," Julie said, and for just a moment she couldn't be sure if he was joking or not—but of course he wasn't. Devil dogs were deeply rooted in the mythology of the Isles. "A fucking Hellhound. Did you see its eyes? They were burning. I mean like fire. Properly burning." A Hellhound was exactly what it was. And, she knew what its presence signified. The green dog had another name, one that Alex knew because of the old woman's invasion in her mind: Cù Sìth. They were harbingers of death that came to bear souls away to the afterlife.

It hadn't been hunting her; it had come for Josh.

Alex looked down at her brother, and realized somewhere between the dog breaking free of the trees and being driven off he had stopped breathing.

When she looked up again, she saw that the boat had brushed up against the shore and the six women were in the process of disembarking one by one, their ethereally thin white gowns soaked up to the knees where they stood in the dead calm water. Each one bore an uncanny resemblance to the other, marking them all as sisters. They each possessed the same fine-boned features, the same long raven-black hair, the same piercing blue eyes, and the same empty expression.

Alex didn't care how creepily similar they were. She only had eyes for the boatman standing on the prow with the tiller in his hand. In his free hand he held a blazing torch that burned brighter than she could bear to look directly at. She'd been wrong, his face wasn't lost in the shadows beneath his hood; his face *was* the stuff of shadows.

The Sisters came up the gray beach two by two; heads bowed.

As they drew nearer the words of their singsong prayer became more distinct. There was incredible beauty in their song. Each voice rose and fell in perfect counterpoint to the others. The words, she knew, came together to weave a spell of life around her brother. She was witnessing her first glimpse of the earth magic that her world had lost, and it was enchanting.

"Save him," she begged, but they did not break their song.

They chanted the creeping presence of death down, driving it out of his flesh in a treaclelike tar that seeped out of the side of the willow bark compress, and kept on chanting as they gathered around Josh to take him in their arms and lift him slowly. They made it look effortless. Her brother lay lifeless in their arms as the six Sisters waded into the water. The surf lapped soundlessly around their legs as they bore him back to the flat-bottomed boat and laid him down on the timbers. One by one the Sisters climbed back into the boat until the final one turned and offered her hand to Alex.

She looked back toward the trees and the lurking presence of the Cù Sìth she knew was still there, and mouthed the words, "Not today," before she took the Sister's hand and joined them in the boat.

43

"We will restore him," Sister Mazoe assured her as they drifted effortlessly through the still sea. The boatman manned the tiller; his deep voice singing a haunting threnody that guided them home. There were no oars. No one rowed the boat. Alex caught snatches of words and phrases she almost understood in the boatman's ancient song. One phrase, *Ynys Afallach,* stood out from the rest because it meant something to the old woman. The Sisters were taking them to the Isle of Apples. It had been the home of Manannan mac Lir, the bearer of the legendary blade, Freagarthach. She felt the knot of fate weaving around them, bringing them to exactly where they needed to be. Alex knew other names for that place thanks to Emmaline Barnes's meddling in her mind: some called it the Fortunate Isle, others Paradise, and in the old tongue *Insula Avalonia.* The most familiar of all named it Avalon.

She didn't say *heal,* or *save,* Alex noticed.

Restore.

Alex didn't know whether that was a significant word choice or if she was reading too much into things.

She wasn't sure she could ever read too much into anything now.

"Where are we going?" she asked instead.

"To the Orchard," Mazoe said, as though that explained everything.

"How long will the journey take?"

"Time has little meaning, Sister, but by your reckoning, two, perhaps three days shall pass in the land you have come from. In that way, it is a long journey. In other ways, it is just over the horizon, though you cannot see it for the enchantments that weave a thick mist around the high tower to keep it safe from accidental travelers."

"He'll not live that long."

Sister Mazoe's smile was gentle, not patronizing but full of certainty. "Rest easy, Sister, he is in our care now. He will come back to you; you have my promise."

One of the other women, Sister Thiten, moved away from her wooden seat to kneel at Josh's side, and placed her hand over the willow bark. Her voice separated from the chorus, lifting above the whisper of the waves to swell all around him. For just a moment, less time than it took for the singer to draw in fresh breath, Alex saw a ghost of bluish light spark between the singer and her brother, a crackle of life moving from one to the other. The boat rocked slightly as the woman moved back to her seat. A moment later the third Sister, Glitonea, took her place at Josh's side. The soft cotton of her diaphanous dress fell across Josh as she leaned forward to place a tender kiss on his lips, breathing her song into him. The fourth Sister placed her hand atop Josh's heart and raised her head to the sky; her voice a delicate susurrus as it called out to the wind to hurry them home. One by one each of the Sisters knelt beside her brother, weaving their ancient magic around him.

At one point Josh opened his eyes, but they were like glass, simply reflecting the gray sky back at her.

He drifted in and out of consciousness as the boat sailed on.

Without thinking, Alex reached over the side and trailed her fingers in the still water. She couldn't understand how they were moving without anyone rowing, but had faith they would arrive at their miraculous destination as the Sister promised. A thoughtful hush settled over the boat as the Sisters' song lulled to a gentle wash of sound no louder than the splash of the prow as it cut through the water.

Alex reached out for Julie's hand.

They didn't speak. They didn't need to. Sometimes something as simple as human contact was enough. It spoke so much more intimately than words ever could. He squeezed her fingers.

And the boat drifted on.

Looking back, she could no longer see the shore.

Looking forward there was nothing to see.

She had no idea how long they'd been adrift, hours possibly. The mist gathered around them, thickening as they sailed into it, until it was impossible to see anything beyond the boatman's torch.

It was a light that would never go out, she realized.

"How did you know to come for us?" Julie asked, breaking the silence. It was a reasonable question. They must have disembarked the island long before the four of them had walked into Coldfall Wood.

"Our lord told us you would come," Sister Mazoe said. At least she thought it was Mazoe, the voice came from her direction but the mist was so thick now it was impossible to make out the details of her face. "It was foretold."

Julie didn't say anything to that.

Ellie hadn't said a word since the attack on the water's edge.

Another hour passed with only the gentle song of the Sisters for company. Visibility dwindled further still, until Alex couldn't see more than two feet in front of her face, beyond that was only shadow and indistinct shapes. She could no longer see if Josh was breathing, but as long as the Sisters sang she had to believe he was still with them. She had no choice but to trust their old ways, which she did far more than her own makeshift medicine.

She caught herself humming along with the gentle ripple of their song, and stopped, self-conscious.

"You are welcome to join us, Sister," Mazoe told Alex. "The more voices in the song, the more powerful its healing properties."

"But I don't know the words," Alex said, feeling stupid.

"You do not need to. The healing is in your heart. It is who you are. So sing if the spirit moves you. It can only help."

"I don't know . . ." Alex said, not so much an objection as doubting her own usefulness. Even so, before too long she found herself humming the healing melody once more and didn't stop herself this time.

And they drifted on, the boatman piloting them home.

Finally, what felt like forever later, Ellie Taylor broke her silence, pointing ahead to a looming dark shadow that turned the sky in the distance black. "What's that?"

"Murias," Sister Mazoe told her. "Where he dwells."

"He?"

"Our lord. Time is broken here. It has been since before he died. Our song now is all that remains of him. His last gift."

The tower solidified as the mists parted before them.

They heard the tolling of a bell guiding them in to shore.

A few minutes later the hull of the flat-bottomed boat ran aground and the boatman extinguished his light.

They were at journey's end.

They had reached the other side.

A seventh white-veiled Sister waited for them on the sands.

"No mortal eyes have seen this place for centuries," Mazoe told her, as she offered a hand to help Alex out of the boat. The water was icy cold around her calves.

The waiting woman bowed her head as they walked ashore with their burden.

She didn't acknowledge their arrival, but rather turned and walked away. At her feet a flame flickered to life between the cracks in a small cairn of stones. Small cairns lined the path all the way up to the door of a crumbling tower. As the woman passed each one, a small fire flickered and blossomed in her wake. Alex couldn't see how she was doing it, but the effect was uncomfortably funereal given their burden. The Sisters walked slowly up the winding path, once more giving full voice to their haunting song.

The mist thinned as they made the climb.

On either side, she saw apple trees. The skeletal limbs were over-burdened with ripe fruit, each tree carrying enough to feed a small army. The red of the fruit was the only color in this otherwise gray landscape.

The tower, Murias, as Mazoe had named it, took shape before them. Alex craned her neck trying to see the very top. The ramparts were crumbling, the stones weathered and broken from the battering they'd taken from the elements over however long they'd stood. Roses grew up the side of the wall, as gray as the stones they clung to.

There were no windows in the first three stories, and no obvious door on this side of the tower.

The Sisters followed the well-lit path through the Orchard, beside a ruin that stood in the shadow of the tower itself. There was no roof, though parts of the beams and cross braces were still visible where they were anchored in the walls. They had turned black with age and calcified like stone. Trees had begun to grow inside the walls of the ruin. They walked slowly along the crumbling wall toward the door of the high tower. It was like something out of a twisted fairy tale, though there was no Rapunzel at the top to let down her hair.

The Sisters approached the door.

The woman who had greeted them on the shore walked to the head of the procession, and rapped on the door three times with her knuckles. The door opened, though they couldn't see who stood behind it, and the procession filed slowly inside one by one.

Alex stood beside Julie. Ellie hung back a couple of steps behind them.

The mist had thinned, reduced now to little more than a ripple of white snakes curling around their ankles as they watched the Sisters' devotions.

The music swelled, the acoustics of the tower changing it, and in it Alex realized she was hearing something that went beyond simple music—if something that stirred the heart could ever be termed simple—and tapped into something more elemental. As the notes swelled to fill the air, they became the stuff of the land itself; this was the Song of Albion.

The tune cut through her like a razor's blade paring away her flesh to get all the way down to her soul.

And in that moment she found herself believing in something

bigger for the first time in her life. Alex hesitated to use the word *God,* as in the last few days her understanding of what that word actually meant had changed substantially. What the song tapped into was *creation*.

She let it wash over her, and in that moment of absolute reverie, she caught a flicker of movement out in her peripheral vision: the emerald dog had returned.

"Do not let it concern you, Sister," the old woman who had led the procession to the bier told her, reading her mind. She offered a gentle smile, her eyes filled with sadness. "The Cù Sìth will not find him within the keep of Murias."

"How can you be sure? It's out there. Somehow it followed us here."

"It is drawn to death, but your brother is under our protection. You have my word. The hound will not claim him today." Alex didn't want to ask the question that was on her mind, put there in no small part by the hound's persistence. The holy woman answered it anyway: "The Cù Sìth lingers because it smells death. Your brother is gravely ill. We cannot heal his damaged organs, but we can hold death at bay, weaving an enchantment around his body while it heals itself. The body needs time. Always. Time is the master."

"But if you can't heal him—"

"The song keeps his heart poised between one beat and the next, freezing time around him like a shell so that his body might recover from its wounds naturally. That is how I know he will live. Every moment we sing the song, he grows stronger. It will take time, but this is the place of immortals. Time is all that we have. He must remain here as long as it takes for his body to be restored. To move him is to risk letting the Cù Sìth in, for it will not leave these shores until it knows that it has been denied. That the dog lingers is a sign that death has yet to relinquish its grip on your brother, but we are stronger than death, Sister." In the distance, the bells tolled on. They sounded like Josh's pain being given voice. "It has no dominion in this place."

44

The police lined up against them in a barricade of blue. Voices carried up and down the line, barking orders, demanding they stay firm. Cries of "Hold the line!" echoed back and forth.

Robin sat on a garden wall, smiling to himself at a job well done.

He peeled a scrap of cloth away from his tattered shirt, tearing it away from the seam and held it up in front of his face. He let go, but it did not fall. The material hung there in the air, held in place by nothing but the pent-up tension in the street, waiting to explode, waiting to fall.

His smile spread at the sight of Arawn loitering between the blossom trees along the grass verge of this perfect slice of suburbia.

This battleground wasn't some broken-down cluster of paupers' shacks; there was wealth here, and comfort. Or at least there had been. Now there was row upon row of riot police shaking in their shoes, as they stood toe-to-toe with the youth of London.

This was good.

This was better than good.

This was bloody *fantastic*.

Robin stretched, making himself comfortable for the coming attractions as the front line pulled down plastic visors and raised equally plastic shields before they squared up to the growing army of kids. It was ritualistic. The trappings of war hadn't changed since he'd last walked this land. It didn't matter if the swords and bows were gone; the rituals remained the same. It was a dance. It always had been. The tension in one side was matched by a youthful swagger from those opposite them. The blacktop of the street between them would become their battlefield, and somewhere in the middle, as they clashed, the blood would spill back into the earth.

There was magic in blood. Nourishment. Life.

And that was just one part of the loss that had leached the magic out of Mother over the centuries. But all of that would change now. This was the first day of a new world. The buildings would fall. The houses would be burned down. The suffocating crap that put a layer between the land and her people would be torn up or pulled down until the factories and their pollutants were no more; the old reserves given the chance to replenish as the voracious appetites of man had been quelled once and for all. Everything they did now, all of the pain and suffering they inflicted, was in the name of a greater good. They were saving the land from the greatest threat it had ever faced—the scavengers and parasites that crawled all over it, stripping her bare with their insatiable hunger. They were fulfilling an ancient vow.

He looked at the kids. They really were his finest accomplishment. They were so ready to die, eager even to be battered down by the truncheons, Tasers, and tear gas of the riot police facing them simply because he had planted the seed in their minds when he had asked them if they were willing to answer the call.

The tension between both groups crackled in the air. The police were trying to kettle the protesters into bottlenecks of streets to minimize their efficacy, but the kids were having none of it. They struck back in the most basic of ways—hurling bricks and bottles at the lines of cops as they crept forward. The police kept their ranks, but it was a struggle as more and more kids piled into the protest. The crowd was easily five thousand strong, and barely held in check, and similar crowds were gathering all across the city, rising up to the call of the old god.

A bottle sailed over the heads of the police, trailing fire.

It shattered, bursting into flame where it splashed petrol all over the street.

They almost broke. They *almost* charged.

But somehow their discipline held.

Robin hopped down from his perch and walked between the ranks of the enemies, putting himself in the middle of the battlefield. He looked at the kids, one face after another, and saw their hunger for the coming fight, before he turned to the police and saw the dread in their eyes.

A boy broke rank and ran at the line of riot shields.

In response, the officers hammered their truncheons off the toughened plastic, raising hell.

There was no rhythm to the noise. It was noise for the sake of noise, aimed at putting fear into the minds of the kids facing them. Each booming sound promised broken bones and pain.

It wasn't enough.

The police edged toward him; one step, another, encroaching on the middle ground.

"I wouldn't do that if I were you," Robin said, lightly enough, like they were all old friends here.

And, as they shuffled another step forward, not quite as one this time, green shoots began to creep up through the tarmac beneath their boots.

"Seriously," he said, sweetly. "It's not a good idea."

But that didn't stop them. Another step, and then another, close enough that they could almost reach out and touch him with the blunt end of their truncheons if they stepped forward into the swing.

The green shoots sprouted up, curling around their feet, tangling with their laces, and climbing higher, to get to the bare skin of their ankles, where they used their thorns to cut open the skin and burrow down. He watched as the green shoots spread like veins through the bodies of the officers, their screams drowned out by the cacophonous banging of truncheon on shield in the ranks of the men behind them.

The men were rooted to the spot.

They couldn't step forward; couldn't fall back.

The green shoots of vegetation wouldn't *let* them.

Now that they had taken root in the men's bodies their growth turned pernicious. Green veins became capillaries and arteries and—hidden by their uniforms—grew up through their groins into their guts, into their armpits, and down their arms so they thickened, clogging up the blood flow into their hands, and up their necks into their faces, growing with every heartbeat until there was nowhere left for them to go except out of the dead men who still swayed on their feet but couldn't fall.

"I did warn you," Robin said. "Okay, kids, they're all yours. Have at it."

He stepped aside to let the children go to war.

Arawn looked on approvingly.

45

It was snowing.

Josh held out a hand to catch a few of the flakes. They didn't melt on his fingers. They settled, gray on his palm. It wasn't snow. It was ash. Ash was falling from the sky. He looked around. He didn't recognize this place. He couldn't remember coming here, wherever *here* was. There were trees. All manner of trees. Oak, sycamore, silver birch, and a different kind of ash altogether.

There was something about the place.

It felt different.

He struggled to think of a word that best described it, but all he could fasten on was mystical. There was an air of the ancient about it.

He walked on into the falling ash.

The flakes reduced visibility to no more than a dozen feet or so in front of his face. He walked slowly on. He was lost. The last thing he remembered was the savagery of the knife going into his side again and again. Not even the pain, just the surprise of the attack and the brutality of the stabbing itself. Everything after that moment was vague, as if it, too, were damped down beneath blankets of ash. There were snatches of conversation, a few images—faces looking down at him—and above it, around it, beneath and inside it, the stench of burning flesh. But, beyond that: nothing.

And now he was here.

He wasn't stupid. He knew what this place was.

"You shouldn't be here," a voice said.

He couldn't see the speaker. The four words swirled around him in a rush. He tried to see through the patterns in the ash cloud. Slowly, up ahead, a shadow began to take shape. He recognized the ragged layers of coats and the magician's scuffed boots as Damiola walked through the ash toward him.

"You're dead," he said.

"And you don't look pleased to see me," the old man joked. "Do I look that bad? I flattered myself to imagine I would return to the dashing figure of my youth when I passed."

It had to be a trick. The enemy, somehow, playing with his mind, taunting him with what he wanted more in the world than anything else, a friendly face.

"I don't—"

The magician held up his hand to cut off any pointless denials or arguments about the impossibility of their meeting here, like this.

"I've waited a long time to see you again, Josh. Walk with me."

A long time? He'd been dead less than a couple of hours, Josh thought, but then remembered how strangely time itself seemed to flow around Glass Town, so why would it be any different in this place?

Josh joined the old man on one of the strangest walks of his lifetime. This was a desperately sad place, he realized. He could feel just how empty it was, devoid of the very essence of life. Of magic.

Damiola led him through trees and thickets of brambles along an old cobbled path toward a circle of standing stones.

"Just watch," he said. In the distance, Josh saw a flickering line of lights, torches burning in the gray night. Cloaked men, dressed in the colors of the forest, walked in a funereal procession toward them, circling the stones once, twice, three times, before entering and gathering at the altar. Josh heard the rise and fall of their chant. They were offering prayer, but to whom he had no idea.

Before they could finish, soldiers stepped out of the trees on either side, their steel swords shining bright in the moonlight.

The slaughter was both brief and brutal; the druids had nothing to defend themselves with. They simply surrendered to the weapons of their attackers. As the last man fell, his murderer turned and seemed to look right at Josh; his gaze piercing whatever veil separated them across time and space. The man's face was inhuman: pale translucent skin; hollow cheekbones, both delicate and sharp; and eyes of the most chilling blue, the only glimpse of color in this entire place.

"What's happening?"

"He is Aos Shee. And those druidic priests that fell before his blade would have been the death of the world," Damiola said.

"How do you know this?"

"Because this is my heritage. I was born here. He is my father. Or was. In the same way that he was your father, and so many more of the children of the Isles. He is Manannan. A hero for the ages and that sword in his hand is Freagarthach, the legendary Aos Shee blade."

"None of this looks heroic," Josh said.

"Unless you know the nature of the dead men, and what they were plotting to do to the land," the old man observed. "Perspective can change even the most brutal of actions. As I said, they were looking to bring about the death of this place. Their song was a chant of undoing. And this place, this circle of stones, like the fairy ring back in Coldfall Wood, is a weakness between the worlds, only what lies on the other side of this veil isn't London, it is the home of the Bain Shee, the enemy of man. Had they breached the weakness here and formed a bridgehead, that would have given them an entire world to conquer, and a way into ours.

"It was a war, lad. A war like none we've ever seen. A war for the land itself, the Earth Mother, the spoils. On one side, there was Macha and the Aos Shee; on the other, the Summer Queen and her king, Arawn, Lord of the Underworld. And between them, ordinary men, mortals, like Manannan. Like you. That war was waged for three generations. And then everything changed with the arrival of a new threat; the Bain Shee, an enemy so dangerous both put aside their enmity to fight them. But, at the last Arawn was sacrificed. The goddess hoped to use his essence to bolster her own magic so that she might have the strength to resist the Bain Shee. He lost his life that day, but was offered a chance at redemption, or cursed, even as his own blood and magic spilled into the land, to come again, to fight at the time of its greatest need. And now the war has begun again and he is returned. This is important. I need you to hear this. He's coming for you here. He's going to tempt you with promises. But, remember who he is; don't let yourself be tempted. The key to it all is in your own hand."

Josh nodded, though the fact that the old man had said *hand* not "hands" jarred. Looking down, he saw again the nub of bone where he'd carved away his finger in the fight against Seth. It served as a permanent reminder of all that he had sacrificed already. And through the space where that little finger should have been, he saw the ground. He realized that his companion left no footprints in the blanket of ash.

The stone circle faded away in a flurry of gray, erasing it from the air. When the wind dropped and the ash cloud cleared he found himself back in the empty landscape.

"Do you know where you are?"

"No. Is this Hell?"

The old man smiled kindly at that. "No. Not Hell. Think of it more as the waiting room. You're not dead yet."

"Are you?"

"No. I'm not dead yet, but I'm closer to the end. I will die soon. It is my time. Again. I can see the light over your shoulder. All I need to do is walk toward it, and then I'll get to wherever I'm going and be done with this life. We aren't going to the same place. You've got stuff to do yet. There are people counting on you. This is your fight. That makes you an intruder here."

"How long until—?"

"It happened a long time ago, I suspect, and my soul is just wising up to the fact that it must say farewell to the flesh."

"Will you help me fight this war?"

The old stage magician shook his head. "It isn't my fight. Now, listen, we don't have long and there is still so much you need to understand," he turned, casting a fretful glance back toward some distant nowhere within the ash. "I can sense his approach. I need you to listen to me, Josh. He is coming for you. He understands that you are key to everything. I didn't see it at first. Now that it is too late, I see everything. I was always a stubborn old fool. I know I told you it was all on you. It never was, lad. I shouldn't have said that, but I needed to make you angry, to make you *want* to fight. I'm sorry. This is on me. All of it. I opened the door when I helped Seth steal Eleanor away. That was my mistake, and my greatest regret in life. I let them through. But I need you to be clever. I need you to find a way to beat him. And when he's on this side, find a way to close the dimgate and keep him here, because these hands," he held them up, then making as though to lock his fingers together, passed one through the other, "aren't going to be closing anything. Promise me."

Before Josh could say a word, an icy chill stole in. The ash thickened noticeably. In seconds it became almost impossible to distinguish any of the old man's features, as though the process of forgetting him had already kicked in, and the world around him shimmered into darkness.

"I promise," he said, but the old man was already gone.

He walked on, trying to find his way back to wherever he had come from, but with no landmarks to orientate himself it was an impossible task. So, he simply walked, haunted by the baleful cries out there in the ash.

In the distance he saw someone waiting.

The man was tall, imposingly so.

Josh walked toward him.

Through the swirling ash, he saw the shadow of antlers begin to take shape around the man's head.

Arawn towered over him.

The cold wind blew a flurry of ash around them, turning Josh's skin gray where it settled.

He glimpsed more shadows through the swirl of ash, slowly re-

solving into the skeletal limbs of trees. He didn't recognize them this time. There were no leaves on any of the limbs. The Horned God stood in the middle of the sacred grove, dwarfing Josh by a full foot and a few inches more. His cloak of leaves was shot through with the rust of autumn, despite the season in the world they'd left behind. "You are dying," Arawn said. There was no joy in the words, no sense of victory. It was simply the truth.

Josh said, "I know."

"It doesn't have to be that way. I feel like I know you. I feel like we should be friends, you and I."

"Why would I want to be friends with you?"

Arawn smiled forlornly. There was more sadness in that smile than in all the tears Josh had ever shed. "I am not the monster here. Like you, I am fighting for what I believe in: to preserve the land where I was born. This place is my birthright, it is in my blood, and it is in your blood, too. If it wasn't I wouldn't have been able to find you here. It may be weak, diluted by the generations between us, but you are the son of my son, and my blood flows in your veins."

In the distance, Josh saw the looming presence of a dark tower. It was one of the four, he thought. Murias in the north; Findias to the south; Gorias in the east; Falias in the west. He didn't know how he knew the names, or which one he was looking at.

"They are part of who you are," Arawn said. "They are part of all of us. It is the blood."

"Kill me if that's what you've come here to do," Josh said.

"Why would I want to do that? I will not lie to you here. I have nothing to gain from lies and everything to lose. I am not the enemy. This is my land. I love it with all of my heart. I am sworn to protect it at all costs, both to me, and to those that do her harm. I was given a chance at redemption, to save myself, for her. She is so much more than us. We are ants on her flesh. Irritants. We come and we will go and she will abide. That is the nature of truth. I have no interest in your death. As I said, I think you and I should become friends in this."

"I don't need any more friends," Josh said. "Besides, like you said, I'm dying."

"Indeed you are, but rather than see you rot, I can restore you."

Josh recalled Damiola's warning, but even in that simple promise there was such strong allure he wasn't sure he'd be able to resist. "Why would you do that?"

"Do I need a motive beyond kinship?"

"Yes."

"Would you believe me if I said it was because you have something I want."

Josh thought about it. He did believe the Horned God. "Why would I give anything to you?"

"Because I can give you something you want," Arawn said, as if it was the most obvious thing in the world.

"What can you give me?"

"Life," Arawn said. "I am a god, after all. It is in my power. Here I have dominion over death. I am lord of this place."

"And the catch? Because right now that sounds far too good to be true."

"I am dying in your world. I have been gone too long, my flesh is crumbling."

"You want my body?"

"You would be my vessel, yes. And together we will save the world."

"So you *are* going to kill me?"

"No, you will give your body to me willingly."

Josh shook his head. "No."

"It is your fate. You will give yourself to me, and in doing so will live for a very, very long time; longer than any man has a right to," Arawn reached out, touching his palm to Josh's forehead and in that moment he saw the land as he had never seen it—vibrant, full of life, full of magic—and he wept tears for what had been lost. Arawn shared the world with him, "This is my land. This is what I would return it to, with your help. Without you, all is lost."

It was beautiful in ways that *his* London could never be.

But the world had changed. Moved on. This wasn't a London capable of supporting 8.5 million people.

"Then why come with your armies to tear it down?"

"They aren't my armies. They are the young; those who can still believe that our land can be saved; that we owe it to the fields and the streams to listen."

"But they aren't fighting by themselves," Josh objected.

"Indeed not, they run with the Hunt, my followers. As I said, I won't lie to you here. Should I fail, the land fails and we all lose. That is my curse. There is a greater threat on the horizon, a threat the land is not strong enough to face without the magic that it lost. If the Bain Shee break through to my home—and make no mistake, that city of yours was, is, and always will be *my* home—it will fall. Without the old ways all is lost. That trace of magic still lingering in your blood will be wiped out, making it harder and harder to reach out to the essence of the land and tap into its richness. The soil will sour, the flowers will cease to bloom, the forests will cease to grow, and all will become dust. The children of Albion must rise up; answer the call, to save her. That is what is happening here. It may appear that everything is being torn down, but out of that chaos comes hope. Rebirth. My land will survive."

"But if I'm gone, why should I care if my body lives a thousand years? It won't be mine. It won't be me in it, I'll be gone."

"That is true."

"So, I might as well die here, now, just surrender to it and be gone anyway."

"Because there will be a moment of transition, where you still live as I begin to take control. It isn't instantaneous, you do not simply cease to be, there is a moment of overlap in which you will possess all of the gifts of a god, and with them the power to save your friends, even if you can't save yourself. That is why you will give yourself to me willingly, because your sacrifice will save *their* lives. Your sister, her lover, you could even save your beloved magus. The flesh I inhabit now cannot last. Out there, back in Albion, I can feel it aging into dust already. I need a body that will live in that world without decay owning it. And we have the connection of blood. We are bonded. Help me."

The inference was clear—*Help me and help yourself*—but he couldn't exactly seal the pact in blood, so how could he ever trust the antlered man?

"Because I promised you," Arawn said, and in that moment Josh understood that the god had the power to simply slip into his mind and sift through his thoughts. Of course he did, gods were omniscient, weren't they? Omnipresent, omnipotent. Meaning there was no way he could hide anything from the deity before him, no matter how desperately he tried to. "You are here for the children. You came to save them," Arawn said. "I'm giving you the chance to do just that. All of the Sleepers; all of the old blood kin borrowed by my Hunters. If you let me in, you can close the gate and return the Sleepers to themselves. You can bring them back. Think about it. You win. You get what you came here to do. You can save the children. It's the only way that happens."

"Is that a threat?"

The Horned God shook his head slightly, the effect exaggerated by the huge crown of antlers. The motion cast deep shadows across the blanket of ash.

"No. It is just reality. If you do not give yourself to me, everything we both love dies. Albion cannot stand. The Bain Shee will devour everything and everyone. Not immediately. But slowly, their deaths will be labored and drawn out to the point of agony. You can stop this. The power is in your hands."

"And if I agree—"

"I will know everything in your mind," the old god said. "Should you try to cheat me, I will know even as the impulse occurs, and it will occur, I am not a fool. It's only natural to try and improve your lot, but the deal I offer is the deal you will accept, believe me. It is your fate, and your fate was sealed before your first breath."

Josh looked down at his hands again, making an effort not to think about anything beyond the offer he had been made and Damiola's warning that the god making the offer couldn't and shouldn't be trusted.

"What would I have to do? Do I have to say a prayer or something to let you in? Some sort of sacrifice?"

"All that is required of you is that you take hold of my staff; it will serve as a conduit for my soul to pass from one vessel to the next."

"Will it hurt?" Josh asked.

"I promised you that there would be no lies here. Yes, the pain will be excruciating, but short-lived. Your soul will essentially be purged from existence; there will be nothing of Joshua Raines left inside the shell. That cannot be done without suffering. I am sorry."

"And I will do this willingly?"

"You will come and seek me out when you return to the world."

"And before then? Will you be watching me? Will you be in my head?"

"Do you want me there?"

"No. Not if these are my last few hours. I want to spend them alone. I don't want some stranger inside me, spying on my every thought."

"You won't be able to cheat me," the old god said, sadly.

"I won't try," Josh said.

"You will," Arawn told him. "But I will honor your wishes. I won't violate your thoughts. You are free to spend your last few hours alone, saying your farewells to your loved ones. Come, find me; I will be waiting for you, son of my blood."

And with that promise, the ash whipped up in a gyre, swirling faster and faster around him. He lost sight of the Horned God within the vortex of ash, and when finally it began to subside, the antlered stranger was nowhere to be seen.

Josh opened his eyes.

46

Alex watched the *wyrd* Sisters perform their benediction around her fallen brother. He lay on a bare mattress on a wooden bed in a room that was barely big enough for the women to gather around the bedside. The walls were bare stone, though a tapestry hung on one: the subject of the woven threads appeared to be a glorious white stag. The Sisters' song didn't falter, even for a second. One tended to the fever sweats on Josh's brow with a wet rag, another to the soles of his bare feet while Sister Mazoe slowly stripped him out of his ruined clothes.

He looked so helpless lying there, broken. It was hard to simply stand back and do nothing, to trust these strange women with their ululating song, but they had little choice in the matter. Sister Mazoe peeled away the makeshift compress Alex had fashioned, exposing the deep wounds with their charred flaps of skin. They looked worse now than they had when they'd bound the wound up. The flesh smelled putrid. Rot had set in. It was happening too quickly, as though the chant was accelerating the sickness, drawing it out. Beads of perspiration clung to Josh's skin.

He wasn't breathing.

It took too long to realize that, to see what was missing: there was no shallow rise and fall of his chest. It was caught between one and the other, empty of life, or full of it, it was impossible to say which.

She grabbed Julie's arm, willing herself to be wrong.

She squeezed his hand.

He looked at her, and understood.

Without another word, he led her down the winding stair and out of the strange tower. They walked through the graveyard at its foot, leaving the weird song behind them, and into the Orchard that took up vast swathes of the Isle, and giving the place its name. Twice, she thought she caught a glimpse of the emerald dog, the Cù Sìth, lurking between the trees, but it never stayed in one place long enough for her to get a proper sighting of it. But didn't the fact it still lurked rather than bounded brazenly into the tower mean that Josh was still alive—or at least not dead yet? She wanted so desperately to believe that somehow the strange Sisters had succeeded in holding back death if only to delay the inevitable a little while longer. Wasn't that what Mazoe had promised, to trap him in the kingdom of the last breath, waiting to exhale into the afterlife?

She wasn't ready to lose her brother yet.

Julie understood that. He didn't offer sympathy or understanding; he just offered his hand and companionship while she wrestled with it all. It wasn't the most romantic of strolls. Josh's fate hung heavy between them. She wanted to say something. He wanted to say something. But nothing either of them could say would offer any sort of comfort or direction. In the end it was Ellie Taylor, coming up behind them, who said what needed to be said; no preamble, no skirting around the issue, she didn't even wait for them to turn around. "I know you don't want to hear this, but we're here, wherever *here* is, and we can't give up now, even without him. I know you want to mourn, but we need to do what we came here to do, and that was find a way to win and bring those kids home if we can. That hasn't changed. And to do that we need to find that sword you were talking about, the one you said could kill this thing." She stopped short of saying *god*. "So, let's find it while the Sisters do their thing. That's got to be better than standing around worrying about Josh. We can't help him."

"You're right," Alex said. But before Ellie could bask in how right she was, Alex said, "I don't want to hear it."

"We've got to believe the Sisters when they say they can save him."

"Do we? Really?"

"Yes. I know it's tough. And it's trite for me to try and pretend to understand, or ask you what Josh would want, but as far as those kids go, we're their only hope. And if you're not going to help me, I guess I'll go it alone. Just tell me where I start looking? What did the old woman tell you?"

"The sword is called Freagarthach. The blade of Manannan. It was forged in the furnaces of the earth by the Mother Goddess, Danu. She showed it to me. I saw it. It was lying on the chest of a dead man. I saw a ruined temple."

"The chapel outside?"

"I don't know. I think so."

"It's not like there can be many ruined temples around here," Julie said.

"Okay, so we're looking for a grave or some sort of stone sarcophagus?" Ellie said, turning back to look up the slope in the direction of the graveyard at the foot of the tower, and off in the distance the ruined chapel that had served it once upon a time. "I say we go and check it out."

Alex nodded, and despite herself, followed Ellie back up the slope toward the ruin. Again, Alex caught a fleeting glimpse of the emerald dog ghosting through the Orchard's trees, circling them. She did her best to ignore it.

The keystone of the chapel's arch had crumbled, leaving half of the doorway on the ground. They picked a path through the stones. Nature had begun the slow process of reclaiming the place, with weeds growing up through the cracks in the stone floor of what would have been the knave. There was a stone bier in place of an altar. Alex walked down the aisle, raising her head to the gray sky. She caught strains of song as the Sisters offered up their beautiful voices in honor of the fallen. She understood the song, if not the words. It was in her blood.

She approached the bier slowly, realizing that a body had been laid out on top of it.

"I don't like this," Julie said, beside her.

"Can't say I'm all that fond of it myself," she agreed, seeing the sword resting on the dead man's chest. He was dressed in the armor of a king, and might have been sleeping, so perfectly preserved was his corpse.

Runes chased along the blade, shimmering in the gray light of this timeless place. The dead man's hands were clasped around the leather-wrapped hilt.

He had shoulder-length black hair shot through with a single lock of white and a day-old shadow of stubble on his hollow cheeks that accentuated the bones. His eyes were closed, but it was obvious that he was not sleeping.

There was something familiar about him, she realized, but until Julie said what, she never would have guessed. "He looks like the old man, doesn't he? Gideon Lockwood." And he was right; there was an almost familial similarity to the bone structure. It was uncanny.

"Coincidence," she said, but knew there was no such thing in this life.

She reached down to take the sword and was absolutely sure the grip of the hands on the hilt tightened. The sudden movement scared the hell out of her. Alex backed up two steps, shaking and half-hysterically laughing at herself for doing that.

"What's wrong?" Julie asked.

"Nothing. I just thought he moved," but when she looked back there was nothing to indicate the dead man had made any attempt to protect the blade.

She stepped forward again, and again the hand clenched around the hilt. They all saw it that time.

"Okay, that's just freaky," Ellie said as Alex tried and failed to claim the sword. Ellie tried, and this time the ancient corpse whispered, "It is not for you," in a dry, dusty voice and refused to relinquish the weapon to the Speaker for the Dead.

"Only the worthy may draw the sword," Sister Mazoe said, explaining the dead man's denial. She didn't seem at all perturbed that the corpse of her fallen hero had spoken in the presence of these strangers. None of them had heard her approach. "Or so the legend goes. I have seen many try down the ages of men; strangers who have come to Murias looking for the ancient blade, believing it is their destiny to wield it against whatever threat they faced, but none have proved themselves worthy of Manannan mac Lir's blade, or the burden that goes with wielding it. As he said, it is not for you. Do not feel slighted, it is a rare soul that has earned the right to draw the weapon." She walked down the aisle, a ghost bride clad all in white, to stand beside the deceased hero. She laid a hand on his heart, her fingers only inches from the weapon. Glyphs the length of the blade shimmered as gray-tinged moonlight chased through the sweeps and curls of their ancient enchantment. "Perhaps you are the one?" she said to Julie. The policeman didn't look convinced.

"I'm nobody's hero," he said, sure she was mocking him and his failures. Alex knew exactly what he meant with that. He'd confided in her, shared his grief over his partner, Taff Carter, and how he'd failed him when he needed him the most, but he'd been there with Josh at the end; he'd made amends. He hadn't run. He hadn't turned Josh over to Seth and his monsters; he'd stood with her brother against them. So, yes, in some ways he was at least one person's hero, and she told him as much.

"Try," she told him, "Arawn marked you for a reason. He *knew* you."

Julie stood beside the funeral bier and looked down at the dead man. Now that Ellie was no longer touching his ageless flesh, Manannan no longer spoke. His eyes were open and glassy. Sightless. There was no spirit or soul or whatever you wanted to call it in there anymore. Julie looked down at an empty vessel. He breathed in deeply, slowly, holding the air in his lungs for a few seconds, until his head started to swoon, then leaned in, and reached out with his right hand for the ancient blade of the last man who had earned the title Godslayer.

And the hand holding it relinquished its grasp.

A soft flame of blue flared within the runes, chasing along the length of the blade and up through the hilt into his hand. The flame blossomed into an aura that enclosed his hand, which then singed away the fine hairs along his forearm as it spread, shrouding him with its ghostly glow.

Sister Mazoe threw herself onto her knees, pressing her forehead down against the weed-riddled cracks in the chapel floor.

On the funeral bier, a fissure appeared in the handsome face, splitting it from cheek to brow. A second crack opened up, stretching the corpse's blue lips in an impossibly wide smile. A third crack and the jaw crumbled, collapsing in on itself, and fourth saw the curve of cheekbone dip, becoming a hollow and finally a dark space in the side of the dead man's skull as, his last task finally fulfilled, entropy claimed the fallen warrior.

Julie stared at the blade in his hand, trembling violently.

"I'm nobody's hero," he repeated, his denial useless in the face of what had just happened.

In the distance the singing stopped and an eerie silence descended upon the Isle of Apples.

And then, grasping what the silence meant, Alex started to scream.

47

Josh was sitting up in bed when they found him, very much alive.

The Sisters tended to his wounds. They had stopped festering, and with their nourishing salves had begun to smell of the sweet fragrances of the Orchard.

Sister Glitonea was on her knees at his feet, washing the dried blood from his skin. Beside her Sister Thiten worked unguent into his hands. Her fingers lingered over the nub that was all that remained of his little finger. "Would you like us to make you whole again?" she asked.

Josh shook his head. "No," he said. It was the first word he'd said in a long time. He saw Alex in the doorway, but his gaze went past her to Julie Gennaro and the sword in his hand. Julie looked different. He couldn't say why, exactly, but there was definitely something about him that this place had changed. "Sis," he said, seeing her stumble and grab for the door's frame at the sight of him.

"You bastard," she said as she straightened. She was laughing and crying at once, unable to cope with the flood of emotions the sight of him stirred. She didn't come any closer to the bed, as though she feared that stepping over the threshold would shatter the illusion her mind had conjured and leave him back on the bare mattress, hair matted to his scalp, chest still.

Josh shrugged, and winced at the pain the moment brought, earning concerned tuts from the women working on his wounds. "Looks like I'm not dead after all," he said.

"How?" she asked, shaking her head. "I saw you . . . you were gone."

"Not quite," the old woman who had led the procession to the tower told them. "Would that we had longer to sing away his ailments, but your brother is quite insistent that you must leave this place. Talk to him, he isn't strong enough to travel."

"I'm fine," Josh objected.

"You are anything but," Alex told him, but Josh wasn't listening. "Where are my clothes?"

"Ruined," the Sister explained as Thiten worked more of the sweet-smelling unguent into the charred skin around the worst of the knife wounds. The flesh, raw and pink beneath the dark scabs, had already begun to knit. "When we have finished bathing you, we will bring you fresh clothes, fear not."

Josh nodded. "Tell me," he said. "This place; the tower. Is it protected?"

That caused the Sister to tilt her head ever so slightly, seeming to consider her answer thoughtfully before she countered with a question of her own, "In what way? Murias is not built to survive another war, if that is what you mean."

He shook his head. "No, nothing like that. I need to talk to my friend, but need to be sure no one, no matter how powerful can overhear us. It is important."

"We can sing an aura of obfuscation around the chamber," the Sister assured him.

"And that will work?"

The elderly Sister nodded. "I believe so."

It was as close as he was going to get to a yes. He turned to Alex and Ellie. "Would you give us a couple of minutes, Sis? I need to talk to Julie about something."

She didn't look happy about it, but she left the pair of them alone in the room.

Josh didn't say a word until he heard the Sisters' song. He looked out of the window and saw that they had joined hands in a ring around the ancient tower, and had their faces turned to the sky as they sang their hearts out.

He turned back to Julie.

"I need you to promise me something. You're not going to want to do it, but I need you to promise me you won't let Lexy change your mind."

"I'm not sure I like the sound of that, mate."

"I'm going to need you to kill me."

Silence.

The policeman looked at him; no flicker of emotion on his face.

"I *know* I don't like the sound of that."

"It's the only way we win," Josh said. He looked up toward the ceiling, as though he expected to see Arawn's naturalistic features melded into the stone, watching them. There was nothing up there.

"You know I can't do that. Alex would never forgive me."

"If you don't, she'll die," he said, and the way he said it made it abundantly clear he wasn't lying. "So will you, the kids, and if what he showed me is true, everyone else."

"What are you talking about?"

"Arawn is not the enemy, or at least not the sum of the evil we face. He came to me when I was dying. He showed me what was coming. The end. There's no other way of describing what I saw. Everything would be destroyed in the war to end all wars. He is just one facet of the conflict the land faces. What you need to understand is that he loves our world like no other."

"And you believe him?"

Josh nodded. "I do. Because of the other stuff he said. He could have lied, but chose to tell me the uncomfortable truth instead."

"So, what do we have to do?"

"Not we, me. I must become the host to his spirit so that he can stand against the greater evil. There will be an hour or two, not much longer, I'm sure, in which we will both be in here," he tapped his temple, "and in that time I'll be blessed with the might and magic of the gods," he offered a smile at the thought. "But after that, as he takes possession of my flesh I'll slowly be lost until finally nothing remains. But we win. We can save ourselves, and you guys get to live happily ever after."

"That's fucked, mate. I still don't think I can do it."

"Don't make me beg." He looked down at his hands, or more accurately the stub where his missing finger had been. "And then comes the most important part, and this is where I need you to stay true, my friend. Do you trust me?"

"Based on what you just said? Not at all."

Josh laughed at that.

"It's something Damiola said. It got me thinking. He said my fate was in my own hand. Not in my own hands. It's a little thing, but I'm not all here."

Julie smiled. "I won't argue with that."

"Arawn is going to consume me, but there's going to be a little piece of me he can't reach," he wiggled the nonexistent finger. "I'm counting on you to find it, and find a way to bring me back with it," Josh said, realizing just how insane it sounded once he said it aloud. "The problem is once he's inside me I won't be able to hide my plan from him. That's why you're going to need to kill me, because if you don't, he'll kill you to save himself."

"Good to know."

"As long as we never mention this outside of this room—don't even *think* about it—we've got a chance that this betrayal might just work. It's vital he doesn't suspect what we've got in mind; otherwise he'll go after Seth first. And if he does that, I'm fucked. That little piece of me is my only chance of coming out of this—" he was about to say *in one piece*. "He's going to be weak for a while. I don't know how long. He said a few hours, but it might only be minutes."

"Or seconds," Julie said.

"Or seconds," Josh agreed. "I'm hoping you'll have a few hours when I can still help you, but I don't know if that's reasonable. He promised me time, but I'm trying not to pin my hopes on everything he said being truthful."

"That's reassuring."

"I know. I'm sorry. I'm just trying to be honest with you. He'll be expecting me to try and fight him, so I don't know how much help I'll be, but I'll try with every bone in my body—"

"Every bone but one," Julie said, and damn him, but the other man was smiling. It wouldn't last, that smile, but it was good to see.

"Every bone but one," Josh agreed. "After that window has closed I don't know if you'll be able to go up against him."

"Well, then we better not find out."

Josh nodded. "Just don't fuck about; take my head off my shoulders with that sword of yours." It was weird talking about his own murder so matter-of-factly, but it needed to be said. They couldn't afford any mistakes. "I know Lexy's going to freak out, but you can't tell her what we're planning. Promise me."

Julie shook his head slowly, but said, "I promise. She's going to kill me."

"I know."

"You're lucky you'll already be dead."

"Some people might not consider that lucky."

"They don't know your sister like I do. Do I want to know where your missing finger is?"

"I gave it to Seth," Josh said, which was technically true, if force-feeding the gangster with it counted as *giving*.

It took a moment, but Julie caught up with him, realizing what giving it to Seth entailed in terms of getting it back from Seth. "Hold on a fucking second, mate. You expect me to what, get banished into the mirror world and go looking for that bastard? Are you out of your fucking mind?"

"You've got a magic sword," Josh said, wryly. "And by the time you find him you'll have killed a god. I'm pretty sure he's not going to pose much of a challenge."

"Famous last words."

"Will you do it?"

"Do I have a choice?"

"Always."

"You're a terrible liar, Joshua Raines. And just supposing I do somehow recover your finger, or the knuckle bones at least, how exactly am I supposed to use it to bring you back?"

"No idea," Josh said.

Julie let out a slow exasperated sigh. "Well, I can't pretend life isn't interesting around you, mate. But I kinda miss the good old days when the only time someone gave me the finger was when I was trying to arrest them."

48

"I will show you the way, Swordbearer, it will be my honor," Sister Mazoe said. "There is a weakness in the veil at Gorias. I believe that is where you will find your way home."

Julie turned his back on the ruin, and stepped into the shadow of the great tower, which stretched all the way down to the beach in the long sun. Without thinking, he reached up and plucked one of the shiny red apples from the branches overhead and took a bite. The fruit was sweeter than any apple he had tasted back home, and so succulent the juice dribbled down his chin. It was heady. Intoxicating. The natural sugars flooded his bloodstream, making his heart beat faster and his head swim. Two bites were enough. The transformation was dizzying. He felt suddenly invincible. Invulnerable. "What is this stuff?" he asked the Sister. "Because it sure isn't a Granny Smith."

She didn't look like she understood the joke. "We call them apples," she said, seriously.

It took Julie a second to realize it wasn't the fruit itself that was different, it was the soil nourishing the tree that was, and that here there was still earth magic in the loam. This was what all the fruit must have tasted like before. The difference in taste and the vitality of the apple was incredible.

"You need to taste this," he said, offering the apple to Alex to take a bite. She looked doubtful, but after a first bite quickly swallowed a second. Her expression changed to one of bliss as the juices spilled down her throat.

"Oh, my God, that's the best thing I've ever tasted."

"Incredible, isn't it?"

"It's nuts. It's just an apple. Here," she handed the rapidly diminishing core to her brother. "Try it."

He did, again taking two bites as he chewed around the seeds of the core. "This is what we're fighting for," Josh said, offering up the remains of the apple. It was a ridiculous thing to say, but in so many ways it was true. It wasn't about the apple or any other piece of fruit in the Orchard, it was about the essence of what had been lost.

They walked on, in silence; each wrapped up in their own thoughts.

Sister Mazoe nimbly negotiated a causeway of octagonal stones that seemed to have been laid by giants, as the waves crashed up against them. This time looking out over the water Julie saw a roiling, churning sea filled with whitecaps being whipped up by the oncoming storm.

The boatman waited half a dozen steps beyond the shore, his vessel bobbing in the choppy surf. He did not raise his head as they approached.

Julie followed the Sister as she splashed into the water, impervious to the shock of icy cold as the water closed around her calves and soaked up through her white dress. She clambered easily into the flat-bottomed boat.

Julie boarded after her, holding out a hand to help Alex and then Ellie board behind him. Josh was the last of them to take up his seat. He was still moving gingerly, favoring his side where the knife had plunged into it. Julie had caught him wincing a couple of times as some ill-thought-out movement pulled at his wounds, threatening to open them again. Each one served as a reminder that, despite the miracle the Sisters had wrought, he was a long way from healed. That made this rush to be home and surrender himself up to Arawn all the more ridiculous. He wasn't in any condition to fight.

The boatman steered them out into the storm, his vessel riding the waves as they splashed up around the sides, some rising up over the top to soak his passengers as the sky turned from gray to black.

Sister Mazoe looked troubled by the subtle transformations of the world around them, but she said nothing.

The winds picked up, blustering across the wide expanse of sea to fold in on themselves, creating a wind funnel around their little boat that whipped up higher and higher walls of waves that it sent crashing against their sides again and again. The implacable boat-man rode out the storm without so much as flinching. He stood on the prow, with his hand on the tiller staring out into the wild waters. They sailed on into the rising tempest. Clouds thickened in the ever-darkening sky, choking out what little light there had been.

Sister Mazoe lit the storm lamp that hung from the pole at the bow, and even as the small flame caught, began to sing forth a brighter light to shine their way.

"What's happening?" Julie asked, after what felt like an hour or more of being tossed around by the sea's tantrum.

It was Josh who answered him, not the Sister. "The world is chang-ing . . . can't you feel it?"

He could. He closed a second hand around the hilt of Manan-nan's sword. Something within the blade was in tune with the ele-ments here, and served as a conduit for Julie through which he could feel the change that as it took place. "It is the magic," he said. "It's being drawn away."

He knew by whom, and he knew where to, and he knew that made the coming fight all the more one-sided as the god drew more and more of the land's lost magic around himself.

They were doomed before they had even begun to fight.

But then, that didn't matter did it, because Josh had no inten-tion of fighting.

The waves rose and fell; the wind rose and did not fall.

And through it all, not so much as a crease in the boatman's hooded robe stirred.

The storm worsened the longer they were out in it. Biting cold winds raged around them. Julie gripped the hilt of the sword, and leaned forward, his forehead resting on the pommel. Every now and then he looked up to see Josh looking back at him. Did the other man sense his weakness? How could he even ask this of him? It was too much.

The way the others looked at him, they knew something had passed between the two men in that tower room, but neither asked what.

Up ahead, he saw the silhouette of another tower in the distance, impossibly far away in the raging storm. The waves crashed against the little boat's hull, bullying it across the sea. It didn't seem to get closer no matter how long they sailed toward it, as though the storm held their boat in place while the sea tossed and churned, filling the air with salt spray and brine. The tower was a skeletally black shadow rising up and up and up. There was a crooked twist to it, or an optical illusion conjured by the storm.

Julie felt the first fat drops of rain against his face.

Beside him, he saw that Alex had a white-knuckle grip on the side, while Ellie couldn't take her eyes off the boatman as he guided them on. She said something, but the wind whipped away her words. He could, however, still hear the song Sister Mazoe sang.

They were taking on water, but the boatman didn't seem the least bit concerned.

He simply steered his course.

And still the tower remained forever out of reach.

They drifted on.

Julie closed his eyes. They were going to reach the tower; they were going to cross back over to the other side of the veil, and the moment would come when he would have to kill his girlfriend's brother and end any hope of happiness he would ever have in life. And he knew he wouldn't be able to do it. It wasn't a shot at redemption, no matter how Josh tried to sell it to him. It was a one-way ticket to damnation. *Then I will do it for you,* a voice sounded in his mind.

He opened his eyes. No one in the boat was talking, and even if they had been, the gale-force winds battering the tiny vessel would have drowned out their words.

He looked over his shoulder, back the way that they had come. The ruined chapel had long since disappeared beneath the tumult, then back to the sword in his hands. Could it have placed those words in his mind? Had he heard the voice of Manannan mac Lir, the last man to slay a god?

He had help, the voice offered, wryly.

The tower was closer now. Above it, he saw strands of red, like veins of raspberry ripple, swirling through the black sky. The heart of the spiral appeared to be directly over the tower of Gorias. The spiral wound itself tighter and tighter, the blood-red stain spreading throughout the sky.

The wind direction changed noticeably. It was no longer battering at their faces, but driving them on toward a distant unseen shore. It was carrying them home.

Julie tried to frame a thought, giving shape to a question in his mind. The best he could come up with in the end was perhaps the simplest way of asking it: *Who are you?*

I have many names; some call me the Answerer, others the Retaliator. I have been called the Godslayer and the Widowmaker, but none of those capture my soul. I am Freagarthach.

The boat dragged across stones, running aground. The shore was still a long, long way away, but the flat-bottomed boat wasn't getting any closer.

Sister Mazoe stood slowly, unhooking the lantern from the pole in the bow, and stepped down into the shallow water. "We must walk from here," she told the others, who followed her one at a time out of the boat.

Ellie reached out a hand to steady herself as she descended, her hand resting on the boatman's, which still held the tiller. "Thank you," she said.

"You are most welcome," the boatman said. His voice sent shivers all the way into Julie's soul.

The rain lashed down, stinging their faces, as they waded toward the distant shore. Visibility was down to a few feet; beyond that, things remained a blur. Above the splash of the sea and their heavy footsteps Julie heard voices. He stopped walking and told the others to do likewise. They weren't alone out here. The voices were raised in a keening lament. He couldn't see anyone for the storm. The disconnected song of mourning chilled him far more than either the storm or the sea. The singers approached them. Out of the corner of his eye he caught a glimpse of movement; a dark shape shrouded within the storm. As he turned, drawn to it, he saw it was a man. Worse, he knew the man. Not so long ago he had called him a friend.

Huw "Taff" Carter stood there: adrift, lost, staring with his blind eyes and seeing nothing.

Julie rubbed at his face. The rain beat down. His shirt clung to his skin. The rainwash stung his eyes.

Sister Mazoe told the shade, "Begone, you will find no peace here."

Taff broke down in tears and wept as they walked away, leaving the shade in the deeper water.

"That was harsh," Ellie said.

They waded on without another word. The storm gathered force, making headway difficult, as the wind battered them back from the shore as though nature herself was determined they should never find their way back to London.

Thunder rolled, and a crack of lightning opened the sky.

Mazoe led them on. In the distance Julie could just about make out a small golden orb of light, like a firefly hovering in the air before them.

They walked toward the light.

They walked for an hour and an hour more until the storm broke and the light streamed down in bright, unbroken beams. On the hillside before them he saw a dark tower, at its foot an orchard and a ruined chapel, each a perfect replica of the one they had left behind at Murias. "Gorias," Mazoe said. The light was a lantern, much like the one she held in her hand, and the woman—Not just any woman, surely? Surely, he was looking at Sister Mazoe's twin?—holding it, beckoned them ashore.

The women bowed to each other.

The eye of the storm seemed to be centered above the tower, which he realized on closer inspection was different in subtle ways to the one at Murias, with a deep fissure running up its twisting spire.

"Where is the dimgate?" Josh asked, without preamble. "Our way home? Where is it?"

"This way," Mazoe said, leading them toward the tower.

There was no door, Julie realized, as her path took them around the base of the huge dark tower.

She continued her strange path, walking a second lap around the base of the tower, anticlockwise.

"What are you doing?" Julie said to her back. Above them the red swirl broke and spilled out into the sky, staining the firmament blood red.

"Opening the door," the Sister told him without looking back, and as they finished their third pass, sure enough there was a door in the base of the tower that somehow they had missed when they'd walked past the same spot not once but twice before.

She opened the door.

Josh was the first to step through. Ellie and Alex followed him. Julie didn't. Not at first. He waited to be sure they were gone, then asked Mazoe, "This sword? Can it? I mean . . . is it . . . alive? Can it talk to me? In my head? Or am I losing my mind?"

She smiled at him. "You need to leave now."

"You're not going to tell me?"

Mazoe turned her back on him and walked away. "It is your choice, walk through the door, or stay, but if you do not decide soon, the choice will be taken for you. The gateway cannot stay open forever."

We don't belong in this place, the voice of the sword urged. *Not when there is a fight waiting on the other side of that doorway.*

Julie went through the door.

49

And stepped into the movie set world of Glass Town.

Or, more accurately, into the scaffolding and bare boards behind the set itself, where all of the magic was made incredibly mundane. The others were waiting for him. "This is it?" Alex asked, ducking beneath a two-by-four as Josh led them out into the actual lot, which had served as Eleanor Raines's prison for a year of her life—one hundred years of theirs.

"This is it," Josh said, turning around and spreading his arms wide as though offering it up. "Not much, is it?"

"Not much?" Alex objected. "It's a piece of London that was lifted out of time for a century and hidden in limbo. I'd say it's more than much."

"What is this place?" Ellie asked. She, of course, was the only one who hadn't at least heard of the mythical Glass Town that had haunted the Lockwood and Raines families since the fall of Ruben Glass's cinematic empire and the disappearance of a young actress that led to an obsession that refused to die.

"It was going to be London's version of Hollywood, once upon a time," Josh told her. "Things didn't work out the way the owner wanted," Josh explained. "Now, it's the way home."

He led them through the streets, past the rows of parked cars and painted façades, the whitewashed steps and neatly trimmed hedgerows that never grew because they were as fake as everything else in this place. He led them to where the fissure had opened out into the street where, for him and Julie at least, it had all begun.

Now, rather than a tear in the illusion, there was a street corner. There was nothing magical about that. They emerged amid a blare of horns. It wasn't cars this time. The horns belonged to rioters. It was impossible to tell how many there were, because what should have been a busy high street in the heart of London looked more like the depths of Coldfall Wood.

An entire forest had grown in the time they had been gone.

The street was still there, and the shops—but the windows were gone, smashed, and vegetation grew everywhere, climbing up the walls and in through the empty windows, weeds, vines, and moss. Infinite shades of green and brown, all so filled with life.

The magic is returning, the voice of the sword told Julie. *Can't you feel it?*

He could.

It was in the air. The tingle prickled his skin. The thrill stirred the fine hairs all along his forearms.

It was here, and not just in the presence of the Hunt, either. This went deeper than the chalk brothers and their kin. This was rooted all the way down in the land herself.

And that couldn't be good.

Julie saw the fallen sign of a coffee shop farther up the street, and between them and it, the surface of the road had been torn up by the sudden profusion of roots that had forced their way up through the surface. Through the trees he saw the dirt-smeared faces of the kids, armed with sticks and stones. They looked feral, the grime of the streets like war paint smeared across their cheeks.

"How long were we away?" Alex asked her brother. She turned from the feral children to look behind them, not that there was much difference in the view: more trees, thick boles of oak and sycamore and a carpet of acorn caps and winged seeds.

"I don't know," Josh said. "But by the looks of it, a long time."

"I can't even . . ." Ellie said.

"No," Julie disagreed. "Not long. Days. Maybe weeks. But it doesn't matter. It's not about how long we've been gone; it's about it being long *enough*. Can't you feel it? This place is different now. It's changed. Or changing."

"I can feel it," Ellie said. "But I don't know what it is that I'm feeling."

"The magic is returning," he said, echoing the sword. "And it's happening *fast*. It started with us, with you being able to speak with the dead," he told Ellie. "And with you trapping Seth in the mirror world," he told Josh. "But it's moved beyond that now. It's reaching out like the roots of the trees there, working its way into every aspect of the city, and this," he swept his hand out to encompass the forest that had spilled out into the city overnight, "is the result of Arawn's presence here. It's only going to get worse the longer he's allowed to walk these streets. He doesn't belong here. We've got to find him, and end this."

Josh nodded, and rather than say anything else, turned and walked toward the ruin of the coffee shop and the kids hidden within the trees. As he approached them, he called out, "I want you to take me to him." When they didn't immediately answer, he named the Horned God. That was enough to draw one of the boys out of hiding. He wore the remnants of a prep school uniform, his faded red-and-blue-striped tie around his scalp like a bandanna, chest bare, skinny arms covered in cuts and scratches from the new undergrowth. "And who the fuck are you when you're at home?"

Josh said, "I am his new host. Without me he dies."

50

She knew Arawn would send his Hunters after her.

Blundering about in her wake, Gogmagot and Corenius weren't particularly adept at stealth. She'd been aware of them for some considerable time now, lurking, trying to build up the courage to face her. She even caught snatches of their conversation; each trying to goad the other into taking her down. They sounded like children with their borrowed voices, but then Arawn had always believed so firmly in youth, in the vitality and innocence it represented, whereas she had preferred the wisdom of age.

"Come out, come out wherever you are," she called, knowing they would hear her.

The May Queen decided to make it easy for them, and followed the steps down into an underpass. The tunnel beneath the roads was dark, with barely any light at the end because of the way the steps doubled back on themselves to create a roof. It stank of piss and shit and all of those mortal stenches. The walls had been painted with crude graffiti—not words or gang tags this time, but offerings to her kind, as the children answered the call to rise up. She recognized attempts to paint the antlers of the Horned God in broad brushstrokes of black behind the silhouette of a faceless man, and so many garishly colored flowers around him it could have been the heart of summer. She liked it. If the meadow was her palace, this dank piss-stinking tunnel was her chapel. She could work with it.

She plucked a flower from the painting on the wall, willing it into substance in her hand. It was a beautifully simple daisy; one of her favorites.

She raised it to her nose and savored the sweet scent, then whispered a word to draw down the first bee into the tunnel. It came, along with a second and a third, answering her call. Soon a dozen buzzed around the delicate flower in her hand, and still more came down into the darkness to taste its pollen. Fifty. Hundred. The buzzing intensified, amplified by the cramped confines of the tunnel, growing louder and louder by the second as more of London's bees freshly woken for the season, came down to draw pollen from the daisy. Within a minute there were easily ten thousand bees crawling all over every inch of her skin, tangled in her hair, and climbing on top of each other and burrowing beneath to taste the skin of the May Queen.

Their tiny wings vibrated against her eyes and cheeks as she watched the two fools enter the tunnel. Their silhouettes transformed them into brutish shapes, closer to their natural form as she remembered it.

In this aspect, they were no match for her. The old woman they could have hurt, possibly even ended, bludgeoning her with their crude blows, but renewed, they didn't stand a prayer. They had no inkling what they were going up against, and but for the fact they had murdered five children before coming for her, she would have pitied them. Now, with the blood of the Sleepers on their hands, they deserved everything she was about to do to them. And more.

She let her fingers trail over the petals of the flower in her hand, ignoring the bees as they swarmed around her, and plucked them one at a time, as though playing a game of he loves me, he loves me not. She didn't need the petals to tell her how he felt. He had come back to save her in his own sweet, twisted way. For all their differences, they wanted the same thing: to protect the land, though where she chose to nurture and nourish the soil with little acts of love, he chose blood.

"We can smell you," Gogmagot said, his voice carrying down the tunnel. "Your *heat*."

"Ripe for the plucking," his chalk giant brother, lumbering menacingly toward her, mocked.

She didn't move: not toward them, not away from them. She let the stem of the denuded flower fall from her fingers, and the bees gathered close enough so that they became a living glove.

"Did he send you?"

"You know he did," Gogmagot said.

"True, I just wondered if you'd try and lie."

"Why would I do that? I don't have anything against you in *this* form."

"And yet here you are, intending to kill me."

"It's not personal," Corenius said.

She saw the crown of leaves the giant wore, and even from this distance could identify bean, broom, burdock, chestnut, hawthorn, meadowsweet, nettle, oak, and primrose.

"You brought me an offering? How kind of you," Macha said, holding out her bee-gloved hand.

"Oh, it's not for you, only to help us find you."

"And here you are, and I'm telling you it is mine," she said sweetly. "Give it to me, or I shall have my little friends take it. I don't think you want that to happen."

The chalk giants didn't move, and she had no interest in drawing things out, so with a whisper sent the bees swarming. They filled the air between them, swelling to fill every inch of the tunnel. Ten thousand must surely have been closer to thirty thousand and more by the time the first settled on Gogmagot's bare arm. The chalk giant crushed it beneath his hand.

"That was a mistake," she said, as the smell of death drove the other bees wild.

"I don't care what you think," Gogmagot sneered.

"And that's your final mistake, my old friend. They will willingly die for me, like all creatures great and small. They understand that there needs to be sacrifice. And there are a lot more of them than there are of you." The giant in a boy's skin laughed, his voice booming out to drown out the humming of the bees.

"Do your worst, woman," his brother said. "See if you can do your magic tricks after I've snapped your neck."

"Sometimes strength has nothing to do with muscles," she said, opening her mouth and letting a single bee settle on her tongue. She swallowed it whole. "Sometimes it comes from being able to ask for help, and now I am asking," and with that whatever had been holding the bees back lost its hold on them, and as they swarmed around the chalk giant they began to sting. At first it was only one at a time, but in the few seconds it took her to walk to where the brothers lay on the piss-stained paving slabs, writhing around in agony, hundreds upon hundreds of her hive had descended to sink their stingers into the two Hunters.

They slapped at their arms and faces, turning and turning on the spot, losing their balance even as more stingers sank into their skin. They fell up against the tunnel wall and slumped down against it, clawing at their faces, their eyes, mouths open to scream, but instead of desperate cries going out, bees swarmed over their lips and teeth, filling them.

Their deaths weren't pretty, but then death shouldn't be.

She watched impassively, as their skin reddened and as more and more venom poured into their bodies; anaphylactic shock took them one after the other. It was an agonizing death that she wouldn't have wished upon her worst enemies, but some good could come of it, she thought, as she recovered her crown from the fallen giant. As soon as it settled on her brow, the leaves and buds blossomed into glorious life.

He would feel it, she knew, just as she felt his growing strength; such was the bond between them. She and he might not be lovers in this lifetime, but they were joined in ways that went beyond mortal comprehension. They were part of the endless knot of life, indivisible, inseparable, unending. It was only a matter of time before her ancient betrayal demanded a reckoning in his mind and the dance would begin all over again, the knot consuming itself like a serpent eating its own tail.

Would it be her turn this time, or his again? It was difficult, sometimes, to remember that though their methods and means differed so vastly, they both essentially wanted to bring the magic back into the world so that it might survive the coming days.

Crouching down beside the fallen brothers, she ran her fingers across the damp corners where the ground and tunnel wall met, digging out a few inches of mossy fungus, that she then sprinkled into the open mouths of the dead Hunters. Her touch brought new life to the moss, causing it to flourish in the dampness of their throats, and in moments all manner of mushrooms and toadstools had begun to sprout out of every orifice as the brothers became a breeding ground for the slugs and snails, worms and flies.

She stood and turned her back on the Hunters. She had taken two of his pieces out of the great game, even as her most potent player had returned. In this moment, she was winning. She could feel the magic bristling in the ground beneath her feet with an urgency that had been missing for centuries. It was flooding back into the realm, and that was his doing. At dawn, all of the birds in the sky had cried out as one, their song announcing the return of Manannan's blade, the Godslayer. With Freagarthach in his hand, she had a hero to stand against her lover in the endless conflict between the Aos Shee and the Bain Shee.

They were the same, and yet so different. It was more than just light and dark, they were counterparts; together they made up the whole. They were chaos and order. The Aos Shee were the ancestors of the forest, of nature and the land, who had retreated into the Otherworld. They were staggeringly beautiful, godlike in their perfection. They still lingered in our understanding with the faces more commonly thought of as angels. While the Bain Shee had taken refuge in the lands of the dead, they were the rot that riddled the landscape and the decay that ate away at Mother's natural beauty. They were the foul stench that came with putrescence, and unlike their kin theirs was a terrible beauty—hideous and deep rooted—bearing the masks of demons in our more basic mythologies. But one could not exist without the other. And no matter what aspect of their kind they represented, they had abandoned our world. They did not belong here.

She could sense their presence, pushing at the veil. It was only a matter of time; the one thing the Bain Shee had an abundance of. Their exile could not and would not last. And when they finally broke through, the world—her world—would need every shred of magic spilling back into it now to resist its ancient enemy.

She had never been afraid of loss. That was for her aspect as a mother. In this skin, she was full of that same youth and beauty Arawn so cherished, and because he was so predictable, she had always been able to manipulate her love.

She dismissed her bees, sending them out into the world to cross-pollinate the miraculous seeds she had conjured into existence, knowing that each bud and blossom they brought forth would enrich Mother.

She took the stairs, emerging from the underpass. The fresh air was heady in her lungs. She felt like her body must surely rupture, spilling out all of its richness, so intense was the fragrance of the newly grown forest all around her. Everywhere she looked she saw fresh signs of beauty returning, replacing the sickness of man.

She *would* prevail. She had no alternative. She *must*. For all of their sakes. She was willing to give everything—even the deity she had loved body and soul for her entire existence—for this place. That was the fundamental difference between her and Arawn. He always thought there was another way to go about things, and clung stubbornly to that need, even when it was as guileless as drawing a sword and bellowing "Charge!" Even so, she knew that her time here was growing shorter by the hour; the maiden aspect could not live forever. In all things there is a season, and summer must come. It would not be held back. Not now. All she could do was take some small comfort in the fact that so much had already been accomplished. She just had to look around her to see the burned-out shell of all of those temples of avarice, gutted by the cleansing fires of Arawn's army of children. Across the avenue newly blessed with fresh woodland, she saw the endless row of chapels dedicated to greed with their gaudy displays of wealth overturned. This place wasn't what it had been, but they were moving in the right direction at least, back toward a simpler time when the land was all anyone needed and they were content to dedicate their lives to serving Mother.

There was still so much left to be done; but this was a beginning.

In the distance she heard dogs barking. Above, the sky was filled with starlings.

Arawn had called out to the creatures.

51

As one, all of the birds in the sky—thousands upon thousands of starlings, rooks, crows, and more—loosed a chorus of tortured song that was deafening. It was answered by packs of wild dogs across the city and by the feral youth who took up the ululating howl as a war cry. The cacophony was utterly bone-chilling. The creatures of the city answered the call.

Robin savored the sheer beauty of it all.

Cockroaches crawled out of the woodwork, thousands upon thousands upon thousands of black-carapaced insects scurried and skittered and chittered between the new forestland, climbing the limbs of the trees to give them a second constantly shifting bark. Then there were the tomcats that prowled along fences and the mice that ran along beside them like a Tom and Jerry cartoon. But the worst of it by far was the rats. They spilled out of the sewers and nests in compost heaps and discarded trash: slick-bellied, bloated, and skinny critters that swarmed over each other in a race to find the light. At first, they came like creatures from the ark, two by two; but quickly two became four and four became eight as they poured up the steps of the abandoned Tube stations at Down Street, Brompton Road, and Wood Lane; at Swiss Cottage, Charing Cross, and Aldwych; until the sheer weight of their numbers was so much that it forced through barricades that had stood in place for decades. By the time they reached street level, they were a flood; a writhing mass of black and brown fur that surged out of the dark places beneath the city, and still they kept coming. There is a myth that there's a rat for every Londoner, meaning more than eleven million of them living beneath the city, some as long as two feet, these giant, mutant rodents like something out of a James Herbert novel. The reality was far fewer, but still in the millions, and seeing them all rise up like this in a sea of black, the difference was negligible.

Robin couldn't see the cracks in the pavement for the rats. He couldn't see the double yellow lines in the gutter for the rats. He could barely see patches of the white line down the middle of the road, turned into a Morse code message—the long dashes broken up into staccato dots. *Save Our Souls* painted on the tarmac.

With the rise of the rats, people started running; panic filled the streets. They were all trying to find higher ground, shelter, somewhere the vermin wouldn't crawl over them if they stood still, even for a moment. He saw them surging up around their ankles, their claws tearing at the seams of tights and hooking into the denim of jeans as the rats scrabbled upward.

And still more of them came out of the darkness, their chittering chorus like the tinnitus of madness in his ears. He had no intention of silencing it.

This was the world he loved and so much closer to how he remembered it.

Robin walked on. Estate agents, banks, charity shops—all of the windows were gone, all of their differences erased over the nights of violence. Now they were just empty units.

The natural order had changed beyond recognition.

Another chorus of rabid barks rose angrily in the near distance, no more than two streets over. The savagery of it changed, and he knew without doubt that the animals had found fresh prey and were tearing into it.

More people ran through the undergrowth that had been the High Street, forcing a path between the trees and the concrete bollards that once upon a time had served to stop the traffic from driving down the pedestrianized stretch of the street.

The rats danced to his silent tune, as though he was some weird Pied Piper in his torn, bloody, muddy clothes. He knew that he must have looked like he'd been dragged through hell backward, kicking and screaming, and out the other side. Though this place was no better than the inferno now. His legs were splashed with dark stains that could have been blood or mud or other bodily fluids that had dried in. Robin looked back over his shoulder, whipping up his arms and cackling as he watched the rats swarm around his feet. He called out for the rat chorus, in the clutches of a religious experience. He ignored the rats that he crushed beneath his feet, throwing his arms around as though conducting some invisible choir that only he could hear.

More and more of the vermin emerged from the city below in front of him, and in streets off to the left and to the right, converging on him as he walked. The city was vast, and the sewer system beneath it every bit as vast. Now that the rats had answered Arawn's call there was no stopping them. It was the stuff of nightmares. It was impossible to plant a foot down without treading on the back of a rat or a roach or tripping over a cat or facing the bared incisors of a rabid dog.

And more of the hidden dwellers of the city were emerging by the minute.

There was no road to follow now, only a churning writhing tidal mass of tiny furred bodies that broke and swarmed around the trunks of the trees and over the ripped-up tarmac where the roots had torn through from below. The constant chittering was everywhere, echoing off the high buildings, and amplified by the ancient acoustics until the entire city sounded like it was alive with rats.

They tore open garbage sacks and gnawed through the plastic bins to get at the rotten food they contained. They spilled out of the drains along the side of the road, bringing up the filth of the sewers clotted in their fur. The stench was overpowering.

A couple of times he caught a flicker of movement, a shadow across the periphery where the canopy of leaves thinned. He heard more dogs baying. They were moving in packs. They sounded closer now than they had a few minutes ago. All of the animals were coming together, converging on a single point: the lightning-struck tree in the heart of the Rothery. He saw them a moment later: the Gatekeeper with the wooden warrior, the Knucker, prowling at his side, heckles of bark raised as they, too, walked toward the old tree, drawn to it.

The rats were the only creatures not eager to crawl all over the ancient tree, giving it a wide berth even as more birds settled in its high branches.

Everywhere he looked, there was life—brilliant, vibrant, animal life. Root and branch; claw and tooth: life.

This was Arawn's kingdom.

52

Josh walked the ancient wood.

Julie walked beside him; lost in his own world of silence.

Alex and Ellie brought up the rear, Ellie on her radio. She looked distraught, arguing with the voice on the other end without being able to explain where they'd been or what had happened to them. She kept dancing around the subject as her superior officer chewed her out. Every third or fourth lie out of her mouth was broken by the same "I know, sir. I'm sorry, sir." But that wasn't appeasing him. Josh felt like taking the radio off her and demanding of the man, "Have you looked out of the window today?"

Eventually she killed the radio.

Of all of them, Josh was the only one who really grasped what was happening here with the incursion of the forest into the streets of the city. It wasn't the miracle the others thought it was. It was a different sort of miracle altogether. It was a rebirth. A return.

The trees might have sprung up overnight, but the forest wasn't *new*.

It was as old as the land itself, and far, far older than the paved streets its roots encroached upon. Albion had awoken. Her ancient forests, the primordial lifeblood of the eternal giant, were once more vibrant and filled with life as dawn by dusk by dawn Mother awoke and found her strength returning.

The land was finding a new balance. The ecology of London reverting to what it had been before Mother's youngest children had come swarming over her body like parasites. He could feel it in the air; taste it on his tongue as he breathed it in. The first strains of magic were there again, subtle, emanating from the old trees. It would only grow stronger if it were nourished. And Arawn's version of nourishment was blood and sacrifice. The blood of this London would seep into the ground, deep into the dirt only to be absorbed by the endless root system of the ancient wood that was spread out beneath the concrete and steel, to be released into the air through the green shoots and leaves.

Blood magic.

The Coldfall Wood that Arawn and his disciples had walked in those long-forgotten days had been so much more *vast* than the Coldfall Wood Julie Gennaro looked out over through his new lounge window and Josh and Alex played in as kids. The woodland had died back naturally in places, but in so many others it had been harvested to make way for the cemetery and the houses of the Rothery, the primary school across the way, and the endless commercial developments of greed, shrinking and shrinking until almost nothing remained. Even a hundred years ago it had covered hundreds of acres more ground than it did even last week. Today was different, and try as he might, Josh couldn't think of that as a bad thing.

He reached out to touch one of the tree trunks, then another.

The wooded streets were infested with rats, but they kept their distance, swarming over each other to make room for Josh to pass, watching him. Recognizing him for what he was, dogs bayed as they neared, their endless barking giving the impression of an honor guard.

"I hope you know what you're doing," Julie said, finally breaking his silence.

"I don't," Josh admitted. "And I can't think about it. Not when I face him."

"*We* face him."

"No. I've got to do this alone."

"Then what was the point of getting this fucking great big sword? We're in this together. One for all and all for one," he brandished Manannán's blade.

"The world's saddest musketeers," Josh said. "Don't argue with me, Julie. You know what you need to do."

"You've changed," Julie said, and the way he said it made it obvious he didn't mean it as a compliment.

Josh nodded.

"I hate you," Julie said.

"With good reason," Josh agreed. "But that doesn't change the fact that this is where we part ways."

He hadn't realized that his sister had closed the gap between them and had heard everything.

"I don't fucking think so," she said.

"Please, Lexy," Josh said, resigned to one last fight with his little sister. Why should it be any different? It was what they did. A smile flirted with his lips, but he could see that was just going to piss her off and he needed her on his side. "I need you to go with Julie. I can't tell you why, but when you are far enough away he'll explain it all to you. He's going to need you to be strong, Sis."

"What are you going to do?"

"To kill the king, you must become the king," he said. "So I'm going to become the king."

She looked at him then—really *looked* at him—and nodded. "Are you sure it's the only way?"

"It is."

"And it will work?"

"Probably not."

"But what you need us to do will make a difference?"

"All the difference in the world. Put it this way, if you don't, I'm dead."

"No pressure then," Alex said. "Okay, we'll do it. Whatever it is. We'll do it. You can count on us. We won't let you down. You worry about what you've got to do, not about us, okay?" He nodded. "Just promise me one thing, please."

"What?" Josh asked.

"That this is where it ends."

"I promise," he lied. Sometimes lying was a kindness; other times it was a torment. He wasn't sure which kind of lie this was, other than a necessary one.

They hugged, the embrace going on too long. He felt the tears threatening to come, and pushed her away with a hollow grin. "Don't make me get soppy, Sis."

He watched them go, heading off toward the hall of mirrors within Damiola's mausoleum. It would take them a couple of hours to get there. His part of this would be over by then.

He walked on toward the Rothery, knowing where he would find the old god. There was only one place he would be by: the lightning-struck tree outside The Hunter's Horns. So much of it came back to the old woodland, and that tree was the oldest in all of the ancient forest. The first tree.

He walked familiar but different streets, knowing that it was the last time he would pass all of these familiar landmarks that had been signposts for so much of his life. He passed the old secondhand bookstore on the corner where he had spent his pocket money as a teenager, only now it wasn't a bookstore, it was a chain store coffee shop and all of the fantastic worlds were gone. He stood on the corner where he'd had his first kiss pressed up against the wall by a girl with too much alcohol on her breath and across the street he saw the black hole that had been the window of the electronics store where all the men had gathered at four forty on a Saturday afternoon to watch the football scores roll by on the teletype, worshipers at their chosen altar. Then there was the dilapidated husk of the old Latimer Road cinema with its posters of Myrna Shepherd still on display behind the cracked glass of the box office. These streets were haunted by his personal ghosts. They were the streets that made him. His mind played tricks on him, offering glimpses of his childhood, the flickering shades of friends past walking by on the other side of the road. He would have done anything to be able to call out to them, to live just one more day in their company without a care beyond whatever obsession drove the twelve-year-old Joshua Raines.

And you will, if that is how you choose to use the magic that will flow through you, Josh. If that is what you want, that is what you shall have.

"You promised," he said. "You promised you would stay out of my head during these last few hours. You gave me your word that you wouldn't spy on me."

I did, but it isn't important, is it? You don't have anything you are trying to hide from me, do you?

"No," Josh lied. "But seeing as I'm going to die, I want to spend the last few hours alone with my memories."

And you don't want me seeing the pretty little girl you used to lust after, or the lies you told to people who thought you were their friend, the ugly thoughts that won't go away. I can understand that. No one wants to share their ugliness. Or is it your blood kin? Is that who you are trying to hide from me? Is it Seth Lockwood? Because I already tasted that memory—your grandfather's funeral, your mother's murder—it is there in the front of your mind all of the time, that final moment where you could have robbed him of his life but chose a punishment far worse and the fear that doing so cost you your soul. You have no secrets from me. Not now. Not ever. Now come to me, let us finish this. Our enemies will not wait for you to dwell among your ghosts indefinitely. We must be ready to fight for our beloved Albion. Are you ready?

Josh saw the tall figure of the antlered Arawn standing in the shade of the lightning-struck tree, waiting for him. The others were already assembled: the Gatekeeper; the Knucker, the impossible wooden warrior; Robin Goodfellow. And they were surrounded by so many other creatures; all of them waiting to witness Josh's sacrifice.

"Yes," he said, knowing his voice couldn't possibly carry, but knowing that it didn't need to.

Then come; give yourself to me.

53

"Take it, it's yours; it always was," Arawn told Josh as he hesitated.

The dense cloak of leaves and the clothes of moss, grass, and bark beneath gave the figure substance, but in the shadows of his face Josh could see he was fading. And fast. He wasn't made for this place. Time here tore at him, peeling away the layers of skin like flakes of dust. Soon there would be nothing left but the eighteen points of the antlers that curved wickedly away from Arawn's temples, and the bleached white bones of his skull, which, too, would crumble to dust and blow away on the swirling winds. Arawn held out an elaborately carved staff for Josh to take. The bulbous head had been hollowed out to resemble the same antlers that grew out of his skull.

Josh reached out, closing his fingers around the rowan staff.

And felt the thrill of possession, as the Horned God's essence flooded into him, overwhelming his sense of self. The entire world reeled around him. Nausea purged his gut, vomit staining his borrowed clothes. He couldn't let go of the staff; the muscles in his hand contracted around the ancient wood so tightly nothing would be able to pry it out of his dying grasp.

He felt himself dying one muscle at a time. The agony was unbearable; the realization that he'd been lied to, worse.

There was no grace.

The god swelled into him, filling every inch of his mind, devouring him, even as the leaves of his cloak began to burn and curl and the moss of his shirt slowly rotted away, stinking of mold as it crumbled. He stared into the god's eyes, seeing himself there, and he still couldn't break the connection; his hand stubbornly refused to relinquish its grip on the rowan staff, even as it was killing him.

You lied to me, he fought desperately to remain himself, flailing around inside himself, in search of anything that might anchor him to himself, so that he might stay Joshua Raines just a few seconds longer.

Of course I did, Arawn said. *I am a god. You are nothing.*

Josh threw back his head and screamed as he felt himself diminish. The world around him narrowed down to two points of darkness: Arawn's eyes, burning into him. He saw his own pathetic body twisting in pain as the ancient Lord of the Underworld took possession of his bones. The golden leaves turned brittle and fell away; all the seasons of their life happening in just a few seconds, until nature's cloak was nothing more than dust on the ground and Arawn stood before Josh, naked and vulnerable. There was fear in his face—an impossibly young face, broad featured, handsome, but more than anything, innocent—as the god that had been holding back the years abandoned the last body it had stolen, giving it to time. And like all things, it became dust.

Yes. Yes. Yes. Arawn was rapturous inside his mind. Josh felt it disappear one memory at a time; his life snatched away and consumed by the Shee creature. He desperately tried to cling on to something: a memory, one thing, just the one that would let him linger. But the sheer force of King Stag's will was enough to drown him beneath a tide of so many other memories that didn't belong to him. He tried to fix on Eleanor's face, on her red dress, as she'd rushed away down the rainswept street the first time he'd seen her, but like the headline on the newspaper stand, the details bled into each other, losing all shape and substance as the rain wept down. When the memory girl looked back at him, she didn't wear the hauntingly familiar features of Eleanor Raines. She wore the face of the old woman, Emmaline Barnes, in her hospital bed, though it, too, melted beneath the memory of rain, becoming younger, a beautiful summer child, and then maturing, the lines of life deepening as she wore the nurturing face of a mother that could have been any of a thousand women he passed on the street every day, but could only ever have been a young Emmaline Barnes.

She reached out to him.

He took her hand, but it wasn't him in the memory, it was Arawn. Josh had been replaced. The parasite was consuming his existence one experience, one thought, and memory at a time.

He fought his way back to the present, to the lightning-struck tree and the boy crumbling to dust before him, and knew that the only time he had left could be counted out in those flakes of dust. As the last hit the ground he would be gone.

Consumed.

In that moment there will be only me. And I am everything.

You made me a promise, my life for the children's.

You care so much about them?

Time narrowed down to a single second. When it passed, he would be gone.

In that second, he was both god and man.

In that second, he had the powers of both.

And that second would last.

Josh thought like a god, reaching out with his free hand to freeze that last flake of dust in the act of falling, and all around him the world stood still.

Very good. See, I did not lie entirely. Time is a construction of the mind. We are outside of time. We exist.

Show me the children.

No.

Show me the children.

No.

Show me.

No. Show yourself. Look. The Sleepers are gone. If you are determined to save them, you must bring them back. Reach out. Find their souls. Reclaim them from the mist. Give them flesh once more.

He didn't ask how. He was a god. The divine spark burned brightly in him, even if only for a single second. That was all it took. Josh sent his essence hunting, focusing his mind on the five Sleepers who had held open the door. They were there. Frightened. Alone. Confused. Wandering. He whispered a word of joining, not knowing how he knew to vocalize it, and in five mortuaries across the city, five girls, all of the same age, all having fallen into the same tragic locked-in state and been murdered in their beds by the chalk brothers, heard his call and opened their eyes. It felt like it should have been more miraculous. All it took was a word, but then, in the beginning that was all there was, the word.

They weren't the dead god's only victims, he realized, thinking of the children who had been stolen to become the hosts of his Hunters, and found himself swimming with Jenny Greenteeth through the litter-clogged water of the Thames, only she wasn't Jenny at all, but rather Penny, a young girl Arawn had drowned with his own two hands before welcoming the spirit of his water witch into her corpse. Josh sank down into the dirty waters, enveloping her sleek body as she swam and swam, darting between vessels sailing the river, and even as, eellike, she skimmed the bottom in the shadow of Parliament, he brought the rockweeds to life, reaching up to snag her ankles and tangle in her hair and fill her mouth even as she tried to curse it. The rockweed fronds burst as he closed her mouth, their salty sweetness filling her throat. She gagged on it, coughing, and as the coughs wracked the swimmer's body, he used his godlike power to drive the parasite out of her mind and into the seminal fluid that spilled over her tongue. Her body purged itself.

With the Huntress gone, there was nothing left within the

swimmer; no intelligence to control her muscles or mind. She didn't breathe. Dead, she floated there like so much flotsam.

Go home to your body, he sent the thought out into the Underworld where Arawn was truly king, and as its lord had no problem in finding the lost soul that had been Penny Grainger. She seemed not to understand, or not dare believe, so he repeated his message, his words like a silver thread that led all the way back to her body. *Go back to the tree and wake Charlie; take him home, you will be safe there. Tell him his love for you saved you every bit as much as your love for him kept him safe. There is happiness waiting for you, Penny. For both of you. Live the lives you were always meant to. You did a good thing for him, Penny. Live brilliantly. You deserve to.*

He saw her leave the water and run, and keep running and knew that she would find the boy waking in the protective arms of the tree in the heart of the great wood.

He found the chalk brothers underground.

They had become an entire ecosystem with insects and fungal growths sprouting from every orifice.

Open your eyes, he whispered, and they did, choking and gagging on the mushrooms in their mouths as they tried desperately to breathe.

Live.

It was a command they could not refuse.

The last one was Puck, the trickster, Robin Goodfellow, King Stag's red right hand who he watched dance at the head of a huge pack of rats, picking a path around the perimeter of the newly grown woodland to the ancient tree. Mud and blood clung to his clothes. This time he used the rats, causing them to surge up Robin's back and drag him down, their bloated bodies swarming over him, teeth and claws biting and scratching, and as they drew blood, offered the parasite a way out of its host body. They supped fragments of the Hunter into dozens of their hungry mouths, and dozens more, dividing and diluting the trickster until his essence was spread out among a hundred rats, forming a tainted pack within the pack.

Danny Ash lay on his stomach, unmoving. For a moment, Josh

thought he was dead; his breathing was barely perceptible. Then he heard the teenager weep and felt the wave of absolute loss as the boy grieved for the life the parasite had promised him. He looked up, looked at Josh, and actually seemed to see him. "I was whole," he said. "For the first time in my life I was complete. And you took that away from me." His heartbreak was absolutely devastating.

Josh reeled away from his grief and anger, recoiling so forcibly he saw again the lightning-struck tree and the last flake of dust from the boy that had been Arawn suspended in the air before his eyes. And kept on spinning away until he saw the bark-and-branch-encased body of a boy, on his knees, growling like a dog, and beside him his keeper, the Gatekeeper. He reached out to draw the soul of the boy out of the wooden cage, searching for his spark in the ether. He called out, but as he opened his mouth, his tongue twisted, and the two words that emerged bore no resemblance to anything he had ever said: *Hwaet! Áríseaþ!*

The answer that came was desperate, broken; a sob, a single word from the mouth of Jamshid Kirmani. "No."

He focused on the voice in the mists, using it as a lodestone to draw him forward until he found the wretched soul that had started so much of this in the name of supposed honor. The boy's soul was tortured; he bore the cuts and lacerations of a thousand thorns and brambles that cloaked him as the Knucker, but they were no match for the wounds the murder of Ollie Underwood and Aisha Kahn had inflicted upon it. The boy's demons were written everywhere on his skin, refusing to heal. Beneath the armor of bark there was blood, lots and lots of blood where the thorns had scratched the skin raw. He cried tears of blood. And in those tears Josh saw the crimes the boy had committed and how they had twisted his soul beyond breaking.

It doesn't have to be this way, he promised the boy. *There is redemption here. You can be different this time. You can make amends. All you have to do is return with me, open your eyes.*

Or at least those were the words he thought, but what Jamshid Kirmani heard was something else entirely: *Hwaet! Áríseaþ!*

And those two words terrified the boy because listening to them the first time was where it all began to go wrong for him.

"Leave me alone."

Hwaet! Áríseaþ!

This time the response was a tortured wail as Jamshid slammed the heels of his hands into his temples, each punishing blow punctuating the next word out of his mouth. "Just. Let. Me. BURN."

And the force of each word was enough to char the wooden armor; raising smoke, then flame, from the great beast's carapace. The air around him turned black, and from the black-sprung flame, Josh used what little magic it took to banish the Knucker and leave the boy to die.

The Gatekeeper was less and more than the others. He was broken in ways that Josh couldn't bear as he touched what little remained of the boy Tommy Summers had been. He found him hiding in the mists, a tiny frightened child of a spirit that had died long before his flesh had been stolen. A boy that had lost his innocence to the abuse of his supposed protector. It sickened him to the core, and made Tommy every bit as much a victim of his life as the boy he'd sacrificed to open the dimgate. His stunted soul was in such sharp contrast to the man who strode across the green with the slavering Knucker at his side, eager to inflict pain.

Josh coaxed the boy forward, promising him that he was safe, that he would always be safe now, that it should never have happened to him, and the boy listened, though did not willingly return to his flesh until the Gatekeeper was long gone and the twisted version of Tommy Summers he had been was gone along with him.

He was broken, but he would heal.

There, Arawn said inside the last tiny cavity of his mind. *You can't save them all. But not everyone deserves to be saved, Josh. Some people need to own the terrible things they do. But you kept your side of our pact; you brought the Sleepers back. I allowed you to restore the flesh playing host to my kin. It is done. Now I will keep my side of the promise, I will save Albion. You should be happy; what you have done with your life is more than many ever accomplish. Now it is time to welcome oblivion.*

He wasn't ready.

This moment of grace was all that he had. It wasn't hours, or days, it was a single moment that couldn't last forever and which, when it was gone, was the end of everything.

There was so much more to do if he was going to save himself.

Arawn laughed bleakly, enjoying the desperation driving that thought.

I told you; you can't cheat me.

But I can try.

I would be disappointed if you didn't. But it is all there in your mind. I know the desperate gamble you have made, putting your trust in a coward and a liar, and I have seen it fail already. Do you forget that I am a god? There is nowhere a thought can hide from me.

That's what I'm counting on, Josh thought, earning a sharp bark of laughter from Arawn.

Now that he had started, reaching out to the children Arawn had used to tear this world apart, the temptation was to undo it all, to reach back in time to a point before his life had fallen apart and rebuild it. It was in his power to save his father from Seth's meddling in that corner shop robbery, he could bring him back and get to have the normal childhood every kid deserved. He could undo the moment when Boone fell down the stairs. He could stop his great-grandfather from being in the crowded marketplace the day he caught that glimpse of Eleanor's red dress and recognized her, meaning that the old man died without ever writing the confession that plagued his family for years to come. There was so much he could do. Infinite possibilities. Infinite outcomes. He could protect his mother from that hideous incubus Seth fashioned from the stuff of the Annwyn to set on her. He could save her from that brutal death, alone in the old house on the Rothery. He could go back further, to the point of stopping the idea of a movie studio even occurring to Ruben Glass, or making sure that Eleanor Raines never set foot before Hitchcock's camera lens. Without that first meeting, there was nowhere for obsession to grow, and without obsession there was none of this. There was no *one for one* that allowed an ancient being to slip through the cracks and return to this world. There was no Wild Hunt. No once and future king, no white stag, no *anything*. There were so many ways he could influence the future by meddling with the past, but there was only one life he knew that he *had* to save so that Julie stood a chance of saving him: Cadmus Damiola.

And just thinking the man's name was enough to tear Josh's divine consciousness away from the moment to a place lost in the swirling mists between worlds.

The void.

The old man's soul walked the mists, still looking for the light.

He burned black in the gray world.

He wore sadness like a veil as the torments of his existence assailed him on either side. He let them lash at him, with burrs and spikes of self-loathing as sharp as any knife. This was his doing. All of it. The ills of the world were on him. He was an old fool. He didn't belong in the light. He deserved the agony, skin peeled from muscle, muscles flayed from bone, all of it, all of the pain. He deserved it. But it couldn't be fast. Pain needed to linger. So, each lash when it came was an eternity from the one before, and from the next, allowing him to suffer forever because that was how long it would take for the last ounce of meat to be peeled away from his bones.

Josh saw the invisible lash open a tear across the back of the old magician's layers of coats, biting deep. There was no blood, only a sticky saplike substance that oozed from the open wound.

Damiola's head came up and he cried out, but he didn't stop walking. He shuffled on, believing himself justly punished.

His soul light was the one intense flame in the endless roiling smoke of limbo. Where everything else came and went, flicking in and out of existence, as it followed its path to journey's end, there was no such luxury for the magician. He was in a hell of his own making. There were no cabinet walls to contain him, no chains or water torture chamber, but his suffering was every bit as creative.

Josh stood before him, waiting for the old magician to approach.

The mist curled around his feet, snapping at his heels like a terrier. He walked slowly, dragging his feet. He had his head down again as though he couldn't bear to see this hellish landscape of nothing, and was simply waiting for his soul to cease to be. "We really have to stop meeting like this," Josh said. "People will start to talk."

Damiola refused to meet his eye, no doubt believing him to be yet another punishment of this dark place sent to drive him out of his mind.

"I failed you," Damiola said. "There. I admit it. Now leave me alone."

"I can't do that," Josh said.

"You weren't this much of a bastard in real life."

"I've got a sister who would argue with you," he said. "Now stop feeling sorry for yourself, you aren't finished yet. I need you."

This time the old man did meet his eye, and Josh saw the flicker of hope extinguished and in its place the flames of fear burn bright. "Joshua? Is it . . . are you *real*?" and then a heartbeat later, "What have you done?"

"What needed to be done," Josh said, even now grasping the difference between this conversation and the others. There, he had only needed to subvocalize the words; this time he actually spoke to the damned. "Listen to me, old man, you don't belong here. Whatever you think, there's no nobility in this. You have suffered enough. This torment you are putting yourself through, you don't deserve it." Before Damiola could argue, Josh pressed on. "You want to be redeemed, then save me." He reached out, resting his fingers against the magus's forehead in blessing, and commanded his spirit to leave this place.

He stood alone in the darkness.

I have had enough of your sentimentality, Arawn chimed in his mind.

And snuffed him out.

54

Damiola opened his eyes and saw Julius Gennaro looking down at him.

"Why couldn't you just let me stay dead?" The words came out as a croak; his voice hadn't been used for a long time.

He tried to sit up, but his body refused to obey him.

A single candle burned in the middle of the burial chamber.

"It wasn't my choice," Julie said, and the old man realized the police officer was shaking.

"You look like you've seen a ghost," he said gruffly.

"No fucking kidding," Julie said. "I did not expect to meet Zombie Jesus in here. Not after last time."

Damiola saw the huge two-handed greatsword in the other man's grasp, and the ancient Celtic runes inscribed along the length of its blade. He recognized the ancient script, and knew well what it meant, but for the life of him could not understand why that should be. "Do I want to know where you got that?"

"Not really."

"But it has something to do with why I am back here?"

He nodded.

"Everything," Julie looked at the two other people inside the cramped mausoleum. At first, he thought Julie was seeking their permission to explain, but then he realized they didn't know what he was about to say, and because of that didn't know how to go about saying it.

"Spit it out, Officer Gennaro," he told Julie.

Julie didn't look at him. Instead he looked at the curious arrangement of mirrors that had been used to imprison Seth Lockwood. They were out of place, rearranged by Josh the last time he had been in here. The mirror Julie Gennaro looked at himself in had a web of cracks spidering through its silvered glass. "Josh needs you to undo whatever you did to make that," he said.

"Why would I want to do that?" Damiola asked, meeting his gaze through the backward land of the mirrors.

"He thinks he knows how to defeat the Horned God. He told me that to kill the king, he must become the king. He made a deal for our lives," Julie wasn't looking at the mirror now; he was looking at Alex. "He traded his life for ours. He's given himself to Arawn."

"That's what he meant when he said I wouldn't like what he had in mind? And you let him?" Alex said quietly, the full weight of what their last goodbye had meant sinking in. "You didn't try and stop him?"

Julie shook his head. "I did. I tried. But he has a plan."

"Oh, well, that's just fucking peachy, then," she said. "He's just turned himself over to a god that wants to destroy every living thing and feed the blood to the land because he thinks it will bring the magic back, but it's okay because he's got a plan? Well? What is it? What's my brother's plan?"

Julie looked over at the empty mirror. "Seth."

Alex shook her head. Then she looked at the old magician and grasped the true meaning of his resurrection. "He's dead, isn't he?" she said flatly. "He's already dead and we weren't there beside him. We just *left* him."

"No," Julie argued. "He's got a plan. He bought us time. We can't fail him. Not when he needs us the most."

"Needs us? He's gone. The old man is proof of that, isn't he? He's here because my brother isn't."

"Yes," Damiola said. He didn't bother telling them what he'd seen in the mist. It wasn't important now. "Arawn has taken over his flesh, body and soul. He's snuffed Josh out of existence. There is no room for him inside his body anymore, and nowhere for his soul to hide. The boy bought our lives with his sacrifice, so yes he's gone."

She didn't cry, which he thought she might. She was made of sterner stuff.

"Then how can we help him? That doesn't make sense."

"He could have killed Seth the first time we were here," Damiola said. "But he didn't. It wasn't mercy. None of this was," he meant the mirror prison and everything else. "But he wasn't prepared to risk Seth finding a way out of Hell, not today, not in one hundred years' time; not without knowing there was someone watching. Someone who would stand against him if they had to. Because Seth couldn't be allowed to walk free. A year in that prison might be a hundred out here, but that wasn't punishment enough for what he'd done to his family. He fed Seth something, a bone from his finger, dividing his body so that out here he would never die, not for as long as part of him still lived in the Annwyn." He understood Josh's plan then; it all came painfully clear in all of its desperation. "He might have surrendered himself to Arawn, but the god doesn't possess *all* of him. By god, that's a risk. Stupid, stupid boy. But there's still that single bone; a piece of him free of Arawn's essence. We have to get that bone if we're ever going to have a chance of bringing him back."

"That was his plan? Find a piece of his fucking *finger* and use it to magic him back into his body? You have to be fucking kidding me, Julie. You agreed to this?"

"I didn't have a choice," Julie said, looking down meaningfully at the sword in his hands. "And if we fail, he begged me to end it once and for all." He looked at the old man. "So, will you do it? Will you free Seth?"

"What choice do I have?" Damiola said, but he was anything but happy about it.

He crouched down beside the candle, placing both hands flat on the stone on either side of it and blew out the eternal flame. For a moment it looked as though it might reignite, the wick threatened to burn again, but he pinched it out before it could. The old man remembered the words of the chant he had used to seal the tomb. How could he not? He said them again, this time as part of a ritual of undoing. He had no idea if it would work until he saw the filaments of bluish light emerge from the cold stone. The light *smoked* as it chased along each and every crack, drawing the miracle back into his flesh. The enchantment undid the latticework of raw energy that had enclosed Seth Lockwood in the mists of the Annwyn.

He looked into the mirror, into Seth's prison.

And like the last time Josh had tried to summon his personal demon, there was no sign of Seth's rage-twisted face in the cobweb of cracks.

"Show yourself," the old man demanded.

That earned a ripple across the surface of the mirror and two fresh cracks through the glass before it turned supple and ultimately liquefied. Damiola rose slowly and walked across to the mirror's face, pushing the flat of his hand gently against the surface. The glass molded itself around his fingers like dough. He pressed more firmly and the rippling surface parted around his hand, resealing itself around his wrist.

The way was open.

But still there was no sign of the gangster.

"Officer Gennaro? A little assistance, please."

Julie moved up beside him, peering into the lightless square. "What do you need me to do?"

"Bring the bone back," Damiola said, and before Julie could argue or ask how, Damiola pushed Julie with all of his strength, unbalancing him. With the huge sword in his hands Julie couldn't reach out to break his fall without dropping it, and Manannan's blade wasn't about to be cast aside by a mortal hand.

Julie fell face-first through the glass, and kept falling.

The liquefied glass sealed itself behind him, trapping him in that Otherworld.

There was no cry of outrage; the two women in the mausoleum with him were too shocked by the sudden betrayal to voice actual words. "It had to be done," Damiola said, heading any objection off with brutal pragmatism. "Point one, Joshua would not thank us for liberating the killer of his parents, no matter his need. That justice offered him some semblance of peace. And, point two, we have no idea what the ramifications of Lockwood's release would be. All we do know is that every time we interfere with the natural order something terrible happens. The ripples of our actions are undeniable. They have been ever since I first opened that crack into the Annwyn to fashion Glass Town for Seth. That moment is like the ripples in a lake when you drop a stone into its still surface. At first, they are concentrated very close to where the stone disappeared, but gradually they roll out and out threatening to undo everything. And that is what is happening now. I would rather not be responsible for the end of everything. Would you?"

55

Julie fell.

And fell.

Into the black.

There was no grace to it. No sensation. No wind through the hair. No flailing arms or kicking legs.

He simply fell.

Until he wasn't falling anymore.

"Well, well, well, if it isn't the little bent bastard," a voice mocked. It seemed to come from all around him at once. With no light source to help orientate him, Julie was lost. He tried not to panic, gripping the sword's hilt tight. "Did they finally get fed up with you, too? Decide you were too much trouble and banish you to their own little private prison to rot? You're here sooner than I expected. It can't have been more than a year since your lot banished me. I would say it feels like forever, but for me it's only been a couple of days and time really does drag when you've got absolutely nothing to occupy your mind except thoughts of revenge."

"Seth?" he said, hating the weakness in his voice.

"In the flesh, so to speak."

"I can't see you."

"That's because it's dark, Julius. That's how this whole light and dark thing works."

"I need your help," Julie said, earning a roar of laughter from the unseen man.

When he finally stopped, he asked, "Why the fuck would I help you?"

Julie didn't have a good answer for that, or at least he hadn't, until he'd fallen into this place. Now, maybe he did. "Because one day you'll be free of this place, and you don't want Josh waiting around for you when you finally get out."

Silence hung heavy in the darkness, dragging out and out, even though the reality of it was no more than a few seconds. "Tell me more," Seth said, finally. "But I'm making no promises."

"Josh gave you something."

"He didn't give it to me. He forced it down my throat. There's a difference."

"Right. Yes. And you know why? If his body is divided between the two places, he won't age the way he should. He'll be around, waiting, even if a year in here is a hundred out there. He'll be there as long as there's a *chance* you might escape."

"Yes, yes, I know all that," Seth said impatiently.

"But what if it didn't have to be like that? What if I offered to help you out? Take that bone out of here, meaning that his body is no longer divided?"

"And you'd do that out of the kindness of your heart?"

"Something like that."

"You're a lousy liar, Julius. At least Taff was straight up about what he wanted, even if he sold his soul for a fuck. So, strikes me, if you want that piece of young Joshua back, there's a pretty fucking important reason, which means I've got the leverage here. And leverage is important in any negotiation. That, and frankly, I don't trust you. Not after last time. So, I want more."

"What?"

"I want out."

"Not going to happen," Julie said.

"Too bad. Can't help you then."

"I could just gut you and root inside for the bone," Julie said. "I don't need to wait for you to shit it out."

"True, and that's a mighty impressive sword you've got yourself there, but there's one thing you haven't considered in all of this."

"What's that?"

"Maybe that's what I want?"

"I don't buy it," Julie said. "Not you. That's not how you work."

"People change," Seth said, laughing again. This time it was little more than a chuckle that rippled through the darkness.

"People do, you don't," Julie disagreed.

"What's so important about this bone? Why all the fuss?"

How was he supposed to answer that without admitting that Josh was dead and without it they couldn't bring him back?

"You wouldn't believe me if I told you."

"Try me."

"We need it to fight a dead god."

The laughter this time was all-consuming. It filled the darkness. It rang like tinnitus in his ears. "You're right," Seth said finally, "I don't believe you."

Julie tried to think of a way to explain it that didn't drop Josh in the shit. He opted for the bare minimum in terms of detail. "This enchantment, it's a two-way street," he said. "When the magician made Glass Town for you and Eleanor, two creatures from there, traded places with you, hiding out in our world. We need that bone to fight them before they become too strong for us to banish him."

Seth thought about it for a moment, and in that moment Julie saw a flicker of light and shadows melded around the gangster's chiseled face. Those rage-filled eyes started at him. "And I should care why, exactly?"

"We lose, the door back for you is closed forever," he lied.

"The bad news is that I haven't taken a shit since I ended up here. It's still inside me. Now you can wait for nature to take its course, but frankly it could be another six months in 'real time' before I crap my cuz's little finger out, and somehow I don't think you've got the luxury of waiting six months. So, if you want it, you get me out of here. That is assuming you have a way out?"

Julie said nothing.

"Oh, wonderful; the bastards just tossed you in here with me, didn't they? You guys are the least organized heroes the world has ever seen. You don't have a clue, do you?"

"The door's open," he said, hoping it was true.

"And do you even know *where* the door is?"

"I know enough," he lied.

Julie's grip tightened on the leather-wrapped grip of the ancient sword.

Seth said, "You do realize that this conversation has lasted a good few hours back there. More. They're going to start thinking you failed soon. Time isn't your friend, Julius. So, here's a compromise I can live with: you let me piggyback your way out of this place, I'll give you your precious bone, but you have to help me with something before we go, because I've got no intention of going back there and dying in a couple of days as time catches up with me. Remember, I know how this place works. I know better than anyone. So, this is what you're going to do: we're going to take advantage of this trick Josh pulled, leaving part of himself here," Seth held out his left hand. "A finger's enough, you follow?" Julie nodded. He had no idea if the gangster could see him. "Good, then that's settled. You'll help me leave a little piece of me in here before we go, and you won't tell anyone."

"Why would I do that?"

"To save my precious cousin," Seth said flatly. "What? You're surprised? Come on, Julie. Think. You're here. You wouldn't be if you weren't desperate. Believe me, there's no way Joshua would risk opening the prison door, not for anything, which means he's out of the equation. Doesn't take a genius. So, you want his finger, you give me what I want, and I want my freedom."

"Give me your hand," Julie said.

"I don't fucking think so. Just a finger."

"Don't you trust me?"

"About as far as I can throw you." Even so, Seth Lockwood took two steps forward and seemed to shimmer out of the darkness, becoming more substantial; the subtle shades of shadow picked out by some unseen light source. No, not unseen, he realized looking down at the blade in his hand. The runes along Freagarthach's blade glowed an eerie blue. "A finger," he repeated.

"Like I said, you're not in a position to bargain. I could just gut you like a fish."

"You could, but you won't."

"Won't I?"

"Not when you don't know the way back to the mirror. I do. You could find it, sure, but it'd take you time. And time in this place is past one hundredfold back there. It's the one thing you don't have. So, like I said, you're not going to do anything stupid—"

Before Seth could finish his rationale, Julie lashed out, swinging the greatsword in a wild arc that would have taken Seth's head from his shoulders if he hadn't ducked and thrown his hands up to protect his face. As it was, the wickedly sharp blade bit into skin and bone, paring the muscle and parting the joint as it cleaved through, taking Seth's right hand off at the wrist.

The gangster's screams were unbearable.

Julie wiped the blood from the blade on his jeans.

"Show me the way to go home," he said, echoing the old music hall song.

"You cunt, you absolute cunt," Seth gasped, the bloody stump of his wrist clamped between his legs as it pulsed out his life. He wasn't handling the pain well.

"You'll want someone to look at that, it's a nasty cut," Julie said. "Chop-chop. Time waits for no man and all that."

Seth didn't say a word. He tried to pull his shirt over his head, and wadded it up over the stump. It filled quickly with blood. Gritting his teeth, the gangster wrestled with his belt, working it free of its loops with his one good hand and used it to fashion a makeshift tourniquet. With one end of the belt clenched between his teeth, Seth cinched it so tight the leather bit deep into his skin, cutting off his circulation.

"All good," Julie said. "Think of it as an incentive for you to get me out of here. You get what you want and I got to hurt you just a bit for what you did to my partner. That's what we call a win where I come from. Now, let's get out of here so you can shit that finger out and I never have to see you again. Complain, even once, and I'll ram the sword through your belly and fish about in your intestines for the bone. I'm really not in the mood to play nice anymore. Like you said, I don't have the time. And now neither do you."

Seth was forced to lean on him as they walked together in the dark, making their way back toward the rippling skin of the mirror and the tear that would lead them back into Damiola's mausoleum.

56

Mel Banks was an island of tranquility in a Situation Room of utter chaos.

But that calmness was a lie.

Beneath it simmered a wellspring of rage.

She stared down at the phone in her hand, not quite believing that after days of radio silence Ellie and Julie had finally turned up, and then had the temerity to hang up on her when she demanded an explanation as to where the hell they'd been for the last few days. She put the phone back in the cradle. There was a half-eaten protein bar on her desk beside a cold cup of coffee. It wasn't much in the way of breakfast, and less in the way of lunch. The cup left a ring of brown on a Post-it note as she lifted it to swallow another mouthful, forgetting how vile the cold machine coffee actually tasted. Within the brown ring, the name *Emmaline Barnes* was written in her tight scrawl.

She wasn't sure how the old woman's disappearance fit in with everything else, but the fact that Julie Gennaro's girlfriend, Alex Raines, was on her primary care team, and Alex was missing, right along with Ellie and Julie, meant she was almost certainly part of the puzzle even if right now Mel wasn't seeing an Emmaline Barnes–shaped space in the jigsaw of crime all around the room. But just because you didn't see it, didn't mean it wasn't there.

Tenaka drew a bright red line through one of the names on the board.

Another dead lead.

And it wasn't as though they didn't have enough crap to contend with right now without wasting time chasing shadows. The world was going to hell, and seemingly a quite literal one at that.

The gaffer was pulling his hair out.

Social media was going crazy. The latest reports had the numbers up around fifty thousand teenagers on the streets last night, tearing the place up. The numbers were amplified beyond reason. Media hubs buzzed with the impossible forest that had sprung up in place of the pedestrianized shopping zone. It was all portents and end-of-the-world preachers, the kind of stuff that drove her crazy. She was practical. If something happened—even something as utterly out there as a forest growing by hundreds of acres overnight—there had to be a rational reason for it. Some bizarre prank by a TV station maybe? Again, just like the Emmaline Barnes link, just because she couldn't see it, didn't mean it wasn't there.

The reality was that fifty thousand kids could do—and had done—a lot of damage.

Tenaka had been forced to draft in support from neighboring constabularies, and had riot police manning the barricades, trying to break the tidal flow of violence as it surged relentlessly on through the boroughs. She'd never forget the sight of people staring down from the highest windows of a burning tower block and realizing that they had no chance and choosing to jump rather than burn.

She'd been caught up in it as well, trying to make what should have been a routine bust on the Rothery that ended up as a reenactment of the Alamo because Granny Underwood came looking for justice for Ollie.

London blazed; it didn't just burn.

And they had no way of controlling it. It was all they could do to go out night after night and try to minimize the hell playing out on their streets, but confronted by the casualties they were taking, it became increasingly difficult to strap on the riot gear and go out into the streets.

Last night alone, a dozen landmarks of the city burned to the ground; photos of St. Paul's dome crumbling, as the fire took down Wren's most iconic creation, showed the violence at its most heartbreaking. It wasn't just the beautiful buildings, either, the bedsits of Paddington and cheap tourist hotels of Bayswater burned just as well. The destruction hadn't reached the shops of Oxford Street and Regent Street yet, but it was only a matter of time before either the fire, the youthful rioters, or the impossible trees won the race to tear up those famous streets.

Mel Banks had made another note when St. Paul's had burned. It said simply *Oranges and Lemons*. What it meant was less simple, and she wondered if there was a clue to what was going on in the old nursery rhyme. The churches had all burned in the first two nights of rioting: St. Clement, St. Martin, St. Sepulchre, Shoreditch, Stepney and Bow from the newer version of the rhyme, St. Margaret's, St. Giles, St. Peter's and Aldgate, Whitechapel, St. Helen's, St. Anne's, and St. John's from the oldest version of it. Fifteen churches in the city had burned to the ground, all fifteen of them made famous by a nursery rhyme that itself was about child sacrifice.

The boards behind her had changed a lot over the last couple of days, reflecting the violence. The faces of the lost and missing switching places with the suspects, the suspects moving into the ranks of the lost and missing, and new evidence was going up all the time. It was a constant battle out there and making sense of it was proving near impossible. Most of it consisted of sightings of Jamshid Kirmani, Danny Ash, and Tom Summers, who, if all the reports coming in to the crime room were to be believed, were everywhere at once and responsible for most of the crimes of the last week. They had photographs of Danny Ash conducting the rioters, right up at the front of a sea of rats like some mad Pied Piper.

She crossed the room to the incident boards, looking at two of the very familiar faces up there: Julie and Ellie, both of them listed as missing since Julie had taken the call in this very room and said he was off to rendezvous with Ellie. Radio triangulation had pinpointed their meet at the old Ravenshill Cemetery, but when Tenaka sent a crew up to scour the place, they turned up nothing, and local CCTV footage recovered from a street camera up the road from the cemetery gates showed the pair of them leaving shortly after. Following their digital footprint proved impossible as in both of their cases it simply ceased to be. It converged on the old wood not far from the station, and then disappeared. Her biggest fear—and one she'd been reluctant to vocalize—was that the reason for that was that they were buried under so much rock and dirt that the satellite could no longer pick up the signal. They'd gone days with nothing while the riots gathered momentum and aggression, and it became more and more obvious they weren't coming back. And then suddenly both of their phones came online, triggering a series of alerts back in the Situation Room. They'd woken up a couple of miles north of where they'd disappeared, in the weird old fake world of the movie studio.

She took their pictures down and carried them back to her desk.

Tenaka saw what she was doing, and for a second the look of dread on his face mirrored her own conviction that they were dead—a conviction that had only been laid to rest by Ellie hanging up on her a moment ago. "They're okay," she said. "Both of them. Taylor just called in."

"Where the *fuck* have they been?"

"Your guess is as good as mine, she wasn't saying."

"Not good enough. They can't simply up and disappear like that. Jesus Christ, we've wasted time and money trying to track them down. I don't even want to think about how much manpower we've diverted into looking for them that could have been put to better use. Like looking for, oh I don't know, how about the fucking *killers*!"

She stared him down. "No need to shout at me, boss. I'm not the one who fucked off in the middle of an investigation. I'm the mug who got left behind to pick up the pieces." She knew she was taking her frustrations—and relief—over her friends out on Tenaka, but someone needed to bear the brunt of her anger and he just happened to be in the right place at the right time, making him more than worthy of a bit of verbal. He was a big boy. He could handle it.

He looked like he was about to bite back, but instead threw up his arms in frustration and turned his back on her.

He went over to the bank of people mapping out social media reports in real time on an interactive map.

"Boss," one of them said, calling him over.

"What is it, Mullins?"

"I'm not sure how I'm supposed to record this one."

"Try me?"

"It's about one of the kids, the lock-ins. Bethany Laws. She's woken up."

"How? That's not possible. Unless someone's royally fucked up, the girls are all dead," Tenaka said, looking back at the incident board where the Sleepers all had the word *Deceased* recorded beside their names.

"She was in a drawer in the morgue," the constable said, "when the coroner heard frantic banging and screams from inside."

"You're taking the piss, right, sunshine? Tell me you're taking the piss. I can't take much more of this shit."

"That's not all of it, gaffer. There's some seriously weird shit going on out there."

"I don't want to know, Mullins," Tenaka said, but of course he did.

"I'm seeing loads of weird reports about the wildlife, sir."

"Weird in what way?"

"Well first there's a lot of photos being shared on Instagram and across Twitter with what look like streets filled with *rats*," he tilted the screen so Tenaka could see what he meant. Tenaka scratched a fingernail in the valley between eye and nose, not really wanting to see what was on the screen. "Then there's reports of dogs converging on the Rothery, sir."

"Strays?" he asked.

"We're talking hundreds of them, sir, so I don't think so," and again he offered photographic evidence. This time he scrolled through half a dozen poorly framed photos showing packs of dogs running wild. There must have been fifty or sixty of them in those few photos alone. In the last one, the animals appeared to be prowling in a circle around a fallen animal of some description; it was difficult to tell from this angle. "The chatter is rife. Loads of people reporting that their pets ran away this morning. Dogs slipped their leashes; cats disappeared over rooftops and fences. I've got no idea what it means, but tracking the sightings, it looks like there's a pattern to it all. They are making a beeline for the Rothery," he said.

"We'll make a proper copper of you yet, Nathan," Mel Banks told the young constable.

"Thanks, ma'am," he grinned.

She wasn't sure what it meant, if anything, but combined with the attacks on the churches, those migrating animals felt as though there was something fundamental happening here, almost like the city was casting off the shackles of Christianity and returning to much older ways. She couldn't help but smile at the notion of animals forming the heart of a new faith. Or old faith.

"Sir?" another voice called from the back of the room.

"Do I want to know?"

"Kate Jenkins and Annie Cho," he said.

"What about them?"

"Both names just came up as alerts," the officer explained.

Tenaka crossed the room to where she was working feverishly at the keyboard to clarify exactly what was coming through the wire.

"If you're about to tell me what I think you're about to tell me, do me a favor, don't. Just don't."

The young officer shrugged. It was a particularly eloquent gesture, all things considered.

"Oh, for fuck's sake. Seriously? What the fuck is wrong with me?

I died didn't I? Somehow. And just didn't realize it. Now I'm in Hell and I'm being tormented for eternity by unsolvable cases with fucking miracles there just to fuck with my head. Fuck my life."

"Maybe it's some sort of poison, sir, like that blowfish that mimics the symptoms of death for days, slowing the heart down so much it's barely perceptible?" Mel offered helpfully.

"It's better than the alternative," Tenaka said as the phone on Mel Banks's desk rang again.

Everyone turned toward it as one.

No one said a word as she answered.

She listened. She nodded.

Tenaka couldn't take his eyes off her.

She nodded again.

Said, "Yes."

She pointed at the board, at Kirmani's photograph. This was it. A credible sighting of Jamshid Kirmani. "We've got him," she mouthed. Tenaka moved excitedly toward her, as if he couldn't wait for her to relay the message. She hung up the phone. "Kirmani is in the Rothery," she told him. "And he isn't alone. He's with Ash and Summers."

"Then what are we waiting for, let's bring them in."

"There's no rush," Mel told him.

"How so?"

"They aren't going anywhere."

"We can't—"

"Kirmani's dead, guv. The other two are out of it."

"How credible are we talking?"

"One of our own," Mel told him.

She looked at the dozens of red lines looping from one name to the next to the next across the incident boards, until those red lines tangled in a violent web.

Dead changed everything.

57

Julie held the bone in his clenched fist.

It was still warm.

He didn't want to think about where it had been.

Seth was with him, clutching the charred stump of his ruined right arm. Damiola had done something with it to stop the bleeding. He didn't want to know what. Frankly, he'd have been more than happy if the gangster had shuffled off their shared mortal coil before he'd passed Josh's finger bone, but such were the disappointments of life. Like the song said, you really couldn't always get what you wanted. The only consolation was that Seth looked like shit. The old man walked two steps behind him, keeping an eye on the East End gangster. Alex and Ellie brought up the rear.

"Bet you never thought you'd see this place again, did you?" Julie asked as they approached the outskirts of the Rothery. So much had changed since they'd last been here. They walked toward the house that had once been Taff Carter's, and a few streets away where Seth had murdered, not one, but two people that the woman he loved had loved. The whole situation was utterly fucked up.

"I never gave up hope," he said, the words laced with heavy irony. "But if we're talking about doing things we never thought we'd do, butchering your girlfriend's brother with a sword has to be right up there. You think you can handle it?"

"Yes."

"I could do it for you, you know," Seth offered, "if you're having second thoughts?"

"I'm fine."

"You sure? I really wouldn't mind. I've fantasized about killing Cousin Josh for quite a while. I think I'd enjoy it."

"I'm sure you would."

"Just trying to be helpful."

A new forest spilled out into the streets, rich and full of life. Julie had walked the beat here for most of his professional life, working with community outreach, running the youth club out of the back of the old church hall, getting involved with sports clubs and even the boxing and martial arts stuff being run out of the old gym over by the railway arches, but the place was unrecognizable. He heard movement all around them—scurrying, tiny paws and claws—but the trees hid their followers from sight.

"You ever feel like you're in trouble?" Seth asked, offering a wry smile. "I mean, given what you told me, you're about to get your ass handed to you on a plate by a fucking *god*. This isn't going to end well for you, Julie. I could conjure up some help, if you wanted, a little backup? I'm sure you didn't destroy the carousel and all of the cutouts, did you? Or did you?" Julie said nothing. "Ah, that would be such a waste. There was some real power there, those conjurations. Hell, if I were going to go up against a god, I'd want to send the Reels in first, to soften it up. Not that I'd even then stand a chance. I'm not an idiot. You can't fight a god, even with a fucking greatsword. How does it feel to know you're going to die in a couple of minutes?"

"You tell me?"

"Ah, Julie, it's a shame you're not going to be around much longer. The more time I spend with you, the more I think I could really grow to like you."

"Shut up," Alex said from behind them.

"I'm just saying, he's my kinda guy."

"Julie?" she said.

"Yes, my love," he said.

"We don't need him anymore. If you want to practice on him before you face my brother, I won't cry about it. We're not a close-knit family."

Julie smiled. "Anything for you," he said, milking the moment by raising the sword to his lips and kissing the curls engraved into the blade.

"Less of that, thank you very much," Seth said, but she was right, they didn't need him anymore. "You've got to start changing the way you think of me. I'm one of the good guys now. Didn't you get the message? You couldn't do this without me. You save Cousin Josh; it's down to *me*. I showed you the way out of the darkness; I gave you the bone in return. That wasn't out of the good of my heart, I did it for my *freedom*."

"I think you should shut the fuck up," Julie said softly. "Because in case you forgot, you murdered my partner and no matter what else has happened between then and now, I still haven't forgiven you for that."

Seth stared at him; he couldn't quite believe he was still being blamed for Taff's corrupt soul getting him killed by that demonic Hollywood heartbreaker. "You cut my fucking *hand* off, I'd say that makes us more than even!"

"Let me explain something to you, Seth," Julie said, far more reasonably than he felt, "I am going to kill you. Maybe not today, maybe not tomorrow. But I *am* going to kill you. I'm going to do it for Taff, and for Eleanor, for Isaiah and Boone and Josh and everyone else you've fucked with during your life. It's going to happen. Believe me. And here's something you might appreciate, I'm going to enjoy doing it."

"Okay, I'll shut up now," Seth said.

"Wise decision," Julie said.

"But one last thing before I do. I just wanted to let you know that instead of frightening me, that little speech of yours just convinced me that you and me, we could have had something, Julie. I'm talking a friendship for the ages. The kind of thing they write songs about."

"Murder ballads," he said, bluntly. "No, thanks."

"Between us we could have ruled this town."

"London doesn't need rulers," he said, ending the conversation.

Up ahead he saw the familiar signpost that offered a welcome to the Rothery.

It was completely tangled up in green shoots that curled up around the sign's metal legs in a corkscrew of verdant vines. Purple blossoms had opened up to obscure the bottom curl of the *e* and the tail of the *y*. Beyond it, the first row of houses looked like they marked the edge of a kill zone. Julie saw the black smears of burns on the red brick, and the twisted wire frames of mattresses and other junk that had been dragged out into the open and set alight. There were six houses in a row, each one of them gutted.

They crossed over the imaginary line into the Rothery.

Julie could feel the tension in the air.

Contact with the blade heightened his senses. The thrill of the old earth magic prickled the fine hairs along his arms and nape of his neck. "He's here," he said.

"I should hope so," Seth said, then looked wounded when the others turned on him. He shrugged, opening his remaining hand and turning it palm up. "I mean, seriously, that's why we're here, isn't it? For the big showdown. It'd be a bit anticlimactic if he *wasn't* here, that's all I'm saying."

The walked on in silence, crossing the wasteland that had been the car park between the single-story line of shops and the pub, making their way toward the green and the lightning-struck tree outside The Hunter's Horns.

Up above, city birds congregated into one huge flock that cawed and cried as they circled endlessly—banking and rising, banking and falling—around the perimeter of the ancient woodland beyond the estate.

They could hear movement in the new trees that spilled out around them, too. Animals prowling. The effect was eerie: the constant rush of sound; the whisper of small bodies up against the long grass and through the thickening hedgerows. It was all-pervasive.

And utterly *natural*.

But that was the problem: the Rothery was a concrete jungle; it wasn't some equatorial rain forest.

He saw Josh standing beside the twisted tree, bodies at his feet.

He seemed to be lost; listening to a voice none of them could hear.

He held a wooden staff in his hand, and had his face tilted up to the sky.

He was watching the birds.

He didn't turn as they approached.

From the back, he didn't look any different, so for just a moment Julie allowed himself to believe that somehow nothing had changed, that Josh was still Josh and that he'd turn around at any moment and smile that infuriating wry grin of his and shrug as though to say, *Hey everything's fine, I don't know what all the fuss was about.*

But when he finally turned around it was obvious nothing was fine.

"So this was his plan?" Josh said, looking down at the sword in Julie's hand. "How utterly tragic." With a flick of the wrist, Manannan's blade was wrenched out of Julie's grasp and sent skidding across the grass toward the ancient god dressed in his friend's body.

It stopped spinning at his feet.

He looked past Julie at the magus behind him. "Ah, have you come to die *again,* old man? I would have thought you'd learned your lesson the last time, having your ties that bound your soul broken."

"I'm a stubborn bastard," Cadmus Damiola said, moving forward. He held out his hand. A small blue flame danced across his fingertips.

He stood between Seth and Julie.

"Well, I'll just have to be sure to kill you more thoroughly this time; make sure death sticks," the god said.

In the distance, they heard sirens. The police. The station house was no more than a minute or two away. They needed this done before Melissa Banks and the others turned up with riot shields and batons and got themselves killed. They couldn't let more die at the hand of the ancient one than already had; the price was high enough.

"You can't win this," Damiola told Arawn. He didn't sound like he believed it. The blue flame along his fingertips flickered as he spoke, flaring until it surrounded his whole hand. "Not in the long run. Kill us, more will come."

"No they won't," the god disagreed. He sounded like Josh. He looked like Josh. Even the half-wry twist of the lips was so familiar, and yet so wrong. "Not until the veil comes down and the Bain Shee find their way here. And by that time the land will be rich with blood, and magic will have returned. I can live with that. Shed enough, and there might just be enough power left in this blasted place to survive the fall. No promises."

The old magician held out his hand, and to Julie it seemed as though his soul stepped out of his body—the blue flame spread, growing, doubling in size between heartbeats and doubling again and again, until it was the old man's ethereal doppelganger. It moved to meet the god.

Josh raised the elaborately carved staff and spoke a single word, which called down the birds.

Starlings swept in fast in a flurry of wings, beating and battering them in a vortex of feathers as more and more of the birds churned through the air.

Julie couldn't see more than a few feet in front of his face except for wings and small-feathered bodies, and never for more than a fraction of a second as more and more of the god's creatures flew at them.

He threw his hands up to shield his eyes as more wings flapped and beat against his face.

Through the ever-shifting gaps, he saw the ghostly blue shadow of Damiola's spirit charge the god.

And lose.

It seemed to tear apart, shredding, then blew away with the wind.

But it bought him precious seconds of distraction.

Julie forced his way forward, only thinking about the sword.

He'd promised Josh.

He wouldn't fail him.

All he had to do was put one foot in front of the other, and again, and again, forcing his way through the pelting wings and the frenzy of caws and clawing talons.

He caught flashes of blue as the tendrils of Damiola's doppelganger smoked, writhing and twisting and coiling as they tried to find the god's flesh to anchor on. They simply melted away, no more solid than the stuff of illusion.

Smoke and mirrors, without the mirrors.

The old man was showing the god what he wanted to see, but none of it was real.

The birds kept coming and coming in a fury of wings and feathers. Julie kept his head down and kept on walking one step at a time.

And then there was a sudden moment of peace, with no avian assault. It lasted one, two, three seconds, and then he dared look up.

All the birds in the sky were in the agonizing process of fusing into a single tortured shape. It was so much greater than their tiny parts of brittle wings and beady eyes. Julie wrestled with the enormity of it; the thing's wingspan stretched all the way across the green, from the lightning-struck tree to The Hunter's Horns. It was huge. It reared back in the air, holding position; wings creating massive downdrafts as they beat slowly, and loosed a deafening shriek from its thousands of beaks.

He was still ten feet from his fallen blade.

It felt like ten miles with that thing hovering over it.

He risked a glance to his left and saw the magician, the blue tendrils of his soul light crackling and sparking, sizzling and reeking, with the most awful odor as they lashed against the rowan staff the god used to defend himself.

Then came the moment—the realization that the tendrils were nothing more than paper-thin trickeries.

Beyond them, Julie saw the sleek bodies of the rats circling. They weren't alone. More of the city's wildlife had converged on the tree, drawn here by the rebirth of the ancient god, finally in skin that could survive in this place and ready to reclaim his kingdom.

Josh whipped the staff around, changing his stance so that he could sweep the rowan weapon around in a vicious semicircle to drive Julie back.

Julie didn't flinch.

He took the hit on the ankle.

Their best hope—their only hope—was to do this together, all of them.

"Josh!" he yelled. "Josh! Can you hear me?" It didn't matter if he could or couldn't, what mattered was the fraction of a second's distraction his cry caused, and the slightest turn of the god's head toward the sound.

Damiola understood.

He seemed to draw deeper on the reserves of his spirit to launch, doubling the intensity of the illusion, dividing the soul light into a thousand smaller flames, and battering the god with them. His body collapsed under the debilitating strain as the ties that bound flesh to spirit stretched to breaking point; but this time he was ready, this time as the god loosed his own spirit animal, the mighty King Stag, to take Damiola head-on, the old magician scattered the shreds of his soul and gave them wing, like the birds that had battered at him only moments before. The effect was such that as King Stag's great blazing halo launched with its horns down, the birds of Damiola's soul simply fluttered around it, breaking up only to reform, enveloping the mythical beast rather than taking the brunt of its brutal assault head-on.

It wasn't a fight he could ever win, not for more than a few seconds, but it wasn't one he was *trying* to win. He'd already died; he was more than prepared to die again if it bought Julie the few precious seconds he needed to get to the sword.

They had to be enough for Julie to make a difference.

He couldn't stand there watching to see if the stag shredded Damiola's soul birds, or suffocated beneath their blanket of smoke and translucent feathers as they closed around the radiant creature, or if the whole illusion just burned out to nothing.

Julie ran for the sword, skidding across the grass like a baseball player sliding in for home plate.

The god wore his friend's face. He couldn't think about that. It wasn't Josh. Josh was dead. He had to keep his word. His word was everything. Fail now and he would damn Josh to an eternity masquerading as a god's meat suit.

His hand closed around the hilt of the ancient blade, and in one fluid motion lunged upward, ramming the unwieldy sword into Josh's gut and forcing it home against the sickening resistance of bone.

The knotwork of runes along the length of the blade reacted to the god's blood as it spilled into their runnels, shimmering as the slick redness sizzled and burned away. What remained were the blood-red scars of writing cut deep into the steel.

And he pushed deeper, harder, until the cross guard dug into the god's stolen stomach, and he felt the torn flaps of skin brush wetly against his knuckles. In that moment, with the blood on the blade and the blood on his hand, he was connected with Arawn and the Underworld. He could feel it pulsing through his body, surging with electric intensity down the length of the blade into his arm, into his blood, into every ounce of his being. He was joined with the earth. He was joined with the Annwyn. He was joined with the soul of the land. It was a great, powerful, unknowable entity: a force that surrounded all things; infused them. It was the magic of Danu, the Earth's mother. It was the essence of all things. There was no beginning; there was no end. He felt the soul of the land burn bright inside him, and it was *glorious.*

He was filled with the energy of life.

It was nothing more magical than that.

And yet it was the most magical of all things.

This is why the boatman returned us from that other place, the voice of the ancient blade chimed in his head, savoring the moment every bit as much as Julie was.

Arawn's hand closed around the cutting edges of Freagarthach, breaking the moment.

Julie looked up at the blade, seeing where it cut deep into Arawn's palm as his grip tightened.

More blood spilled between his fingers, making the steel slick.

And up above, the great conglomeration of feathers came undone, each and every one of the starlings, pigeons, and other city birds scattering from the gigantic gestalt to take wing. Some settled on the rooftops nearby, others on the tree limbs, watching. The last of them landed on the gable of the Lockwoods' old pub across the way, close enough to see everything.

"You dare?" The god drew the sword slowly out of his stomach, shaking his head with disappointment that they would try something so utterly pointless as stabbing him with a mortal blade. He cast it aside contemptuously, and turned the full force of his rage on Julie, who was on his knees at the god's feet.

With a scornful gesture, Arawn plucked him up off the ground, lifting him to his feet and then up a few inches more so that his toes kicked uselessly against nothing but empty air as he hung there, flailing impotently against the invisible bonds restraining him.

"Any last words?" the ancient one mocked. "A message for the woman you love?" Julie screamed as first one wrist snapped, the sound of the bone breaking like a gunshot, then the other snapped. "I'll take that as a no," Arawn said as Julie's shoulders dislocated, the blades parting like butterfly wings. His body bucked forward as the joints were wrenched out of place. His world was reduced to a single sensation: *agony*. He ceased to exist outside of it. There was pain, nothing else. And still his body continued to contort, bones bending beyond the point of breaking as Arawn concentrated on breaking him one bone at a time. Ankles and knees were next, and then the staccato rattle of each rib shearing apart one after the other, like firecrackers.

The skin tore, unable to contain the spreading bones as they opened up.

And Julie stopped screaming. His cries went beyond agony into the afterlife as his head fell limply forward, lolling on his chest as the vertebrae in his neck snapped one after another. Arawn drew Julie's arms up at his sides until he hung spread-eagled in the air, dead, and turned his attention on Damiola and his diminished soul.

"You thought you could win? How truly pitiful you are, you creatures of the modern age. *This* was your desperate plan?" He wasn't talking to them. He was talking to the man whose body he had stolen. "I expected . . . *more*. For just a second you were a god, and this was the best you could do?"

Arawn let Julie fall.

58

Alex picked up the fallen sword.

No one was looking at her.

She saw Ellie Taylor running to Julie's side. She couldn't look at him. If she let herself see what had happened to him, to see the ruin of his body, she'd break every bit as brutally as any one of his bones. She looked down at the sword in her hands. It was so much lighter than she'd expected. She looked up at her brother. And that was who she saw.

Josh.

The same Josh she'd played Eggyman with when she was little more than a baby and couldn't really say Superman as he flew her on his knees; the same Josh who used to pin her down and pretend to fart on her chest and would tickle her until she was on the point of peeing and begging him to stop; the same Josh who convinced her the birds that had nested in the attic were really the ghost of an old woman and had her believing that their little council house in London was actually built on an ancient Indian burial ground despite the completely illogical notion that the Native Americans would sail over to England to bury their dead; the same Josh who stood on the sidelines as she cheated in the egg and spoon race at school, running with her thumb over the top of the boiled egg so it wouldn't fall as she raced to victory; the same Josh who used to play nerdy role-playing games on a Sunday and whose best mate she'd totally crushed on, baking brownies to try and win his heart; the same Josh who had taken her out to her first nightclub and warned her years after the brownies against losing her virginity to another "best" mate. There were a billion memories, large and small, that tied them together. They were brother and sister, and they were all each other had now.

Her hands shook violently.

The sword's tip dipped, scraping across the ground.

She felt a tingle—a thrill—chase up her arm.

The world around her reduced to the two of them, out on this green outside the pub where they'd played a thousand times growing up together.

Family.

The bonds of blood, the ties of shared grief, the weight of most painful memories of all, the memories of the future not shared.

She took one step. Two.

"Oy! Cuz! Over here, you ugly bastard, come on, you and me. That's what it's all about isn't it. Family. So, come on, fucking face me," Seth roared from somewhere over by the pub. She'd just assumed he'd run when he had the chance. He had nothing to keep him here. So his challenge, a modern, crass war cry, had surprised her as much as it had surprised the monster inside her brother's body.

Josh turned to face the more imminent threat, leveling the bulbous end of the staff at Seth. She expected thunderbolts and lightning to shoot out of the tip, or a flamethrower-type venting of fire to scorch the earth between them, something *spectacular*. For a moment, it looked as though nothing was happening. Then she saw the roots that had grown up from out of the ground to tangle around Seth's ankles, rooting him to the spot, literally.

Josh was already fighting on two fronts, deflecting Damiola's illusions and pinning Seth down, when Ellie yelled her own challenge, but hers was different in so many ways. She shrieked like a banshee as she ran from Julie's broken body, stumbling on traitorous legs, straight at Josh. She held her hand out in front of her. She held a gun. No, not a gun, Alex realized, as twin wires fired out of the end of the device, arcing across the distance between her and Josh, the probes slamming into Josh's wounded chest. The barbs bit deep, a huge current surging through the high-voltage wires that jerked and twisted his body regardless of any divinity.

Josh's entire body bucked, his head thrown back, arms pinned to his sides, as the charge ripped through him.

Alex couldn't think about what she was doing.

She strode across the intervening distance, raising Freagarthach, both hands wrapped around the hilt. The outside of her forefinger pressed up against the cross guard. Her brother's blood dripped down across her hand.

She raised her arms, bringing her hands up level with her cheek, the sword's blade stretched out long in front of her, and swung.

Freagarthach's edge parted the skin and muscle where Josh's neck met his body, cutting the thick artery as his head lolled, unsupported by the bone the blade had bitten deep into. Blood gouted in an explosive arterial spray, spattering across Alex's face and arms.

It took a second swing to sheer through Josh's spinal cord and a third swing to hack his head off his shoulders.

She gasped from the exertion. It wasn't clean.

Staring down at her brother's face at her feet, she started to laugh hysterically, and couldn't stop laughing because of the image that bubbled up in her mind. Suddenly, she was confronted by memories of Josh and their grandfather, Boone, playing kickabout on the green with a battered old leather football; Josh pretending to be whoever Orient's latest greatest striker was at the time, running around, arms windmilling, as he scored a goal between their jumpers that had been laid down as goalposts.

Behind her, Alex heard an anguished wail.

She looked up to see a beautiful young woman racing toward them through the tangle of trees, her hair streaming out behind her, skirts—no not skirts, she realized, it was a medical gown—flapping around her bare legs.

Wordlessly, the woman threw herself to her knees at the feet of the decapitated Josh. His body still hadn't fallen. The Taser wires sagged as their charge was finally spent.

Alex looked down into eyes as deep and old as time itself, and knew them even if they didn't belong with this young beauty: Emmaline Barnes. The connection between them burned bright in that moment and those shared memories.

The sword felt suddenly heavy in her hands, and all Alex could think was: *What have I done?*

59

It wasn't over, even if the god was dead.

He wouldn't fall.

He stood there, headless, swaying, but not going down.

The Speaker for the Dead dropped the Taser and went back to Julie Gennaro's body.

She knelt with her hand on Julie's broken chest.

She could see his shade standing over Alex protectively as the young woman curled her arms around Josh's legs and lowered him to the ground. He was talking, but she couldn't hear him. Again and again, his lips moved trying to deliver the same message, until she finally managed to read them: *the bone.*

The bone.

Josh's finger.

Ellie looked back to Julie's corpse with all of its broken bones and wondered how the hell she was supposed to tell one fragment of bone from another. It wasn't like he had it clutched in his hand when he went into battle. She rifled through his pockets, ignoring the blood, as the sound of sirens grew louder. They couldn't be more than a minute away, if that. They were going to have a lot of explaining to do. There were bodies everywhere. Jamshid Kirmani, Danny Ash, Tommy Summers, Julie, Josh, and beside him a naked boy she didn't know.

She had no idea how she could even begin to explain what had happened here.

She rooted around in Julie's pockets, rummaging for anything that felt even remotely bonelike amid the collection of coins, keys, and lint. It wasn't in either of his front pockets, which meant she was going to have to turn him over. She felt sick as she rolled him. Without the bones to hold his body shape, he rolled like a sack of potatoes. She found the half-inch of bone in Julie's back pocket, wedged in alongside his wallet. She palmed it and stood up.

Standing, Ellie broke contact with Julie's body, causing his shade to fade, leaving the two women and the headless corpse the last ones standing beneath the limbs of the lightning-struck tree.

No, that wasn't quite true. There was something else there, too. She saw it in the blood that spilled into the ground from the gaping wounds in Josh's corpse, thickening in the soil. She could see the trails drawn back up into the tree itself as Arawn's blood nurtured the soil, replenishing it with the dead god's magic. And in that way, he was right, there would be magic in the soil, put there through sacrifice, before the Bain Shee came. If they ever came. She watched a few seconds, seeing the threads drawn up through the roots into the ancient tree, the grand old oak that had once been at the heart of the wildwood, and in the creases and shadows of its thick bark imagined she saw a face take shape; the true face of Arawn, the portrait in bark of a young man who had died not once but twice for the land he loved.

Perhaps there could finally be peace for him now? If anyone deserved that soft eternity, it was the young man who had been denied it for a thousand years and counting. It was never black and white. There were no villains, not even Seth was the enemy here, despite everything that had gone before. It was too easy to write someone off as evil. Even Arawn, the threat he had posed, had been acting out of love for the land. From his aspect, he was the hero of this futile fight, and those that stood in his way an enemy far worse than they could ever consider themselves.

Ellie knew what had to be done, even if she had no idea how it would—or could—work, not now that Josh's head had been separated from his shoulders.

She crouched down beside his head, taking it in both of her hands, and heard him gasp.

Only of course, he wasn't inside his body; he was standing over her, very much whole.

She pried the head's mouth open, and forced the bone inside, re-uniting it with at least part of its body.

Nothing happened.

She looked up at the ghostly Joshua, shaking her head. "What do I do? What do I have to do?"

"I don't know," he told her.

"You promised Julie. You said that if we got the bone back, if we killed Arawn, we'd *save* you."

"I didn't have a plan. I only wanted to keep my sister safe. To save those kids if I could. You. Julie. Even the old man. Buy you time. It was never about me. And we did it. We won. The cost doesn't matter. We won. Now I can go. I'm done here."

"You can't leave like this. You can't do it to Alex. She just lost her lover and best friend and all the futures they should have had together; she can't lose her brother, too; not at her own hand. That's just cruel."

"And he won't," the May Queen finally looked up at the ghost, still cradling his body. "To kill the king, you must become the king," she said. "Now you must become the king."

"I let him in," the ghost said. "I gave him my life. I became the king. That's the trade I made."

"No, you became a shell, like the cap of an acorn to the seed itself. Now you must become *my* king. That was always the Summer King's destiny, to stand at my side at the fall of Albion, the last hope of the land, and you robbed Arawn of it. So now you must become the Summer King. The May Queen needs her sword arm. Come to me, Ghost, you must live again in this ruined body of yours."

The woman laid her hands on the open cavity of Josh's chest, and with tender words the weeds of the land slowly crept across the torn flesh, drawing the ragged edges together and knitting them. A chain of daisies stitched the wound; the yellow centers of their beautiful flowers were like a smile across his pain.

Alex stood behind them, the sword at her feet.

Her brother's blood was on her hands.

She couldn't see what was going on; she couldn't see the ghost of her brother or the face in the tree, and she only heard half of the conversation, but she understood that something miraculous was happening with the land healing Josh's wounds.

"Do you want to live, my king?" the May Queen asked, seemingly talking to the headless body in her arms. "Do you promise to stand at my side against the ancient enemy as my king? Do you swear to give your life time and again in service of your queen, and thus promise to love her with all of your body and soul?"

Ellie Taylor looked from the ghost to the beautiful young woman with flowers in her hair, and back, trying to understand what was happening here. Everything about the moment was so tender and yet so macabre as well.

"I do," the ghost pledged his troth with two simple words, two simple syllables that meant more than death. This here, now, this was his sacrifice. And it was the kind of selfless surrender that might, just might, save a land.

She took the floral crown from her head and placed it like a ruff at Josh's neck.

There was a solemnity to the ritual.

The blood stained the petals.

"With this kiss, we are wed," the May Queen told the ghost, before she took the dead man's head from Ellie, holding it in both of her hands and planting a tender kiss on those bloodless lips. "Now you must come back to me, my king." She nestled the head into place, and traced a gentle finger along the wound where Freagarthach had claimed its second god, urging the flowers to grow, to knit, and weave: the bean, broom, burdock, chestnut, hawthorn, meadowsweet, nettle, oak, and primrose fusing with the skin, a black line of root and thorn stitching the dead man's head back onto his shoulders, and continuing to grow and flourish as long as the May Queen breathed life into her blooms. "Come with me into the Kingdom of Summer, my king," she whispered.

And Joshua Raines opened his eyes.

He had become the Summer King, consort of the May Queen.

"What have you done?" he said, the first words of his second life.

"I . . . I am *empty*. I . . . there's nothing inside me. I am a hollow man."

"I have done what you wanted, my king," the May Queen said. She helped him sit up, cradling him tenderly. It was almost possible to mistake that tenderness for love, not ownership. "Only that. Nothing more. The old king is dead, long live my Summer King."

Josh suddenly cried out, doubled over in pain. He clutched at his temples, screaming.

Alex saw the shadow on the ground stretch out on either side of his head. At first, they were finger thin, but they thickened, spreading until they looked more like two hands, fingers spread wide from his temples, and continued to grow, stretching out from his head as the eighteen-point antlers grew.

She barely recognized Josh as he turned to look at her.

The antlered man looked bereft.

Haunted.

Josh had inherited his kingdom.

"I will always be here. If you find yourself lonely, look for me in the rich soil of the forest, in the wild grasses and the vibrant flowers of summer. Look for my face in the veins of every leaf and tree," he said softly. He was staring at his sister. The words were for her. Alex nodded. "Listen to my voice on the soft summer breeze and hear that I love you, that I would do it all again for you, to keep you safe. See my spirit in the ripples of the river and the crystal blue surface of the lakes. Feel my love for you in every sunrise. Feel my sorrow that I cannot sit beside you and tell Boone stories or remember Mum every sunset. But know that I will be everywhere you need me to be." A single track of tears ran down her cheek as she still nodded. "I must go. This is not my place anymore." He turned to the old man, Damiola, and said simply, "I understand. Finally. It all makes sense. I know who you are. I know your nature; I know your sacrifice. I could help you remember. Just say the word and your past shall be my gift to you."

Damiola shook his head.

"As you wish. I would not force memory upon anyone, especially not a soul as old as yours. It will come back to you, given time."

"I hope not," the old man said.

And with that, the Summer King stood and took his queen's hand.

Together they walked away in the direction of Coldfall Wood.

60

"Fuck me, that was intense," Seth Lockwood said. "Who'd have thought Cuz could be all noble like that? Not me. I always thought he was a bit wet. Goes to show what I know. Funny though, in an ironic sort of way, that I'm free and he's the one in a metaphorical prison now . . . Well, I'd like to say it's been emotional, but with the law rolling up, I'm out of here. Try not to miss me. After everything, I can't quite believe I've finally got my life back."

Alex ignored him.

She watched her brother leave her for the last time. Finally, the two of them, Josh and the rejuvenated Emmaline Barnes, were gone. Lost to the wildwood.

The sirens were on top of them now. Ellie could see Mel Banks and Sara Sykes leading the line of cops running into the common ground; Tenaka in their wake.

She walked up beside Alex, the last two women standing, and put her arm around her. "I've got no idea what you're going through," she said softly.

"I'm not sure I do," Alex told her.

"Do you want to say some kind of goodbye to Julie? I can help you. Make sure that he hears."

"Oh, God . . . Julie . . ." Alex turned her head, and saw, properly saw, what had happened to him, for the first time and sagged a little against Ellie. "I . . ."

"Come on," Sara said.

She led Alex over to where the love of her life lay broken on the ground. Looking down at him, Alex realized she would never be whole again. That all of the miracles of the world had achieved one thing and one thing alone: they had succeeded where Seth Lockwood had failed; they'd robbed her of everything.

Ellie took hold of Julie's hand; then with her other hand, tangled her fingers with Alex's, making a bridge between the living and the dead.

"Can you hear me, Julie?" the woman asked.

Alex bit back on a scream when she heard him answer, "That bastard broke a lot of things, but my ears are still pretty good."

Ellie smiled. "She wanted to talk to you. You don't have a lot of time." Mel Banks was no more than three hundred feet away, and running fast. Tenaka, too. He moved like he had the devil on his heels. "So, make it count."

"I can't beat what Josh said," the ghost joked.

"I can," Alex said. "If there's a way to save you, a way to bring you back, I'll find it. I love you, Julius Gennaro. You were supposed to be my happily ever after."

"I love you, too," the ghost said. "And because of that, I'm going to ask one thing of you, just the one. Promise me you'll do it for me."

"Anything."

"Please don't. Let me go," and those were the last words the ghost of Julie Gennaro said.

He said one thing, but she heard something quite different.

"I promise," she said.

EPILOGUE

Across the endless age of mortals
The distant sound of thunder resonated
Drumming, drumming, drumming
Carrying from shore to mountain and back to shore
While the ancient enemy searched for a way to pierce the veil
He waited
It was his curse

The Summer King stood in the long shadow of the wall that was not a wall; his queen at his side.

He felt whole.

Seasons came and seasons went, as seasons are wont.

And still they waited as the leaves turned from green to gold to brown to green again.

All the while, a sound deeper than thunder rumbled the length of the immense structure, seeming to come from within the stones themselves. They could not hold. Again and again the thunder came, amplified by the peculiar acoustics of the endless curve, each rhythmic clash of sound rolling out across the great gray plains of the Annwyn, through the first trees of the wildwood all the way to the calm oceans and beyond to the Isles and the four sacred towers: Murias in the north, Findias to the south, Gorias in the east, Falias in the west. It was the sound of the world's pain.

The antlered warrior stood impassively, waiting for the first inevitable crack to undermine the wall.

It was coming.

He had seen it already: a thin line of black running through the bricks pitted with thorns and climbing plants that clung to the imposing structure to lend it the illusion of life, when of course it promised anything but that. The wall was a manifestation of the veil, the divide between the realms, and it was failing and no amount of magic could prevent it.

Now it was all about sacrifice.

He held the rowan staff in his left hand. Death held no great fear for him; he had experienced it more times than any mortal man had the right to. He reached out with his free hand for his queen. Her hand felt so small and delicate inside his, but there was more strength in it than in the wall they faced. Summer King and Queen, they would fall before the blades of the Bain Shee together, the last children of the Aos Shee.

The wind whistled through the long grass.

Birdsong filled the air.

Fallen leaves—turned to gold already—crunched underfoot, as their kin gathered at the foot of the wall, the tension in their muscles palpable. Every spirit animal joined them—waiting, watching, unmoving—as another deep blow shivered through the wall.

The chalk giants, Gogmagot and Corenius, stood with him at the last, along with nature's tiniest warriors, the bees and wasps that had killed them in that last short life of theirs back in the Summerland. At his side, the ever-faithful Robin had amassed the smallest creatures of the forest—the rats and foxes, the voles and weasels and badgers, rabbits and mice—to fight at their side along with the elemental spirits and the sprites of the ancient wood, the Children of the Forest. They emerged from the trees with their leafy faces gaunt and fashioned by fear, unable to take their gaze from the crumbling wall and knowing what it would mean when that first brick fell. The black dogs and emerald hounds at their sides, prowling as the Wild Hunt assembled. The mud people came next, clawing their way up out of the stuff of the battlefield, lacking bones or faces, these raw golems stood side by side with the wooden warriors of the trees. Frost-rimed warriors and ocean serpents came next, the mightiest of them, the Knucker, adding to nature's song as the great beast flew, untethered, unfettered, free, spreading her incredible wings wide and casting shadows long that blocked out both sun and moon in those great gray heavens.

It was not alone up there. The owls gathered in their parliament, a murmuration of starlings muttered their discontent as a boil of hawks spiraled. Shoals and squalls and nests emptied to watch.

The echoes of crashing waves came to them next, carried across the continent of lost souls all the way to the wall to join in with the great song. Mother was afraid, and her fear ran deep. It was infectious, spreading through each and every one of her children as they waited.

The breeze ceded to a great wind, and the great wind did *howl* adding its voice to the Song of Albion.

They didn't have a single weapon between them, these brave children, but they would fight to the death when the time came.

And come it would.

Then, when it did, when the dying was done, their blood and the blood of their enemies would soak deep into the soil of this place, into the root of every tree and every flower, into the bellies of the worms that churned up the dirt, and then antlered king's love would draw on it, reaching into the shimmering pathways of the ancient leys, drawing deep of Mother's reserves, all the way to the mighty stone henges, and fight back.

The antlered king knelt and laid his rowan staff on the ground. He closed his eyes, drawing on his love of the land, and whispered a word of changing as he ran his fingers across the grains of the wood and feeling out the nature that resided within. The wood slowly returned to the stuff of magic it was fashioned from, and in that moment could have become anything, but he knew what the situation required, and summoned forth the great green serpent. The snake licked at the air with a flick of its bright-red forked tongue and slithered away from him toward the giant fissure that opened up, as another hammer blow struck on the other side. The land screamed her protest and pain as the huge stones crumbled and fell, opening the way to the void.

More of Albion's sons and daughters answered the call: polecats and bats, squirrels and shrews, boar and stoats and deer joining the throng. Adders and slowworms and spiders followed, filling the land.

The ley lines and earth nodes hummed with life; the stone circles and chalk men and horses were ready to fight.

The bean nighe who foretold the death of mortals joined their number. The black dogs of the fae—who barked once as a warning, twice as a threat, and a third time to doom their foe—prowled through the long grass. The Alp-luachra, that crawled down its victims' throats while they slept to feast on their last meal, and the Dearg-Due, that once beautiful woman who killed herself to escape hell, crawled free of their graves to join the hunt. The church grims and the Nuckelavee, that twisted creature with the torso of a man sewn onto the back of a rotting horse, brought its blight to the coming war. The boggarts, brownies, corn dollies, ettins, green men, hag stones and redcaps, Black Annis and Jack o'Kent, Barghest, witches and giant killers came to fill the swelling ranks, leaving their drowning pools to take up arms against their immortal foe, remembering all that had gone before; all that had been lost.

The Summer King was that memory.

This was his land.

And still they came, answering his call.

A figure, tinged with an ethereal blue light emerged from the mists and walked across what would become the field of battle. He held the ancient blade Freagarthach in his hands. The runes along its length shimmered, alive with the magic of this place. The blade was ready to taste Bain Shee blood.

Julius Gennaro struck an imposing figure, more so than he ever had in life, as the animals parted to allow his passage to his rightful place at the side of their lord. He had changed beyond recognition, carrying the scars of life into death, but in so many ways he was still the same, just like the man he fought for. Men of both worlds. Men of none.

"You took your time," the Summer King said, without turning

to face the most recent sacrifice to join the swelling ranks of the ghosts of Albion.

"Dying took a little bit out of me," the warrior said, offering the antlered man a wry smile.

Beside him, the rapturous light on Macha's upturned face left her creatures in no doubt that she was the embodiment of the season, their queen. She had garlands of beautiful summer blooms tangled in her hair and the white cotton skirts of her flowing summer dress lapped around her legs. Her gaze was haunting. She was so much stronger than all of them. But even she was not strong enough to face what waited in the void. She never had been.

Deep tremors shivered along the wall as the Bain Shee hammered away at the very stuff of existence, determined to tear down the veil between the ancient realms.

That there was any color in this place was one tiny victory; the first glimmers of magic returned, but it wasn't enough. It could never be enough.

The fissure widened.

Within it, the antlered king saw the gaunt ghosts with their lava-pit eyes tore at the veil, clawing their way through into life even as the stones on the edge of the fissure crumbled and fell.

The snake slithered up the wall, coiling around the vines that climbed all the way up to the gaping black smile of the fissure, striking with venomous fangs at the first face that appeared, its deadly poison claiming the first victim of the *woruldgewinn*. His mistake had been in believing that the earthly war would be fought in that other place. It wouldn't. It would be fought here. It would end there. The snake slithered away from the wall, returning to its master's hand where its forked tongue once more became the glistening red berries of the rowan's fruit.

More stones fell as the great wall bowed and buckled.

And still the thunder rolled on, booming out across the land.

"Are you ready, my love?" his queen asked of him.

He was.

He closed his eyes to let the Song fill him, drawing on every sound that together made up the music of life, and soul swell, bursting with everything that made the land at once the most beautiful and perilous place.

"We do this together," he promised, still holding the hand of the woman who owned him body and soul.

"Always," the tripartite goddess agreed.

"And so it begins," Julie said, lifting the great blade.

As they came, more and more of them with their vile aspects, clawing their way into his realm, the lord of this place raised his hand. His Hunters fell silent; hungry, eager to hear whatever rousing words passed his lips.

But he offered none; instead he said simply, "Let's get this over with." It was an utterly Joshua Raines thing to say in the face of death.

THE END

ACKNOWLEDGMENTS

Okay, right up front let's start this one with a huge "Oh, my God, I can't believe I spelled one of my best mate's names wrong in the back of *Glass Town*'s confession." So, to Thomas Allwin, I am mortified. Obviously, all the nice stuff I said in the back of the last book about coffee and friendship was for a damned imposter. Still, this time you get a paragraph all to yourself, and you're ahead of the editors and agents. So, score!

Right, where were we? *Coldfall Wood.* Let's face it; it's bonkers. So, I have to apologize to Peter Wolverton, my long-suffering editor, who seemed quite happy when I pitched him a book about the return of the Once and Future King that had absolutely nothing to do with the Rothery, Glass Town, Josh, Julie, any of it. The two weren't linked at all until they were. I won't mention now that there's a line in this one that has my subconscious screaming, *I know what happens next!*, because sometimes you need to go out leaving 'em wanting more. And frankly what's better than a Butch and Sundance last page? Nothing. Ever. So, I promise, Pete, no more mad ideas that take over two whole years of my life. The same apology goes to Jennifer Donovan, who gets to do all the fun stuff like wrangle the fragile egos of us writers as we stare into the pit of despair that is the internet, convinced that everything we try and say is in fact shite and doesn't need to be said. Jen's great. Pete's lucky to have her on his side. If you read this, Pete, she deserves a pay raise for putting up with us. The rest of the team at St. Martin's, notably my cover artist, Ervin Serrano, who with *Glass Town,* happened upon the greatest moment of serendipity ever—assuming you have *Glass Town* close at hand, take a look at the cover. See the cobbled street and the sign above Eleanor's head? That street is Yxsmedsgränd. It's in Stockholm where I live, and the sign is for Grändens Café. My old office when I was working for a gaming company in

Stockholm was on that street and that sign was my view. Ervin had no idea. He just found a street he thought looked cool. And the true unsung hero of *Glass Town* and *Coldfall Wood* is Su Wu, my copy editor, who is the reason there aren't a thousand continuity errors in these two very elaborate books, and who caught every instance of me changing the mythology on myself and saved me from looking very stupid. But that's what you want. That's why you surround yourself with brilliant people.

Then there's my agent, Judith Murray, at Greene and Heaton in the UK, who has probably forgotten what I look like by now, as it's been so long getting from our first chats about the future to here.

Unsurprisingly, the wife hasn't noticed the offer in the back of *Glass Town,* so we'll keep that as our little secret.

I'm lucky. I know I am. I'm surrounded by good friends who make the loneliness of my chosen career a little less lonely, and by new friends that blow me away with their generosity. So, to the new: I owe so much more than a glass of decent whiskey to Jan Smedh, the man behind The English Bookshop in Uppsala, which only went and won the London Book Fair's Bookstore of the Year in 2018—I like to think it was because of the events we've done together. *Shhh,* don't ruin it. People like me can't survive doing what we do without champions like Jan, Stina, Christer, and the gang. There isn't a better bookshop in the world. It's official. You've got the plaque to prove it.

And, the old: Mike, Stefan, Stephen, Andy, who probably think I'm a figment of their imaginations since I've been gone so long, and, of course, to my family, all of them, scattered across the world. Well, Europe at least. Well, England and Sweden. That counts as Europe. It should. Well, until next year when the politicians drag us kicking and screaming back into the 1970s with their stupidity.

That's about it this time of asking, apart from to use these last couple of lines to put out an advert to anyone who's read this far: Steven Savile will write for food. Doesn't even have to be great food. As long as it's not McDonald's. So, editors, publishers, fools with lots of money they want to transform into little money . . . you know where to find me.

And to readers, the folks we do this stuff for, the last thank you is for you. Please, if you're of a mind, drop by Facebook and say "hello," hit my website and say "wotcha," hit Twitter and say "hi"— got to be mindful of the character count on Twitter after all. Honestly, just thanks for taking this adventure with me. It's been two years of my life, and a lot more from the first moment the idea of Seth and Josh and their twisted little family came to life in my mind. Without you, I'd just be sitting in a small room talking to myself: *What do you mean there's no one there . . . ?*

—*Steven Savile*
Sala, Sweden